THRICE BOUND

THRICE BOUND

A ROMANTIC PARANORMAL SUSPENSE

NICOLE E. KELLEHER

jewel lake books

Jewel Lake Books LLC
www.jewellakebooks.com

Cover Design by Kanaxa

Thrice Bound | Nicole E. Kelleher—1st ed.
ISBN Print 979-8-9988658-1-7
ISBN Digital 979-8-9988658-0-0

Dedicated to my family.

Acknowledgements

So much goes into publishing a book, far past the words
written by the author, so I would be remiss if I didn't thank my
two editors, Kay and Cindy, for their exceptional notes, and
my cover artist, Natalie, who always manages to create the
perfect face to capture the vibe for my books.

Most importantly, I would like to thank the readers,
like you, who give new authors a chance, and read and
review our books.

Author's Content Note

Thrice Bound is a paranormal suspense and, as such,
contains violence. There is an early-term loss of pregnancy
in Chapter Twenty-five.

CONTENTS

Chapter One

Lakeside Health Center, Chicago, Illinois

Exhausted, Natalia Waever resisted the urge to shove Adrian Shareff out of her office—the man set her teeth on edge.

"Trust me, your brother needs people like me on his side," Shareff touted. "I don't mean to condescend, Natalia. Not that there's anything wrong with"—he waved an *all this* open palm in her face—"you being a Non...non-Fascina, I mean. I suppose you do add some value being appointed to the board—"

Perhaps a knee to the groin, she amended, then a shove. "What Chris needs *on his side* is his business, Shareff," she said, using his surname because calling him by his first name, as he always insisted, was an intimacy that made her skin crawl. As always, her refusal to acquiesce nettled him. Before he could respond, she added, "Since you brought up the board, I will remind you that this is neither the time nor place for this conversation. You are, no doubt, aware that sidebars such as this are completely against Fascina protocol, as stated in the bylaws, as well as being subject to censure enforceable by the National Order."

"I don't need you to—"

"Besides, there is a general meeting this week. And you are welcome to put forth any concerns at that time." She put her hand on the door and started closing it, slowly forcing the man out of her office.

"You know it's impossible to get new items on the agenda. And your twin never returns my calls."

"As the appointed liaison between the Fascina Community and the Norms, my brother's schedule falls outside my purview."

Halfway into the corridor, he put his toe against her office door. "I've asked you nicely, Natalia." He leaned in, breaching her personal space. His Fascina power buffeted against her, weak though it was, trying to break through her resistance. He believed she wouldn't know it for what it was, that she would simply and unknowingly give in to his persuasiveness. But her twin, probably the most powerful of Fascina, had *warded* her. Even if he hadn't, Tally had always somehow been immune to Fascina persuasion.

She gauged how she should respond. Ignore it, and Shareff might complain to the Fascina Council that her brother and Bane had used their gifts on a Non—a derogatory term for someone without supernatural abilities who was born of Fascina parents. No, with Shareff, she sensed, his powers were weak. She could fake her reaction.

Tally frowned at him, then let her features slacken for a moment as she slowly blinked. A satisfied cast stole over his face. Then she shook her head as if coming awake and stared at him. "I'm not my brother's admin. I suggest you call him and make an appointment. Goodbye, Shareff."

He narrowed his eyes at her and started to push back into her office, but she was too fast. She shut the door in his face and engaged the lock. He slapped his palm against the frosted glass, then jiggled the door handle. "This isn't over, Natalia," he yelled before, she imagined, storming off.

"Thanks for the super end to my day," Tally groused to herself, looking at the stacks of papers she'd sorted into three piles—the Lumina Foundation, otherwise known as the Red Tape Black Hole, the Pediatrics Volunteer Coordination stack, and another simply marked URGENT. The latter was the largest and was filled mainly with details regarding the upcoming annual gala. Sadly, the Peds pile, representing the volunteer work that sustained her, was tiny in comparison to the other two.

Tally rubbed her temples, trying to ward off the coming migraine. She shot off a quick text to her twin, warning him about Adrian Shareff, then grabbed her noise-cancelling earbuds, kicked off her shoes, made herself comfortable on the cushy loveseat across from her desk, and then cued up the latest calming meditations her best friend, Bane, had shared with her. Immediately, her senses were lulled by soothing musical tones, and she pulled her legs into position and set her hands above her knees. *Breathe in through the nose and open right palm, and out through nose and left palm, and then reverse—* again and again as she imagined a sphere of air slowly arcing in a simple back-and-forth juggle.

She'd graduated to non-guided meditation and was trying out new soundtracks. Gradually, she lost herself in her breathing and the somewhat gloomy music and visualized shedding each stressful moment of her week, working her way backward through the day until her mind was blessedly blank.

Her eyes fluttered open, and her first thought was that the battery in her earbuds had died, but the way the sound seemed sucked out of the room told her that they were still working. Her thirty-minute session had flown by. She took out her earbuds and placed them into their charging case. After a few neck rolls, she uncrossed her legs and got up from the sofa.

Forcing herself to ignore the work on her desk, she reached for her laptop and tucked it in its designated slot in her leather courier bag. She locked her office behind her before turning toward the elevators near the reception area. The rest of the hospital might be a twenty-four-seven operation, but at five o'clock on Fridays—6:03 p.m., she amended, peeking at her phone— the administrative suite was deserted. The motion sensor engaged, washing the neutral-toned lobby in soft light. As she waited for the elevator, she rubbed her ears, trying to rid herself of the feeling that her earbuds were still in and dampening the constant noise of the hospital's forced air system. Even the soft chime of the elevator as the doors opened seemed muted.

She pressed "G1" for the garage level where her reserved spot was located.

Finger scrolling through the multiple emails that had come in since the Lumina meeting ended nearly two hours ago, she stepped off the elevator, registering the G1 plaque on the doorframe. The doors slid closed behind her, and she glanced toward the valet booth.

Tally frowned. This wasn't the garage. She stared down the stark, dimly lit lobby, trying to get her bearings. In either direction were double doors, each with frosted windows and no light in the corridors behind them. "What floor is this?" she asked aloud, hating how even the sound of her voice seemed deadened. She force-yawned and swallowed a few times in an attempt to pop her ears as she pressed the button to recall the elevator. The UP arrow illuminated, then winked off. She pressed it again. Same thing. She jabbed it repeatedly, as if the elevator had sense and would hurry to her floor. The light stayed on as she did this, then frustratingly winked off when she stopped. "Oh, for Pete's sake!"

She checked the time on her phone—6:13 p.m.—and waited. Even if the button's bulb had a short, the elevator would eventually arrive. The newly constructed hospital's mechanics were state-of-the-art, and she continued to scan her emails. At least five minutes must have passed. "Make that ten," she muttered upon noting the time on her phone. The screen flickered, then went completely dark as her battery died. "Unbelievable."

She looked from side to side, then marched down the carpeted lobby toward the doors on her right. She pushed on one and was relieved when it swung open. The motion detectors caught her, and the recessed lighting flared spotlight-like on her head. "Where *am* I?"

She strode toward the reception counter before her, hoping to find a phone. While she contemplated who to call, the overhead lighting tracked her progress. But the desk was bare...no phone, paperclip, or pen.

The motion sensor near the double doors timed out, turning off the entryway lights. There had to be a phone somewhere, and she peered down the dark corridor ahead. Behind her, another light blinked off. Even if she didn't manage to find a phone, she would eventually come to a stairwell. Lights strobed on as she walked down the long dark hall, trying each door handle along the way, only to find them all locked. Behind her, lights flicked off as she progressed.

Somewhere ahead of her, the distinct click of a door latch sounded, and she halted, peering into the dark. "Hello?" she called, aware that if anyone was down there, the motion sensors should have turned on the lights. Rattled, she looked at her dead phone, mildly freaking out. "Get a grip, Tally." Her words sounded dull.

She took another step, then keys jangled ahead, the sound strangely crisp and sharp. "Okay, then," she whispered, fear creeping up her back. Something told her she did not want to meet whoever it was down that hall, so she hurried back the way she'd come, the motion-activated lighting picking out her progress. She pushed at one of the double doors, had a moment of panic when it didn't swing open, then realized she needed to press the break-bar. She made it to the elevator lobby just in time to see the car's doors swish shut. "What the hell?" Behind her, the ceiling lights had all gone off. She stabbed both the up and down buttons, just in case the car was still there.

Through the frosted glass panes of the doors, a faint glow illuminated the far end of the corridor. The windows of the entrance she hadn't taken were dark. "Make a decision, Tally." Then she remembered the mace that her friend Bane had pressed her to carry, the little can at the bottom of her bag.

"My bag!" To her right, the light had gone out. She must've set her satchel down when she was searching the reception area. Her laptop and keys and that tiny aerosol deterrent were all out of reach. No way was she leaving those behind. She went back the way she'd come and had her hand on the door when, midway down the corridor ahead, another light strobed on, then off. It was hard to tell, but someone dark moved under it. And they were moving fast.

Tally scrambled backward as, faster and faster, the overheads flashed on and off—whoever they were, they were barreling toward her. She fled to the doors on the left. The fact that the motion sensors did not activate the lights was a relief, for they would pinpoint her location, and there was enough exit lighting that she could see down the corridor. She followed the arrows, rushing to find the stairwell and fearing that, at any moment, the lights would flick on in the elevator lobby.

Halfway down the corridor, she nearly missed the turn when the EXIT sign's arrow pointed to the right. No sooner was she around the corner than the double doors behind her banged open. There was a terrible crash, as if someone was throwing furniture. She could almost feel the blast of air percuss against the back of her neck. She took a step and winced when her shoes clicked on the laminate floors. Kicking off her heels—she now had a weapon—Tally hustled toward the next EXIT sign.

So much for the motion detectors—lights were coming on behind her, strobing closer and closer. Finally, an exit sign with an arrow pointing to a door. She pushed it open and entered yet another, narrower corridor just as the hallway behind her lit up.

Afraid to look back, she started moving, trying door after door, zigzagging back and forth down the arced passageway in search of one that would open. The hall followed the curved shape of the building and obscured her sightline, but the slam of the door she'd come through pounded against her ears. Her neck prickled at the sense of malevolence that bore down on her. Whoever it was had to be Fascina...how else could they manipulate the lighting? But why would they want to hurt her? She was a Non—no one of consequence. Her twin had inherited all the power from their parents.

Tally kept moving. She could hear her pursuer, stalking her, soles pounding the tiles, making a squishing noise with each step. Images of blood-covered ER floors came to mind and how the non-slip shoes the nurses wore would squelch in the gore. Her heart would be sure to burst if she didn't turn around to identify the man pursuing her. But she was more afraid of knowing who it was.

She whipped around another corner, speeding down another deserted hallway. Finally, an unlocked windowless door. She shouldered it open, praying that he would run past the room. Closing it as quietly as possible, she engaged the simple push lock on the doorknob, knowing it to be but a tiny defense against a powerful Fascina.

She shivered in the cold quiet and clamped her jaw tight to stop her teeth from chattering. Then, she stretched her arms out in the pitch-dark room, blindly searching back and forth for a place to hide, until she ran into a wall of cold steel. She ran her fingers over what seemed to be square metal panels, then found a...a handle? "Shit," she whispered, as she groped over the rectangular doors stacked one on top of the other, spreading out along the entire wall. How in the hell had she made it to the morgue?

From under the crack at the bottom of the door, the corridor lights blazed hotter and hotter, marking the Fascina's approach. Her eyes adjusted just enough for her to see the metal tables, organized precisely end-to-end, side-by-side, with not a trace of warmth for their silent, supine occupants. In the middle, an empty table with a sheet folded neatly at one end sang to her, a cruel, coaxing lullaby. Unable to resist its plaint, she climbed onto it, rested her head on the hard block, and drew the sheet over her body and face. The cold metal stung the small of her back where her blouse had inched up; despite the sheet covering her, she felt utterly exposed. She waited. And waited.

Tally let out the breath she'd been holding when it seemed that he'd passed by the door, but she dared not move. Then she heard it, a key sliding into a lock and the door slowly opening.

Click.

Click.

And then another...*click*. The fluorescents flickered on, growing brighter until her eyes hurt from staring at the blinding white of the sheet covering her face. He was here. All the pressure in her ears whooshed away as his hand touched her shoulder.

"Tally?"

Her eyes flew open, and she gasped, choking on the very air she was trying to breathe. Disoriented, she looked all around, only to discover that she was still in her office.

"Hey," Bane said, sitting next to her and rubbing her back.

She searched his face, tried to calm her breath, imagining the arc again. But her once open palms were now curled into fists. Bane pried them open, revealing that her nails had cut into her flesh.

Chapter Two

Bane grabbed a couple of tissues and pressed them into Tally's palms. She'd clenched her fists so hard that she hadn't even noticed the pain. But she couldn't allow Bane to examine the wounds because, in a few moments, they would be gone. Tally had no idea why, recently, she suddenly possessed the ability to heal at an accelerated pace. She was non-Fascina, wasn't she? After her nightmare, the thought caused an irrepressible bubble of laughter to burst forth, and Bane's eyebrows drew together with worry.

"I'm texting Chris," he said, pulling out his phone.

"No. Don't. I'm okay." She kept her hands fisted, and when he tried to check her wounds, she deflected. "I just need some water. Can you grab one for me?"

"Sure," he said, opening the door to her office mini-fridge. "Looks like you're out."

She'd known her supply was gone but needed him out of her office for a few minutes. She gave him a sheepish look.

"Cafeteria?" he asked.

"Thanks."

"I'll be back in a few minutes," he promised.

"More like twenty," she said after he left her office, knowing how busy it would be at this hour. She got up and walked to her desk, pulling out her first aid kit from the bottom drawer. After dropping the blood-spotted tissues in the bin, she used an alcohol wipe to clean her palms. She watched as the moon-shaped cuts knitted together. She put gauze pads on, then wrapped her hands to conceal her lack of wounds. By the morning, there wouldn't even be scars.

"What's happening to me, mom?" Her mother had died years ago, but it didn't stop her from having the occasional one-sided conversation with her deceased parents. It was her mom who'd been in the forefront of her mind more and more of late.

Tally's mom, Mallory Waever, had been one of the strongest Fascina in the modern era, and though Tally hadn't inherited any of her powers, she did carry her DNA. Before she had died—been murdered—her mom divulged that she'd extended a few protections around Tally. Her immunity to people like Shareff, for one; and, except for the migraines she suffered, her robust health for another. But lately, like right this minute, if she got hurt, her body healed itself, and at lightning speed. Hence, the reason behind getting rid of her best friend for a few minutes to hide the evidence.

But this strange new gift came with a price—increasingly terrifying nightmares.

The air pressure in the room dipped, and Tally gripped the edge of her desk and shuddered, remembering the same feeling she'd had in her nightmare. But instead, Bane *slipped* back into her office, the smoky dark cloud of his essence recombining before her eyes until he stood solidly before her with a six-pack of her favorite flavored water. *Slipping* wasn't a rare power, but neither was it common. What *was* rare was when a Fascina could carry another person or thing along with them, as Bane could.

"You shouldn't do that in public," she warned him. "What if someone saw you leave my office only to find you here again?"

"It's Friday evening, Tally, and the floor is deserted," he explained. "Besides, the line was too long at the cafeteria." He handed her a cold can of water.

"Thank you."

"Want me to take a look?" He eyed her makeshift bandages.

"I didn't realize healing was one of your gifts," she teased.

"You know it's not," he countered, still serious.

"I'm okay, really. My first aid kit was out of Band-Aids, so I improvised." Before he could ask, she added. "I used an alcohol wipe and then added antibiotic ointment. Satisfied?"

"I guess. Fingernails are disgusting crevices for all sorts of germs."

Tally laughed. "Stop it, Bane. You and I were lab partners in that petri dish experiment. Remember? When was that, like eighth grade?"

"Seventh," he replied with a grin.

Bane had been her best friend since the fourth grade, ever since the day she'd had the temerity to come to his aid, when he was being attacked by three sixth-grade boys.

Most Fascina came into their gifts between the ages of seven and nine. There were exceptions: the prodigies, like her twin, Chris, who began demonstrating control over his powers when he was only five. For Tally, five came and went. So did six, seven, and then eight. By age nine, their school deemed her both non-Fascina and non-Norm, or the slightly derogatory Non. She was an in-betweener. There were others like her, and because they were related to Fascina families, they were kept in the same schools. Bullying was strictly prohibited, but that didn't mean it didn't happen. Names like Noni and Nona were bandied about.

The non-Fascina weren't the only ones who were bullied. Anyone deemed weak was also a target. Though Bane Caron was one of the most powerful Fascina in the Chicago Order today, his gifts had been slow to emerge. Tally always wondered if his parents had somehow dampened them—it was horrible, and totally something they might do.

She watched him as he folded his lean, rangy frame to sit on the loveseat. "Damn, Tally, you were dug in deep. I called your name several times. What were you listening to?"

"One of the new meditations you sent me. I must have dozed off."

"You didn't seem to be sleeping." He picked up her phone.

"The battery died," she told him, and frowned when the screen lit up.

"I didn't send this to you." He shared it to his own phone, then deleted the audio file from her list. "I'll check it out later. Are you okay?"

"Yeah. Maybe. It was like a nightmare, but real. I guess I was just super tired." She remembered that her office door had been locked and used the fact to change the subject. "Did you also slip in earlier, Bane? What if someone had been in here with me?"

"You worry too much, Tally."

"I don't want you to have any trouble with the Order. What was so important that it couldn't wait until tonight?"

"Look, you didn't show up at Chris's. We both texted you. And you're *never* late to anything, so I got worried."

"But we're not meeting until seven."

"It's nearly eight, Tally."

She grabbed her phone from him to check the time. "That was supposed to be a thirty-minute breathing meditation."

Bane consulted his phone. "It's over an hour long."

"Before you go all security-consultant expert on me, Bane, I have no idea how I downloaded that. I haven't given my phone to anyone."

"Maybe not, but has anyone AirDropped anything to you lately?"

She got up and looked away.

"Uh-huh. Too many people to count, I'm guessing. Let me take your phone and run some diag—"

"No way. Not with the gala coming up." She leaned back against the edge of her desk. "I'm just overworked. And then I had to deal with Shareff."

"Shareff?" Bane shot up to his six foot-plus height and frowned at her. "What did he want?"

"An audience with the king, what else?" They smiled at her joke. It was what they called Chris when they wanted to remind her brother that he wasn't their boss just because he presided over the Chicago Order of Fascina, or C.O.F., a responsibility he'd not only inherited when their parents had been murdered but had earned as well.

"Come on," he said. "Let's get you home."

Tally grabbed her satchel as they headed out to the elevators. Except for the relieved pressure in her ears and Bane by her side, everything was exactly the same as it had been in her dream.

First into the elevator, she hesitated before pressing G1. But the car gave a soft lurch as they descended to the garage. The doors swooshed open, and she just stood there, the wall with its G1 plaque in the garage lobby exactly where it should be.

"Hey, are you sure you're fine?" Bane asked again, and she nodded and stepped out of the car. She let loose an easier breath when the attendant at the valet booth looked up and smiled at her. Bane walked before her, taking her keys from the attendant. "I know how much you love driving, but you're not getting behind the wheel tonight," he said, and for once she didn't argue.

"Always protecting me," she said under her breath.

"Someone has to. Hey, I was joking," he assured her when she frowned.

She truly *was* exhausted. This was Bane. Her best friend.

"Besides," he went on, "I like to think of it as my civic duty—protecting everyone on the road by not letting you get behind the wheel."

His comment finally elicited a smile from her. It was a running joke between them, that she was the safest speed demon in the Midwest, and proud of it.

Chapter Three

Orson Sedge slammed the gavel on the table so hard that the mallet's handle cracked and sent splinters flying.

Shouts of "Ask the Non!" were followed by an equal number of calls of agreement and gasps at the disrespectful term. Tally, sitting in her place next to her brother at the head table, ignored the insult—again—and looked across the room. Representation at the Chicago Order general meetings had grown too large, while the board that governed them had grown too small. It was nearly impossible to accomplish even the simplest task. As the Order's chairperson, her twin, Christian, was unsuccessfully trying to present a motion that membership should be capped and the vacant spots in the ruling board filled. Orson, the vice-chair, would make sure it was seconded. Both knew that if the current situation didn't change, and soon, her family's legacy could crumble. Unfortunately, the membership was focused on murder and not management.

Chris glanced her way and shook his head. Tally could sense his frustration and hated that he was being forced into yet another delay to resolve the issues that threatened the C.O.F. Didn't these people realize that he had their interests at heart? Orson nodded to them, mouthing the words, "next time." He'd always been the voice of reason at these meetings and one of her brother's most loyal supporters. But even Orson seemed to be losing his patience. The Chicago Order was too riled to do anything but decry the incidents that had been taking place in the Norm community—a series of gruesome, ritualistic murders.

"They doth protest too much, methinks," Bane whispered, leaning in to fill her water glass. She and Chris relied on his staunch support, and because most of those present feared him, her own admittance to the board was tolerated.

She mentally catalogued the angry faces. There were those in the Order's Council who resented her inclusion, charging that since she possessed no special powers, she was not truly Fascina. Her mother had insisted that her power lay not in the supernatural, but in her strength of character. So, here she was, acting submissive and ignoring the barbs thrown her way, and here she would remain. Her brother counted on her for her counsel.

Under the table, Tally kicked Bane's shin. "Quoting the Bard at a time like this?" she whispered back.

Tally didn't want to think it, but the mutilations and murders had to have been committed by someone with supernatural powers. And with that truth came the knowledge that every person in the room was a suspect. Everyone but Bane and Chris—during more than one of the attacks, they'd been with her. As far as she was concerned, that gave them ironclad alibis.

"Enough," Orson bellowed, causing the assemblage to retreat into a disgruntled silence. "By the way you are carrying on, one would think the perpetrator was amongst us."

"Told you," Bane said quietly.

Tally gave him a look. She shouldn't have—her wry expression was not lost on her enemies. They might abide her presence at the meetings, but never her opinions. Sometimes, she wished that Orson hadn't fought for her assignment as liaison between the Fascina and the Norms.

She followed Bane's gaze as he gave a hard eye to the four or five people who had dared sneer at her. They all looked down, afraid to meet his gaze. Like Tally, Bane Caron was not wanted. Not here. Not anywhere. People would always distrust the son of Sebastian Caron and Giselle Coyle-Caron. But Bane's power and financial influence, not to mention being the issue of a powerful family, had guaranteed his seat at the table. Not only was Bane the chief financial officer for the board, he was chief security officer as well. Handling Chris and Tally's personal security, running interference for her brother, warding Tally's house, and providing them with the most secure tech available were just a few of the myriad things he did.

Bane's name floated upon some of the disgruntled whispers. He had long ago accepted that he would bear the stain brought on by his father, the man responsible for the murder of Tally's father and a failed attempt to wrest control of the Fascina from the Waever family. Thank God for Orson; he had rallied their supporters and had come to her mother's aid. In the end, Sebastian Caron had been banished to the Null—like the French oubliettes of old, it was a fate worse than death.

Orson had a grudging respect for Bane, but only due to Chris and Tally's insistence. The three of them had been inseparable growing up, sharing their hopes and dreams. Tally held close to her heart the memory of the day that she and Chris had finally teased Bane's dream from him—he wanted to be a Viking. Chris had razzed him for days, but Tally had understood. After years of abuse from his father, Bane wanted to be nothing less than fearsome. The truth of it had always been that Bane was made of sterner stuff than his father would ever realize. He might even be more powerful than her brother.

She suppressed a shudder at her growing headache and hid her frown. Bane would only ever see her as a female non-Fascina. He caught her eye, and she rallied her features into a speck of a smile. He winked back at her, just like an older brother would. She jotted a quick note on her phone for him to read. She knew sending him text messages during the meeting could cause repercussions, but nearly everyone had been doing it this evening.

What'r u looking 4?

He texted back.

Guilt

She wasn't surprised. He was doing what he did best at these council meetings—reading the room. No one was better at surreptitiously studying people. He'd perfected his brooding mien over the years, then added some much-needed bulk to what was once a beanpole-thin teenaged body, Tally thought appreciatively. Now, when he was ignored, nine times out of ten, it was because people feared him. And if not him, his family's reputation.

The meeting was well on its way to the three-hour mark, and he cast another glance her way. Sensing the serious weight of his gaze, she drew back her hand when it trembled as she reached for her water. She tapped out another quick text, not wanting him to be distracted by her.

I'm fine. Wish they would stop yelling.

Bane took her at her word and focused his attention on the room.

While Orson Sedge continued to coax the assembly into order, Tally took a moment to compare the two most important men in her life. Her twin was an ethereal light to Bane's dark Mediterranean roots. Bane was slightly taller, but both were built and athletically slim, like their fathers. Tally's own coloring was like her brother's, including the way their ashy blond hair bleached out in the summer sun. Fortunately, they had complexions that tanned instead of burned, with pale, green-blue eyes.

Chris was one of the most sought-after bachelors in the Fascina community. And he knew it, though Tally wondered that his current girlfriend, the sultry Jacqueline Silva, was lasting as long as she had.

Now Bane, she thought, turning her attention to the incredibly handsome man next to her. Well, *she'd* always been attracted to him, at any rate. More than that, actually. She'd long ago given up trying to deny the fact that she was in love with him. Thinking about why they could never be together, legally and morally, while knowing she would break Fascina law in a second if he expressed even the slightest interest in her, led to a rabbit hole she avoided at all costs.

The yelling in the room turned to angry shouts, and Bane continued to focus on the rest of the room. A text popped up from him.

Pay attention to the quiet ones

"Why should we help the Norms?" Comford, a low-level bureaucrat, asked.

"Maybe it's the work of a maliker!" a woman yelled, amid shouts and pounding fists.

Tally searched the faces to find the person who'd made that audacious claim. Malikers were the monstrous issue that resulted when a male Fascina and a female non-Fascina mated, and the reason she could never risk having children. As toddlers, they aged at an accelerated rate, their growth and development extremely painful. It was theorized that this caused their lack of empathy and their violent tendencies. Generations past, children who exhibited maliker traits were euthanized around the age of two. It was barbaric. No one knew how many innocents had been killed. It'd been Bane's great-grandfather who discovered how malikers came to exist, and laws were enacted. The harsh punishment for defying the decree forbidding procreation between Fascina and non-Fascina was extreme, but effective.

Orson banged the broken gavel, desperate to regain control of the room.

"Why doesn't the Non answer?" someone shouted in a derisive tone, and Tally tried without success to determine who it was. No one ever referred to her as a Non at these meetings. That they did so now, and several times, was blatant disrespect, and not only to Tally, but to Chris's leadership as well.

"Isn't it her job to know what the Norms are thinking?" someone from the opposite side of the room accused.

She glanced at her brother to see how he was taking the insult, but he was tête-à-tête with his girlfriend du jour, oblivious to the calls for Tally to respond. And she couldn't say a word until the floor was officially ceded to her. Across the room, Rene Grossomm, one of the newer appointees to the council, sat with his arms folded across his chest, wearing a smug smile. Quiet ones, indeed.

The gavel hammering continued, and with her headache moving into migraine territory, Tally resolved to buck protocol. She stood, and the room suddenly fell silent. Bane shook his head in warning, but she'd had enough and remained standing, waiting patiently until her brother looked her way. Jacqueline looked like she could spit nails.

"The Chair recognizes Natalia Waever," Chris finally acknowledged, but only after he gave her one of their silent twin-speak looks. She returned it with one of her own. The murmurings of discontent began almost immediately; but it took only one hit of Orson's gavel to silence the hoard.

"My thanks to Chris and our esteemed council for ceding the floor. It has long been the Fascina tradition to have at least one non-Fascina in attendance to act as liaison with those outside the community," she reminded them, as levelly as she could. "And I am honored and proud to serve you ."

She deserved an Oscar for keeping her disdain hidden from those who constantly ridiculed her behind her back, not to mention being impervious to the "We're talking about this later" look from Chris.

"I spoke with Mayor Greene," she continued, not mincing words. "At this time, the police have no leads. They do not think it is a maliker because they have no idea that such creatures ever existed. They are in the preliminary stages of profiling the killer, and the last thing they want is to create wide-spread panic. Mayor Greene only requested that the Fascina community, with its unique resources, will assist the CPD with their investigation."

She sat, relinquishing the floor and making it impossible for any to question her. Again, against protocol. Though Chris was annoyed with her, he shook his head impatiently at Jacqueline when she leaned forward to tell him something.

"A task force to investigate these crimes will be convened to assist the police," Chris stated. "Rumors of a maliker being involved will no longer be voiced. Orson, I leave it to you to select the members."

Chris looked ready to take the gavel from Orson's hand to signal the end of the meeting. Thankfully, Bane, knowing the ruckus it would cause to go against centuries of Fascina tradition, rose to his feet. "I move that we create a task force, formed by Orson, to investigate these attacks." He started to sit but, with a glance at Tally, added, "And that tonight's meeting be adjourned."

"I second the motion," Adrian Shareff called out ingratiatingly, standing with the appropriate amount of pomp. Before another word was spoken, Orson slammed the gavel on the table.

Chris was already up and on his way out of the room, trying to catch up with Jacqueline, as Shareff waded through the crowd to get to Orson. Tally looked up at Bane for help.

"You're as pale as a ghost," he whispered. "And definitely not fine."

"I need to get out of here." She couldn't stop her hands from shaking as what felt like a freight train barreled through her skull. Half the room was packed near the main exit.

"Come on," Bane said, helping her to stand.

Keeping her face a mask of calm under the strain of the mother of all migraines was a struggle.

"Back exit," he added.

She clenched her teeth and managed to nod without passing out or, worse, vomiting in front of all and sundry.

He steered her past the few members who lingered. They lowered their voices to whispers as he squeezed by, most likely speculating on what appeared to be a rift between Chris and Tally.

"Caron. Miss Waever!" Shareff called out from across the room as they pushed through the swinging rear exit doors. Tally stumbled, and they ignored him. As soon as they were through the service doors and out of sight, Bane scooped her up and into his arms.

"Hold on a little longer," he said in a hushed voice. "And close your eyes. I'm going to slip you out of here."

"Absolutely not! It's not worth risking censure."

"Let me worry about that. Besides, the coast is clear. No one will find out." Before she could refuse, he used his powers to instantly move them both into her living room, where he carried her to the couch. "What can I get you?" he whispered, gently removing her shoes, then drawing an old crocheted blanket over her. "Other than a Coke and pretzels."

She gave him the faintest smile, her color already improving. "Am I that predictable?"

He went into her kitchen, grabbed a glass and a can, filled the former with ice, and poured, waiting an interminable amount of time for the fizz to dissipate before topping off her beverage. After tossing some sourdough pretzels into a bowl, he returned to her side. "You're already looking better. How's the melon?"

"Oddly enough, I started feeling better when you told me to close my eyes." She pinned him with her stare. "Bane, you really shouldn't have done that. You're not the only one who would suffer if you were caught."

"No one saw us," he assured her. "And if I had waited, we would still be there, extricating ourselves from Shareff. I don't know why he always feels the need to sidle up to me after every meeting."

She stared at him over the rim of her glass, lifting her eyebrow.

"What? No. You think? If it were anyone else, I would be flattered," he stated thoughtfully. "But not Shareff. Besides, you know that's not how I roll."

"That's not my point. I've never seen him date anyone. Have you?" She took a sip of Coke. "Maybe that 'Mr. Dark and Dangerous and every girl's dream' thing you have going on works for him, too."

"I think your migraine is causing you brain damage," he teased, pushing her legs over to make room to sit. "Most women think I'm a nightmare. Besides, he's even better looking than your brother. He would never look twice at me."

"I guess he's handsome," she said.

"So, you've noticed how attractive he is?"

She made a gagging noise. "Please. I mean, sure, if you're into that sort of studied perfection, which I'm not."

"No?"

"Gorgeous, but way too exhausting. A woman wouldn't be able to keep up."

"So, you don't like him because he's great to look at."

She threw a pillow at him, which he easily deflected. "I don't like him because he's an entitled, pompous ass."

After she propped herself up on the cushions, he handed her a pretzel. "Where's the mutt?" he asked, scanning the main floor for Dusty.

"Probably in the garden, waiting for Michelle to come home. Poor thing. She won't be back for a few more weeks."

Bane snorted. Michelle Bruce was Tally's upstairs tenant, renting the converted attic while she studied design and sustainability at Roosevelt University, and Dusty was her twenty-five-pound Maine Coon cat who hated everyone except Michelle and Tally. The two women had grown to be close friends, and Tally would cat-sit Dusty when Michelle visited her mom in Florida. As if the cat needed to be watched: he was the toughest inside-outside beast in the neighborhood and sported the tattered ears to prove it.

"You're lucky to have found Michelle; she's a good tenant."

"And friend," Tally agreed. A few years back, Michelle returned to Chicago after visiting her family in Florida, only to discover that her building had been condemned. Tally had been biking along the shore near Belmont Harbor when she rode past the young woman sitting on a park bench with two suitcases and a crate, staring at the lake and silently crying. She was holding a thin leash, and at the end of it was the largest cat Tally had ever seen. Michelle had moved into the renovated attic that evening.

"Chris still hasn't forgiven me for renting to a complete stranger without running a security or credit check," she added unabashedly. "I can't imagine what he'd say if he knew how little I'm charging for rent. But some things are more important than money."

Tally stretched. "Michelle has drawn up plans for a moveable chicken coop. Three Rhode Island Reds, max."

"Just make sure the beast doesn't mistake the hens for dinner." He crunched on one of the pretzels. "I can never figure out how you eat these things without making a mess."

"I take tiny bites and brush off the crumbs when you're not looking," she said and laughed.

There was an almost imperceptible change in the air pressure. Tally looked down the hallway; her brother had slipped in. Her twin-senses were almost as acute as a Fascina's when it came to detecting her sibling. She got up and went into the kitchen to prepare herself for whatever excuse Chris had concocted for his rudeness at the meeting.

"How mad is she?" Chris whispered, loud enough that his voice carried.

Bane wasn't so circumspect. "I love you like a brother, but sometimes you're a total jerk. You take advantage of Tally because, deep down, you know she'll always forgive you. Look, I get it. You're trying to impress Jackie, but seriously, Tally is always here for you."

"That bad, huh?"

"You wish you were that lucky."

"I'm not mad at all," Tally said, turning to them both. "I'm just resigned to the fact that I have to put up with your BS all over again."

Her brother was about to protest, but Bane held up his hand. "She's right. Don't even try to deny it. Every time you think you're in love, you end up treating your sister like crap."

"Like I said...not mad," she insisted, wondering why Bane, who usually stayed out of the arguments between Chris and her, was butting in. She shot him a questioning look, but he shrugged and took the cheese-and-cracker board from her hands and set it on the kitchen island. Tally opened a bottle of Syrah and placed it next to the food.

Bane poured two generous glasses, one for Tally and the other for himself. He handed the almost empty bottle to Chris.

"I'll get another bottle," Tally said, starting to rise.

"Like hell," Bane countermanded, but then chuckled. "You should rest."

"I'm sorry, Tally," Chris started. "I didn't know you were having an attack."

She rolled her eyes and gave him an exasperated look. "I do not have 'attacks.' You make it sound like I'm some wilting damsel. Between Bane's overprotectiveness and your cluelessness, the migraine could come back any minute. Knock it off, both of you. Now, would you like some more wine?"

"No, thank you," Chris said, somewhat subdued. "I can't stay anyway."

Tally remained silent, thoughtfully sipping her wine.

"Look, something else came up. Damn it, Tally, Jackie said you would try to make me feel guilty if I backed out of movie night."

"You don't need me to make you feel guilty, Chris. I see right through what you're trying to do. I always have. You are a grown man, capable of making your own decisions, and you don't need my permission to skip sitting here with me and Bane and watching some dopey movie we've seen a thousand times. Just go on your date already."

Chris stared at her for a minute, looking like he was trying to come up with some argument. He finished his wine, and then stood. "Hey, I apologize for earlier at the meeting," he said awkwardly. "I was distracted."

"Another tiff?" Tally asked. "What about this time?"

"More of a...difference of opinion," he replied, his answer confirming at least in her mind that Jacqueline Silva had been complaining about her. "You know, this is the longest relationship I've ever had with anyone?"

Tally nodded.

"I really like Jackie, but there are times when we don't see eye to eye."

"You're trying to work things out, Chris, something you would never have done before. She must be good for you."

Her brother gave her a curious look. "That's what tonight is about. At least I hope."

"Call me tomorrow and fill me in on the details."

"Really?"

"Of course, Chris. I'm always here for you. You know that."

"Thanks, Talz. I love you, sis."

"Love you, too. Now go, before you're late."

Bane waited until Chris slipped away, then asked, "How's your headache?"

"Much better. Though I probably shouldn't be drinking red wine."

"Stella?" he asked, walking to her fridge.

She pushed her barely touched wineglass toward his, knowing he would finish it for her.

"That was nice of you to let him off the hook like that again. I wonder what they were arguing about."

She took the beer from him, drank a long pull, then settled back into the deep couch, the remote for the TV in her hand. "Chris hasn't said anything specific, but I get the feeling that Jackie doesn't approve of me."

"Well, she doesn't approve of me either, so you're in good company."

"The best."

"Nice try. Hand over the remote. It's my turn to pick the movie."

Chapter Four

Tally stared down at the package sitting on her kitchen counter. Her name, Natalia Lillian Waever, stared back at her in her mother's neat script. She forced herself to relax her white-knuckled grip on the paring knife, then slid the sharp blade through the tape.

Inside the box was a small envelope, and she undid the metal clasp and shook the contents into her palm. A flash drive and a folded sheet of her mother's stationary. Her hands shook as she unfolded the paper.

> *Dear Tally,*
>
> *By now, you're beginning to experience some changes. This flash drive will provide you with answers. Forgive me. Everything I did, I did to protect you. When the time comes, you'll know who to trust with your secrets. Never forget that.*
>
> *I love you.*
> *Mom*
>
> *P.S. Do not remove the rose from the canister. Its thorns are deadly. Lock it away until you have need of it.*

Her hands shook as she lifted the preserved rose. Its withered petals had faded from near-black to dusty gray. A memory of a long-ago night flickered in her mind and winked out before she could remember the details. She reread the note, lifted it to her nose, hoping it would smell of her mom's perfume, knowing that after a decade and a half, it wouldn't.

She opened her laptop and plugged in the drive. It contained one large file—a video. Double click. Play. After the first ten minutes, she hit pause. She poured herself a bourbon, then took her drink and her laptop to the couch. Another thirty-two minutes and seventeen seconds later, the last frame of her mother's tear-dampened face smiled regretfully at her. Her final words echoed those in the note. *Never forget that I love you.*

Tally downed the rest of the bourbon, relishing how the liquid scorched down her throat, making her eyes water. She had lived her entire life believing that she was a powerless non-Fascina. Had even come to terms with the anger, the sadness, and, she could now admit, the jealousy she'd felt for her brother. "And don't forget the loneliness."

And then this package arrived. Forty-two minutes of video, and life as she knew it somersaulted. A codicil to her will, Mallory Waever had called it in the video. A message she'd intended to give to her daughter personally, when she deemed her ready. But Sebastian Caron had changed all that when his lust for power led to the murder of Tally's father, and then the death of the one person he coveted most—Mallory Waever.

The gist of it had always been that the sainted Mallory Waever had purposely muted Tally's Fascina abilities before she'd even taken her first step, all to protect her from some terrifying unidentified fate.

According to her mother, Tally's gifts would manifest one by one until she became even more powerful than her brother. She smoothed out the sheets of paper she had crumpled in her hand. A prescribed list of reading material for Tally to review. Books, her mother had said in the video, that would explain why she had had to suppress Tally's powers when she was only an infant. Some of those books rested in the box on the counter. And even though Tally was furious with her mom, she realized deep down that her mother had been right to steal her gifts. Had probably even saved her life. For a toddler with untold power always led to destruction and ruin. It was still hard to believe that only a little more than twenty-five years ago, Tally would've been branded a maliker.

Her mother had been strategic, leaving Tally with the ability to ward off common ailments, such as allergies and colds, and an immunity against falling victim to persuasive powers, like those possessed by Shareff. Unfortunately, this caused her body to be constantly at war with itself—accelerated healing battling to right the wrong perpetrated upon her by her mother. And the side effects? Debilitating headaches.

"Thanks for leaving me to figure this out on my own, Mom." Yet another point which her mother had tearfully regretted.

Her head spun with possibilities of how this would impact her life. She rewatched the video once more before locking it away with the rose in the safe in her office. She grabbed the books and, skipping dinner, went upstairs to her bedroom to read.

• • •

Tally pulled her belongings from her hospital locker and stepped into the narrow gap between the end of the row and the window. She loved ending her day here, taking in this hidden view overlooking the sprawling city. Below her, silver, ridge-roofed trains of various lengths rocked forward on the maze of elevated tracks, spitting their sparks as they groaned and screeched like hungry dragons. She hadn't taken the L today. The pouring rain had seen to that. Her sporty little A4 was in the garage, just waiting to speed her home.

She checked her phone. 7:22 p.m. Though the streets of downtown were moving at a slow but steady pace, Lake Shore Drive would be a nightmare. Still, it would be better than taking Clark to—

"Sir, only staff members are allowed there. I'm afraid you'll have to—"

"I'm looking for Miss Waever. I know I saw her come in here." Tally recognized the voice, and the last thing she wanted was to be trapped in a conversation with Adrian Shareff again, especially considering how grueling her day had been. It'd taken over an hour to recover from her *work*, locked in her office to ensure that no one interrupted. Tally didn't know what else to call it. After noticing how quickly she could heal her own wounds, she discovered that she could influence the healing process of others. She was being careful, not wanting to risk exposing that her mother may have tampered with her genetic make-up. But she'd been secretly helping with the worst cases in the pediatric ward. Her few attempts had yielded astounding results, but each effort had left her completely drained.

"Sir!" There was a scuffle behind her, and the door slammed open. Even though she was confident that Shareff couldn't see her, she drew herself tighter into the confining space. Bane hadn't been lying when he noted how handsome Shareff was, but something about the man made her just a little queasy inside.

"I could've sworn I saw her come in here. Is there another exit?"

"No, there is not. And as you can very well see, the executive lounge is empty. Why don't you ask Reception to page her?" Tally heard the door ease shut and let go of the breath she'd been holding. What was Shareff doing in the hospital anyway? Her phone vibrated, and she nearly jumped out of her skin. She answered it just before the final ring, then fumbled it and watched as it ricocheted off the window and lockers. Bane's name flashed up at her from the screen, which, thankfully, hadn't cracked.

"Tally? Tally?"

"Hi. Sorry. Dropped my phone."

"You sound flustered. Are you okay?"

"Yes. I was avoiding Shareff. He's here, at the hospital, looking for me."

"That's why I'm calling. Orson warned me that he's on the new task force and that he planned on liaising with you. Coming from Shareff, it sounded a little creepy, so I thought I would give you fair notice. Where are you?"

"Holed up in the exec lounge. He's probably lurking in the lobby."

"Are you alone?"

"Yes," she said, knowing he was about to slip in, "but you shouldn't—"

Bane ended the call, then appeared across the room.

She shook her head at him. "You can't keep rescuing me like this, Bane."

"Twice isn't quite a habit. So, how was your shift?"

Already, the fingers of exhaustion inched their way up her neck and into her brain, causing her muscles to tighten even more. He seemed to always know when she'd had a rough day. "Nothing that a hot bath, a glass of wine, and a *Law & Order* marathon can't cure."

"That bad, huh?" he asked, opening the door a crack and looking toward the nurse's station. "The children's ward or Lumina Foundation red tape?"

"Both." She tucked her phone into her pocket. "The most rewarding time of my week is spent with those kids. It's also the most heartbreaking. I want to help them all, but I can never seem to do enough. Is Shareff still out there?"

"Unfortunately," he replied, closing the door he had cracked open. "Ready?" She nodded and closed her eyes, and he pulled her into his arms and slipped them both to her living room. "You work too hard. I have never known you to not visit every single kid on that floor when your volunteer rotation is up."

When she started to sink onto her couch, he took her by her shoulders and turned her in the direction of her stairs. "Go take a bath, and I'll pop back over to get your car." She tossed him her keys. "You can tell me all about your day when I get back. Or we can binge *Law & Order SVU*."

"I knew you were a fan," she called back to him as she trudged up her stairs.

"No way. I hang out with you for an entirely different reason."

"My scintillating conversation?"

"'Fraid not. It's your impeccable taste in wine."

Tally laughed at that. Half the wine she possessed had come from Bane. He was constantly discovering some new winery on the West Coast, or in New York, or even Virginia. But his favorites were the old vineyards in

Europe. He would go away for the weekend, meet some struggling vintner in the Massif Central of France or the Rioja region of Spain. If they got on, he would offer capital for a stake in the business. He rarely talked about his investments, but Tally knew he was more than comfortable. How else could he afford to do what he wanted, when he wanted? When asked about his portfolio, he would shrug and say he only invested in the vines because he loved the grapes. Tally knew better—he liked helping people to succeed.

She climbed the stairs, making her way to her en suite bath. She had really splurged on this room, knocking out a wall to a tiny bedroom. The added space allowed her to accommodate an enormous walk-in closet. After removing her shoes and socks and tossing them in the hamper, she wiggled her toes into the ultra-plush carpet. She headed for the glass-enclosed shower instead of the bathtub and turned on the water. It was hot in seconds, and she stripped, then stepped into the spray of multiple shower heads. She stood there, hands on the marble wall, head hung down, letting the pulsing spray beat down on her neck and shoulders until the low-grade headache that had been creeping up the base of her skull was pounded into submission.

She'd pushed herself too hard today, and lately, it seemed to take longer to recover. Then again, she'd been testing the limits of her capabilities with the children in hospice care. It was worth every yawn, tired muscle, and headache if it meant that one more child would survive. She wished she could help them all, forever taking away their pain, but if she did, people might take notice. And the last thing she needed was to be found unconscious in the hospital locker room while her body repaired itself. Discovery was *not* an option.

Tally shut off the massage heads and turned on the rain shower. She shampooed, scrubbing away the antiseptic reminders of the hospital, towel-dried her hair, and stepped into comfy yoga pants with a slouchy tee. When she caught a glimpse of herself in the mirror, she added an oversized cardigan to her ensemble—she was bra-less, after all. It was that thought that had her stopping short. She had never worried about what she looked like in front of Bane before; why'd it matter now? Because that damn video from her mother had changed everything.

She could hear him downstairs—the pop of a cork being pulled from a bottle, the tossing of stovetop popcorn, and the clinking of wineglasses—and she pictured him carrying all three items to the coffee table. The television came on, and she smiled at the iconic *duhn duhn* of the *Law & Order* theme music.

Maybe she should give her hair a quick blow-dry. "Knock it off. It's just Bane." She took a deep breath, then skipped down the stairs to plop onto the other end of the couch from where he sat. Normally, she would have curled up next to him or thrown her feet in his lap—his shoulder and neck massages were second only to the magic his fingers wrought on her feet. He gave her a look, then pushed her glass closer to where she sat, keeping the bowl of popcorn for himself. He turned his attention to the show, settling back into the cushions, and sipped his wine. Tally's sigh was audible even over the clatter of Elliot throwing a chair at a perp. The corner of Bane's lip twitched. She gave in, sliding closer to him and holding out her hand. He put the bowl between them, and she finally relaxed, holding her wine in one hand and nibbling her snack with the other. Sometime into her second glass of wine and second episode of SVU, she nodded off.

• • •

"Hey, Dad, you there?" Bane addressed his own reflection in the half bath off Tally's front hall. He didn't know why, but he could never look at himself in a mirror without seeing his dad stare back. They shared the same mocha-brown eyes, with a hint of soot that stole away any warmth.

He sometimes imagined that Sebastian Caron had survived being nullified. That his atoms could re-combine to peer at the world through mirrors. It was utter nonsense, but it didn't stop Bane from holding the occasional heart-to-heart chat. "Sebastian. Sebastian. Sebastian," he said three times, mockingly.

"Nada, just like always," he said and sneered. He washed his hands and then banished his father from his mind to really study his own reflection. For once, he liked what he saw. A man relaxed and comfortable. Not his normal outward mien. Only around Tally and Chris did he let down his guard, and that was happening less of late with Chris. Around other Fascina, he bristled. He knew what they all thought of him and what they called him behind his back. But he didn't care; their digs at him meant nothing. It was an entirely different matter when they took aim at Tally for being the victim of a simple trick of genetics.

Thanks to a single toggle switch in the evolution of man, his kind existed. Every Fascina family could trace its lineage back to ancient times, at least as far as humankind's ability to record its history. Fascina were spawned from every corner of the world—South America to Egypt and the Middle East, Asia and Europe, and North America, too. They came from the same peoples who built the henges and pyramids, the Mo'ai and Nazca lines. And the Norms of the world hadn't an inkling of what the strongest Fascina were capable of doing. They only knew of the parlor tricks, the low-level ESP. If it were discovered that they could slip from one place to another faster than Kirk could tell Scotty to beam him back up to the *Enterprise*, the world would never be the same.

Genetics. Tally had the switch, but it remained in the off position. Unbeknownst to anyone, he'd spent years trying to find a way to activate what he believed was within her. He stared at the wadded tissue in the little trash can and wondered if there would be any of her DNA on it... No. He had to stop. Continuing meant delving deeper into the atrocities his father had engineered.

His best friend was a non-Fascina *in extremis*. It was the way of things with Fascina twins—invariably, one of the pair's skills far outweighed the other's. Because of it, Tally's childhood had been nearly as painful as his. They'd both borne the taunts and jeers of their peers. If it hadn't been for her friendship, his life would be entirely different.

He rubbed his hand over his five-o'clock shadow, remembering that hot and humid summer afternoon when Giselle Coyle-Caron had given him up. Tally and Chris had been on holiday, visiting relatives in England. Their mother had taken one look at him, and then thanked Giselle, asking her if she would like to come in for a cup of tea, as if handing over her tweenaged son with nothing but the clothes on his back were the most natural thing in the world. Having settled the particulars the day before, Giselle had declined the invitation and, without another glance at him, abandoned him to another's care. Mrs. Waever had pulled him into her arms, and held him for the longest time, right there in the opulent foyer of their grand, old home. Though she had healed his bruises and cuts that day, it had taken many more years for his heart to mend.

She had also insisted on calling him Braeden, even though he told everyone he preferred Bane. The moniker was his protection, his armor. Mr. Waever had understood and had abided by his wishes. But not Tally's mom. The funny thing was, he loved her more for it. She'd died nearly a decade past, and he missed her still. She had loved him like his mother should have, even if she didn't think he was good enough for her daughter.

Bane turned off the bathroom light and went back into the living room, where he'd left Tally sleeping as the second episode of *SVU* drew to its conclusion. She was thrashing against the blanket that he had pulled over her shoulder—it had somehow become wrapped around her head.

"Tally," he called softly, helping to free her. "Shh. It's okay." He had just tugged the blanket away when she swung out with her fist. He barely managed to dodge the blow that probably could've broken his nose.

"Easy," he soothed. "You're having another bad dream. I'm here. Nothing can hurt you." She opened her eyes, and the terror in them tore a hole through his heart.

• • •

"Bane?"

He nodded and pulled her into his arms, smoothing his hand in comforting circles on her back. She drew in a deep breath. She'd had that same dream, the one she'd had when she'd fallen asleep meditating, four times that she could remember. Twice now, it had been Bane waking her. She pushed him back.

"Another nightmare," he asked. "Want to talk about it?"

"It was the same one that I had in my office. He'd found me and was pulling the sheet away. And then I woke up to you. Again."

"Who was it?"

"No idea. Did you ever have a chance to look at that meditation file from my phone?"

"Sorry. I must've accidentally deleted it."

She stared at him for a minute; her gut told her that he was hiding something, but she was too tired to pursue it. "The dream is so real. And I always wake up before I can see his face. My subconscious must be afraid that I'll recognize him."

"It was just a dream, Tally. It...he can't hurt you." He stood and held out his hand. "Come on, it's late, and you've had a long day. Let me help you upstairs. I'll come back down here and clean up, and then I'll sleep on the couch so you won't be alone."

She allowed herself to be drawn up the stairs to her bedroom. He tucked her in and turned to leave, but she snagged his hand. "You know you could stay in the guest room down the hall?"

"I'll be up and out of here before 5:00 a.m. and don't want to wake you."

"Bane...thanks for staying."

"Anything for you," he replied before heading downstairs to a night on her couch.

Chapter Five

Chris didn't want to hear the truth, Tally realized with a jolt. There was a time when she knew exactly what he was thinking, was sure of his opinions and beliefs. But lately...not so much. She supposed the best way to answer his question about the murders was to be blunt. "Six, that they know of."

"My God," Chris breathed, sitting down.

"There was another one last night," she said. "The police don't want to cause a city-wide panic. The mayor is withholding the details from the joint task force for now. She only told me because she trusts me to only tell you." Bane snorted from across her kitchen, and she rolled her eyes at him. "Correction...to only divulge the information to those who need to know."

"You, the mayor, now us. The police. This will leak," Bane predicted.

Tally shook her head. "Not from the police. They only know of the three murders in Chicago. Detective Haneluk linked the other cases, all cold and all spanning the last ten years."

"And now three in the last seven months. And you're absolutely sure that they don't suspect that this could be the work of a maliker?" Chris asked. "Not that I believe it is. Ever since the ban, there hasn't been an occurrence of one in years...maybe decades."

"That you know of," Bane interjected. "There's a reason some Fascina live on the fringes, even though the cities are safer for us."

"Just so that they can break our laws and risk creating a maliker?"

"Love is love," Bane said dryly, and Chris scoffed at him.

Tally's annoyance at her brother's attitude grew. The Fascina had hidden their malformed offspring from the entire world.

"You both know that the Norms will eventually blame us for this. Then the C.O.F. will blame me," Chris insisted.

"Is that all you can think about, Chris? Innocent people are dying," Tally reminded him, none too gently. "You're better than this. Than them."

"As you seem to keep reminding me lately," he pointed out.

"I shouldn't have to, should I? Mom and Dad—"

"Are not here, are they?" Chris shot back. His phone dinged with a text, and he flipped it over without reading the message.

She looked to Bane for an assist, but he did what he usually did and stayed out of it. "Nice," she mumbled to herself. Something was going on inside her brother's head, something he needed to work out on his own. Tally took a long, even breath. "Chris..." she started.

"You don't know, Tally. The rumblings. The pressure from the National Order. Keeping the peace with the Norms. Hell, stopping the infighting within the Fascina. And now this."

"You're right. I don't know. Because you stopped talking to me."

"Please don't bring Jackie into this," Chris said with more weariness than anger. It was the tiredness in his tone, more than anything else, that had her biting back her retort. Her twin gazed up at her from where he was sitting on her couch. Those damn eyes, eyes that mirrored hers and could see through her, those eyes reflected the same exhaustion that she'd been feeling lately. "Talz, you and I fighting isn't helping. Can we just get through this and then work on whatever it is that's bothering you later?"

"Excuse me? What the ever-loving fuck? *I* didn't bring Jackie into this. *You* did."

"That came out wrong," Chris back-pedaled hastily. "Of course, you're right. We need to help the mayor. This is more important than National Order interference and politics."

Tally narrowed her eyes at him but held her tongue.

"They have no leads," Bane interjected, steering the conversation back to the murders and safer ground, at least for her brother. "Not a single hair or skin cell. No fibers. Nothing. Every scene was sterilized. The only traces belong to the victims."

Tally narrowed her eyes at him. "Been trespassing into the evidence locker?"

He shrugged at her.

"The crime scenes are so clean," Tally relayed. "Haneluk and Greene think it's someone in law enforcement."

"And thus their desire to control the narrative, I'm guessing," Bane added.

"So why bring you into it?" her brother asked, then quickly added, "and when I said *you* just now, I meant the Chicago Order by extension."

"Because one of the victims was Fascina. Maybe two."

"Who?" Chris exclaimed, incredulous.

"Lorna Winters," Bane answered. "You probably don't remember her—"

"She moved to Galena over a decade ago," Chris furnished. "I remember everyone in the Chicago Order. Didn't you go out with her?"

"Hardly. She was at least ten years older than us," Bane quickly corrected. "But she called me once. It was weird...she wanted to offer condolences about my father."

"Who's the other victim?" Chris asked.

Tally blanched. She still felt sick when she recalled the crime scene photos of Lorna's murder.

"She had a daughter named Melissa," Bane said. The gruesome statement hung like an evil odor in the room. "The girl was only nine when Lorna was killed. She seems to have disappeared off the face of the earth. For the police, she's a cold case."

"Detective Haneluk worked in Rockville years ago and had heard about it," Tally explained. "Last week, he drove out to Galena to look at the file; he believes that Lorna's murder was the first. The daughter was never found and is presumed dead."

"Chris, you know as well as I do that this is the work of a powerful Fascina," Bane stated, leaving no room for argument.

Tally had already come to that conclusion, but her position on the council was tenuous enough already. No need for her to proclaim that the serial murderer was a part of *their* community, maybe one of its elite. She watched her brother closely, needing him to say it out loud.

"It's one of us," he finally conceded. "Look, I don't want anyone else to know, not even Orson and the task force. Not yet. We follow Mayor Greene's lead and keep this to ourselves."

"Chris—" Tally started.

"Hear me out first," he asked, slanting a look at Bane.

Bane crossed his arms over his chest. "Why do I think I'm about to be asked to do something I would rather not do?"

"Do you really want the National Order poking around our city?" Chris asked. "Because that's precisely what will happen if this gets out."

"A separate investigation?" Tally asked. "Just the three of us?" Her brother nodded. "Then I need to know where both of you have been at the times of each of the murders."

"I don't think that's necessary," Chris said.

"Fine," Bane agreed at the same time. He turned to her brother. "It'll be the first question that's asked once this comes to light. Best get our alibis in place."

"Good," Tally said when her brother nodded. "I'll email you with the dates." Her phone pinged, and she looked at the message. "Damn. I'm so behind. We'll talk later. Now, get out of my house, so I can get ready."

"Do you need a ride to the gala?" Bane offered. "I can come back after I change."

"Your date would *love* that, I'm sure."

"It's not a problem. Trust me."

Tally was tempted. The big charity event for the hospital was tonight, and she had a little under an hour to get ready before her friend and colleague, Marc, arrived. She could just text him to say that she would meet him there, but she knew how much he hated events like the gala. She was his *de facto* date whenever his partner was out of town; asking to meet him at the museum was akin to giving him the go-ahead to stay home.

"No, thanks, Bane. Marc's picking me up."

"How's the good doctor doing?" Chris asked. "You know, I still secretly harbor the hope that he'll make an honest woman of you one day."

"You know that'll never happen, so stop saying it. It's not even remotely funny."

"I don't mean it to be. Look, you two are good friends. Sure, he's not a strong Fascina, but his talent lies in being a great surgeon. Dating a weak Fascina might be the answer for your...situation."

"My situation? You mean, being a Non?"

"Don't get mad. You have the hospital in common."

"And on that note, I'm outta here," Bane said, and slipped away.

"WTF, Chris! Marc is gay, so stop suggesting that we would be good together."

"I know, but Ryan is always traveling; it might not last. I just want to see my sister happy. Is that so wrong?"

"They're engaged, Chris." His helpless look only made her angrier. "Would you be happy in a platonic marriage? What if Marc needs to get laid? What if *I* need to? What then? Are you suggesting that we have an open arrangement?"

She almost laughed when her brother paled when she mentioned having a sex life of her own. "Yeah, you don't want to think about that, do you?"

"Okay, I get it. Marc is not on the menu. That doesn't mean—"

"Go, Chris. I'll see you at the gala. Please get out of my house. I don't have enough time as it is."

Even before her brother departed, Tally was climbing the stairs two at a time, her mind already working out how she could simultaneously dress and do her makeup. Thank God she'd gone to the stylist to have her pale blond hair set in her preferred, messy up-do before Bane and her brother arrived. She had but a half an hour before she would have to be on the porch, where she would wait for Marc to pull up.

She rarely let Norms into her home—it was just too much of a hassle asking Bane or Chris to reset the protections that kept her house hidden from the world. Michelle, of course, could find their house, but others, when looking for her address, simply couldn't locate the building and would find themselves blocks away before realizing they were on the wrong street. The huge foursquare with Victorian accents was perched upon a coveted double lot on a cul-de-sac near a park, with the nearest neighbor's house set on the far property line. Add to that the established trees and boxwoods, and her backyard garden was a secluded oasis. Even so, hiding it was a power of the highest caliber, creating the ongoing illusion that her address didn't exist, especially as Michelle's unit upstairs had to remain quasi-accessible. But Bane took security seriously. Michelle, happy to have an urban oasis in which to grow things, a home for Dusty, and rent that was affordable on her student budget, never complained. Not even when Bane imposed a training schedule to explain the security measures and had her sign a NDA.

Dusty must have heard her thoughts, for the massive cat wound his way between Tally's legs.

"That day was the first time that I ever saw Bane distracted," Tally said, reaching down to scratch the purring beast's head. Five minutes into Bane's presentation, he'd noticed Michelle's green space design in her open portfolio. What followed was a three-hour discussion on Michelle's business plan—she hadn't even begun to think about one—and a promise from Bane that if her ideas were sound, she could count on him for backing. Since that day, he had become Michelle's mentor, encouraging her to take additional classes at Roosevelt in business administration.

As the epiphany slammed through her brain, Tally stared at her reflection, her hand paused mid-application of mascara. "Damn, he truly cares about people," she swore to her reflection. Not just about Fascina, but about Norms, too. She'd never paid attention to that. He operated quietly and without accolade. And just like that, the threads shrouding his charity fell away from her memories.

"He's concealed the best of himself from everyone," she told Dusty, nudging the cat toward the cushy chair in the corner. It was a type of power that she hadn't thought possible. The ability to maintain such a delicate illusion was genius. It must be related to his ability to mask things, like her home. "You know what, Dusty? Tonight, I'm going to take a good, hard look at our friend Bane." And the thought of doing so filled her chest with a bubble of excitement, making her laugh out loud.

"*Meeerorrh*," Dusty joined in.

The timer on her phone went off, and she jumped. She looked back at her lopsided eyes—one with mascara, the other unpainted. She was still in yoga pants and a tee. The sheath of muted platinum silk still hung from a hook on her closet door. Tally sighed. As quickly as possible, she finished her makeup and donned her silky sheath. It was when she was securing her strappy heels that she noticed that she'd forgotten about her mani-pedi appointment that morning.

"Well, crap, Dusty," she complained, closing her eyes and imagining the perfect nail polish color—*Oy Ve, Oysters*. "Too bad glamouring isn't one of my talents."

When she studied herself in the floor-to-ceiling mirror that covered one wall of her bathroom suite, she gasped. Her fingernails and toenails shined with a pale pearlescent shimmer. She touched her now enameled nails. This wasn't a simple glamour; this was real.

"Another thing to figure out later, Dusty," she said. "You be a good kitty, and I'll give you tuna tomorrow." As fast as she dared, she skipped down the stairs. She was on her porch and off the stoop just as Marc's Mercedes pulled up to the curb.

He lowered the passenger-side window and whistled. "What's the occasion?" he teased, coming around the car to hand her into the passenger seat, looking more handsome than should be legal.

They kissed cheeks. "You don't look too bad yourself, Dr. Changara. Ryan is missing out." Ryan, a low-level Illinois politician with high aspirations, was attending a conference in the capital.

"He's flying home tonight. Gets in at 12:38 a.m."

"From D.C.? I heard there's a big storm headed to the Mid-Atlantic. Won't his flight be cancelled?"

"What a man won't do for love," Marc sang. "He managed to reroute to Charlotte, then a connection to Dallas/Ft. Worth, then back here to Midway."

"That *is* true devotion," Tally agreed.

They made it to the museum in record time, and Marc came around to hand her out of the car as the valet opened the door for her. He tossed the keys to the young man.

Halfway up the steps to the main entrance, the hair on her nape suddenly stood on end, and her skin prickled. Raw emotion pulsed toward her and Marc—anger, jealousy, lust. She looked first at the valet, but he was already driving away. Across the street in the park, under a light that had burned out, she could've sworn a shadowy figure pulled away into the trees and shrubbery. And almost immediately, the eerie feeling evaporated.

"Brr," Marc said, and she nodded. "Let's get inside; that's some chill coming off the lake."

"Must be," she agreed. "And it's nothing a glass of champagne won't remedy."

• • •

"Here, you look like you need this more than I," Marc said, sliding what Bane hoped was a good dose of scotch in a rocks glass across the high cocktail table.

"Thanks," he said, leaning forward and using Marc's body as a screen.

"Your date's not *that* bad." Marc laughed, and Bane cringed at the knowledge that he'd been found out. "Pretty and polite. Has all the finer points of small talk mastered. She's—"

"Talking about how many children she wants."

"Ah."

"Chris warned me, and I thought I'd made it clear that I wasn't interested in—shit, she's found me." He tossed back the scotch to bolster his resolve before she reached them.

"There you are. Come on, the band is only playing one more song and—" Antonia started when she was still ten feet away, just as Chris, Jacqueline, and Tally arrived.

"Don't forget that you promised me at least one dance tonight, Bane," Tally announced, weaving her arm through his and gently nudging him toward the dance floor while Antonia looked daggers at her.

"I did, didn't I?" Bane said with a grin, taking the lead as they stepped away from the group.

"Try not to sound so relieved," Marc whispered as they passed by.

On the dance floor, Bane turned in a graceful circle and pulled Tally close, holding her hand. She settled her other hand on his shoulder, and he reached around her waist to press his palm against the small of her back. He tensed for a moment upon realizing there was nothing but bare skin under his fingertips. Did he imagine her quick intake of breath when he touched her? He must've, for when he gazed down, she smiled back up at him, her face composed.

"Thanks for the rescue," Bane said. "I owe you one."

"Chris should have warned you about Antonia. She's husband hunting."

"He did, sort of." He expertly steered her around the overly crowded dance floor. The orchestra played the modern waltz exquisitely. But not everyone dancing knew the steps, forcing those who did to navigate the area as if it were an obstacle course. Even so, he witnessed several collisions. Tally, of course, had waltzed with him before, and knew him to be a proficient lead, so she gave herself completely into his protection as they glided through the dancers.

"You look lovely," he said, stating the obvious, as he maneuvered them past a couple rocking back and forth. It was a Fascina requisite, knowing how to waltz. And he was always surprised that more Norms did not wish to learn how.

Across the floor, Marc was dancing with Antonia, and she seemed content to have a partner for the last orchestral performance of the evening before the musicians packed up and the more modern band took over.

"Thank you," Tally said simply, reminding him that she was as light as a feather in his arms. "Dog and pony show for the donors, and all that. There seems to be a direct correlation between how much skin I expose and the size of their checks."

"Then you must've raised a record amount for the hospital this year," he said appreciatively. "You are easily the most beautiful woman in the room."

"You're the only man here who could say that to me without leaving me all greasy feeling. Well, there's Marc. And Chris, but..."

"But he's been avoiding you tonight." The waltz was at an end, and he drew them to a stop to clap for the musicians. From the corner of his eye, he saw another couple, clearly inebriated, careening toward Tally. He pulled her close against him, turning so that he took the brunt of the collision. They both heard the rending of fabric at the small of her back.

"Is it bad?" she whispered, her eyes wide, and he steered her toward the edge of the room.

Bane swallowed. All he could feel under his fingers was a smooth expanse of naked skin perforated by the thin silk of, God help him, her thong. She reached back and gasped. He shrugged out of his tuxedo jacket and then swung it over her shoulders. They walked over to the bar, and Bane ordered for them.

"Oh my gosh," she said, astounded, taking the glass of champagne he held out to her. "Just think, if that had happened while we were dancing. The checks would have been enormous!" She began to laugh.

Bane still hadn't quite recovered from having touched her so intimately, but she didn't seem to notice. He laughed with her, hoping he didn't sound like a lunatic. "You'd've earned enough money to build a new wing!"

"There you are," Marc interrupted. "What's so funny?"

"Wardrobe malfunction," Tally admitted. "You look ready to go."

Marc held up his phone and the app showing the nearly completed arc of Ryan's flight. "I just came over to let you know that I'm headed out. Tell your brother I said thanks for giving you a ride home. See you next week." They kissed cheeks, and he was gone.

"Why are you scowling?" Tally asked Bane.

He drew a long breath in through his nose, then exhaled to control his impatience.

"Chris left, didn't he?" She sighed.

"About a half hour ago. Look, Tally, I know you don't like to get mad at him, but—" He stopped at the expression on her face. "Come on, let's get your cloak; I'll see you home."

"What about Antonia?"

"I was running late, so I met her here." They scanned the room for his date.

"There," Tally said, nodding toward a grouping of tables. Antonia must have sensed their scrutiny because she looked over and flipped them off before turning back to her friends and laughing.

"I hope that was meant for you and not me," Tally said.

Bane frowned and shot off a text, and, across the room, Antonia reached for her phone.

Bane's phone dinged. She peeked at his screen and laughed when the middle-finger emoji populated the screen with an echo effect. "What did you text her?"

"I asked if she was sober enough to drive." He looked down at her. "Can you walk in that gown?"

She nodded.

They made it to the curb, and Bane looked at the valet stand, where countless guests were waiting with tickets in hand. A long line of limousines waited to take people home, and he approached the driver of one, handed her a bill from his wallet, and turned to Tally with a wide grin. "Your pumpkin awaits..."

"But what if the person who hired—"

"You live thirty minutes away; she'll be back before they can get their coats. Besides, it'll be another hour before the party winds down."

The chauffeur opened the door for Tally. "He's right, ma'am. I've been bringing this fare to the gala for five years now, and never once did they depart before one a.m."

"If you're sure," Tally relented, getting into the limo.

Bane slid in after.

"I'm Amanda," the driver introduced. "There's champagne, so please help yourself."

Bane checked the label—Perrier Jouet Rose. Nice. He poured two servings.

"Pretty glasses, Amanda," Tally noted.

"Thank you. The limo's mine, and my mom suggested that I upgrade the appointments to attract a better clientele. I sunk every last dollar into this car."

"And did it work?" Bane asked, taking note of the luxurious leather seats, the gleaming wood accents, and the subtle lighting.

"I only accept fares from my regulars now," she said proudly. "Paid off my student loans and bought a condo."

"Do you have a business card?" he asked.

"In the compartment located in the armrest," she said, and he pulled out a card, running the pad of his thumb over the elegant lettering. Embossed. "Unless I get a call—which I promise you I won't—you have me for the next hour and a half. It's a beautiful night for a drive along the lake, so I'll head in that direction before turning west toward your neighborhood." The partition went up, the interior lights dimmed, and the privacy glass on the exterior windows lightened, showing them the sights as the limo glided effortlessly through the light evening traffic toward Lake Shore Drive.

"This is really nice. Thank you, Bane." Tally slid closer to him so that she could better see out the window and sipped from her glass. "Don't wait too long before calling her."

"Who?"

"Amanda."

Startled because he had just been thinking the same, he glanced down at the business card before putting it into his wallet. "What do you mean?"

"You're going to make her dreams come true."

"Tally, I don't—"

"First, you'll set up a meeting with her, go over her business plan, mentor her, then invest. And you are going to make her very rich and very happy."

Bane was speechless. After all these years, she somehow managed to see through his glamour. He gave a little shrug; no sense in denying it. But then Tally threw him for a loop. She set down her empty champagne flute, took his face gently in her hands, and gave him a quick kiss on the lips, one that was entirely dissatisfying.

"You're a good man, Bane," she said and relaxed into the cushy leather seat, completely unaware of how his heart hammered in his chest.

Managing to tear his eyes away from her, he leaned back to stare out at the glistening lake. He could easily *obscurate* her memories of the moment—it was a trick at which he excelled—but he held back. She'd sussed out what he'd been doing and hadn't made a big deal about it because she knew that he wouldn't want her to. She would simply let him go on helping people in his own quiet way. He could feel the warmth of her, sitting next to him, and he pressed his lips together, tasting where hers had touched an abbreviated, "champagne laced but only friends" kiss.

"*Philosi*," he murmured.

"What was that?"

"Nothing. Just something your mom taught me years ago."

Philosi—deep and lasting friendship. He'd been young and wanted to know why his parents didn't seem to love one another the way Tally's parents did, and Mrs. Waever had explained that some Fascina believed that the highest form of love, *agapia,* or the ultimate bonding two souls, was only possible when comprised of three distinct forms—*philosi, erosa,* and *pragmalia.* When he wanted to know more, she took him to their library and pulled out an ancient tome from the shelf. That was her way— never giving the easy answer. And in opening her home to Bane, she had forced him to open his own heart to possibilities he'd never before considered.

He glanced at Tally. *Philosi* was the easiest form of love. Friendship. But what if he needed more? What then?

Chapter Six

The low cut of her gown was indelibly etched into his brain. All that exposed skin, he thought, his mind racing with possibilities. He was too keyed up to not take some sort of pleasure in what the city offered him. But where should he begin?

He ignored the dog he'd taken from his last victim but then laughed when it growled as he walked past. "Good girl," he praised, then refilled her kibble and water. "I don't like you much either." He strode into the paltry space that passed as a kitchen in his secret bolt-hole, then stopped. "How about Jessie?" he asked the designer Labradoodle. A low rumble emanated from its chest. "No? Come on then, dog. I'll let you out back. But no barking! I don't want you to bother the neighbors."

He opened the back door, and she edged warily past him. She was a smart dog, and contrary to what he'd said, he liked her for distrusting him. He turned and stared at the wall above his kitchen table where he'd hung his special dartboard. Each concentric circle was marked with a different letter, A through G. He tossed a dart, planting it in the third ring from the center in the number 2 wedge. "C-2," he said, and then went to consult his map, running his fingertip over the neighborhoods and fondly reminiscing about the places he'd visited before. He hummed as he used his index fingers to trace down from coordinate C and across from 2, then lifted his head. "Hmm. Jefferson Park. Not one of my usual haunts." He glanced at his phone. "Only 12:48—plenty of time to find a nice bar, settle in, and meet someone new."

He rubbed his hands together, then immediately dropped them. "Not so cocky that you make a mistake," he mused aloud to himself. "Finding the right person can take days, weeks even." But he was kidding himself. He was too amped by thwarted plans for the doctor to take it slow. Tonight would be about sex, quick and brutal, all about relieving the ache between his legs. Since he was in a good mood, maybe he would give his partner some relief as well. He called out to the backyard, "Jessie, come." And to his delight, the dog obeyed.

He was about to leave when he noticed the groceries he'd bought the day before were still sitting on the counter. "Stay, Jessie," he commanded as he grabbed the handles of the paper bag. The dog sat, but its gaze followed him down the hallway until he stopped before a monitor on the wall. He pressed his hand to the touchscreen, then tapped the app that controlled the glass door. Like a polaroid whose image slowly develops before one's eyes, he waited, peering into the dim room behind the one-way glass as it came into focus. He touched the bulb icon on the screen, and every light in the small bedroom blazed. Next, he unmuted the mic and spoke, "I told you the last time you did this, if you hide behind the bed, I'll have to remove it again. Only this time, it'll be gone for good."

She slammed herself against the glass door so ferociously, he shrieked and staggered back. After all these years, she was still so spirited, hiding like that against the wall. She must have heard him, for she laughed, convulsing before the door in her threadbare pajamas with the cartoon smiley faces. Pajamas that were just a little too tight. She'd grown from a gangly girl to a skinny teenager and was now a slim young woman in her early twenties.

He touched another icon, and the privacy glass cleared so she could see him studying her. When the dog disobeyed and joined him, his captive frowned, trying, no doubt, to understand what it meant that he had a pet. Most likely, the newness to their routine set off warning bells in the workings of her brain.

"I brought you a treat," he said, and set the grocery bag in the painted, iron-and-steel pass-through—an old-time milkman cubby from the fifties. He'd found this one in the cellar and had repurposed it for his ward. "I'm afraid it melted." She grabbed the bag, rooting through the food he'd brought her and ignoring him when he walked down the hall to another room.

When he returned, she was drinking from a cardboard container. "It's called ice cream."

She scowled at him, still refusing to say a word. She hadn't spoken in over five years, the very last time she'd begged him to let her go. It was her grand silent treatment. "I've brought you something new to wear, Missy. The pajamas you have on are indecent for a woman of your age." She stared at him with an equal measure of fear and loathing that had him smiling. "Set the ice cream down for now. I want to see if it fits before I leave."

She took her time but went to the pass-through. "Go ahead," he ordered. "Use the corner if you need privacy." She bolted away, and he touched the screen to change the view to another camera as she unrolled the lacy negligee. She covered her mouth with her hand, biting down as she trembled.

"If you make me wait, I might just forget to bring you food again." He watched her shed her old pajamas, saw her perfect breasts and the dark tangle between her legs.

When had *that* happened, he wondered, slightly shocked. Had he grown so bored with her that he neglected to see the changes? She clumsily shrugged into the negligee, and he watched as the realization that their relationship was about to change came into her eyes. He would toy with her for months, drawing out and inflating her fears, until when it was time, she would embrace her final breath as a welcome relief.

She stuffed the old pajamas into the pass-through and came to stand before him. "Arms at your sides," he instructed. "Now turn. Let me see all of you. That's so much better, isn't it? Lovely." To think, he'd been entertaining the idea of getting rid of her. But now, after all this time, she'd grown interesting again. "Good girl. I have a new book for you." He touched the screen, bringing up an app, then selected Margaret Atwood's *The Handmaid's Tale*, making sure to loop the audio, stopping the story just before the protagonist had something for which to hope. He raised the privacy tint again.

"Go lie on the bed." She hesitated, staring at the groceries: a thin paper bag full of nutrition bars. "You can put your food away later; do as I say."

She obeyed, reclining to stare at the ceiling. The glaring bright lights bore through the white silk, making it almost translucent. He tapped another command on the screen, and the lights dimmed and shifted to a red glow. Much better. "I want you to listen to this new book five times without moving. And if you're obedient, I might bring you another treat." The book, he knew, would continue to replay the section he'd selected over and over, running nonstop until his return. A week, maybe two.

He turned off the two-way view mode of the door, and Jessie whined. "Something will have to be done with her hair," he said, petting the dog. It had grown too long again—he could see the dark roots. Yes, next week, he would give her something to make her sleep, and then he would slip in for a little grooming time. Maybe buy extra hair dye for certain other areas on her body.

Chapter Seven

It had been almost three weeks since Tally had seen Bane—the night of the gala, in fact. The limo had dropped them off at the park across from her home, and Bane had escorted her inside. But he hadn't stayed.

She'd emailed the dates of the murders to him and her brother the next day, but neither had replied. After that, she'd exhausted all the legitimate reasons for contacting him and had accepted that he would get back to her when he had time. He had a life of his own, as did she. She couldn't always take advantage of their friendship. If he was continuously at her beck and call, he would never find someone to love, another person with whom to raise a family.

Tally finally acknowledged that it bothered her more than she cared to admit. She missed him. Around the second week, she had asked Chris about his whereabouts. Her brother, usually forthcoming, was vague in his reply. Tally persisted, expressing her worry that he might be injured or sick. Chris had rolled his eyes and told her not to fret.

"Condescending jerk of a brother," she said to her reflection. "As if I would *ever* fret."

She leaned forward to apply mascara, forming an *O* with her lips. Bane had seen her do it once and asked why. She explained that it helped her to keep from blinking. Later, he had given her some scientific explanation having to do with the oculomotor nerve stimulating the trigeminal nerve in the jaw. That was Bane—never one to accept the easy answer. She slid the mascara wand home and stared at herself. Twenty days and not a word from him. Her emotions ranged from concern to ire and back again. Now, she was mostly pissed off.

After light swipes of lipstick, she popped her lips to even out the color, then pursed them.

"And to think that I was so nice to him when we left the gala!" She froze and stared at her reflection. Could that be why he was avoiding her? She'd had a little too much champagne, the night was beautiful, and he was such a good person, so she had kissed him. A nothing kiss. An embrace between friends. A simple *bisou*, albeit on the lips, she recalled.

"Damn it, Mother," she said to the ceiling, or heaven, or wherever her mother had gone when she died. She was going to be late for the council meeting if she didn't leave soon. For once, she didn't care and walked to her office instead to watch the video again. Her feelings for Bane—feelings she herself had suppressed all these years—had been stirred up by the recollection of that simple kiss.

The image of her mother appeared on the screen of her laptop.

The inevitable tears welled.

She hit mute and tamped down her emotions. She could hear her mom's words in her head. She even whispered along with some of them.

...I foresaw my death before you were born...your father never knew; he loved you so...to protect you and Christian...I hope you'll one day understand...

Nothing about falling in love. No. Her mother had been bent on protecting her. Never once considering that, believing she was a non-Fascina, Tally could never entertain the idea of being in a romantic relationship with another person. The ban against non- and Fascina couplings was strictly enforced. Tally slammed her laptop shut. She shouldn't have watched the video, not before a council meeting. Not when Chris had been so patronizing of late. Not when Bane had abandoned her.

"Where did that come from?" she asked herself. But she knew; had always known. An entire life of having feelings for Bane and not being able to do a thing about them. She'd come to terms with it long ago. Good thing, because her mother managed to put the *kibosh* on the idea even now.

First, she had to master her powers. And she had to do this with no outside help, for her mother had warned her against revealing that she was full Fascina until she could protect herself. She couldn't even tell Chris.

Twins were not a cause for celebration in the Fascina community. It was believed that they diluted the bloodline. In a few cases, the more dominant of the twins got everything. Such was the case, or so everyone thought, when it came to her and her brother. But as powerful as Chris was, he wasn't the dominant twin. Tally was. Such children were beyond rare, and their strengths were feared more than malikers. If discovered, they were removed from their families and taken away to institutions where they were stripped of their powers.

Tally remembered the hope that had sprung into her heart when she first heard her mother's words: "*...and your gifts will eclipse those of your brother's.*"

At the time, she had not thought about all the years of condescension, of derision, of toleration of her presence at the council meetings. No. The very first thought that bloomed in her heart had been for Bane. And then her mother's voice on the video cut through her joy. *"...must not tell anyone...loss of life...Christian, Braeden, you. You must give yourself time to harness your power so that it cannot be corrupted by others who would wish to use you. You must hide your gifts until you are ready. You will know when to reveal yourself."*

"Yeah, Mom," Tally muttered. "When will that be?"

Her phone chimed. It was Bane.

Need ride to mtg?

"No, I don't need a ride! Especially from you!" she yelled at her phone, then switched it to DO NOT DISTURB. She stomped down her stairs and out the back door to her alley-access garage. She was in the mood for speed, so she climbed into her little black Audi. She took the long way to get to her destination. But then, traffic seemed to magically move out of her way. Even the police car that she passed—fifteen miles over the speed limit— ignored her. She was poised to take the corner and pull up to the valet, but saw that Bane was standing on the sidewalk and, thankfully, looking the other way.

"Nope." She shifted gears, cutting across four lanes to reach the down ramp as her A4 dove to the lower drive. Downshifting at the garage entrance, she expertly zipped into her reserved spot near the elevator bank. She tossed her keys to the attendant in the booth, then punched the up button on the call panel. Bane had been waiting for her...she knew it in her gut. Well, he could wait all night for all she cared.

• • •

No reply. She must be driving. When the high-performance purr of Tally's car revved behind him, Bane resisted turning around, even though he wanted to make sure she made it safely across the busy surface street. He climbed up the steps to enter the main lobby of the Chicago Order's headquarters and then strode through the doors into the large meeting room where the monthly board meeting took place. "Parking," he said, and Chris nodded back.

Bane sat, poured himself some water, and gingerly leaned back. He wore his habitual scowl and kept his sunglasses on. He'd sported them before to meetings, letting the others believe they hid bloodshot eyes from drinking all night, or worse. The more fantastic their ideas about him were, the better. It kept people at bay, if not a little afraid.

No one would guess, not even Tally, as she took her seat with nary a glance his way, that he had a black eye, a fractured wrist, and three bruised ribs. He'd lost count of the stitches sewn across his shoulder, where he'd been knifed. Two days ago, he had slipped into the good Doctor Changara's condominium.

Marc had taken Bane at his word when he said his ribs were only bruised. He stitched him up, set his wrist, and gave him enough painkillers to put down an elephant. They'd knocked Bane out for about four hours. It wasn't the first time Bane had paid the doctor a visit in his home, and now Marc kept an ambulance-worthy med kit on the premises. As far as Bane knew, Marc had never told Tally about the reverse house calls. Everyone had secrets.

"Pass the water, please," Tally asked of him as the room began to settle. He reached for the pitcher, remembering too late that his wrist was broken.

"Take mine," he said a little roughly, earning him a curious glance.

She took his glass, but then stretched for the pitcher, the delicate scent of her wafting under his nose, and poured him another. Then she set it down within his reach before scribbling a note to him.

You look like shit.

She narrowed her eyes at his scraped knuckles and swollen fingers before he had a chance to hide them.

"Damn it, Bane," she whispered. "Is that a black eye? And what's wrong with your hand? Is that a cast under your sleeve? I can't be pissed at you if you're hurt."

He smiled at that, then doodled a picture of a dove with an olive branch in its beak on the pad. In reply, she drew a rain cloud over it. He wrote back:

I hate to ask...but I need a lift home.

"Fine," she whispered a little too loudly.

At the end of the table, Orson gave them a censorious look and cleared his throat. "First order of business. You'll find a copy of the task force's progress in the binder. We've been providing an assist but haven't been able to come up with any tangible insight—at least not that we can give to the Norms."

Bane knew his intelligence gathering had surpassed that of the task force. Chris had asked him to check in with Giselle, his mother, for she had kept up some of his father's more below-board acquaintances. He had hoped to have more to share, but the only thing he'd come away with from his visit was his current physical state. In the end, she had only confirmed that a maliker's power came from their malice, infusing their physical strength. Any power they possessed was raw and clumsy. *Brute force*, she had said with a satisfied smile.

It was what Bane had suspected all along, so he had thanked her and made to leave. But then she'd asked him that which she asked every time he was sent to her to ferret out information—she asked him to stay. And Bane had replied the way he always replied. No.

Only this time, she surprised him with a new tactic, one that had him incapacitated for over a week. For the first time in his life, she'd accepted some responsibility in how he was treated as a child, and she apologized to him for her part in making him unhappy. Fool that he was, he half believed, half pitied her and, in the end, had accepted her invitation to stay for dinner. He should've known better when she came out of the kitchen with his favorite dessert. She must've been planning the ambush for months, just waiting for the perfect opportunity. And thanks to the drugs she'd put in his food—just enough to slow his reactions—her latest groupie was able to get the jump on him. A hypodermic needle pricked his skin, and chemicals flooded his system. The last thing he saw was the half-eaten slice of angel food cake in front of him as he fell forward and lost consciousness. Seven days later, he came to in a garbage-strewn, rat-infested alley, beaten, bloodied, and bruised, and still smelling of his favorite boiled raspberry icing. He'd had just enough strength for one slip.

The scrapes of chairs drew him back to the present with a jolt. He'd tuned out the entire meeting, but no one seemed to have noticed his lapse. Except Tally—she faced him with worry-filled eyes, regarding him the same way her mother had all those years ago.

"Orson," Chris called out as the others were leaving the room, "can you hang around for a few more minutes?"

"Sure, what's on your mind?"

Chris tapped his binder. "Tell me what's between the lines."

Orson sat back down, a bit wearily. Bane waited, not knowing where Chris was taking this. "I think you've already figured it out," Orson said— *Ah*, Bane thought.— "The killer must be one of the Fascina."

Chris steepled his hands. "Is this your conclusion alone?"

"Preston and Comford might suspect it. Shareff is clueless. He believes our community is *above* such conduct." Orson shot an abbreviated look at Bane.

WTF, he thought.

"Shareff is a blockhead," Chris said unkindly. "I don't want you operating in the dark, Orson, so I'll let you know that I've come to the same conclusion. It's vital that this doesn't get out. The C.O.F. isn't ready for this kind of news. And neither are the CPD and the Norm community. The repercussions alone... I don't even want to think about it. I say we keep this under wraps until we have proof, and then we take it to Mayor Greene."

"I suppose it could be someone from outside Chicago," Orson noted, but not before shooting another dark look at Bane. "How would you like me to move forward with the others on our task force?"

"Carefully," Bane replied, not liking the vibe he was getting from Orson.

"Keep it between us for now," Chris directed. "If it comes up, instruct the task force to put a lid on it until you have concrete evidence."

Orson nodded and made his goodbyes. At the door, he paused. "It would be helpful if we could eliminate suspects, starting at the top, by collecting alibis for the nights in question." Again, he glanced at Bane, longer this time.

"I already did that," Tally said swiftly. "At least for Bane and Chris. They were with me during several of the attacks—I checked my calendar. So, unless they can be in two places at once, they're in the clear."

"Wouldn't that be something," Orson said mysteriously. "I'll make a list, starting with the board."

Bane got the feeling he wanted to say more. Tally must've thought so too because she asked, "What is it, Orson?"

He glanced at Bane. "Nothing. It's nothing, I'm sure."

"If you have something to say about me, Orson, best to get it out. God knows I'm used to the rumors."

"That's just it, Bane," Orson said. "It's not a rumor. And it's not about you. It's about your girlfriend."

"I don't have a girlfriend," Bane stated.

"He doesn't have a girlfriend," Tally said at the same time.

"Your date, then," Orson said.

"My date?"

"From the gala. Antonia Benedict. I heard that she wasn't exactly happy with you that evening."

"Great. What's she been saying?"

"Nothing. At least not recently," Orson said. "She went away for a weekend trip to her parents' beach house." He looked around as if others were within hearing and lowered his voice. "George and Catrin were worried because she didn't come home, so they checked the beach house, and it looks like she never made it there."

"When was this?" Chris demanded.

"About two weeks ago. Look…I'm sure she's fine. George even said she's done this before—going off on some adventure or another to reset at the end of a failed relationship, but her—"

"There was no relationship," Bane said flatly.

"You asked," Orson said, putting up his hands. "It's just that you've been gone, too. If she doesn't turn up, people are going to start asking questions."

"Orson!" Tally cried. "You can't think that Bane has anything to do with Antonia going off the radar again."

"No, of course not."

"Thanks for filling us in, Orson," Chris put in. "Let's focus on clearing the names of those on the task force first." Orson nodded. "I mean it, my friend. Thank you for always having our backs. I don't know what we would do without you."

"You know you'll always have my support, Chris. Tally. Have a good night." He nodded to them all, then closed the door as he exited.

"Why didn't you tell him about the other attacks?" Tally asked, putting a point to what was running through Bane's mind.

"I will, but not yet. Let's keep that to the three of us for now. Did you really check on our alibis?" Chris asked.

"Well, yes. When you both ignored my emails, I did some backtracking. One or both of you were almost always with me, enough times to rule you out as suspects."

"Thanks, Talz," Chris said, glancing at his watch. "Hey, sorry. I've got to get going."

"See you," Bane called after him as he rushed out the door. He turned to Tally.

"Do you need to lean on me, old man?" she asked.

Bane tried not to laugh. It hurt too much.

Chapter Eight

"This isn't the way to my place," Bane remarked as Tally picked up speed.

"That's because you never have anything in your fridge, and you need to eat if you're going to heal after the beating that you obviously took but aren't telling me about," she said in one angry breath. "Go ahead."

When he gave her a curious look, she added, "Black eye, broken wrist, scraped up hands, bruised jaw..." He touched his jaw as if he hadn't noticed. "Typical. What else?"

He sighed, drawing in a deep breath and wincing.

She swore under her breath. "Damn it, Bane. Broken or bruised?"

"Bruised," he finally admitted. "Three ribs. And...a few stitches."

The silence as she drove through the city was uncomfortable. When she turned into her alley, she asked, "Why? Why do you go back?" He didn't answer. "Ah, Chris asked you."

"I would've told you, but I know how you worry."

She pulled into her garage. "Stop. Just...stop. You went missing. Someone *should* worry. And to think that I thought it was—forget it." She got out of the car, walked around, and opened his door, giving him her hand to help him out of the low-riding vehicle. Instead of walking to her back door, she cut through the side yard and crossed her street to the broad park that her house faced. Bane remained silent but caught up with her to walk the half block to her favorite restaurant. From the outside, the only indication that there was a business in the three-story building was the modest wood sign hanging above the entrance with the name, Nonna Lucia's, painted on it in an elegant script.

"Take out, or can you handle dine in?" she asked.

"Dine in."

"You're paying," she said as she held the door open for him, then followed him into the intimate neighborhood restaurant. The owner immediately ushered them to a table in the back courtyard, passing by the open kitchen where the aromas of oregano and garlic and tomatoes intermingled.

Tally loved the house-made pastas and breads, and *Nonna Lucia's* gelatos were so delicious, it was a crime. A year ago, they had closed for a few months, and Tally had worried that they had gone out of business, but then she received an invitation to their grand reopening. Gone were the Tuscan-themed murals, Italian pasta bowls converted into pendant lights, and the ubiquitous red leather banquettes that seemed to plague so many family-owned restaurants. Diners were greeted with authenticity, right down to the terra-cotta tiles in the new alfresco dining area, the imported wood-burning oven, and the glazed Italian pottery on which the excellent food was served. She turned to say something to Bane, but he was chatting with the chef, Frank Carilio.

"Your usual Chianti?" the server, who also happened to be the owner's daughter and wife to Chef Frank, asked.

"Sure. Thanks, Kathy." She watched as Bane clapped Frank on the back before joining her at their table. "And a Negroni, please."

"I'll be right back. Oh, make sure to save room tonight. Joanie made cannoli." She acknowledged Bane with a nod when he took his seat.

Tally pinned her gaze on Bane as he removed his sunglasses. "You invested here, too," she accused, frowning at the ugly puce-colored mottling under his eye. There was a gash on his cheekbone, though it apparently hadn't been deep enough to warrant stitches. He patiently endured her scrutiny.

"Just don't mess with the pasta," she capitulated, knowing her anger toward him wasn't about the restaurant. "Or the desserts."

"Understood," he promised. "The food here was never the issue. The facelift is only a reflection of the simplicity of the flavors that come out of Frank's kitchen. There's already a waitlist for reservations—Fridays and Saturdays are booked three weeks out."

"I'll keep that in mind."

"Tally, you don't need a reservation here. Ever."

Kathy appeared and took their orders, from antipasti to gelato. "No cannoli?" she asked.

"An order to go, please," Tally stated. "Bane is paying, after all."

He laughed, then rubbed his jaw.

Tally just managed to stop herself from reaching out. Instead, she turned her attention to the courtyard, now illuminated by various up-lit potted trees and a pergola strung with old-fashioned lights artfully crisscrossing the space above them. The candlelit tables were spread out far enough that conversations would remain private and intimate. And, as she gazed at the couples dining together, romantic.

"I wanted to—" she started.

"What were you—" he began.

They fell into an awkward silence, which was weird because they'd never been uncomfortable around each other. Kathy rescued them by arriving with the appetizers, inviting their conversation to turn toward the food. Salads followed, then entrées. When they finished their gelatos, Bane settled the bill with Joanie while Kathy chatted with Tally near the entrance.

He handed her a pastry box. "Your cannoli," he said, then opened the door for her. "So, what did you want to tell me earlier?" he asked as they strolled through the park.

"You go first."

Bane was silent for a minute and then drew her to a bench. "I'm sorry I didn't tell you where I was going."

"If you had, I could've helped you."

He smiled ruefully.

"Ah. I see."

"My mother isn't exactly a stable person. If you got hurt...I couldn't..."

"She could never hurt me, Bane. She couldn't." Tally brushed his scraped knuckles with her fingertips.

"You put too much stock in the friendship she had with your mother. My father's banishment, her disgrace...it changed her."

Tally stared at her hands, hating herself for keeping up the lie. Giselle Coyle-Caron couldn't hurt her. Tally was simply too powerful. Healing and parlor tricks aside, she was discovering that she could also sense emotions and intentions. And she could move things—like the texting truck driver who had swerved into her lane and nearly driven her into a concrete barrier on the Kennedy. She'd almost tried slipping, but she'd chickened out, afraid that she would end up inside a wall. Not knowing how her gifts worked made her afraid to use them. She didn't say any of this to Bane. Better to let him think she was counting on her mother's past friendship with Giselle to protect her.

"Come on," he said. "Let me get you home so we can eat these cannoli."

At her place, she uncorked a bottle of wine while he plated the pastries. They sat on the couch, watching nothing at all on the television but not really talking either. She could feel the exhaustion pouring off him. "You're staying here tonight," she ordered. "No couch. It's the guest room for you." She stood and held out her hand. He took it and rose with a groan.

"And you are going to let me check your injuries, Bane. No arguing." Had she not been holding his hand, she would not have noticed the spike of anger that flashed through him. Before she could check her instinct to heal, she reached out to soothe him. It was instinctual; she'd been helping patients at the hospital for years without even knowing it. But this time, the experience wasn't one way. Emotions flowed back. A feeling from Bane...something she'd herself felt her entire life—longing.

And not the everyday *needs* that most people carried around with them, either, but heart-and-soul-wrenching *want*. She was so surprised that she forgot to guard against the flowback, and some of her own aching sluiced back into him. The weight of his stare had her afraid of meeting his eyes.

"Tally, please tell me what you were going to say earlier?"

"Nothing. It was stupid." But he wasn't going to let go of her hand, nor would he let her words go unstated. "I, uh, thought you were avoiding me."

"Avoiding you? Why?"

"It's ridiculous...never mind." She tried to turn from him, but he touched her cheek, then tipped up her chin so that their gazes met. "You're going to laugh. It's that dumb."

He waited.

"I thought I might have offended you...in the limo...when I, uh, kissed you."

But Bane didn't laugh and continued to stare at her. She could barely stand his intense scrutiny, and then he took a step nearer.

"*Bane,*" she whispered as his head tilted and his lips slanted toward hers. All she had to do was move, less than an inch, and their lips would touch. She could feel the warmth of his exhale, though, like her, he didn't seem to be breathing. Her lips parted as he moved to eliminate that last bit of space between them.

"*Hey, Tally. I saw the lights on. Are you awake?*" The words crackling through the backdoor's intercom felt like a bucket of ice had been dumped over her head. "*It's me. Michelle.*"

Bane stepped back, and Tally, bewildered by what had almost happened, gave herself a mental shake. "Um... I-I have to..." She trailed off and went to let Michelle into the kitchen. Behind her, Bane cleared the dishes and wineglasses, setting them on the counter near the sink.

"I'm sorry to bother you so late, but—"

"You're not bothering me, Michelle." She somehow managed to say it without stuttering, because, holy crap, Bane had almost kissed her. "What's up?"

Michelle, holding her cat, looked back and forth between her and Bane. "It can wait until tomorrow. I'll just..." Dusty squirmed and dropped to the floor with a loud *plunk*.

"I was just leaving," Bane announced, and Tally barely managed to keep her jaw from clenching. "Are you working tomorrow, Tally?" She shook her head, rendered temporarily mute. "Great. I'll see you for breakfast. I'll bring the bagels and schmear." She nodded at him as he strode to the front of her home, where he would pretend to leave via the front door and instead slip away unseen by Michelle.

She stared at the spot where he had disappeared down the hall. Dusty snaked between her ankles, then padded haughtily up the stairs to the bedrooms like he owned the place.

"Aw, Tally, I'm so sorry I interrupted the two of you."

"What? No. You didn't." She accepted a glass of wine that Michelle had poured and followed her friend to the couch.

"Please. Do you know how long I've been waiting for you guys to hook up? Since the day I met you and he dropped by." Michelle sat there, grinning from ear to ear. "C'mon. Don't tell me you're not attracted to him. I've seen the way you look at him when you think no one is watching."

Tally blushed.

"Ah ha! I knew it! Look, I get that you all, your family and people, have all kinds of weird rules about who can date who, but there's no reason you can't have some not-so-innocent fun. I mean, he is one smokin' hottie."

"But we can't just...and he doesn't—"

"Doesn't what? Look at you the same way you sneak those peeks at him? Get a clue, girl. He is so into you."

Suddenly, Tally worried that others could see it, and she frowned.

"Uh-uh, don't be thinking that way. No one else has noticed."

"But you did."

"You think Fascina are the only ones who can sense things? My grandmum could read tarot cards. I'm just extra sensitive to people in love. Or lust."

"You won't tell anyone, will you?"

"That's your private business, isn't it? I won't say another word except, damn, Tally, it's about time. And I'm so happy for you. Bane is a great guy."

Tally grinned. "I kissed him, just a peck, after the gala. It was innocent. But I've been thinking about it, and I think he has too."

"So, did you kiss for real tonight?"

Tally pulled a face.

"Dang it. I *did* interrupt."

"It's okay," Tally said, laughing. "He's bringing bagels tomorrow, remember? Anyway, it's better that we talk first." She sipped her wine. "So, do you need me to watch Dusty?"

Michelle nodded. "Yep, for a couple weeks. I need to de-catify upstairs because my little sister is coming to stay while my mom gets a much-needed vacation with my stepdad."

"Kayla, right?"

"That's her. But she has asthma, so Dusty is banished. I'll need a few days just to remove all traces of him from my place. Are you sure you don't mind?"

"It's my pleasure. I love that cat. Whether or not he likes me..."

"He likes you. Bane, too, come to think of it." She finished her wine and stood. "Thank you, Tally. You're the best landlady in Chicago, and an even better friend."

"Can I get that on a mug?"

Michelle hooted, then gave her a quick hug.

After her friend departed, and Tally finished cleaning up, she washed her face, brushed her teeth, and pulled on her pjs before plopping on her bed. She closed her eyes and then did something she hadn't done in ages. She imagined what it would be like if Bane kissed her. Only this time, she had more material for her imagination. She pressed her fingers to her lips, pretending it was Bane who touched her. Tracing her other hand down over her breasts, she paused at her nipples for a moment, then slid lower to tease herself until she called out his name. And this time, that crushing emptiness did not envelop her, reminding her that they could never be together. No, this time, she fell asleep with a smile on her face because, after all these years, there was a chance that he wanted her as much as she wanted him.

Chapter Nine

Deep in the shade of the oak trees, with their noble limbs arcing over the spot where he'd parked, he waited. He checked his watch again. She must be sleeping in, or perhaps she was having one of her migraines. Usually, Sunday mornings found her taking a walk to the neighborhood diner, an old standby for Chicagoans, one that still had a faint scent of cigarettes, even though the city had banned smoking from restaurants years ago.

Beside him, he looked at the beautiful roses sitting on the passenger seat next to the breakfast pastries he'd picked up. "Now or never," he announced, grabbing the box and bouquet and climbing out of his car. As he neared her house, a delivery van pulled up. A person hopped out, looked at his phone, then directly at her house, and then back at his phone. He scrolled, then made a call, walking a few steps away and looking down the street. He turned, stared, and then climbed the very steps that led to Natalia's front door. He waited a minute or so for someone to answer. When no one did, he set the package out of sight on the porch, and then skipped down the steps, humming some tune that only he could hear, thanks to his earbuds. The delivery man climbed back into his vehicle and sped away.

When the van finally turned the corner and drove out of view, he exited his car and climbed the steps and spied a small box. There was a tiny card with Natalia's name spelled out in elegant by-hand calligraphy and a brief note of apology for missing breakfast. He removed the lid to find a small bouquet of violets within.

A posy—how quaint.

And intimate.

There was no name indicating who had sent the flowers. He surprised himself by pulverizing them and throwing the pieces over the side of the porch. The crushed box followed its ruined contents. He stomped down the steps and stalked up the sidewalk to where he had parked, throwing the dark roses he'd brought for her into the nearest storm drain.

One day, when Natalia was his—to own and command—he would make her understand how every act he'd committed had been for her. In turn, she would worship him. He peeled out of her neighborhood, driving much too fast for the narrow street and almost colliding with another vehicle. But then he was on one of the broader diagonals, speeding through yellow lights and ignoring horns and angry gestures. Maybe Natalia had ordered the flowers for herself, he thought, but even that idea annoyed him. Why tiny, nothing violets? She deserved so much more.

"Stupid!" He should have swapped the two bouquets. He tore recklessly down the alley that led to his home away from home and then pulled into his garage. Once in his backyard with its high privacy fence, he surveyed the make-shift greenhouse he'd installed. It had taken him years to duplicate the color of the infamous roses, and he'd tossed them into the gutter like worthless trash. There were only another ten or so buds that had yet to bloom; he would have to use them sparingly.

The dog had sensed his arrival and whined to be let out. "Were you a good girl?" he asked when he opened his back door. The animal sat and thumped her tail, waiting for permission to exit the house and do her business. He'd had to retrain the mutt, and was pleased, if not growing bored, with her superlative behavior. "Out." The dog stood, walked past him, her tail wagging as she went by the narrow space on the stairs, and bounded to the back corner where she did her business. It was time to clean up there again.

It'd been a couple of weeks since he'd thrown dog excrement over his fence and into his neighbors' backyards. One neighbor was a decrepit octogenarian, the other a college student whose parents owned the house and who had any number of roommates living with him. The kid took no pride in his yard. And what did his parents do? They paid thousands of dollars to a landscaper to come in and plant vinca vines. What were a few dog feces to a plant that provided a safe haven for rats?

"Come, Jessie. Good dog," he crooned as the mutt swiped past him. In his kitchen again, he picked up a dart to throw and missed the target completely, hitting just below the number sixteen. That meant consulting a different map, one that would take him farther afield. "Platteville, Wisconsin—four hours away, six if traffic is bad," he complained, and catching his mood, the dog sat next to him and lifted her front paw. "Let's get you fed. Then we'll go for a ride. Would you like that?" The dog cocked her head, her eyes brightening.

As he walked down the hall, Jessie followed, but gave the right wall a wide berth, whining as they passed the control screen and door.

"Well, shit, Jessie. I completely forgot about her in all the recent excitement." It'd been over two weeks since he'd given Missy any food.

He knew that she hoarded what he gave her, thinking him unaware. She couldn't have starved yet. He paused, unmasked the monitor, and tapped the screen. Missy wasn't in the bedroom, so he switched to the bath-cam.

There she was, drinking water directly from the tap—he'd never given her a cup, or any plate or utensil, for that matter. Her nightgown was filthy, having not been washed in weeks.

He thought for a moment—there was nothing in the house except kibble. He went back into the kitchen and grabbed the bag. From the bedroom next to Missy's, he opened a drawer and pulled out a clean negligee and a pair of lace underpants, these more revealing than the ones she wore now. Then, he walked to where the pass-through waited and switched the camera back to her main room. She was there, looking more vulnerable than he'd ever seen her.

When he opened the hatch, depositing the negligee and turning the bin, she heard the scrape and stumbled to crouch behind her bed.

"Put it on," he said dispassionately. He watched her on the monitor, how her eyes darted to where the door was located, waiting for him to reveal himself. When he didn't, she scuffled over and grabbed the negligee, heading to the bathroom. "No," he ordered. "Right where you are standing." She didn't move, and he was about to threaten her, when she finally pulled her arms free of the dirty nightgown's straps.

"Everything," he stated breathlessly, and in his mind, replaced her image with that of Natalia's. She was beautiful as she stood naked in the middle of her room. Her slim waist and full breasts, perfect in every way, and he grew hard, thinking they would finally be together. The new negligee had been selected especially for Natalia—it was just the right shade of ivory. "Put it on, my love," he commanded and watched with pride as she obeyed him.

"So beautiful." The negligee was a little too short, he noted, staring at her feet. His eyes traveled up her slim form, and—

Disgusting, he thought, as Missy's face stared, hollow-eyed, back at him. He'd lost interest in his houseguest and all the plans he had for her. Soon, he would have to come to some decision about Missy, and do so before the day came that he completely forgot that she was here.

He picked up the bag of kibble and poured its contents into the pass-through's receptacle. Then, he turned the handle, and dog food rained down onto the floor in Missy's room. He had to hand it to her. Even half-starved, she didn't race to the food. Instead, she dropped to the floor, buried her face in her hands, and wept.

Pitiful. Even Missy sensed that her time with him was nearing its end.

He pressed the mic button and spoke, "When your day comes, I don't want you to worry. I'll make sure it's special. Though I don't love you, we'll be together, because you deserve me. And afterward, I'll set you free."

"Please," she begged, finally breaking her years of silence. "Tell me what I did wrong."

He pressed another menu command, and her pleading was cut off. Jessie sat patiently, staring at the door.

"Come on, girl," he said jovially. "I promised you a ride."

Chapter Ten

She was doing it again. She'd never been a toe tapper before, Tally noted, taking a deep breath while she waited on the uncomfortable couch outside the mayor's office. Her stomach grumbled, reminding her that she'd missed bagels with Bane. There went her foot again. No breakfast, and now it was pouring rain outside. She had wanted to hug the mayor's assistant, Ken, when he asked if she wanted anything to eat while she waited. She'd settled for a strong cup of coffee. Ken nodded, raised an eyebrow at her swinging foot, and promised to return with a plate of Danish, just in case she was hungry. Tally had always liked Ken. Unfortunately, it wasn't hunger that had her stomach in knots. Something in the case must have broken.

It was a few minutes later that two FBI agents exited the mayor's conference room. One could always tell who they were from the much-too-studied casual demeanor to the friendly smiles, but searching eyes. Tally wasn't afraid of the pair of agents, but she wasn't happy to see them either. They turned and stared at her as if waiting for her to do something. And then she understood—they thought she was the receptionist. She smiled politely, then resumed flipping through the pages of the *Chicago Magazine* that she was studiously not reading. Her feet were planted firmly on the thick rug, behaving.

In that moment, she'd sized them up. It was clear that the older agent was in charge. He stepped forward, standing above her—close enough that it might feel intimidating, but far enough away to avoid appearing rude.

Definitely feds.

"Good morning," he finally said.

"Is it?" Tally replied without looking up from the glossy pages of the tourist magazine. "The rain is quite awful."

"I'm Special Agent Reiss, and that's Special Agent Lima."

She almost smiled...rice and beans.

"Nice to meet you," she replied, purposefully not offering her name as they sorted through their mental catalog of criminals. Her family, and most of the Fascina Order, were wary when it came to the federal government. Chicago, like most large metropolises, did not require a Fascina registration.

Not so in other areas of the country, where fear and suspicion of anyone different still held sway. Regardless, the feds kept files on all the prominent families in her community. As she possessed no special talents—as far as anyone knew—her name would have only been an aside. And if the mayor hadn't told them that Tally had been called in, she wasn't about to reveal her identity and give them time to check her out. Lima pulled out his phone, ostensibly to check his messages. Tally lifted the magazine to block his camera.

As he moved closer, Ken returned, carrying a tray. He wedged himself between the agents and Tally in order to set her coffee on the table. Tally flashed a grateful smile when he rolled his eyes. She had an entirely new appreciation for the man.

"Cream and sugar?"

"That would be lovely. Thank you, Ken." He filled a porcelain mug bearing the Seal of Chicago with dark, strong coffee, added the accoutrements, then gestured to the pastries. She lifted the hot beverage and breathed in the delicious aroma, her brain popping awake at the scent of the caffeinated beverage.

"Mayor Greene asked me to show you out, gentlemen. This way, please."

Tally could feel their disdain as they stared down at her, but they departed. Soon after, Detective Haneluk entered. He held a disposable cup of coffee in one hand and a dripping umbrella in the other.

Detective Barney Haneluk hung his trench coat on the hook next to Tally's and sat in the chair nearest the couch. Tally held out her plate of Danish, and he happily wolfed down two in short order. "Thanks," he said gruffly. "I needed that."

"Late night?"

"Tally..." he started, and she knew something bad was coming. "Did you know about them? The malikers?"

Her silence was answer enough.

"You should have told us. You made Greene look like a fool in front of the Bureau."

"It wasn't relevant to—"

"Not relevant? There are deranged magical people running amok in my city, and you don't think it's relevant? That wasn't your call. I thought we trusted one another."

"There aren't 'deranged people' running amok, Barney. And there's no such thing as magic. That's just ridiculous."

He gave her a look that told her he thought she was splitting hairs. "Oh, yeah? They have one in custody. The feds caught him. More than one, if my source is right. Not just here, but in New York, and L.A., too."

"That doesn't make sense. There hasn't been a—" Before Tally could finish, Ken returned and waved them into Greene's office.

The mayor's usual warm smile was in place, but it didn't quite reach her eyes. She slid a thick file across the conference table. "Tally, your brother should have told us about these... I don't even know what they are."

Still on a first-name basis—that was at least a good sign. Then Tally opened the folder and winced. "Janice, I don't know what to say. There was never a need to talk about them because it's been years...decades even since—" She stared down at the gruesome pictures, slowly flipping them over in the file.

One of the photos showed the broad, misshapen face of a maliker, bruised and swollen. Underneath, in the space reserved for a suspect's name, a string of numbers had been written—he hadn't even warranted a John Doe designation. The poor creature's gaze was cast down and away— Tally could swear he was cowering. If she had to guess, he was in some sort of mobile holding cell, one made of metal sheeting and riveted, like the inside of a shipping container. The photos of the victim highlighted the frenzied violence that had taken place in the train yard. The woman had been beaten to death, strangled, her head bashed against the concrete. Her clothes were torn and shredded, but her bra was still in place. So was her thong, though the scrap of fabric that charaded as her skirt had been shoved above her waist. Tally read the report and the witness statements. Things weren't adding up. Then, a few more photos of the maliker—on the ground, tasered into submission; another with zip ties cutting into his wrists. It was in the final shot that the photographer had caught his gaze. As she suspected, it was devoid of any emotion, save animalistic fear. This shouldn't be happening to him. He should've been safely locked away in one of the special institutions that could care for him during his blessedly short life.

"The victim wasn't raped," Barney pointed out. "The witnesses found him on top of her with his hands around her neck. But judging by the blood under her head, she was already dead."

"Tally," Mayor Greene started, "we've known each other a long time. I don't know what to think about this. Why not tell us about these malikers? This man—"

"He's not a man. Despite his looks, he's only thirteen years old. Maybe twelve." She paused. "I have to...I can't... This is bigger than a single maliker. I must speak with my brother first. Please, Janice. Please trust me that I'll explain everything later."

"When?"

Tally checked the time on her phone. Chris would be in his office, on his second or third cup of coffee. Bane would be there as well. "Noon?"

"Ken?" the mayor asked.

"I'll juggle a few things on your schedule."

Tally needed Chris and Bane at the meeting. It was time to come clean with the mayor, and with Haneluk, and she wasn't going to do it on her own. She scribbled down the address to Nonna Lucia's and handed it to Ken. "They're not open until five, but Bane can get us in. It's private."

Tally rose from the table. "Janice, I'm sorry for not being open with you. Your friendship means a lot to me. Yours too, Barney. I just..."

"I'm not happy with this situation, Tally," Janice stated. "I expect a full explanation at noon."

She nodded, then turned back before leaving and pointed at the mug shot. "While I don't know if he murdered that woman, I am positive that he's not your serial killer."

"I was afraid you were going to say that," Janice admitted.

Barney nodded. "Our killer is too precise. He would never beat a woman to death in a train yard. It doesn't jibe."

Janice closed the file and handed it to Tally. "Take this—Ken already scanned the contents. I have a feeling you might need it to convince that brother of yours to come clean."

"Thanks. I'll see you in a couple of hours."

She headed straight to her car and set out directly for Chris's office. She pulled into her reserved space, spotting Bane's car. A blossom of warmth filled her chest upon knowing she would see him in a few minutes, but she set it aside. She had a job to do. People had put their trust in her, and she would get her brother to Nonna Lucia's if she had to knock him out to do it.

Chapter Eleven

The elevator doors swished open, and Tally strode past the receptionist without giving her usual warm greeting. She continued through the offices and workspaces where her brother's employees toiled and ignored his assistant as she rose to intercept her. Twenty feet away, the door to Bane's office—the one he kept when working on C.O.F. business with Chris—was open. He was already up and walking toward her. Tally turned the doorknob to her brother's inner sanctum and marched in. He looked up, surprised by the interruption. Jacqueline was perched on the edge of his desk, one shoeless foot on her brother's knee.

"Leave, please," Tally ordered.

"Who do you think you—"

"Now."

"It's alright, Jackie," Chris soothed. "Give us a minute, okay?"

Tally didn't bother hiding her disdain as Jacqueline pouted at her brother.

"Fine, but only because *you* asked me." She slipped her bare foot into her high-heeled shoe and, as she walked out of the office, glared at Tally.

Bane entered and shut the door as Tally tossed the file from the mayor on her brother's desk.

"You didn't have to be rude."

"I'm tired, Chris, so please spare me the social niceties lesson. I was just ambushed by two feds in Greene's office."

Bane opened the folder. "Damn. How much do they know?"

"Enough. And this guy...he's not the first maliker they've detained."

"They admitted that?" Chris asked, sitting back down.

"Barney told me."

Bane snapped pics of the photos. "Hey, there's another image behind this one. They're stuck together." He carefully peeled them apart and, after taking another picture, cast them all onto one of the wall monitors. He scrolled to the image that had been stuck and zoomed in on one corner, where an unknown man wearing a military uniform had not been cropped out of the frame.

"Fuck," Chris said, summing up Tally's exact feelings in a single word. He started flipping through the photos and stopped at a close-up of the dead woman's face. He paled. "Bane, you need to…"

Tally hadn't really examined the images in the mayor's office—they were too gruesome. But she did so now. "Oh my God." Her hand covered her mouth in horror as she studied the bite marks on the woman's face and chest. The skin on her midriff had been clawed open. And still, Tally did not want to acknowledge what she knew to be true.

"Antonia Benedict," Bane stated.

"You're sure?" Chris asked. "Look at her clothes."

"She's been dressed up to look like a prostitute," Bane said woodenly. "She was tortured, and it was made to look like that maliker had done it."

"Take it down," Tally said quietly. "Take it down. Please."

"Of course. I'm sorry." He swiped the images away, one after the other. Chris pulled the photos together and closed the folder.

"Who would… Why…?"

"Tally, can you sit down, please?" Bane asked. "Chris, it's time you told her."

"Told me what?" She was suddenly worried that she didn't know everything she thought she did. Worse, they were deliberately withholding information from her, and Bane didn't look happy about that fact. "You have exactly"—she looked at her phone—"ninety-seven minutes to tell me what's going on, prepare your statement to the mayor, and get your asses to Nonna Lucia's by noon. So, start talking, or I go back to Janice and Barney and tell them everything I know. Which right now, I'm beginning to think, isn't all that much."

"You can't do that," her brother warned. "You've sworn to protect the Fascina from—"

"We've only suspected for a few weeks," Bane explained, cutting her brother short. "So it's not like we've kept you in the dark all this time."

"Quibbling," she said. "You either trust me, or you don't." Her brother made a grunt of exasperation.

"About two months ago," Bane said, stepping between them, "there was an incident involving a maliker—the first in decades."

"As was done in the past, we handled it within the community," Chris added. "Norms weren't affected. We thought it was an isolated problem…someone using bad judgement, a botched sterilization. But then another incident popped up a week later."

"And more," Bane said, putting up a map of the U.S. on another monitor. He touched his tablet. "The green stars designate the places where there is currently no Fascina registration." He touched the screen again, and Tally watched as multiple red dots speckled the larger, reg-free cities. And more telling, the dots were absent everywhere else. "Chris has been in contact with the other Orders, and they are just as baffled."

"But Antonia..." She stared at the screen. "These are maliker sightings. Have you mapped the murders?" Bane was one step ahead of her, and a series of blue dots appeared. They were all clustered in and around Chicago. "This means..."

"Yeah," Chris said. "We've got more than one problem here. A local killer, plus a national operation to turn sentiment against the Fascina in the safe zones."

"You went to your mother about the malikers, didn't you?" Tally asked Bane. "Not because of the murders."

"Both, actually. Believe me, the opposition to Chris's leadership gains nothing by creating malikers. That much was clear to me by what I discovered during my visit."

"Detainment, you mean." He acknowledged her with a wry twitch of his lips, and for the first time since entering her brother's office, she thought about those lips almost kissing her. But now was not the time for such thoughts, and she scowled at him. He and her brother had withheld information from her. She didn't think they could ever do such a thing. She hated being wrong about that. And then she remembered her own secret. "Shit," she said under her breath, feeling like a hypocrite on top of being a liar.

She rose from her chair to study the map of dots more closely. "So someone is dropping malikers in Fascina safe zones."

Bane raised an eyebrow. "They made a critical mistake—we weren't meant to see this photo," he said and walked over to the map. "The other cities have kept a lid on the maliker presence."

"You would think the National Order would've warned you that government agencies are working in tandem to sway public sentiment toward forced registration," Tally added.

"I'm afraid it's much worse than that," Chris worried. "We think they're completely unaware of this new threat. At least we can count on Mayor Greene to stand firm, even if the state folds. She's always been a friend to us."

"That was before we breached her trust," Bane pointed out. "And there's an election next year. You can bet that the feds have already cherry-picked an opponent to run against her."

Tally was still staring at the map. "So many, all of age, and all at once." There hadn't been more than one or two malikers born per year over the last few decades, and none in Chicago. Those few *accidents* were put in special homes. There, their suffering was eased with medication given by caring professionals, and in a safe place for parents to visit.

"We noticed that, as well, and thought my mother could provide some insight," Bane explained.

"Because of your family's research."

He nodded. "For all her faults, she abhors the idea of producing a maliker."

Reluctantly, Tally plucked up the photo of the poor, disfigured boy who'd been left to fend for himself in a strange and hostile world. He was hogtied on the ground, covered in blood and dirt. She brought the photo closer to her face, then handed it to Bane. "Can you put this one on the screen again?"

They gathered around the image, and Tally asked, "Any missing children from the institutions?"

"No," her brother provided. "I checked with what few there are remaining."

Tally leaned in closer. The boy's shirt had ridden up, revealing burn marks on his skin, some older than the beating he'd taken during capture. "There, in the lower-right corner." Tally's stomach turned when Bane enlarged the section.

"Is that a cattle prod?" her brother asked, aghast.

"He's been tortured. No wonder he attacked." Panic gripped her chest, and she sat down heavily, fishing out the photo of Antonia. She stared at it, then threw it on Chris'sesk as if it was coated in acid.

"What is it, Tally?" her brother demanded.

She gazed up at him, then at Bane, who'd apparently already figured it out. She pointed to the woman's stomach. "Those claw marks...they look like they came from the inside."

"You can't be sure," Chris said, sounding like he was trying to convince himself otherwise. "She's only been gone for a few months."

"That's long enough, isn't it, Bane?" she asked, and he nodded grimly. Then, she pointed to the areas of skin not damaged. "Every woman knows what stretch marks look like."

"If they're breeding malikers—" Chris started.

"No longer *if*," Bane corrected. "They need two important things: a male Fascina and a female non-Fascina. In Antonia's case, the genders were reversed, hyper-accelerating gestation and ensuring a nonviable result. Sterilization is a harsh sentence for breaking our rules, but necessary, for this combination of genders is always fatal to the woman. Only non-Fascina women can carry a maliker to term and remain alive and re-impregnable. Antonia was an experiment."

Chris and Tally stared at him, open-mouthed. He'd said it so clinically.

"My father's work...he..."

Tally watched as Bane shuttered his emotions. She closed the folder as he removed the image on the screen.

"Agent Lima tried to take my picture," she said and swallowed. "Just how many of us have they taken? And why hasn't anyone noticed?"

"I suspect because most non-Fascina live outside the reg-free cities. No one much cares what happens to them." Bane must have realized how he sounded and immediately crossed the room to her. "I'm not saying it's right, Tally. And you are a definite exception. It's just an ugly Fascina truth."

"Damn it," Chris swore, saving Bane from having to say more. "We're going to have to take this to the National Order."

Bane's phone buzzed, and Tally recalled that they were on a deadline. "We have less than an hour before meeting with the mayor. What are you going to tell her?"

"I can't believe that I'm saying this," Chris said, "but maybe we should come clean. About everything. The malikers. The serial killer being Fascina. All of it."

"All?" Tally asked. "Slipping, healing, the lot? Janice is my friend, but even I don't believe the world outside the Fascina community is ready. Intuition, low-level ESP, a bit of trickery, that's one thing. But knowing someone could sneak into your home, or out of a jail cell. Bane? Back me up here."

"She's right. We're already seen as a threat by most people in this country. You think the feds are pressuring us now? Think of the fear and panic they could stir up. Where is this coming from, Chris?"

"Look, it's not like I want to. But there are those who are tired of hiding. Some of the head councils in the other cities mentioned it. It's going to come up at the annual conclave."

"This is what happens when there's a weak National Order," Bane stated.

"Chris, you have to fight this. You know that, right?" Tally took his hand, unable to stop herself from sensing his stress and worry. "I know it's a lot for one person, but there's a reason you hide your true abilities. If the military is breeding malikers, it means they are already holding people from our community and are forcing them to mate, or extracting eggs or sperm, or—oh dear God, this is horrible. And if they are doing that without compunction, think what they would do if they found out about your powers, or Bane's, or any of the head families' skills. They might not be able to take you, but there are others out there who are not so well-protected."

"I know, Tally. You're right. And I'm sorry we didn't tell you everything. It was my decision. I was only trying to protect you."

Tally sensed a tiny lie. And it didn't take any special powers to detect it; it was in his voice. Something was eroding the trust they had in one another.

There was a knock on the door, and it opened. Jackie stepped in, not looking at all apologetic for interrupting a private meeting. Payback, Tally guessed, having just done the same to her.

The folder and its contents had disappeared. She glanced at Bane, but he gave a slight shake of his head. Was this why her brother was hiding things from her? Was it Jackie's influence? She wondered if it was Jackie's family, the powerful Silvas, who were pressuring her brother to reveal their true powers to the world. If that was on Jackie's agenda, then she was a very dangerous woman. And worse, she was using Chris.

"Who died?" Jackie joked, no doubt because of their grave expressions. "Oh, Chris, I'm sorry. Did the serial killer murder someone else?"

"No," Chris said, coming around his desk with a smile worthy of a politician. "Not at all."

"Thank heavens for that. Ready for our lunch date?"

"I'm sorry, J, but I have to bail. How about later tonight? You could come over to my place, and I'll cook a romantic dinner."

Chris rarely let people visit Rosegate, their family estate, and Jackie's eyes lit up at the chance. "I guess if you're willing to cook for me, I can forgive you."

Tally rolled her eyes but was saved from commenting when Bane offered her a ride.

"Where are you all off to?" Jackie asked.

"Order business for me," Chris said.

"Tally and I are going to grab a bite. Want to join?" Bane asked.

"Oh, no. I couldn't," she said, sounding panicked by the idea. "But thanks for the offer," she chirped, recovering quickly. "Rain check?"

Tally couldn't help but reply to the insincere platitude. "Oh, let's do," she said cheerfully. "We should have coffee or something. I'll tell you all the terrible things my brother did when he was a kid." Jackie's smooth countenance cracked. Even more so when Tally stepped forward and gave her a perfunctory hug. "I'm sorry I interrupted earlier," she half whispered. "Family drama, you know." And then she and Bane herded Jackie toward the elevators. But that brief embrace had told Tally one important thing: Jackie truly cared for her brother. She had sensed it. Sure, there was annoyance and even jealousy, but nothing more nefarious than ambition.

"I'll see you at seven," Chris called out to Jackie as he closed his office door. Her brother would slip directly to Nonna Lucia's a few minutes before noon.

Bane was on his phone, making arrangements, and they waved to Jackie as she sped out of the parking garage.

"Let's go to my house first," Tally suggested as she slid into the leather seat of his sleek Mercedes. "Michelle won't be home until next week, so you can park in her spot." She would have to come back to retrieve her car later.

Before Bane folded his lanky frame into the driver's seat, he shrugged out of his suit jacket and rolled up his sleeves. Tally couldn't stop herself from staring at the powerful flex of his muscles and tendons as he shifted gears to pull out onto the surface streets.

He was so damn hot to watch, and she couldn't believe how wound up she was getting, just thinking about them in her house, together, alone. She swallowed and dragged her gaze away to look at the passing cars. Considering what they had just discussed, her feelings were so inappropriate. That's when she felt the tension rolling off him. "Are we being followed?"

"No."

His terse answer had her sneaking glances at him as they sped through the city. His jaw was clenched as he concentrated on pulling into her garage. After entering her house through the back door, they stood there for a minute, facing each other. He was so much taller than her, but she'd always liked that about him. He made her feel like he could block all the rude comments, stares, and pitying looks from the other Fascina, simply by moving in front of her. She had to do something. Jumping on him came immediately to mind and a laugh bubbled out. He smiled at her, finally relaxing. Some.

Tally scooted back, then jumped up so that she sat on the kitchen island. This was much better, for now they were looking at one another eye to eye.

"I'm sorry," he started, and she remained silent. "For many things. For what I said in Chris's office. For not convincing your brother to tell you about the maliker resurgence. For not trusting you. And most importantly"—he took a step forward until he stood between her knees—"for missing our breakfast the other day."

His fingers traced a path down her arm, causing the hairs to raise in the most delicious way. "I'm beginning to understand your brother and Jackie...about what it's like to feel that way."

"What way?" she asked, her voice thick. She leaned closer.

"Besotted." He lifted both hands to her cheeks. "Tally, this thing I feel for you. It's not new. And even though I know that I'm going to kiss you, I also know it's wrong."

"Why?" she whispered. "Why is it wrong? If I feel the same...if we're careful—"

"Because you deserve more than what we could ever have together. And it's wrong because I don't care. I'm going to kiss you anyway."

Pleasure spiked inside her, and it took everything she had to stop herself from sliding forward to press herself against him. He hadn't even kissed her yet. Her chest rose and fell as he held her face. Then, finally, he tilted his head and touched his lips to hers. He didn't so much pull back as he did break contact, a mere millimeter. Then, he closed his eyes and kissed her again. This time, dragging his lips over hers, then kissing and tugging and nipping, pulling away, then coming back for more, again and again.

She waited for his tiny retreat, and advanced, taking his lower lip in her teeth, and giving it a shy sweep of her tongue. Her hands gripped the edge of the island, afraid that if she touched him, she wouldn't be able to control the ebb and flow of her emotions, because...this kiss. His kiss. It devastated her.

He nipped her back, a little harder this time, and then the tip of his tongue met hers. She moaned, and he slid one hand behind her head, the other down her back, and set to plundering her mouth. She dragged in a breath, here, there, when she could, when her own tongue wasn't exploring the taste and feel of him—coffee, mint, linen, power.

Bane growled, pulling her heated center against him, and she felt the hard ridge of his cock. And still, she held onto the edge of the counter as if her life depended on it. He withdrew his marauding tongue, setting little trailing kisses along her jaw to her ear and down her neck. There, he pressed his lips to her skin, not moving except for his heaving chest.

Tally had never taken drugs, but this euphoria...she could easily become addicted. He eased away, his hand on her back still holding her to him as he searched her face for some answer. She gave him a tiny smile and forced her fingers to flex. Then she touched her hand to his cheek, sending him all her love, through her eyes and her touch, briefly, though, just enough to erase the uncertainty in his eyes. He captured her hand, pressed a kiss to her palm, and they both shivered.

There was no going back for either of them. Not now.

"We should talk," he said, and their phones dinged at the same time. "It's your brother. He's ready to head over. Hey, have dinner with me tonight." She nodded, agreeing to everything, and he grabbed her hips and set her down on the kitchen floor. But he didn't release her.

"Bane, you shouldn—"

He slipped them both into a tiny room, one she recognized as the women's restroom at Nonna Lucia's. "You could get us in trouble."

He pulled her closer. "In case you haven't noticed, we've crossed that bridge already." Then he kissed her soundly before letting her go. "Give me a couple of minutes, then join me in the back courtyard."

He left her there, standing by herself. She turned to the mirror to tidy her tousled hair and paused. Something was different about her eyes, and it took her a moment to realize what she was seeing—happiness. And just as quickly as it came, the feeling disappeared. Happiness was one emotion she didn't trust.

Chapter Twelve

An emergency board meeting had been called when a few of the head families somehow got wind of the meeting with the mayor. Tally kept quiet—Chris didn't need reminding that Jacqueline had been in his office. He was doing everything possible to prove that those who thought they could do a better job at running things than he were wrong.

All this time, Tally had assumed that the hushed conversations that stopped as she walked by had been about her. But now, she wondered if this odd shift in sentiment wasn't more—a deliberate chipping away at her brother's control of the C.O.F.

They had about ten minutes before the meeting would commence, and Chris was bringing Orson up to speed on the newest threat. "That's horrifying," Orson cried. "Who would do such a thing?"

"It's what we've been trying to determine," Chris replied as Orson paced.

"You should have told me sooner. I could've helped." He stared out the window.

Bane glanced at his phone. "I'm going in, Chris. The Fortunas and the Prestons have arrived."

"See you in a few minutes," Chris said.

Tally was about to join Bane when Orson mumble something.

"What was that?" Chris asked, hearing it as well.

"The timing of it all," he repeated. "The murders, the undercurrents, the malikers. All coming at your family from different sides, undermining you. Maybe they're connected."

"How so?" Tally asked, drawing near him. Just what did Orson mean by undercurrents?

"If someone powerful, someone who would prosper with your removal..." He looked toward the door that Bane had just gone through, then at Chris. "No, the threat to the community from forced registration is too great for one of us to ally themselves with those demanding it. Never mind my rambling. I must be getting paranoid in my old age." He turned to

Chris. "I meant to ask, have you thought about what we discussed on Wednesday?"

"I haven't had much time, given recent events, but I will. I'll see you in the meeting," Chris said, shooting Tally a look that meant he wanted her to stay back. She closed the door after Orson departed and turned to her brother.

"What's up?" she asked.

"Orson's right. We need to be careful, Tally."

"What did you and Orson talk about before?"

"He suggested a few compromises that might assuage the dissenting voices. At least until we—"

"Find a serial killer? Discover who's breeding malikers?"

Chris smirked at her.

"What?" she asked. "Too soon?"

"Just...keep an eye on Orson for me; he's getting older, and I don't want him hurt. I think he might know more than he's letting on and is trying to protect us," Chris added.

"It feels like before, when it was the Waever twins against the world."

"And Bane. Don't forget that we have Bane on our side."

Chris's trust in their friend filled her with relief. "Let's go. They'll be getting restless."

They headed toward the door to the conference room. "What did you decide about the concessions Orson suggested?" she asked.

Her brother frowned. "I don't think that now is the time to concede anything. Jackie agrees with me, by the way." He stopped and touched her arm. "Please believe me when I say that she's not your enemy, Tally." And with that statement, he opened the boardroom door and the eyes of a dozen-and-a-half people homed in on them.

The minimum number of ruling families for any region was five. But in a city as large as Chicago, where a dozen or more families should have been included, there were only nine head families. The Waevers had ruled for five generations, when Tally's great-great-grandfather had proved a stronger and steadier leader than Delacourt Sedge. From what she knew, it had been a peaceful transition, and the Sedge family maintained their chair at the table.

Currently, one power seat was empty. The Coyles' spot had been vacant ever since Bane's mother had been forced out. Bane always came alone, managing to represent both the Carons and Coyles, handling his mother's family's interests. Down to eight board members, each with a second, if one was available or trusted enough. Tally was her brother's, and by naming her liaison, he ensured that she would be welcome at every meeting.

If Tally had to rank each family—their combined power, including political and economic status—her family and Bane's would be near equal, followed by Orson Sedge's family, and then the Grossomms. That left the Silvas, Fortunas, Ryans, Baptistes, Prestons, and Coyles. Of course, it was the Grossomms who were making the most noise right now.

The meeting dragged on and on. Rene Grossomm was his father's second, and his goading whispers had the man interrupting every attempt to move the agenda forward. It was eight o'clock already, and she sensed Chris's growing frustration. Hell, the whole room was about to break out in fisticuffs—the silly word brought a smile to her lips, and Bane drew a *?* on his notepad. She sketched out a simple line drawing of two men with raised fists. He circled the question mark. *Fisticuffs*, she wrote, feeling foolish. He snorted, earning a raised eyebrow from Chris. Bane slid her note closer to him, and Chris's lips twitched. They were the only people in the world who understood her sense of humor. Chris made fists with his hands, and Bane coughed to smother a laugh. Now was not the time to get the uncontrollable giggles. She took the pad and wrote to her brother: *This meeting is taking an eternity; I bet you're in trouble with J!*

Buzzkill, Bane scribbled out to her when Chris refocused on the latest rant.

"Enough," Chris called out to the room. "We can argue all night, but the fact is, a decision had to be made to protect the sanctity of our community. If disclosing certain facts to Mayor Greene—a person who has championed us and our integration into the city and allowed us to continue to govern ourselves and mete out our own judgments when it comes to our people—means owning up to the existence of malikers, then I say it is a small price to pay."

"But a Norm on the council!" Surprisingly, this came from DJ Preston.

"Detective Haneluk won't be on the council," Bane repeated wearily—they'd already argued this point *ad nauseam*. "He'll be a liaison, like Tally, if and when there's a crime involving both a Fascina and a Norm. He's a good man—honest, incorruptible, and circumspect."

"But Chris will allow him to attend meetings," Jean-Christophe Grossomm argued as he leaned forward.

"That is not what I said," Chris stated, his frustration rising to the surface.

Finally, Tally thought. She watched as her brother projected, drawing on his gift of aural enthrallment—a useful talent when one needed to take the reins and make people hear reason. His voice took on a siren-like quality, but his words were infused with the strength of his family and the authority of his position.

The bickering ceased. Bane leaned back and crossed his arms, his mouth set in a satisfied line. Chris was a master, and no one even realized that he held them in his thrall. "The mayor is on our side and deserves to know about the malikers—she trusts that we can handle our own. Detective Haneluk will join the board meetings when, and only when, anyone in our community commits a crime that affects his people. And it goes both ways, for he will be our point person with CPD when we have a problem with a Norm." He paused, and Tally watched as he dialed back his hold and wondered for the first time if she had that power. "Now, if there are any other concerns, send an email to my office. Have a good evening."

The board members filed by. Orson was one of the last to leave, and Tally caught his eye, hoping to find out what he'd meant earlier. "I keep forgetting to ask... How are the grandkids?"

"Growing like weeds," he said, pulling out his phone to show her the latest pictures. "Georgia's pregnant again."

"Her third, right?" she asked, and he nodded proudly. Over in the corner, Bane and Chris were deep in conversation. "I wanted to ask about something you said in the foyer about the timing of everything. You mentioned 'undercurrents?'"

"Undercurrents? Oh, you know, just the usual rumblings. Nothing for your brother to worry about."

Tally loved Orson, but he sometimes viewed her brother as needing his guiding hand in all matters, and right now, they needed answers. She focused on Orson and pitched her voice a little lower, speaking melodically, trying to infuse her words with the same enchantment her brother had so deftly crafted. "I'm so happy that Chris has you as an advisor, Orson. I bet it was the Grossomms stirring up trouble."

He nodded, blinking.

"Not surprising," she agreed. "Anyone else? For instance, have you noticed if they've been cozying up to any of the other families? You know, having dinner, setting up marriage contracts for their kids?" She laughed as if it was the funniest thing in the world and a completely innocent question, but it was one that needed answering.

"No weddings that I know of," Orson said with a chuckle.

She'd managed it! And he didn't even realize what was happening.

"Just the usual weekly soccer games for the kids. Mary Fortuna is a coach in my grandkids' league. Bane's company sponsors them." Then he blinked again as she eased off, a slight frown on his brow. "Are you worried about something, Natalia?" he asked. "You know you can tell me anything, and I'm here for you. And your brother, of course."

"It's good of you to ask," she replied without answering as Bane and Chris approached. "You must love watching your grandkids play. I expect to see more pictures next time."

"Of course," he said, looking for a moment at his phone. "They're growing like weeds," he repeated.

She still couldn't believe that she'd done it! She hadn't even needed to raise her voice. "Maybe we could come to a game. What do you say, guys?" she said, including Bane and Chris in the conversation. "A Saturday afternoon at the park? Hot dogs, soda pop, and soccer. I bet Caron Corp could treat both teams to ice cream. Right, Bane?"

"Uh, yeah. Sure," he agreed. "Sounds like a fun day."

"I'll send you the schedule—I think our game is at two, but on Sunday, not Saturday."

"I have it already," Bane said. "I'm the team sponsor, after all."

Chris's phone buzzed. "I have to take this call. Excuse me."

"I should get home," Orson said, nodding goodbye to Chris as her brother hung up and ran his hands through his hair. "See you Sunday."

Bane gave her a shrewd look. "Tell me why I just volunteered for snack duty for a kids' soccer game?"

"Just a hunch. The Grossomms have been increasingly vocal lately. Rene seemed a little too pleased with himself and was passing a few sly looks right before Chris went all Jedi on the room."

Bane laughed, and Chris, having finished his call, smirked. "Just wish it worked on you when we were kids, Talz. Let me guess, he was looking at the Ryans?"

She shook her head. "Fortunas." She let that sink in. "The Grossomm kids are coached by Mary Fortuna."

"So, it's ice cream and soccer this Sunday," Chris said.

"You should bring Jacqueline," Tally suggested. "Or at least offer."

"If she's even talking to me after tonight."

"Wine, pasta, and chocolate," she advised.

"And flowers," Bane put in.

"Just show up at her door and stay put until she opens it," Tally added.

"Thanks, guys. Who knew the two of you had a romantic streak? Remember to text me the *deets* for Sunday." He slipped away, missing Tally's blush.

Beside her, Bane shook his head sorrowfully. "This maliker problem has me behind schedule, and I need to make some calls. I'm sorry, but we won't be able to have dinner tonight."

"No problem," she said, trying to hide her disappointment.

"How about I bring a late dessert and wine over when I'm done? We have some unfinished business to discuss, don't we?"

"I guess we do. Text when you're heading over."

•••

Bane parked his car. It was nearly ten o'clock by the time he'd finished up and texted Tally to see if she was still awake. Standing there after the meeting, alone together, he'd wanted to sweep her into his arms. She had looked so beautiful with the blush on her cheeks. But there might've been people still lurking about the lobby.

It was 10:46 p.m., according to his phone. The night was beautiful, clear and star-filled, despite Chicago's constant light pollution. Nights like this were made for walking, not slipping in and out and missing the cool air of the city on one of its rare days without humidity, so he hadn't minded parking three blocks away.

He climbed the steps to her stoop, where a dark furball greeted him. Dusty wended his way between his legs. "Out carousing again?" He set down the wine he'd brought and bent over to scoop up the cat, but the beast jumped off the stoop to race into the backyard. "Good hunting."

Something in the garden bed caught his eye, and he went down the steps to pick up the crumpled cardboard. Made runny by over a week's worth of morning dew, he could still make out his neat script where he'd addressed the florist's card with Tally's name. No wonder she had never mentioned the flowers—she never saw them or his apology note. Or maybe she had.

The hairs on his nape rose. He turned, noting that the cicadas had gone silent, and even the breeze had stopped ruffling the leaves. The stillness was unnatural and seemed to push out toward him from the park. Briskly, he crossed the street. Two of the park's lampposts lining the central parterre were out. Bane eased forward, not sure what to expect, when he heard a faint *meow*.

"Dusty," someone called in a soft-but-frustrated voice. "Here kitty-kitty-kitty."

It was Tally, and she was in the park, alone. He stood still, opening his senses and letting his eyes adjust to the gloom. Someone was hiding behind a tree that she'd just passed.

"Dusty, you are in so much trouble," she warned.

Bane crept closer as another shadow shifted on the other side of the path, lurking. A man dressed in a dark hoodie, skinny, with sloped shoulders, stepped out, blocking Tally's way. She froze. Two others revealed themselves, surrounding her on three sides. She relaxed her stance, setting her feet to either run or attack. Her arms were loose, like he'd taught her. She was skilled enough that he had no doubt she could handle herself against one attacker, maybe two. Three? No. Especially when he sensed that they were Fascina. Why wasn't she running?

"Lose your pussycat?" one of the men asked as they hemmed her in.

Bane didn't hesitate and slipped next to her. He collared the front man first, then took out the second two before they could react. They struggled and cursed, trying to escape the invisible bonds that held them to the ground. Tally stared at him with wide, frightened eyes.

Grabbing her hand and pulling her toward home, he didn't ask if she was okay. He couldn't. He'd almost eviscerated the three men in front of her. And as he handed her the bottle he'd left on her stoop, the urge to send the three men to the Null was overwhelming. Without a word, he turned to deal with the mess he'd left behind, slipping back, his dark aura momentarily reaching out like black tendrils of smoke as he disappeared from Tally's foyer. Less than a second later, he stood in the park.

The men were gone.

And that gave him pause.

No one had ever broken free from him. *Ever.* Only someone with tremendous power could break the hold, and he knew, beyond any doubt, that it was not one of the three bound men. He knew because whoever had set them free had left a calling card. A single rose, one that was a darker red than any florist bloom he'd ever seen. He snapped a picture, then sent the rose to a secure place where it could do no harm.

That's when he noticed that the park lights that had been out, brightened the shadows again. The cat. The lights. The three punks and their escape. And that black rose. This wasn't a crime of opportunity. Someone had orchestrated the attack. Worse, they had almost succeeded.

He sent a coded text to Chris. His phone dinged back almost immediately—Chris was fine.

Instead of slipping into Tally's home, he walked. He needed the time to clear his head. His phone vibrated again. It was from Chris.

> T safe? U?

> *Yes x 2. Will explain all in AM*

> I can come over

> *Not necessary. 10AM@office*

> IAD

IAD? It took Bane the time to make it to Tally's porch before deciphering Chris's text: *It's a date.* He shook his head. Chris and his SMS. At least the diversion had allowed Bane's emotions to settle. He was about to ring Tally's doorbell when she opened it and pulled him into her foyer, shutting and locking the door behind her.

"What happened? Are you hurt?" She ran her hands down his arms, then his sides, as if checking for broken bones. Finding no wounds, she let go a huge breath.

He stared down at her. If they had hurt her, taken her—if they—

She shook her head at him as if sensing the direction of his thoughts. "They never touched me. Just wanted to give me a scare."

Her words angered him. "Scare you? Tally, what were you thinking? Going off by yourself this late."

"I heard Dusty crying, like he was hurt." She stood tall and squared off against him. "Michelle is trusting me to—wait one second. It's only eleven. This is my neighborhood, and I'll be damned if—"

"Dusty was on the porch when I got here. Whoever was making the cat noise was not Dusty. And even if it was, Michelle would be the first person to tell you that your safety far outweighs her pet." He raised his voice, hoping to make her see sense. "You can't just—"

"No."

"What do you mean, *no*?"

"Just, no," she repeated, crossing her arms. "I won't be a prisoner in my own home any more than I already am. Just how many security measures do I need, Bane?"

"Apparently, more than I thought."

"Wow. Why are you being such a jerk?" She stood there, toe-to-toe with him, waiting.

"Oh," he said, "you want an answer. I thought you were being rhetorical." Her eyes narrowed dangerously, but he ignored the warning sign. "Fine, I'll tell you. You don't take precautions, Tally. You forget your phone at work, leave it where anyone can mess with it. Or you forget to take it with you in the first place. You chase after a cat in the middle of the night and—"

"It wasn't the middle of the night," she snapped back.

"You didn't notice that the park's lights were out. You work yourself to death at the hospital. You—"

"I have to do something," she shouted at him. "I have to at least help people. I can't sit around with this inheritance and do nothing. I—"

"You take crap from Chris. All. The. Damn. Time. And don't let me get started on the way you drive."

"That's crossing the line, you jerk! I'm an awesome driver. Never an accident, or a ticket, or—"

"That's because you drive too damn fast for the cops to catch you, Mario!" She didn't reply, and he had to explain. "As in Andretti."

•••

"That might be the nicest thing you've ever said to me." Tally stared at him, waiting for him to let go of his anger as she had just done. "You had better kiss me right now, Bane, or I'm going to burst out laughing." And then she did laugh, as he stood there trying to down-shift to keep up with her. "Come on." She grabbed his wrist. "Let's open that wine and talk. You can tell me how much you admire my incredible driving skills."

Did that count as their first argument? She pulled him toward the kitchen. But he snaked his free arm around her waist and pulled her hard against his body. Her laughter died away as he gave her a desperate look.

"If anything had happened to you..."

"Nothing did." She lifted on her toes, wound her arms around his shoulders, and pressed a kiss to his lips. "I promise to be more careful." She kissed him again. "To keep better track of my phone." Another kiss. "To kick Chris's ass once in a while." She nibbled at his lower lip.

"And to slow dow—"

She silenced him with a kiss that demanded he return it with equal passion. And as their tongues tangled, he ran his hands down her back and over the swell of her ass, pulling her closer so that she could feel his growing arousal. Heat spiked inside of her, and she very nearly ground herself against him. She gave voice to her desire and moaned as he massaged her with strong fingers. And when he dipped them lower, she lifted a knee and set her foot on the built-in bench in her foyer.

He half fell, half sat on the bench, pulling her down with him so that she straddled his lap. The juncture between her thighs felt so hot and heavy that, if she didn't get some relief from the delicious ache, she would scream. She lowered herself the rest of the way, feeling every inch of his jeans-encased cock through her maddeningly thin palazzo pants. His hands girded her hips, and he lifted her against him, letting her drop down the holy-shit-long length of him. She gasped at the exquisite friction, and he took her lips with his mouth, drinking in her moans.

This wasn't Tally's first rodeo, but, *damn*, it was the hottest. She couldn't believe how close she was to coming, and they were fully clothed. Hell, he hadn't even touched her bare skin except where their mouths were locked together.

Bane growled, pulling his mouth away. He didn't say anything, just holding her tight against him and not letting her move. She tried to wriggle against him, and he shook his head.

"Uh-uh," he whispered, and she thought she would die of embarrassment. But he lifted her above and away from him, holding her immobile.

He slid a hand between her legs to caress her. She tried to kiss him. "Wait," he murmured, watching her face as he applied featherlight strokes to the heat between her legs. "Put your hands on the wall," he ordered. "And don't drop them."

"I can't, Bane. I—"

"Just do it, Tally." She bit her lip but did as ordered. He used both hands to pleasure her—one in front, the other behind. All through the fabric of her pants. "You're soaking, Tally. And I'm going to keep doing this"—he scratched his nails over the fabric, causing the most intense tickling sensation, along her seam and up over her clit, and back toward her rear— "over and over until you're almost ready to come."

She gasped, already there, but somehow he knew, and he adjusted his touch, moving his fingers maddeningly away, circling them in a holding pattern until her gasps downgraded to pants. "I've fantasized about doing this to you for years," he murmured. "Ever since I helped you to restore this damn bench."

His finger pressed against her center, like he was making a "come here" gesture. Then, two fingers, one after the other. She lost focus when he finally brushed his thumb against her throbbing clit. She was so close to coming that she didn't notice his other hand had come around front, searching her waistband.

"Side zipper," she managed on a gasp.

She heard the agonizingly slow release of metal teeth, felt the loosening of fabric from her middle, then whimpered as his fingers worked underneath the waistband. He smoothed them over the sheer silk covering her pussy and lower. And this time, he groaned. "You're sopping, sweetheart." And then he dipped his fingers inside her panties.

She cried out, and when her hands dropped to grab his shoulders, he paused, waiting, one brow lifted, until she pressed them back in place. His fingers slid lower, ignoring her clit, and running through her slick heat.

"Please, Bane."

"Please what, Tally? Do you want me to let you come? How should I do that? Should I play with your clit or fuck you with my fingers?" One finger eased in, just a tiny bit. Tally's legs were trembling with the strain to not grind down against his hand.

"Yessss" was all she could manage at his inciting words. And he obliged by inserting two strong fingers into her, then withdrawing and stroking them in again. The pressure built, deliciously, and her muscles clamped down around his fingers. He thrust them in again, deeper than before, twirling them as he pulled them out. She was going mad from the invasion, in and out and in and out, until she screamed out her climax, tightening and clenching as he worked her through the final spasms.

Her arms gave, and she dropped down against him. He tucked a lock of her hair behind her ear. She could feel him against her, all of him, and as much as she wanted to curl into a ball to take a nap, she wanted something else so much more. She wanted him inside her.

But she couldn't. They couldn't. Not yet. Not until after they talked. Bane still thought of her as a non-Fascina, and knowing him, he would want to outline their interactions, setting guidelines and rules. Bane would never cross that line if the result might be the creation of a maliker. He'd told

Tally once, about a half-sister, the issue of his father and some woman in California.

So no, Tally thought, there would be no ripping off his jeans tonight. Not until they'd parsed out their relationship to his satisfaction. Or, she revealed to him that she was Fascina as well. Could she? Her mother had warned her against telling anyone, even those closest to her, at least until the time was right.

"What are you thinking about?"

"Time."

She couldn't give them what they both wanted. She couldn't even give him the truth. But she could give him something to remember. She smiled lazily, holding his gaze, and slid her hands down to his jeans, where she started undoing each button on his fly. He started to protest, but she put one finger to his lips. "I know," she whispered, "but you're not the only one with fantasies about this bench."

She reached back down to free him. He was magnificent, and she applied light strokes of her fingertips to his length. He leaned his head back against the wall, his eyes closed, his face, for once, at ease. At least until she slid off his lap to take him in her mouth. She ran her hands down his jean-clad thighs and went up on her knees. And when she stole a peek at him, the intensity of his stare sent a wave of pleasure coursing through her. She went back to working him with her hands, then her mouth, and felt his fingers on either side of his head, gentle, touching her hair. And she let that touch be her guide, not allowing him to pull her away when he climaxed, taking all of him deep into her mouth and throat. He shouted out her name, and something snapped inside her, in her heart, mind, and soul, like a perfect chord plucked on a guitar. A falling into place. Right there, on the built-in bench in her entrance hall.

He pulled her up, held her in his arms, and they sat together, neither speaking. His chest rose as he took a deep breath, preparing himself for what she knew he was going to say: *they had to talk.* But her phone pinged in the kitchen, and his vibrated in his pocket.

"Shit," he swore. "Your brother is on his way over." Then he lifted her to her feet, catching her pants before they slid off her hips to puddle to the floor at her ankles.

She laughed and smiled at him like a sated cat who'd been caught with nothing but yellow feathers hanging from its mouth.

"You go change. I'll set out glasses and wine and turn on the TV."

"Bane, we didn't do anything wrong. We didn't break any laws. You don't need to make it look like we are innocent because we *are* innocent." He opened his mouth to say something, but she was already heading upstairs to change. When she came back down, he had two glasses of wine poured. A third empty glass sat nearby, waiting for Chris's arrival.

Bane stood when she walked to the couch. He took her hand, kissed her palm, then drew her to him so that he could kiss her properly. When he finished, he put some space between them. "I wasn't feeling guilty. Or regretful."

"No? What then?"

"When your brother finds out, he'll kick my ass. And I'm going to have to let him."

"Why would he want to kick your ass?"

"Whose ass?" Chris asked, slipping directly into her kitchen.

"No one's," they replied at the same exact time.

"What's up?" Tally asked. "I thought that you were spending time with Jackie tonight."

"I am. I was." He narrowed his eyes. "You look a little flushed, sis. Bane, you said she wasn't hurt."

Oh, Tally was flushed, alright. But it had nothing to do with being cornered in the park. Bane turned away before her brother could see his grin. He poured Chris a glass of wine and, composed, handed it to him.

"So, tell me what happened?"

"Just some thugs in the park," Tally said.

"Someone set a trap for your sister," Bane said at the same time.

"You don't know that it was a trap," she protested.

He turned to her, his previous seriousness back in place. "They lured you out there, Tally. If Dusty was on the porch, how could we have heard him meowing in the park? The lights had been extinguished. Three men, all waiting for you, each possessing low-level skills. You've been around us enough to know what they were."

She stared at him, unable to refute his words. "But they could've been waiting for anyone. They probably just wanted money."

"Maybe," Chris said. "So, what happened?"

"Bane arrived, incapacitated them before I had a chance to find out who they were, then escorted me home. How did you do that, by the way?"

"More importantly, where did you put them?" her brother asked. "I want answers."

"When I returned to the park, the lampposts were back on, and they were gone."

"Shit."

"What?" Tally demanded.

"No one breaks free from Bane. Someone powerful must've orchestrated it."

"But you still can't be sure they were after me, specifically."

"Oh, I'm sure. They left a calling card." Bane pulled out his phone, tapped open an image and showed it to Chris, then to her. Chris drained his glass. Tally sank back against the couch cushions, staring at the picture of a nearly black rose.

"The mal de nuit," she whispered.

"My father's nightmare rose," Bane confirmed.

Bane's father, it was rumored, had created the flower as a tribute to Malory Waever. He'd sent dozens of them to the memorial service and the funeral. Hell, he'd even sent them to their mom at their home. Then, it was discovered that Sebastian Caron had been behind the murder of her father, and the subsequent poisoning of her mother. It had been Bane who had lured his father to a place where the council could trap him and send him to the Null—the place where Fascina who committed only the most heinous of crimes were sent. Bane never talked about that night, nor about what his father said to him before he was banished for all eternity.

If a mal de nuit rose had been left behind, it was a surety that Tally had been the target. Just what they wanted with her, she shuddered to think.

"Where is it now?" Chris demanded.

"In a safe place," Bane replied. "It'll be scanned for prints, DNA, residue. Full works." Tally felt his searching gaze on her face. "It wasn't Sebastian," he vowed. "It's not possible. And I'm pretty sure it wasn't my mother. She wouldn't stoop so low."

Chris gave him a sharp look, as if he knew better.

"She *hated* that flower, but I'm not ruling anything out. It's more likely one of my father's old supporters. And I didn't recognize the thugs. Could be that they're not from Chicago."

"Bane," Tally said, taking his hand, "we've never blamed you for your father's sins."

"And we never will," Chris concurred. "Hell, sometimes I think you were closer to Mom than I was. You're not *like* a brother to us, Bane, you *are* my brother." Tally nearly choked on her wine. Another complication to add to the list of things she would have to figure out if Bane was going to get through this without getting an ass-kicking from Chris. "I've got to head back," Chris continued. "You'll let me know if you find out anything."

"Always," Bane said.

When Chris slipped away, Tally set down her empty wineglass. Despite the revelation, she stifled a yawn. Bane fell onto the couch next to her, catching her exhaustion and letting loose a long, satisfying yawn himself. He took her hand.

"How many people know about your father's rose?" she asked.

"Besides us? Maybe a half-dozen people. But everyone saw them at the funeral services, though only a few of us knew what it meant, and how you were affected by the sight of them."

"I remember all too well. Sebastian had been sending them to my mom long before my dad's funeral." She tried to smother another yawn.

"I'll sleep down here tonight, Tally. You go get some rest."

"Should we talk first?"

"We will." He drew her up off the couch and led her to the stairs. "What we have isn't going away. There'll be time to figure things out later."

She nodded, then kissed him, savoring the feel of the heat that bloomed between them.

"Go to bed. Now. Please. It's going to be hard enough staying down here as it is."

"That's what she said," Tally quipped, quoting one of her favorite TV shows. He smacked her on the butt as she climbed the steps. "Ow!"

When she made it to the top of the stairs, he called up, "Dusty's back."

Michelle's cat must've used the cat door. Poor thing was probably being scanned by some high-tech gadget that Bane's R&D people created.

"She's clean."

"Night, Bane," she called down.

"Night," he answered.

She stripped, then climbed into her bed and fell immediately into a deep sleep.

Tally peered over the edge of the landing. Chris was in his Power Ranger PJs and had fallen asleep next to her from where they were spying on the adults. She'd fallen asleep as well, for the party her parents were throwing was just a little bit out of ear- and eyeshot. It had been the voices directly under her that had roused her from her slumber. The entrance to her parents' study was just below the upstairs landing, and as Tally worm-crawled closer to the edge to peer down between the balusters, she recognized her mom's voice. There was a quality to it that she'd not heard before. Not fear, exactly, but worry, or agitation. The lights were dim, but she could see her mom. And a man.

"You're drunk, Sebastian. Now, please, let me by." Tally heard the low rumble of his laughter—it made her skin crawl. "I mean it, move out of my way. This isn't funny."

"They'll never know, Mal. It can be our little secret."

"For the last time, I married Torbin because I love him, Sebastian."—Tally wished she hadn't woken up. She did not want to see this.—"What are you doing? Get your hands off me!"

Sebastian? That was Bane's dad! And he was trying to kiss her mother. All of a sudden, Mr. Caron was thrown against the wall. Hard enough that a framed photograph fell off and went crashing to the floor. He glared at her mom, then waved his fingers. The beautiful flowers in the vase on the credenza were replaced by roses so dark red that they seemed to drip with blood. "I've almost perfected these for you. I'm calling them "Mal" de nuit. And one day, just like these roses, you'll belong to me."

"Get out of my home, Sebastian. Leave before I do some permanent damage." Her mother stalked off. Her words had held so much power. Tally narrowed her eyes at the back of Mr. Caron's head, hating him for touching her mom. But on her lips, she wore a satisfied smirk. Her mother had just bested the most powerful Fascina male in Chicago. More powerful than even her own dad. Next to her, Chris rolled over with a sleepy snort.

Sebastian Caron turned and caught her spying. His furious expression turned into something sly. His stare pinned her to the spot, and Tally's smirk slid away. She was about to scream, but he did something that took her voice. Literally. She couldn't move her arms, her legs...she couldn't move anything. He disappeared from the hall below, but she knew from the sound of creaking wood that he was coming up the stairs to get her. First, his head appeared, then his whole person, and he knelt next to her. Chris mumbled something in his sleep, but Mr. Caron waved his hand, and her brother got up and walked into his bedroom, shutting the door, seeing nothing the entire time.

"You must be the Non," he whispered. She wanted to recoil at his touch, and he sensed it and chuckled. He twirled a blond lock of her hair around his finger, then gently tucked it behind her ear. "You know what's worse than eavesdropping?" he asked, pulling her so that she lay over his lap. "Spying on your betters. If you were my child, I could discipline you properly, like my own ill-begotten son. But this will have to suffice." And then he spanked her—his palm stinging and bringing tears to her eyes.

"You'll be sore tomorrow, little one, but like your brother, you won't remember a thing." He waved his hand before her face as he had done to Chris, and some small amount of control returned to her arms and legs. "Now go to bed before I decide to spank you some more."

Tally slid off his knees and walked to her room, zombie-like, as her brother had. She shut her door and then collapsed against it. Worried that he would find her there, see that he wasn't controlling her like he had done to her brother, Tally ran to her bed and hid under her covers.

When she woke the next morning, she opened her eyes to a bright and sunny day. On her pillow was a dark, blood red rose. She touched her bottom...it burned and stung. She grabbed the rose and ran into the bathroom to destroy it, watching the torn bits swirl down the toilet. Then she took the hottest bath she could draw. She would never wear her favorite PJs again, and she hid them in the back of her closet to throw away on garbage day.

Sebastian Caron was wrong. She had remembered everything. And that meant he wasn't as powerful as everyone said.

Tally woke with a start, half expecting to see a rose on her pillow. She hadn't thought about that night since she was a child, but the ambush in the park had brought it all back. Sebastian Caron was gone forever and in a much worse place than her parents. He would never possess her mother, and he would never again be able to touch Tally. She strained to recall the old memory. Sebastian Caron had wanted her mother for his own. Had jealousy and lust driven him to kill her father? He'd created the dark mal de nuit rose for her mom. Mal for Mallory.

But he wasn't capable of love—he only coveted her mother's powerful genes for his future progeny. Giselle Coyle had watered down his bloodline, and he loathed his son because of it. No wonder Bane had kept secret his true skills from everyone, save Tally and Chris. His father would have used him horribly if he had known. As it was, Sebastian had perceived his only son to be weak, just as he'd seen Tally.

She walked downstairs and picked up the note Bane had left for her on the counter.

Going back to Giselle's. Send search party if you don't hear from me in two days.

Smiling, she poured herself a cup of the coffee he'd brewed. Bane had always been as powerful as Chris, but no one knew. And then something occurred to her. It wasn't that Sebastian's powers were not as great as everyone thought. No, she was able to remember what he'd done to her that night only because she was stronger. Her mother had been right to mute her gifts. For if the likes of Sebastian Caron had discovered that she could resist him, and at such a young age... Tally shuddered to think what else he might've done to her.

Chapter Thirteen

It was supposed to be her day off. So, of course, Tally had spent most of it in her office at the hospital. Last-minute documents needed her approval, and the funds raised at the gala required earmarking. Her email inbox overflowed with proposals from doctors, departments, and researchers. Happily, it was her annual labor of love, one that took weeks to sort out. It was 2:46 p.m. when she stepped out into the corridor—and smack into Adrian Shareff.

He reached out to grab her arm as if she needed steadying, and her skin recoiled. "Shareff," she said coolly, pulling her arm from his grip before stepping around him to head to the elevator.

"You're a hard one to nail down, Natalia Waever," he oozed, catching up with her.

"I suppose it's because I'm busy...working," she hit back, knowing that Adrian had sponged off his parents his entire life. He was the epitome of the good-looking-but-spoiled, trust-fund brat. He didn't even wince.

"Yes, your little charity is exactly the right kind of diversion for a woman in your position."

"Goodbye, Shareff."

"Hold on, Natalia. You *want* to talk to me."

Tally felt his intention even before the words came out of his mouth...his desire for her to do as he suggested. But his attempt to compel her was crude. "Do I?"

His eyes narrowed, changing his handsome features into something feral and ugly. "You and I *will* have this conversation."

"There you are, Ms. Waever," one of the nurses called out from down the hall. "Everyone is waiting for you."

"Thank you, Joseph. I was just on my way." She joined Joseph where he was holding open the elevator door and threw a backward glance toward Adrian. "No rest for the weary. Have your people call my people and—" The elevator doors swished closed. She turned to Joseph. "Thank you."

"That guy reminds me of this opossum that got trapped in one of our garbage cans a while back," Joseph observed, pressing the button for the third floor, then the parking garage. "Nasty little creature."

"That's a bit rude...to the opossum, I mean." They laughed. "Most people tell me they think he's charming," Tally said, stepping sideways to let him off at the third floor when the elevator stopped.

"Most people are idiots," he replied with a smirk, remaining in the elevator. "I'm escorting you to your car, Ms. Waever. I only pressed the third floor to throw him off your scent."

"Thanks, Joseph, but you really don't need to do that. I can handle the likes of Adrian Shareff."

"Maybe. But why should you have to? Look, I'm not trying to tell you your business, but you should report him to security. The guy has creep written all over him."

Tally studied Joseph with fresh eyes. He shrugged. Only a Fascina with a fair amount of skill would be able to see through Adrian's layers. She looked at his ID tag—Joseph Garban, RN—recognizing the last name but not recalling having met anyone from his family. "I'll think about it." He waited until she belted herself into her car. "Thank you, again."

"Anytime, Ms. Waever." He paused. "For what it's worth, my family supports your brother. Before you ask, no one has approached us, or other minor families that I know of, but we hear rumors." He shut her door for her, nodded, and walked back toward the elevator.

It was nearly four o'clock when she pulled into her garage. At least the sun was still out, even if her brain was on autopilot—key, backdoor, fridge. Leftover Thai. Half a grilled chicken breast that she needed to toss. Not enough fixings for a decent salad. And zero desire to whip up something proper. Besides, it was too late for lunch.

She missed Bane.

Sure, they'd seen each other at the soccer game, but then he'd had to travel with Chris to the National Conclave in San Francisco. Chris was staying the entire week, but Bane had said he'd be home after a few days...days that stretched into six days.

It wasn't that he hadn't kept in touch. They'd been texting, as usual, and they talked every night. But their conversations never touched on, well, *them.* She'd broached the subject once, but he said he wanted to talk when they could do so face-to-face.

Dusty trotted into the kitchen, sticking his big head around her legs and into the refrigerator and eyeing the leftover chicken she'd been about to trash. "Alright," she told him, setting the wrapped piece of meat back on the shelf, "you can have some of it with your dinner."

Her stomach growled at the thought.

Bane had asked her to limit her outings while he was gone, and at the time, she'd agreed. But now? She was tired and hungry and in no mood to cook. Nonna Lucia's. She pulled out her phone to text Bane and headed out her front door.

> Going stir-crazy here. I need a walk, pasta, and a
> cannoli.

Her phone chimed almost immediately. She sat on her stoop to read it.

> *Nice. Pick up one or two for me. Be careful. <3*

> Sure. But if you're not back by tomorrow, I can't
> guarantee their safety.

> *Duly noted. :D*

Hmm. Did that mean he would be back? That they could finally talk? She'd already decided to come clean to him. The timing finally felt right to her. And her gut told her she could trust him. Happy to have something resolved for once, she trotted down the limestone steps to the sidewalk.

Behind her, the front door crashed open, and she ducked. Michelle rushed out, holding a limp Kayla in her arms. "Oh, thank God you're here!"

"Oh, Michelle! What's wrong with Kayla?"

"I don't know. She was watching cartoons, so I went to take a shower and when I went into the family room, she was barely breathing."

Tally pushed her phone into her pocket. "Come on. I'll drive you to the hospital."

Michelle looked completely freaked out. "I called an Uber."

"You can cancel it. Do you have your purse? Kayla's inhaler?"

Her friend looked panicked. "I forgot everything upstairs!"

"Let me take her, and you run upstairs and get your things. Then we'll go in my car." Michelle nodded, handing her sister into Tally's arms, and raced back into the building.

Cradling Kayla against her, Tally lowered herself to the stone bench on her porch. The little girl's lips had a bluish tinge, her breathing was thready, and her pulse weak. Michelle was probably still running up the two flights of stairs to her apartment. Tally looked furtively around, and then she imagined the girl's airways opening and filling with oxygen. Kayla's eyelids fluttered as Tally's own throat and chest began to tighten. "*Shh.* It's okay, sweetie. Your sister will be right back. Just close your eyes and rest for a minute." Tally sought out the root of Kayla's illness and imagined herself drawing it into her own body, where it would be dissolved and destroyed.

Behind her, Michelle tromped hurriedly down the steps and, seconds later, her friend emerged breathless from the entryway. "How is she? I should have called 911. I thought an Uber would be faster. I couldn't find my keys."

"She's going to be fine. Look. Her color is improving." Tally carefully handed Kayla back to Michelle. "I think the worst is over. She doesn't look so ashy, and her breathing is stronger."

Kayla opened her eyes and stared up at her sister.

"You scared me, Kay-lay-la," Michelle sang. Tally smiled as Michelle hitched her sister up onto her hip, and Kayla wrapped her gangly arms and legs around her. Behind them, an Uber pulled up to the curb.

"You should get her checked out at the clinic," Tally suggested, starting to feel the effects of her intervention and willing the rising bile in her throat back down.

"Thank you, Tally! I don't know what I would've done if you weren't here." She climbed into the waiting car. "The hospital, please. It's not an emergency."

Tally waited until they were out of sight, then turned and vomited over the edge of her porch. She'd never rooted out an entire illness before, delving past its molecular level all the way to a person's genes, but she hated to think of Kayla suffering another attack and dying.

Her front door stood open, and she lurched into the outer vestibule, kicking shut the thick oak-frame door with its heavy, leaded glass. As her lungs seized from the echoes of Kayla's attack, Tally's vision wavered, and she fell. The mosaic floor that she had painstakingly restored looked odd from the angle where her cheek rested upon it. Tiny chips of colored glass, lapis lazuli, jade, and pastel marble pieces glinted in the light. Then, everything went dark.

• • •

Bane stepped from behind the tree where he'd been about to text Tally, intending to surprise her by treating her to lunch. He stared at her porch. A thousand different explanations for what he'd just witnessed whirled through his brain before settling on the inevitable conclusion. And once determined, her episodes of fatigue after visiting the children's ward at the hospital suddenly made sense. *Tally was a healer.*

And if she was a healer—and from what he'd witnessed just now, she was a powerful one—*then she wasn't a Non.* All these years. A Fascina. As the utter sense of betrayal hit him, he slipped to the privacy of his living room. Of course, the first thing confronting him was a picture of him with his two best friends when they were kids. It was the beach vacation that the Waevers had taken him on. Waterlogged, wrapped in oversized beach towels and sprawled out on folding lounge chairs eating ice cream out of huge waffle cones, they looked supremely content. His dark hair contrasted against their twin towheads, backlit by the setting sun and glowing pink. Bane had known from that day on that he could love no person other than Tally.

The picture was taken before he had moved in with the Waevers. And only the pure love that he felt for her had gotten him through the rest of the year with his abusive father.

Bane strode straight to his office, poured a drink, then opened his safe to pull out the leather photo album. He dropped the heavy portfolio on his desk and sat. He took a gulp of scotch, nearly choking when he swallowed more than he should have.

There were more pictures, many of the three of them, even more with just him and Tally. She'd been his prom date—no one else at the school would go with them. He flipped the page, where, mounted in the next section was the handwritten letter from Mallory Waever. It had been delivered to him by the Waever family lawyer after her funeral.

Dear Braeden,

By now, you must realize that I have come to love you as much as I do Christian and Natalia. And I see that you, in turn, love us like a family. But when we were at the beach, I saw more... I saw the truth of your feelings for my daughter. Such depth—it reminds me of how I feel for Torbin. It hurts me to know that in the coming years, your heart will suffer for this love. Like Romeo, you are a star-crossed youth.

Natalia will grow to love you as you do her. But she is special, Braeden: no one knows how much, except for me, and perhaps you. She is so strong, stronger even than her brother, though she won't realize it for many years. And when she does, her life will change. Bear with her, help her through the years when she will struggle. There will be times when she will need you to keep her safe more than she will need your love. But most important of all, she will need your trust.

There is so much good in you, Braeden. You, the boy who somehow managed to take only the best parts from your parents. I pray that those same parts keep you safe.

Love,
Mallory Waever

He'd read it hundreds of times, one day interpreting her words as a warning to keep his distance from her daughter, another day seeing that which she'd written as a promise. Now, after years of keeping it locked away, he studied the short letter with fresh eyes.

"She knew!" he shouted, pounding his fist on his desk. "And she thought I suspected." He scanned the letter again, finally interpreting Mallory Waever's words in a completely new way. It wasn't a warning to stay away from her daughter—she was asking him to be patient. She hadn't said that he and Tally could not be together; only that it would be difficult. And, somehow, Tally didn't know about what she could do, or least not until recently. Maybe.

He closed the album and locked it back away. His last glimpse of Tally had been of her staggering into her foyer and shutting her door.

"How could I have left her like that?"

Visions of her choking on her vomit or at the bottom of her stairs with a bashed-in skull from a fall taunted him. He loosed his energy and slipped to the middle of her kitchen. Only silence greeted him until Dusty meowed from the front hallway. Bane ran to the foyer and found Tally, collapsed and unconscious on the cold floor, her face in a pool of her own vomit.

"I'm sorry I left, Tally," he whispered, scooping her up into his arms. She was breathing, but her skin was tinged blue. If she was a healer, she didn't need a hospital. She needed warmth and quiet and time to recover on her own. He carried her to her room, laid her gently in her bed, exchanging her soiled and vomit-reeking clothes with a comfortable T-shirt and a pair of yoga pants. He washed her face and neck with a warm cloth, then pulled her sheets and a light blanket over her. Dusty jumped up onto the bed and curled up next to Tally's hip.

Already, her pallor was receding. Bane sent a quick text, waited for a reply, then leaned over to kiss her forehead. "I'll be right back," he whispered, cupping her cheek with his palm. To the cat, "You're in my spot, Dusty. You have until I get back to move."

• • •

Tally woke. She was in her bed, in clean clothes and under her blankets, and bracketed on both sides by two heavy bodies. She nudged Dusty, the lighter of the two, and the cat immediately started purring and kneading the blankets with his enormous, tufted paws. His low rumble roused Bane.

He must have found her on the floor and brought her up here. He had probably freaked, seeing her like that. She was so relieved that she could finally tell him the truth.

His eyes slowly opened, and he propped himself up on one elbow. "Are you alright?" She nodded. "You were passed out downstairs and—"

She put her fingers to his lips. "I'm okay. It happens when I...we need to talk."

"We will. But not yet. When's the last time you ate something?"

She thought back. "I had coffee this morning. And a croissant at work."

"It's seven o'clock, Tally. You haven't eaten for over ten hours."

Only seven? She felt fully recovered. She didn't even have the raging migraine that usually followed in the wake of healing someone. Bane leaned in, but she tucked her chin.

"I don't care about your breath," he said dryly. "Trust me when I say that I've smelled worse." She punched him. "So, you're strong enough to maybe eat something. Come on, I'll help you downstairs."

"I, uh, need to pee," she said cagily as he drew her up and gave her a wry look. "Oh, be quiet. Even if you don't care how my breath smells, my mouth tastes horrible right now."

She shuffled to her bathroom and shut the door on his grinning face. Screwing up the courage to look in the mirror, Tally was shocked that she looked as good as she did. Great, in fact. She turned up the dimmed lights, fully expecting a shaft of pain to pierce her brain. Nothing. She squeezed some toothpaste onto her brush and scrubbed away the taste in her mouth.

He was waiting for her when she came out, and he scooped her up into his arms. "Better?"

She kissed him by way of an answer.

After carrying her downstairs and depositing her on the couch, he went into the kitchen. She crisscrossed her legs and waited. He came back carrying a tray and set it on the coffee table. Warm, crusty bread and two large bowls filled with steaming soup. Her favorite—*avgolemono.*

Tally's eyes teared up as Bane sat down to eat. He tore off a piece of bread and buttered it, then held it out to her. Suddenly, the weight of the secret she'd been carrying hit her, and she started crying. She couldn't stop. It was horrifying, and she buried her face in her hands.

"Hey. Hey. Come on," he soothed, dropping the bread on the tray and pulling her onto his lap. "If you'd rather start with the cannoli..."

She continued to bawl like a little kid. The whole time, he held her, rocking and making shushing noises.

"I'm s-sorry," she gulped. "It's been s-so hard... I've been lying to everyone. T-to you."

"It's okay, Tally. We can talk about it after you eat. I promise." He handed her a couple of tissues from the box on the console table. She blew her nose, then scrubbed her eyes with the heels of her hands.

"You know?" she whispered, hardly daring to believe it.

"Not everything, but yeah, I saw what you did for Kayla." He looked away, then back at her. "I was mad and took off. But then someone reminded me how incredible you are."

"Who?"

"I'll tell you after you eat, I promise."

She nodded, then picked up the slice of bread, tearing it in half and giving him a share. He took it from her, his eyes never leaving hers. She had to ask. She couldn't make herself swallow until she knew. "Will you forgive me?" she whispered, looking toward the kitchen as her eyes watered up again.

He turned her face back to his. "There's nothing to forgive. Now, come on. The soup's getting cold."

She scooted back into the corner of the couch and took the bowl from him, balancing it on a pillow set on her lap. The *avgolemono* was divine.

As they ate, Bane began to ask her questions.

"You've healed others before, haven't you?"

After hiding her gift for so long, she hesitated to answer. But he was looking at her with those same eyes that had watched her since they were kids. And in them, she saw the unflinching trust that told her they could share anything. She nodded. "In the children's ward."

"No wonder they have one of the top cure rates in the country," he noted. "Have you ever had such a bad reaction before? I mean, I know you get migraines."

"I get the migraines even when I haven't healed anyone. Is there more bread?"

"That didn't answer my question."

How could she tell him what she'd done with Kayla, especially as she didn't understand it herself?

"This must be strange for you, after hiding your abilities for so long. You trust me, don't you?"

"I do." Of course, he knew what she was thinking. He always did.

He stared at her for a moment, thoughtfully chewing his bread. He got up and went into the kitchen, bringing back two glasses of water for them. "I'll tell you what. You tell me something that you can do, and I'll tell you something about me in return."

"You already know I can heal. So, tell me what you did to those men in the park first," she said.

"I can immobilize things."

"Things?" she asked, scooting closer to him. Bane *never* talked about what he could do. She knew he could slip and set complex protections, but she had long suspected other talents.

"People, objects in motion, things."

"See, it's not easy for you either, telling someone else."

"Try explaining what made healing Kayla different," he coaxed.

"Well, it's, um, not something I ever tried before. I mean, I'd thought about it, but I didn't want to raise suspicions. When healing some kid with a tumor, I just imagine the growth shrinking away to nothing. People think the cancer goes into remission...that the treatment is working. I was afraid if I did more, the 'm-word' would start coming up."

"The m—? Oh, miracle."

She nodded. "But today, when I held Kayla, I reached deeper. Past the symptoms and the cause. I found the root. It was like I could see how the gene was damaged. And I...fixed it?" She had no idea how she had done what she'd done.

Bane leaned back and blew out a long breath. "So, your mom used to give me these projects. Mainly assigned reading from old Fascina journals and texts."

"I'm starting to think that my mom did a lot of things I didn't know about."

"An investment in my future, she used to call it." He chuckled. "She would quiz me on the assignments afterward. For the most part, much of what she gave was anecdotal evidence of various powers that the Fascina have.

"There are healers, Tally. And then there are the *sostosi*: people who can fix things that are broken, though the modern term is *recoder*. It's a very rare gift. And those who have it pay a steep price. You see, healing someone simply drains a person. Rewriting a genetic defect involves taking it into yourself and sending part of you, the healthy sequence part, into the other person. In a sense, a cut and paste. You then take on the symptoms until your own body can overwrite the newly introduced damage in you. I have never seen you sick before—other than the migraines and fatigue, I mean."

"I've never been ill. Not even the sniffles," she confessed.

"People who can recode generally have no afflictions."

"None?"

"None. But your migraines. I wonder... Am I right in thinking that your mom somehow suppressed your powers all these years?"

She nodded.

"Then the migraines are a side effect."

Tally leaned back, thinking. "So, who told you that they thought I was incredible?"

"Who else? Your mom. She wrote me a letter...years ago. She didn't leave you to deal with this all alone. She wanted me to help you, Tally."

"I've been so angry at her," she admitted.

"Your mom was a pre-cog," Bane explained. "At least I think she was. Did you happen to inherit that from her, the ability to foresee?" Tally shook her head. "Can you do anything else?"

"Glamouring, I think." She explained what had happened the night of the gala, and Bane quietly listened.

"I'm not saying that you couldn't glamour," he started. "Almost all Fascina can. But that wasn't what you did. It's another rare gift—it's called *kanaekti*. You envisioned yourself ready and made it happen. Glamour is just a façade—like creating an illusion that you look younger or thinner, or having different colored hair or eyes." He took her hands. "There are very few Fascina in the world who are both *sostosi* and *kanaekti*. Do you think that you can show me?" he asked, and she nodded. "I'll clear up this mess and then get some wine for us while you come up with something."

He let go of her hands and turned to grab their bowls. But in their place on the coffee table stood an open bottle of pinot noir and two glasses. Their dinner dishes had been cleared away. Bane sat there, hand outstretched, staring at the table. He closed his mouth, then turned to her with a smile. "You forgot the cannoli."

"I wasn't sure where you'd put it," she admitted.

"Interesting. In order for you to shift inanimate objects or materialize things, you have to first know their location. Would it help if I told you they were in the refrigerator?" She shook her head. "Top shelf? In the usual box from Nonna Lucia's."

Tally frowned in concentration. A muffled clatter sounded from the fridge, and she slapped her hand over her mouth as she swore.

"I'm sure everything is fine." He laughed, and then poured the wine, handing a glass to her. Relaxing with his arm propped up on the back of the couch, he took to twining a lock of her hair around his finger. "Can you—"

"It's your turn to share," she reminded, sipping from her glass and peering at him over the rim.

"I can shadow."

Tally sat up. "What's that?"

"It's like slipping, but you leave a portion of yourself in your original location."

"You can be in two places at once! That's so cool!"

He started chuckling. "Not quite. It's more like an anchor, or a tether. Most Fascina who can shadow are able to split around the fifty-fifty mark, so you can always tell that they're there, but not quite. And most can't pick things up, or even be heard. It's not a very useful skill, so no one tries to master it."

"Except you, I bet." She tucked herself under his arm, cuddling up next to him on the couch. "What was your biggest split?" When he didn't answer her at first, she nudged him.

"Ten-ninety. Sometimes, ninety-ten. And anything in between."

"Bane! That's amazing. Do you ever use it?"

"Yes," he admitted. "Sending ten percent of myself somewhere can be useful in certain business dealings. Ten percent is nothing more than an insubstantial shadow. It's been a while, but when I was cleaning up all the messes left behind by my father..."

"Do you think he could do it?" she wondered suddenly and shivered.

"Maybe. I don't think I got it from Giselle. Have you tried slipping?"

"Not yet. I haven't wanted to do it on my own. I've heard the stories—ending up half in a wall, or missing an arm, or not coming back at all." She could tell he was trying to stop himself from laughing, and she hit him on the chest. "It's not funny. Chris told me that he—"

"Chris was teasing you," Bane said, laughing out loud. "It doesn't work like that."

"You better not be making fun of me, Bane." She pushed away from him, but he grabbed her around the waist and pulled her back. And just like that, their playful banter turned into something else entirely.

He kissed her. "You know, I read once that when two Fascina are together, they can, uh, slip together and the experience is supposed to..."

"Really?" Tally whispered, caught up in the low rumble of his voice. "The times that you took me with you when you slipped, I never felt anything."

"Because I made you close your eyes, and it was only me, not the both of us." He nibbled on her neck, easing her down into the cushions. His hand skimmed up her waist to cup her breast. He fondled her there, through the soft cotton of her T-shirt, and she arched her neck when he nipped her skin. "I could slip now, and take you with me, and you could keep your eyes open this time."

"Now?"

He nodded. "Don't do anything; let me do all of the work, like before. And remember, this time, keep your eyes open. It's very important that you don't try to slip."

She watched him as he came apart. And when the dark, sooty tendrils emanated from him, breaking him into smoke, his essence enveloped her, and her own body loosened and fell away. And in that instant, when she broke apart only to sift back together somewhere else, she saw the beauty of Bane's smoke. Yes, it was the color of night, but that was only because it was made up of myriad vibrant hues—indigo, emerald, sunflower yellow, violet, and so many more—everything coalescing back together in his shape, half-reclined above her. In his home. On his bed.

She set her hand on his cheek, making sure he was looking at her. "You're just so beautiful," she said. "You're not dark, like everyone thinks. I've never seen so many colors."

He dipped his head, and she met his kiss, an equal partner as their tongues slicked against each other. There was nothing to stop them now. He trailed a series of nips down her neck, and he pushed up her shirt until her breasts were exposed. She watched him as he took his time to study her, his eyes growing heavy with lust, and when she was about to press up just to feel his mouth on her, his tongue licked a broad swipe over her nipple. He lifted his face away, then blew on her wet skin. The cool air on her wet areola had her sucking in a breath as her nipple contracted into a tight pebble. He did the same to the other, and Tally shifted restlessly beneath him. And then he attacked her breasts with his lips, swirling with his tongue, scraping the tender flesh with his teeth, and finally, drawing the buds into his mouth and sucking just hard enough to make her gasp in pleasure. She speared her fingers into his hair, holding him to her.

But she wanted more, and she grabbed at his shirt, bunching it in her fists as she pulled it up and off, snarling when it snagged on his chin. He lifted up and peeled off the garment. She stared at the impossibly broad expanse of his chest. Her fingers traced up his side, pausing at the mustard-stained skin where his bruised ribs had healed, then higher until her palm lay flat against his nipple. And because the moment was so intense, she tweaked it. He laughed, and the sound of it filled her heart with joy.

He captured her hand, then licked and sucked at her palm, scratching the surface with his teeth, all the while staring at her half-naked body. He let her go, then drew on one end of the drawstring that held her yoga pants over her hips. Slowly, he pulled, until finally the bow untied so that he could draw down the fabric. He fell forward to kiss her again, his bare chest against hers. Dipping lower, he dragged his mouth down her neck and over her collarbones until he could once again pay homage to her breasts. His hands were everywhere, lightly teasing her skin, and he moved ever lower.

He pressed his face to the vee of silk that still covered her, rolling so that his nose and mouth skimmed her, and drawing in a deep breath to take in her scent. It was incredibly sexy, and she felt herself grow wet for him. As if he sensed it, he ran the flat of his tongue against her, and her legs drifted wider apart at the urging of his hands. He rained kisses over her, through the sheer fabric, licked and lashed and sucked as if trying to draw her taste through the silk. His teeth scraped, and she moaned. Then he put his lips on her still-clothed clit and sucked her into his mouth. Tally's hips bucked; she wanted so much more. She wanted to feel the wet heat of his mouth, and she tossed her head and willed her panties away.

Between her legs, Bane growled his pleasure at having her completely naked. He did unimaginable things to her with his tongue and mouth. If she thought he had been teasing her before, she was mistaken. He eased his sensual assault, pulling her down to the edge of the bed and spreading her thighs wide to either side of his shoulders. Then he plucked at her with his tongue, playing it like the sweetest chord, sucking and laving, only to retreat and swipe his entire mouth over her. His tongue dipped inside, lapping up her juices, until he shifted back to that throbbing nexus between her legs. Again and again, he penetrated her like that, as deep as he could go, then retreated to tease the rest of her with his wicked mouth.

Tally thrashed her head and grabbed one of his pillows to bite down and smother her screams. The heightening pleasure was staggering, and she feared she would never come back together once it broke. And still he fed on her until not even the pillow could mute her cries. With one hand, she reached down and held him to that place where his tongue delved, felt how it curled inside her as he sucked. And the pressure to let go grew so strong, she pressed herself against him for her release.

He reached with his hand, his fingers tracing lazy circles on the flat of her belly, lower and lower and lower. Fingers she knew that were much harder and could go deeper than his tongue ever could. But he stopped just above that place where she throbbed, until he flicked her there, softly, all the while fucking her with his tongue. He reached still farther, taking her little core between his finger and thumb and gently squeezing in time with the thrusting. And she came, her body one fantastic pulsing wave after another. It took her a long time to come down from the heights to which he'd pushed her, and as she did, he pressed his lips to her, gently kissing her there until she settled.

When he crawled up next to her, his hair a total wreck, he wore a satisfied grin on his face, one that had her blushing. He pulled a blanket over her and made to get off the bed.

Oh no, not this time, she thought. Not after waiting so long to be with him.

She didn't know which had been worse: the years of wanting him but knowing it was impossible. Or suddenly realizing they could be together and not being able to do a damn thing about it. She would not suffer another minute without having him completely.

• • •

Halfway to his bathroom, Bane stopped. His jeans had disappeared. He turned, slowly. She was kneeling on the edge of his bed, waiting for him. He thought he was rock-hard before, but nothing prepared him for the look she was giving him now. His cock twitched like a divining rod straight toward her, and seeing it, she lifted an eyebrow and grinned appreciatively. She crooked her finger at him, inviting him back to his bed.

"You're the one who wanted to take turns," she coaxed.

"I was talking about sharing our talents with one another."

"And that's what I want to do. Share my talents."

He stalked toward her, and she lifted her chin when he bent down for a kiss. She skimmed her hands up his thighs, tracing her nails against his skin. Then, gently, she took him in one hand, stroking his length, while with her other, she fondled his balls. Bane groaned, the sound swallowed up by her mouth. She sank down, knees wide, and guided his cock into her mouth.

He drew her hair to the side and off her face so that he could watch her, witness the way her tongue glided over him and circled his tip. Her lips parted to draw him in, again and again, until finally, she let him rock against her in a rhythm that had them both moaning.

But he'd come in her mouth once already. And though it had been glorious, he wanted to bury his cock deep inside her, where her muscles could clench around him as he made her climax once more. He let her go on, loving how beautiful she was with her eyelids lowered in concentration. And when it was time to stop her—because if he didn't, he would explode in her mouth—he slid his hands down her arms and gently lifted her up.

She tumbled back against his bed, and he crawled between her legs, first planting a gentle kiss on her tight curls before slowly easing up the length of her body. He kept himself levered above her, dipping his head to kiss her and reaching down to run his fingers between her legs. She was wet again. Or maybe still wet from earlier. It didn't matter, and he gave her a little of what she had wanted before, sinking first one long finger, then another into her swollen sheath. She writhed beneath him, lifted her hips and ground her center against him. When she dropped back down, he followed, holding himself still at her entrance.

"Please, Bane," she whispered breathlessly, and he reached into his nightstand drawer for a condom, tore open the package, and suited up.

He took his time, rubbing the head of his cock against her folds, opening her little by little as she moaned and sank her fingers into his shoulders. When he was seated just inside, he thrust forward, slowly, easing in, inch by inch, giving her time to accommodate him. He withdrew part way, then sank back into her again. Her eyes fluttered but remained focused on him as he set the tempo of their lovemaking. She was so hot and wet and tight, and he doubted he would be able to last because, finally...Tally. Under. Him.

Propped on his elbows, he stared down at her, closing his eyes for a brief moment when she touched his cheek. Then her hips synced with his, and she bit her lip and squeezed shut her eyes at the pleasure he was giving her. He could feel her body tauten, her hips tilting so that he could bury himself even deeper. He slowed a fraction, wanting to savor the moment of her imminent release, needing to prolong it for her.

"Bane," she growled. He faltered for a moment, but even in the throes of passion, she was too observant. His mouth captured hers before she could ask him what was wrong, and he made her forget everything except how it felt to be filled by him.

She'd drawn up her legs, pressed her heels into his mattress to help her rise to meet him, but now, her calves hugged his pumping buttocks, urging him forward again, calling him home to her. He drove into her sweat-slicked body, dropping his head to kiss her neck, tasting the sweet saltiness of her. She went wild under him, pressing her heels again to the bed and throwing her hips into the air as he pounded again and again. And then she broke, her insides squeezing at his cock as she came, screaming out his name. "Bane!"

He let go of his control, driving deeper, sealing himself against her still-quivering muscles, and came. Hard. Harder than he'd ever experienced in his life, because never before had he been with Tally. Her muscles clenched around him still, drawing out every last bit of his seed until he collapsed on top of her, rolling to the side and wrapping his arms around her until they both stopped heaving. After a few minutes, he slid away, intent on disposing the condom, but she gave him a mischievous smile. An instant later, there was a tiny *plink* in the bathroom. She snuggled against him, seeking his warmth as her breath evened out and she fell asleep.

He knew she'd felt his hesitation when she called him by his nickname. He had felt her try to reach for some understanding. He'd been called Bane for so long, it would be ridiculous to go by any other name. And in business, the moniker had served him well, though he hated his father for giving it to him. Bane detested his name so much that he used it every day. He owned it now, and hearing others call him by that name could never hurt him again.

Except he wanted more from Tally. He wanted to hear his given name drop from her lips.

He thought again about Mallory Waever's letter and wondered if she'd had their being together in mind when she'd written it. Viewed in that context, everything she'd done before, the arcane books about bonding that he'd studied at her bequest, all of it was prelude. He would have to tell Tally, and soon. They already shared the love of friendship, *philosi*. If tonight was any indication, *erosa*—or passion—would never be an issue.

Still, he had a little more time. *Pragmalia* came last, the deep and lasting understanding between two people in love. All words taken from the Greeks and made to describe the rites of Fascina bonding—*agapia*. Mallory and Torbin Waever had done it. And it was a testament to Tally's mother's strength that she'd managed to survive those last years after the death of her bondmate.

Bane had found more on the three stages of love over the years—ancient books and scrolls. They were safe in a hidden climate-controlled room behind one of the walls in his office. He'd long since digitized them and could bring them up at a moment's notice.

Tally settled deeper into his embrace, and Bane realized that there were bigger issues to deal with first. Like deciding how they were going to move forward. No other living soul knew she was Fascina. And something told him that Mallory Waever had been wise to dampen Tally's powers until she was old enough to manage them. But if she were stronger than her brother, and in a relationship with Bane...well, the consequences were more than social. They were political. The National Order of Fascina would undoubtably take note. And if they deemed her too powerful, they might take measures to mute her talents to maintain the balance of power. Unlike what her mother had done, their interference would be permanent. And if they bonded? He didn't want to contemplate the ramifications to them both.

"Are you going to tell me what's wrong, Bane?" she asked sleepily.

"Nothing that we can't figure out together."

She sighed.

"We need to talk, Tally. And soon."

"You keep saying that, and yet, we never do." Then she drifted back to sleep.

Chapter Fourteen

He needed to find a better selection method. When he'd thrown the dart earlier, he'd missed the board again and ended up having to drive here—three hours away from home to Michigan, all the way to the little art community of Saugatuck, where he'd spent his evening staking out the local nightlife. There wasn't much, but on the outskirts, he'd finally found this little club. The Deep was an establishment that catered to gay men. Not that it mattered. Sexual orientation was not something against which he measured a person's worth. In fact, he prided himself on being an equal opportunity offender.

So far, the night was a complete disaster. Two hours of nursing martini after martini and not a single person worth catching his interest. He was about to signal the bartender to close his tab when a man slid onto the barstool next to him. He gave him a cursory scan—silver-fox hair, laugh lines at the crinkles of his eyes on an evenly tanned face. It was a natural tan, too. No reverse-raccoon eyes. Nice looking, handsome. Aging.

He lifted a finger for another martini and made eye contact with the newcomer in the mirror behind the bar. When the crystal-blue eyes of a prowling *manther* stared back, pleasure curled all the way down to his toes.

"Another?" the bartender asked, looking dubious that he could handle more. Truth be told, alcohol had little effect on him. Fascina benefit or curse, he'd never been drunk in his life.

He looked at the man in the mirror and lifted an eyebrow. A slight nod later, and he raised two fingers to the efficient bartender.

"I'm Bernard," the man said. His voice was as smooth as his skin.

"John," he replied ironically. This was going to be a fun night, after all.

"I haven't seen you here before," Bernard said.

"I'm on my way to a wedding in Ann Arbor; it's been a long drive, so I thought I would stop. Seemed like a nice place."

"A little out of the way, coming from Chicago." At his surprised look, Bernard added, "I teach linguistics at Western."

"That's a pretty good ear, since I'm not from the Southside and haven't lived in Chicago for fifteen years," he lied.

They chatted a bit about Chicago and the Lake, and he made up his story as he went along, flattering Bernard. The subject somehow turned to pets, particularly dogs. It turned out that Bernard was a dog lover, too, but allergies had made it impossible to have one.

"You have to meet my dog, Jessie. She's hypoallergenic. And very sweet-tempered."

"I don't know..." Bernard hesitated.

"You'll love her. She's outside in my car. Don't worry, it's cool outside, and the windows are cracked. She has water and her own bed in the backseat."

"Sure. Why not? But only if you promise you're not a serial killer," Bernard teased.

"You found me out," he joked. "But my unmarked van is at the shop, so I'm taking the night off."

Bernard laughed some more, then placed a hand on his knee and gave it a gentle squeeze, before sliding it higher. "I would love to meet your dog," he said, staring at his hand where it rested high on his thigh and not referring to Jessie at all.

At his car, Jessie gave an obligatory wag of her tail upon meeting the stranger, and they decided to spend some more time together to check if Bernard's allergies would remain at bay. Driving separately, he followed the man to his home.

It really was turning out to be a spectacular evening. Jessie was behaving; Bernard wasn't sneezing. As he sipped an excellent vintage from Bernard's wine rack, he eagerly anticipated the older man's terror when he would reveal his true motives for allowing himself to be picked up. Eventually, they finished the wine Bernard had poured, and the manther smiled and pulled out a little blue pill. He swallowed it with a final draw from his wineglass and, thinking himself in control of the situation, began to disrobe. He was a handsome man for his age, taut and toned, but with skin that betrayed his years.

When Bernard reached out to draw him closer, he smiled. Cruelly. He grabbed Bernard's hand and pressed it against his erection. Then he let a little of his mask slide away, purposefully showing a hint of the monster that lurked beneath the façade.

Bernard went and did the unthinkable. Clutching his left arm, he fell back onto the bed and died.

"Well, hell, Bernard!" he fumed. "This won't be as much fun now."

Jessie started whining when he threw up a shield, filling the room with a bubble that would dampen any loud noises he might make while he, ah, rearranged Bernard's bits and pieces. "Quiet!" he yelled at the dog when she started barking.

Jessie whimpered and shrank back from his raised arm. "I'm sorry, pups. It's not your fault that you're in here with me." When he stepped closer to her, she reacted as any cornered animal would and growled, baring her teeth. He released the bubble, and the dog shot from the bedroom. He managed to trap her in the kitchen, but when he reached for her collar to take her to the car, the damn bitch bit him.

She gave a yelp of pain as her ribcage was crushed with one flip of his hand. "Sassy girl. You should not have bitten me. This is your own fault." His hand throbbed as he lifted Jessie's broken carcass to carry it outside to the dumpster in the alley. His mood completely ruined, he returned to Bernard's bedroom, expanded the bubble again, and drew every trace of himself back to his body. He washed his wineglass, wiping it of his fingerprints, and put it away in the cupboard, careful to only touch things with the paper towel. Satisfied that nothing remained for the police to collect, he left Bernard on his bed, naked and untouched, and with a huge death erection pointing toward heaven.

It was a long drive back to Chicago, and he should've gone straight home. But the draw to see her was too great. The motor under his seat whirred as he pressed the recline button—might as well get comfortable during his little stakeout of Natalia's house. Catching a glimpse of her after such a disappointing evening would help mitigate the throbbing in his hand.

Perhaps he could wait until the afternoon, when he knew Natalia would be at the hospital, and ask her to tend to it. Ascertaining her work schedule had been easy...he'd been able to seduce it out of her assistant. And once he had the passcode for her hospital email account, he now knew where and when Tally had meetings and with whom.

In fact, she was running late. She had to be at the hospital by eleven for her foundation meeting. Could she already have gone in? About to start his car and go home, he stopped when a black Mercedes drove past and then halted on her street, finding the perfect parking spot directly across from Natalia's house. He recognized the car immediately, and its driver.

The figure of Bane Caron climbed out of the expensive sedan and walked around to the other side to open the door. He stood there, offering his hand to his passenger, then threw back his head to laugh. After looking up and down the sidewalk, Caron bent down to say something and was hidden from view.

Watching from a hundred yards away, a terrible, gut-clenching feeling began to build in his stomach. Caron stood, grinning, and pulled a slim woman up from the passenger seat. She fell forward in an obvious flirtatious feint, her light-blond ponytail swinging, and into Caron's arms. He held her there, up against him, tenderly caressing her cheek. Her head tilted, as if waiting for a kiss...and then they seemed to remember themselves and drew apart. She preceded Caron up to her door. At the last minute, she turned and took both of his hands, tugging him into her home. Their body language alone...

They would pay, he thought, gripping his steering wheel and forgetting his throbbing hand. Yes, they would pay in ways they could never imagine. First, Bane Caron. Then, Christian Waever. As the head of the Waever family, he should've controlled his sister—kept her pure. After he rid the world of the two men, he would finally take Natalia for himself.

Poor, ungifted Natalia Waever would finally be his. He didn't care that she was a Non. In fact, the idea that she would be completely helpless only made his appetite for her grow. He would train her to do his bidding, as he'd done with Missy. The idea of holding two women captive at the same time had his mind spinning with possibilities. He drove to his home-away-from-home, surprised that he actually missed Jessie's greeting when he unlocked the back door and resisted checking in on Missy. He wasn't sure, in his current state, that he could trust himself where she was concerned, and he detoured to the desk in his bedroom. He stared hard at his computer screen, willing his boiling blood to cool. Two secure emails later, and the ball was rolling on his planned revenge.

Of course, he would have to make another deposit for their experiments—not that he cared what they did with his samples. They needed him, not the other way around. And now he wanted more than just the money they funneled into his hidden accounts. He stripped out of his clothes from the previous night, and then collapsed, exhausted, onto his bed. As he fell into a deep sleep, he thought idly about keeping Caron alive, just long enough to watch him while he molded Natalia to his liking.

• • •

The next morning, they were getting ready to eat breakfast at Tally's. Her phone vibrated at the same time as Bane's, and he took a step back, busying himself with making a pot of coffee. Tally hustled upstairs to change her clothes, feeling that telltale air pressure fluctuation as her brother slipped into her home just as she made the landing. "Be right down," she called. When she returned, Chris and Bane were arguing about the bagels her brother had brought. Only they weren't bagels but gourmet donuts, the dense cakey type, overloaded with frosting and sprinkles. Bane was complaining that just because they were round and had a hole in the middle didn't mean they were donuts.

"And who in their right mind would put bacon on a donut?" Bane demanded. Tally smirked at her brother.

"Please don't go there, sis."

"Go where?" Bane demanded.

"Nothing," Chris said, holding up his hands.

"Natalia?" Bane said, stretching out the syllables of her name.

"Sounding like my mother isn't going to make me talk," she replied. He crossed his arms and stared at Chris until her brother broke.

"Fine," Chris conceded, "but don't say I didn't warn you."

"Chris, don't!" Tally begged. But it was too late.

"This is just like your licorice rant," her brother blithely went on.

"My licor—that wasn't a rant," Bane said, defending himself. "That was fact. If it doesn't taste like licorice, it's not—"

"Licorice," Tally finished.

"Exactly! Twizzlers and other red *non-licorice* candies are called—"

"Vines or ropes," Chris interrupted. "Yes. We know, my friend. You've been preaching this truth since we were kids. Here, have a torus-shaped cupcake. By the way, don't knock the bacon. It's delicious with the maple icing."

Bane grabbed one with pink sprinkles instead, but grinned.

Tally set the pot of coffee on the island while her brother pulled plates and mugs from the cupboard. Bane pointed to the fourth mug.

"Oh, I forgot. Detective Haneluk is joining us," Chris informed them. "He'll text when he arrives, so one of us can bring him in."

The good-natured ribbing that had lightened the last few minutes evaporated. "Did something happen with the case?" Tally asked.

"That would be my guess," Chris replied. "Haneluk said he wanted to meet about a donation to the Benevolent Supporters of the CPD fund."

"Code for: *the feds might be listening*," Bane guessed.

Chris's phone buzzed. "He's here."

"Let me," Bane offered, going to the front entrance.

"What's up with Bane?" Chris asked, and Tally shrugged and sipped her coffee. "I haven't seen him in a good mood in, well, ever."

She was saved from having to answer when Haneluk came in, followed by Bane. "Oh good, coffee and mini-bundt cakes."

"He paid you to say that!" Chris complained. Haneluk remained tight-lipped and reached for a red velvet donut. Tally poured him a mug of coffee and pushed it across the island.

"I couldn't talk over the phone because we believe that Greene's office is compromised, and not trusting that my texts and calls aren't being picked up—" He paused to take a bite and a swig. "I'm under explicit orders to not give you any information," he finished.

"From Greene?" Tally asked.

The detective shook his head. "Pressure from Springfield."

"They have the governor in their pocket, then," Chris said flatly, and Haneluk nodded. "What about the task force?"

"Still in play. Tell your people to take care. Information is being collected on you, whether you know it or not. Leave nothing behind." Almost as an afterthought, he swiped his thumb over the rim of his mug.

"You think it goes that deep?" Bane asked.

"Look, it's no secret the government has been collecting DNA for decades. Who do you think is behind those genealogy tests they sell on TV?" Haneluk was a quasi-conspiracy theorist, but now his ideas didn't seem so farfetched.

"We got a break, finally," Barney continued. "That woman in Wisconsin who was raped and murdered a few weeks ago... The reason they found her was because of a noise complaint. She lived on the outskirts of Milwaukee," he divulged after consulting his pocket notebook. "Don't look at me like I'm quaint," he accused Chris when her brother made a bemused face. "Pen and paper can't be hacked like your phone."

"You mean *your* phone," Bane corrected, spinning his on the marble countertop. "I offered to set you up, Haneluk. Hell, the whole department would be a tax write-off for me."

"Yah, but who's to say you couldn't hack our system if you provided it?"

"I could do that now, if I wanted, so what would be the difference? It comes down to a question of trust."

"You mentioned a break in the case?" Tally asked, steering the conversation back.

"Right, so, as I mentioned, the victim lived on the outskirts, pre-fab houses, trailers, a few ranches. One of the neighbors complained about a dog locked in a car and barking all night. Called in the complaint three times before a patrol made it out there—the last time citing that the dog seemed to be in distress. No make, no model, no tags, dark in color...let's just say the area is not known for its neighborhood watch.

"The locals arrive at 3:04 a.m.," Haneluk continued, looking to his notes again. "No barking dog. But they see the complainant, one Roy Chandler, on his porch, so they go do their due diligence. Roy tells them that a man, carrying a large bundle, departed the house situated across the street. He got into the car with the dog and drove away. Roy then stated that the homeowner, a Ms. Sandra Temple, entertained different men on a regular basis.

"They go to investigate, find the woman, tortured like the others. It was evident that the victim owned a dog. Pictures of the two on the wall, dog toys and bed, leash. The dog's water dish was still there, but the food bowl was missing, as was all the dog food."

"He took the dog?" Chris asked, and Haneluk nodded.

"Yeah. One of those custom designer pooches...a labradoodle. The techs collected the dog hair, processed it. That was five weeks ago. This morning, a cleaning lady in Michigan unlocks the door to one of the townhouses she services. She finds the owner dead in bed. Apparent heart attack. When the police arrive to take a statement, she's busy vacuuming"—Barney paused to shake his head, then took a sip of coffee—"and complains to the officers about cleaning up dog hair which, according to her, is strange because her employer was severely allergic."

"Tell me they confiscated the vacuum," Bane hoped aloud, and Barney nodded.

"When they left, they went back to their car where it was parked in the alley. One of the officers heard a whimper and went to look around. They found a dog, beaten and broken and left to die in a dumpster. But get this...the poor dog had blood on its muzzle and no apparent wounds."

"I'm sorry, Barney, but this still doesn't sound like much," Chris said, voicing what Tally had been thinking. "The guy had a heart attack. It's probably not even related to the dog. Was there torture like the other cases?"

Barney closed his notebook and returned it to his suit pocket. He took another sip from his mug. "You always make the best coffee, Tally." Before she could correct him and give Bane credit, he went on. "No, no torture this time. And I would agree with your assessment except for this—the case was inexplicably taken over by the feds. They seized all the evidence, interrogated the housekeeper, even took possession of the dog.

"I made a call to a friend of mine that retired near Saugatuck, asked her to talk to the vet up there. Anyone wanna take a stab at the breed?"

"Labradoodle," Bane guessed.

"Exactly. And it turns out that she was chipped. National database, too. Guess who owned the dog?" He paused for effect. "One Sandra Temple, our victim from Wisconsin."

Tally sat down on the stool and stared at her friend. "Chicago has to be his home base. Easy to get to multiple metropolitan areas by car. Both O'Hare and Midway to everywhere else in the country. Day trips."

Haneluk nodded.

"Did the witness from the Wisconsin case give a description?"

Haneluk shook his head, pulled out his notebook again for effect, and flipped it open. "Roy said it was too dark. And the streetlights were out. But the responding officers made a note in their report that when they arrived—every lamppost was in working order." He flipped his notebook shut and gave Chris a hard stare. "Those lights being out sounded a little too hinky to me, but I gotta ask—can your kind do that? Turn off streetlights?"

Tally turned away, pretending to get more cream from the fridge to hide her shock. Chris came to stand next to her and gave her a meaningful look.

It was Bane who answered. "A few can, but that kind of power is rare."

"Does Janice know?" Tally asked.

"What? That the killer may be one of you? That you failed—again—to share an important bit of information with us?"

"Barney, I—"

"We just determined it ourselves," Chris answered quickly. "But we didn't want to let whoever it is get wind that we're close." Barney gave him a hard look. "I'm sorry. We were wrong not to tell you."

"You think it might be someone on the task force," Barney deduced. "I get it. You were probably right to hold off telling me. But with this new information, you should be able to narrow down the suspect pool."

"We don't really talk about what we can and can't do," Chris explained. "It's a form of mutual deterrence in our politics. You mentioned trust, Barney, so I'm going to trust you with this—certain families have more power than others. This determines if you get a place on the council. We're not elected, but inherit our positions, at least as long as we have a strong family and strong allies. It happens on occasion that a ruling family's power goes into decline, but their place remains on the council because they manage to hide their deficits."

"You lead the council," Haneluk pointed out.

"Our family is one of the strongest," Tally admitted. "Bane's, too." She cleared the dishes from the island. "It's a good starting point," she stated. "Looking for someone who can manipulate streetlights." She hadn't meant to, but her words sounded a little bleak. "Thanks for trusting us, Barney. Tell the mayor—tell Janice—that we will find this man, and if he's part of our community, he'll pay."

Haneluk nodded. "Find him before the feds do. Because if they get him first, your families will suffer for it. I don't want to live in a world where good people are forced to register their DNA."

"Thanks for that," Chris said.

"For what?" Haneluk asked.

"For grouping us in with the good guys. Come on, I'll walk you out."

Tally gripped the edge of the counter, assessing the latest facts. Something was fomenting in her mind, the clues congealing and blending, but the solution still out of reach. Whatever the end result, it was bound to shake their community to its core.

Bane had started loading the dishwasher but stopped when she began to shake. He drew her into his arms and rubbed her back.

"Aw, Talz," Chris said when he came back. "We'll find him. Don't worry."

She pulled herself away from Bane's arms and turned to face her brother. "You think it's the same man?"

"I don't like coincidences," her brother said. "Maybe you should come stay with me at Rosegate."

"I bet Jackie would *love* that," she said. "I'm sorry, Chris. I didn't mean it to sound like that. It's just not every day that your stalker is probably a powerful Fascina serial killer."

"It's alright, sis. You know, Jackie was really concerned when I told her about the attack. She wanted you to know that she's happy to be your escort to the hospital when you go to work." Her brother chuckled. "But I guess no one's better than Bane at watching your backside. Hey, you could stay at his place! Right, Bane? I would feel much better knowing she's in your capable hands."

"Uh, sure. Or I could bunk here."

"Great. That's settled. Now, when do you want to meet to go over your database?" Chris asked. "I can make time this afternoon, say three o'clock."

Bane nodded, and when Chris slipped away, Tally leaned back against the counter. "Database? Is that even safe? What if it got into the wrong hands?"

"I'm the only one with access, and trust me, no one can hack my system," Bane replied, taking her by the hips and lifting her so that she sat on the counter. "It was Chris's idea, and a good one, considering what's happening with the council. We've been researching the families, writing down any mentions of powers and categorizing them. Most of the information is known—so-and-so's grandparent could heal, that sort of thing. I'm looking at the genetics of the great families, how they've managed to remain strong without diluting their bloodlines by forming strong bonds through marriage. The information can help us on many levels."

"Do you think it's all related? The murders, the person behind my attack, the surge of malikers, even the rumblings on the council?"

"Maybe. This predator is certainly drawing our focus away from the problems with the Order. The task force has been nothing but ineffectual, and that's being viewed as a reflection on Chris's leadership. Orson couldn't find anyone who didn't have an alibi for at least half of the attacks."

"I was positive the killer was on the task force, but that's only possible if they could be in two places at once."

He frowned.

"Knock it off. I think I would have noticed if even ten percent of you was gone last night. No. I can't put my finger on it..."

"What's wrong?"

"I know we ruled him out, but I was thinking...maybe we should take a deeper look at Shareff. My assistant says he calls daily, trying to make an appointment with me."

"An appointment?"

"My fault. He was at the hospital again, and—don't look at me like that. I handled it."

"Just promise me that you'll tell me if he comes at you again." She nodded. "Chris wants me to take another stab at getting information out of my mother, but I don't think I should leave you—"

"Bane, now that you know about me...about what I can do"—he leaned in to nuzzle her neck—"you don't need to spend as much time watching over me. I don't need a bodyguard."

He pulled away and stared at a spot over her shoulder.

"I do need you, Bane, but as a boyfriend. And a lover." They touched their foreheads together. "We'll have all the time in the world for you and me later."

"I'll always feel protective of you. I can't change that."

"I'm not asking you to," she said. "But these other threats need your full attention. You know you're the best of us when it comes to security."

"One condition," he stated.

"Name it."

"You will let me assess what you can do and help you to understand how to use your powers. Have you tried slipping yet?"

She shook her head.

"We can start there."

"Fine," Tally yielded. "But only if I get to name a condition of my own—I get to feel just as protective of you."

"Deal."

Chapter Fifteen

Tally closed the videoconference app and rolled her neck—over three hours was too long to sit in a meeting, especially if said meeting was on a screen. But the hospital board always wanted a thorough recap of the gala and which programs would benefit from the donations.

She was shutting down her home laptop when her cellphone buzzed. Bane had gone to see Chris about visiting his mom and had promised to check in with her before leaving. She flipped her phone over and saw a text from Haneluk.

> Can u meet again today?

> *Yes. When? Where?*

> I'm outside, but damned if I can find your house

> *Be right out*

He was pacing on the sidewalk, one block over. When he saw her, he jogged to her porch, and she waved him inside.

His face was more dour than usual. "How did Janice take the news? It's bad, isn't it?" He looked over his shoulder as she shut the door. "Are you being followed?"

"Maybe," he said. "We know Greene's office has been bugged. I think the station is likewise compromised. I finally accepted Bane's offer." He held up his phone and jiggled it back and forth. "I'm worried about you."

"Me? I'm no one. Wait. Did Bane tell you about my stalker?"

He gave her a hard stare. "First off, let's get one thing straight here— you're not no one, Tally. You've got the ear of Greene, the Chicago Order, the hospital, and two communities. Not to mention more street smarts than anyone I know—except maybe Bane and yours truly. And don't forget money, powerful friends, and family. Unfortunately, that kind of influence gets you noticed."

She slouched on her stool, not liking where the conversation was going and feeling a little queasy. "So, what's going on that you had to go all cloak-and dagger to visit a friend? It's Reiss and Beans, isn't it?"

He nodded. "They're overly interested in your comings and goings. At first, I thought it had to do with the Order and the Mayor's Office. Then I reached out to a friend in D.C. Seems they're acting on some anonymous tip, and it was recommended that I insulate myself from you.

"You're already sitting," he continued. "So I'll just pull off the Band-Aid. You're being investigated—suspected money laundering, tax evasion, fraud."

"What! Oh, Barney! You know that I—"

He shook his head, then set his bear paw of a hand over hers. "It's all bunk, Tally. Anyone who's met you knows there's not an ounce of truth to the allegations."

"Then I should be fine, right? I mean, I've done nothing wrong, so..." Barney was giving her that look again. "Right. They can pretty much make up what they want, and it'll be up to me to prove my innocence."

"If you're defending yourself at a congressional hearing, you can't liaise between the Order and City Hall. Public sentiment is fickle. Your brother and Bane would have to commit resources that would normally be used to keep everyone happy and at peace. Don't think for one moment that Greene doesn't appreciate the support your family has given her."

"But..."

"No buts. She's as loyal as they come. So what's this about you having a stalker?"

Tally gave him a quick recap, glossing over some of the details that would have him asking questions about Bane. Or even her.

"I'll have the patrols in your neighborhood increased," he said, then finished his soda. "Listen, Tally, you'll beat this but call your lawyer. Start an investigation of your own and gather evidence that will refute any possible charges."

"Another distraction," she muttered.

"What's that?"

"Nothing important, Barney," she said as he rose to leave. "Hey, thanks for the warning."

He nodded. "You need anything, you call." He surprised her by giving her a hug before walking to the front door. Barney never hugged.

"What's wrong, Barney? Is there something else?"

"Maybe. I'm not sure. Just an impression that I got from Orson Sedge."

"Orson?"

"Yeah, when he gave me an update from the task force. He said that everyone on it had been cleared, 'even Bane.' I thought it odd, how Sedge specifically named him, but then..."

"You can't think that Bane is—"

"No. No! But others might. He has a certain reputation. Just tell him to watch his back."

"I will. Thanks, Barney," she said, pulling open her front door. "And I'll keep my ears open for rumors."

On her porch, he turned to her. "One of these days, I'll remember what your place looks like, and you won't have to come outside to find me when I get lost." He chuckled and shook his head.

She smiled and waved goodbye, knowing the moment he stepped off her property, he would forget to turn around and commit her home to memory. When she went back inside, she walked straight to her office and turned on her laptop, where it was docked to two large monitors. She couldn't leave everything to friends and family. It was time to do some investigating on her own. She clicked the onion icon on her task bar and opened up the dark web. In the search bar, she typed, *mal de nuit roses.* Images of dark, nearly black roses with abnormally large blooms, stunted leaves and smooth stems with needle sharp thorns filled the screen. Descriptions varied, but she knew what she was looking for, and none of the roses were the real thing.

Recollections of that night when Sebastian Caron had compelled her were as fresh in her mind as the smell of the roses he'd created for her mother. The mal de nuit had taken on near-epic notoriety over the years in the Fascina community. People around the world claimed to have cuttings from the original stock and sold them for tens of thousands of dollars. She clicked on one of the images and was taken to a private webpage where root grafts were offered at the bargain price of thirty-two thousand dollars. The accompanying images of the stock plants showed the horrifyingly beautiful flower in all its glory. But she knew it was a fake.

Tally's phone vibrated. Bane was on his way. The air pressure shifted, and she called down, "Up here. In my office."

She looked up when his body filled the doorway.

"Hi, Tally."

Even as distracted as she was, her skin flushed under the heat of his gaze. She loved looking at him. His tall, slim build hid taut, ropy muscles. Despite her worries, her fingers itched to run up and down his body. He pushed off the doorframe where he'd been leaning, then walked over to her desk and let his gaze drift over her, pausing at the vee of her shirt.

The heat in his gaze dimmed noticeably when he looked at her screen. He cleared his throat. "I got the lab results on the rose left in the park. No prints. But this is a good idea. If you can find the person who sold the flower, I might be able to track down the buyer. Here, let me," he said, and she pushed the wireless keyboard to him. She gave up her chair, but he pulled her onto his lap after he sat down.

"Now let's see." His fingers flew. "This is a good browser, but there are better ones. Taskbar?" She managed to nod, difficult to do while surrounded by all his hot Bane-ness. He added the new icon to the bottom of her screen, then found another vendor selling the cut flowers. Perfect specimens, and like the rootstock, they fetched hefty prices. Bane whistled at the cost of a full bouquet.

"None of these are true mal de nuit roses," Tally said.

"No, those are all gone, thanks to the fire my mother set in the greenhouse. But how can you tell?"

"They're tamer somehow. The thorns aren't as sharp. Besides, the stems on the real ones are darkly variegated."

"I was never allowed that close to them to notice that detail." He paused, looking thoughtful. "The only time Giselle showed any concern for me was when she caught me trying to pick the lock on my father's conservatory, where he grew the awful things. She said going in there was too dangerous."

Tally stared at the images on her screen, then reached over and closed the site, putting her laptop in sleep mode.

"What's up, Tally? It's like you can't even stand to look at them."

"Did your lab discover anything unusual?"

"It would help if I knew what you were looking for."

"Toxins, maybe?"

"Not really."

"Not really?" she asked. "But something."

"One of the techs had an allergic reaction. Broke out in welts and blisters. Nothing an antihistamine couldn't handle."

"Then the rose might've been an actual hybrid of mal de nuit," she said, getting up from his lap.

"Why would you think that?"

She walked over to the closet and pushed the hanging door to the side. On one of the broad built-in shelves, she shoved over a set of ledgers and placed her hand on the blank wall. A moment later, the proximity scanner, coded to her and her alone, revealed a concealed wall safe. She rested her palm against the biometric scanner, then leaned forward for the retinal scan. The door to the safe hissed open, and Tally withdrew a firesafe lockbox.

After setting it on the credenza and a quick fingerprint verification, followed by a six-digit code, the box unlocked. Holding the lid, she stared up at Bane when he came to look over her shoulder.

"The week after my dad died, I woke up to find one of the roses on my pillow. A birthday present from your dad. It was the second one he gave me. I destroyed them both." She opened the lid to reveal a dried rose, its leaves crumbling, but the thorns as deadly wicked as if the stem had just been cut from the plant. "My mom sent this to me along with the codicil to her will. She'd had tests run on the flowers."

"My dad gave you two of these roses. Why would he—?"

"There's more," Tally interrupted. "A bit of parting wisdom from my father when I told him about the flower your dad sent. It was the roses, Bane. Your father...he..."

"Go ahead and say it. It's easier if you just get it over with."

"Your dad created them for my mom. He was obsessed with having her, and my father was in his way. So, he engineered them to contain a deadly toxin keyed specifically to my dad."

"Sebastian admitted to killing him, right before they sent him to the Null. But he never said how. Oh, Tally, I'm sorry." Bane hung his head.

She took his hand and pulled him over to the small sofa in her office. "My mom was a powerful healer, but that very power ended up killing her. When my dad was on his deathbed, she tried to cure him. She took his illness away just long enough for him to become lucid and talk to us one last time. Afterward, when he fell back into a delirium, I stayed by his side. I was alone with him when he woke and grabbed my hand. He pointed to an angry scratch on his wrist and uttered the words, 'mal de nuit.'"

Bane shook his head. "Sebastian claimed that your mom made her choice, and could only hold herself to blame for the outcome. At the time, we didn't know what he was talking about. But he did. He knew your mom was also poisoned."

"She must've taken the toxin into her own body when she tried to heal him. And there it stayed, weakening her over the next few years like an angry cancer eating her away from the inside out."

"Why didn't she...you...tell me about this?"

Tally took his face in her hands. "I never really put it together until I started coming into my own powers. We'd all grown older, and I wasn't completely sure. Besides, why add to everyone's pain? It wouldn't change anything." She closed the box and locked it back in her safe.

"No one could figure out how he'd done it," Bane said, staring at the safe as she closed the closet door. "Giselle must have suspected—she forbade me to ever enter the conservatory. She was protecting me by keeping me from his deadly creation."

"There's more," Tally said, and began telling him about her recent dream. "It was during one of my parents' parties. He tried to seduce my mom, but she rebuffed him and left. Sebastian caught me spying and compelled me and Chris. My father was dead a few weeks later." She cocked her head. "You don't look surprised."

"I'm not. My dad was a predator. Does Chris know?"

"How it was done? I don't think so." She took his hand. "Hey, how do you feel about all of this?"

"I'm pissed I wasn't strong enough to kill the bastard when I was younger."

"But it's not your fault, Bane."

"I know. But knowing doesn't stop me from being sorry." Comprehension filled his eyes. "What Sebastian did to you that night...holding you frozen. No wonder you looked so afraid of me when you saw me do the same thing to those men in the park."

"I wasn't afraid of you, just shocked by what I saw."

He drew her into his arms. "I understand. I can be a scary guy."

She pushed at his chest, but he was made of stone. "Don't ever say that, Bane. There's not been one single day that I've been frightened by you, and you know it. I guess I never thought about what you inherited from your father. Or your mother."

"Some things are darker than others," he admitted.

"So, what brought you over?" she asked, trying to steer them away from the uncomfortable subject. "I thought we were meeting later. Did Barney call you?"

He stepped back, letting her go.

"Where do you think you're going?" She cupped his cheeks and lifted to her toes to kiss him. Softly at first. And just as slowly, she could feel his resistance melt away.

He lifted her so that she sat on the edge of her desk.

"I came over to see if you wanted to practice some of your gifts with me."

"Liar," she accused playfully.

"You caught me. I'm here for this." His lips scorched across hers in a searing kiss. "You're sure you're alright?"

"Are you?" she countered. "I'm stronger than I look, remember?" And then she kissed him as passionately as he had kissed her. When they pulled apart, panting, she added, "I was wondering..."

"What's that?" he said, stepping closer, between her knees so that he could press his torso against her.

"What you did in the park..."

"Tally, would you like me to hold you while I do...things?" He dipped his head and nipped and sucked along the side of her neck. She hummed deep in her throat as he fondled her breast.

"Bane, remind me to—" She meant to tell him about Haneluk's visit, but at his provocative purr in her ear, the train of her thoughts derailed.

"I have this fantasy of you, Tally. Not here on your little antique desk but stretched out naked on mine."

Tally could do nothing but give a little squeak as his fingers pinched her pebbled nipple. "Yes, please," she murmured. He wrapped his arms around her, slanted his mouth to hers and pulled her impossibly close as he slipped them from her home to his. In that jump of space and distance, she kept her eyes open and watched the swirling colors that made up his essence. She wondered what hers would look like, and in her wondering, felt a little bit of what made her dissolve and spread out, intermingling with that which was Bane. Feeling him in a way that her five senses could never imagine.

They came back together in his office with a pop. At least it felt like one, and it left her gasping. Bane, too. He stared down at her, the amazement and hunger blazing in his eyes.

"I can slip!" Tally exclaimed. "I was always too afraid to try it on my own." She realized then how hard he was, pressed against her. "What's wrong?"

"We should," he growled, "not do that again. At least not yet. Not until you've been properly trained. There's, uh, very little written on co-slipping, and it's not meant to be done while traveling from one place to another."

"Then what..." She stared at him, feeling his lust rolling off him in waves. "Oh! Wait. You mean we can do that when we—"

"You're killing me, Tally," he groaned, then lifted her so that she sat on his desk and he stood between her legs.

She giggled as she looked up at him. "Fine. But tell me about this fantasy of yours," she started, looping her arms around his neck. "Clothes on or off?"

He gave her a smile that melted her heart and heated her body. Tally had never been shy, but she felt a blush steal up her neck and onto her cheeks. He saw it, too.

"Definitely off," he said. "But leave your bra and underpants on."

She willed her garments away. "What about you?"

"On for now," he said.

"Will you..." she started, not sure how to ask, but knowing if she didn't, she would never stop having nightmares about his father. "Can you show me what you did that night in the park?"

"You're sure?"

She nodded.

"Then I will, but not quite yet." He pressed her back and posed her while files and notebooks slid and fell to the floor. One leg dangled over the edge, the other he bent at the knee, setting her heel on the desk. He stared down at her for a moment, hungry, and making her feel like the most powerful woman in the world. Leaning over her, he gave her a kiss that left no part of her unsated, taking his time to nibble his way down her neck and over her collar. He teased her breasts through the silk of her bra, tickling her by barely brushing his fingertips over the sheer material. She ran her fingers through his hair, pushing him lower, urging him to take her in his mouth.

• • •

She was so brave, asking him to subdue her, wanting to conquer her fear. When her sighs turned to pants, Bane drew away, caught her wrists and lifted them above her head to hold them in one hand while his other traced down her inner arm, causing the most exquisite goosebumps. His lips and tongue followed the trail. He hooked his fingers under the edge of silk and lace, pulling the bra cup down far enough that he could admire her tautened nipple. He did the same to the other, loving the way her breast swelled up with each of her increasingly heavy breaths. Tally. Spread across his desk. How many times had he imagined her like this? Hundreds? Thousands? And here she was. His. Asking him, begging him, to live out his fantasy.

He hovered over her, his mouth close enough that she could feel his breath on her skin, and she arched. But he moved his lips so that he kissed the pushed globes of her breasts, ignoring her nipples as they strained to be sucked. She tried to draw down her arms, but he held her with his hand as he applied gentle, teasing kisses and licks to her skin. She tried again to break free, and he lifted his head. "If this is too much—"

"Don't you dare stop, Bane," she snarled in the sexiest voice he'd ever heard.

He smiled against her flesh and let her go. Only, her wrists remained fixed above her head as she struggled to break free, gasping when she realized he was no longer physically holding her. And on that gasp, he took her nipple in his mouth, sucking hard. She writhed on his desk, arching her back, and he quickly pushed the band of silk and lace up over her nipples so that they sprang back as the elastic passed over them. Then he devoured them, gently biting and nipping and sucking and laving until she was moaning his name.

He held her only at her wrists, savoring how she looked stretched out across his desk. Finally, he moved to where her one leg hung over the edge, bent at the knee. He wheeled his desk chair around. She lifted her head to stare at him, her eyes laser-focused on what he would do next. Above her head, her fingers clenched and unclenched. He expanded his hold over her, letting her feel the weight of his power across her stomach, and lifted the foot that had been on the desk so that he could drape her leg over his shoulder. The other, he set on his thigh. "You're mine, Tally. You have no control over what I'm going to do, do you?" She shook her head, her mouth open. "But you're enjoying this, aren't you?" he asked, running his fingertips in lazy circles, higher and higher along her inner thigh until he barely grazed the edge of her panties. "You love giving up control."

She closed her eyes, tilted back her head, and bit her lip as he applied gentle kisses to her thigh. His fingers touched her through the tiny wisp of lace. He held her legs, only slightly parted, not enough room for him to go down on her, not properly anyway. And when she tried to further spread her thighs, he expanded his hold yet again. Tally growled. "Tell me, Tally. Tell me how this feels for you. Being held at the whim of another. Tell me that I'm right, and that you need this surrender."

She lifted her head to glare at him. "Only with you, Bane. Only ever with you," she hissed, and when he looked down again, her panties were gone.

He grinned at her and then promptly buried his face between her legs, hitching her other thigh over his shoulder. He breathed her in, tasted her. Used one hand to tease her nipples, while the other spread her open so that he could stab his tongue into her, over and over. She strained, invisibly bound to the desk. And he kept her there so that he could worship her sex.

Teasing and sucking, then working his fingers inside her. She was so wet, and she cried out her frustration as he held her immobile, fueling the pressure that was expanding inside her. She gave out a strangled cry—his name, maybe, or perhaps a curse—as she came apart while completely held together by his power.

He pulled the condom out of his pocket and set it on the desk. "Clothes, Tally," he ordered, standing and lifting her legs so that the backs of her thighs were up against his torso. "Now, please," he commanded when she didn't seem to hear him the first time. Suddenly, he was naked, and he took a moment to suit up. He was so hard, he wasn't sure he wouldn't come the second his cock touched her slick folds. She was still coming down off her orgasm when he entered her and plundered her anew, stoking her fire until she burned again for him. She opened her eyes to stare at him in wonder, and though it was her under his control, he was the one held captive.

He thrust into her, harder, again and again, holding her legs to his front, kissing her calves. He pounded against her, his solid desk creaking with the force, and felt her tighten around him, deep inside. He wouldn't immobilize her there. He never wanted to try. She cried out his name, and her entire body quivered with her second, more powerful climax. He thrust one last time, his own release pulled out of him by the muscles spasming around his cock. "Tally!" he shouted, and then hung onto her, grinding against her until his orgasm played out.

"Bane," she whispered. She must have done so several times, but his blood was still pounding in his ears, so he hadn't heard. He gazed down at her, her chest still heaving and her skin, like his, sweat-dewed. "You can let me go now."

He released her, but she stayed where she was, sealed up against his groin. Gently, he lowered her legs, and she circled them around his waist. He leaned forward, reached for her arms, and dragged her up against his chest. Then, he lifted her and carried her out of his office and through his bedroom to the bathroom and into the walk-in shower. She was boneless against him, and he set her gently on the teak bench. He turned on the water next, blocking the spray until it was good and hot. The entire time, she watched him, a tiny, satisfied smile gracing her lips. He grabbed a thick terry cloth and soaped it up. Then, with painstaking thoroughness, he washed her, massaging and rubbing her skin until he felt her regain her strength. She stood finally, grabbed another cloth, and did the same for him. He hadn't realized how strenuous their lovemaking had been for him, and it was his turn to slump onto the bench she'd vacated. When she was done, she stood before him, curling forward to hold him in the cradle of her body. He reached over, turned the water off, and pulled himself up. They dried each other, then fell into his bed, both drained.

He held her in his arms as she nestled against him. "Remind me to tell you about Barney," she murmured, then fell asleep. He half napped, listening to the steadiness of her breathing, knowing he could never let her go.

He would have to tell her the full truth about the stages of bonding, and soon. Especially as they had co-mingled when they'd slipped here. Even though it had been a mere split second, she had unwittingly set them on a path from which they could never stray.

Chapter Sixteen

"Bane," she whispered, not wanting to wake him if he was asleep.

He blinked open his eyes, coming out of a drowsy state, and frowned. "What's wrong, Tally?" he asked, smoothing his hand over her worried brow. "If you think we're moving too fast, we can slow down."

"It's not that," she said, tracing her fingers over the outline of the tattoo that covered his shoulders. "The last thing I want is to waste more time."

"Then what is it?" he asked, turning and touching his forehead to hers.

"Can you recommend a good lawyer?"

He propped himself up. "What's wrong with your family lawyer?"

"They don't specialize in criminal cases."

"What did you do, sweetheart?"

She sat up and swung her legs over the side of the bed. The endearment had her feeling all warm and fuzzy, and although she loved it, they needed to have a serious conversation. "Barney came back to my place. Let's get dressed, then I'll tell you everything."

He sat up and gave her a salacious ogle. "You're right. We should definitely get dressed."

Bane led her back into his office to collect their clothes. Tally bit her lip—files and papers were strewn everywhere.

"Maybe we should go back to your place. I'm just going to be distracted here, thinking of you, on my desk."

Heat shot through Tally, remembering how it had felt to give him complete control. She swallowed and nodded, and he drew her into his living room. He took her by her shoulders and turned her to face him. "Do you want to try slipping back on your own?"

She'd always been too afraid, but Bane gave her courage. "What do I do?'

"What did it feel like to you before, when we slipped here?"

She thought back to that brief instant. "Like a loosening."

"Good," he said. "That's really all it is. A gentle coming apart. Although, some people feel as if they are tightening, becoming smaller. I've heard that others think they're melting." He stepped back. "Now, think about where you want to be, specifically in your home, then let your mind relax until you feel your body give." He rubbed her arms. "You can do this, Tally. Focus on the area behind your couch; it's an open space."

"And you promise that I won't accidentally rematerialize half in the wall or the coffee table?"

Bane tilted his head back and laughed. "No, honey. That only happens in *Star Trek* episodes. Your essence, whatever shape it takes, possesses a natural tendency to avoid obstacles. You could imagine coming back inside your toaster, and you would end up next to it. Nature will always seek the familiar."

"What do you mean, *whatever shape*?"

"You've seen what I look like when I slip. I sort of explode with dark tendrils shooting out, then implode back until I pop out of sight."

"Dark, but beautiful." She smiled at him when he looked embarrassed. "And my brother...he's more of a swirl that turns into a vapor. So, what am I?"

"I don't know yet. But everyone is different. Are you ready to try?"

"I guess so."

"I'll be right behind you. And do this first slip with your eyes closed. It'll help if you're not distracted by your essence, at least for now."

"But how will I know what I look like?"

"Don't worry, I have no problem watching you." He pulled her up against him and gave her a heated kiss. "And I'll tell you all about it. And even if I didn't, you'll be able to *feel* your pattern." He stepped back to give her room and nodded encouragingly.

Tally closed her eyes. She thought about her home, her couch, the space on the floor behind it. She concentrated on being there, waiting for that loosening feeling. And just when she thought nothing would happen, her mind and body began to drift apart. For a moment, there was a nothingness to her, and she was in a place without sensation. Then, a second later, her feet were once more touching the floor. There was another change in the air pressure around her, and she opened her eyes to see Bane materialize before her.

He was staring at her, his eyes wide with wonder.

"What?" she asked, alarmed.

"You are so beautiful. A shimmering iridescence. And so many colors."

"Like you."

"Only...made up of light." He drew her around the couch so that they could sit. "Okay, now that we're here, tell me who you murdered."

She laughed. "He probably already has plans with Jacqueline, but Chris should hear this, too."

"You call him, and I'll go get takeout from Celestial Thai. Your usual?" he asked, already dialing the restaurant's number.

She nodded, then gave her attention to Chris when he answered. "Hey, we're getting takeout from CTs. You in? Got it...level five spice." Bane's fingers flew over his phone as he ordered Chris's favorite dish, pad krapow with shrimp. He held up his hand and flashed five fingers three times. "Yes, fifteen minutes. See you in a few."

Bane hung up at the same time as she did. "I'll be right back with dinner." But first he gave her a kiss that stole her breath. "Getting it out of my system before your brother arrives."

"Did it work?" she asked, grinning.

"Nope." He stepped away, then slipped to a location near CTs.

Tally looked around, then focused on being in the kitchen. And this time when she slipped, she kept her eyes open. She gasped. Watching herself come together had been like dancing within a prism, only her essence was both the light and the rainbow.

She grabbed plates, napkins, and utensils from the cupboard. Chris was bringing beer, but she made sure she had wine chilling in the fridge for later. Her brother was the first to arrive, and he hefted two six-packs of Singha onto the counter, immediately opening two and handing one to Tally. Bane was only minutes behind and went straight to the task of pulling out the various cartons from the brown paper bag. He'd picked up spring rolls and golden shrimp as appetizers, and slid Tally's pad Thai over to her.

They sat at the kitchen island, dipping the appetizers into the various sauces and drinking beer before digging into their entrées. Bane reached out to wipe something off Tally's chin but made a course-correction mid-reach. Fortunately, Chris didn't notice.

"So, what's up, Talz?" Chris asked.

"Barney stopped by a second time today," she began, then told them of her conversation with the detective.

"You need a lawyer," Chris stated.

"That's what I told Bane," she said and frowned. "I wonder who's behind this?"

"My first thought was the Grossomms and the Fortunas, considering their newfound chumminess. But I don't think they have that much clout. Someone else is pulling the strings," Chris guessed. "Maybe Giselle—sorry, Bane."

"It would have to be someone with more clout than my mother." Bane looked thoughtful. "I'm not saying that she isn't involved. It's just that we're taking hits from so many directions—the feds, the killer, Tally's stalker, the pressure on the mayor, and now this investigation into Tally. I think we need to look for someone with more power."

"Another Fascina Order?" Tally asked, and Bane nodded. "All of this might be coming from Springfield. Chicago has always been an island of progressiveness in Illinois' conservative landscape."

"Maybe," Chris said. "But it would take a concerted effort from all the families in the State Coalition, and the Chicago Order still has the majority of votes when it comes to any policy shifts." He paused, holding his chopsticks in the air, mid-bite.

"What?" Tally prompted.

"Do you think it could be Janine Almarque and the National Order?" He turned to Bane. "At the time, I didn't think about it because she said she used to be friends with our grandmother, but she asked me some personal questions...about Tally and, well, you."

"Like what?" Bane asked.

"The usual small talk. But I sensed an edge to her questions. Like was Tally serious about anyone?" He turned to Tally. "And stuff like whether or not you find your hospital work fulfilling."

"And about Bane?" Tally asked.

"Same, but more pointed. I felt like she was asking me about your credentials. Did they approach you with a job offer or something?"

"As a matter of fact..." Bane started. Tally and Chris stared at him with identical looks of disbelief, and he grinned back at them. "Every other month I'm approached by some Order wanting to poach me from Chicago, so it was only a matter of time before the N.O.F. tried."

"But you won't go, will you?" Tally asked.

"No," he said, slapping her brother on the back. "Everything I care about is here."

"That's a relief," Chris admitted. "But we can now add the N.O.F. to the list of people making trouble for Chicago."

They ate their takeout, no one speaking while they thought of the implications of the C.O.F. without Waever leadership. Tally set down her chopsticks. "If someone is pressuring even one of our nine families, it could be enough to turn the entire board. I don't like it, Chris. I think they're coming after me to hurt you. We need to put an end to this as soon as possible."

"Like yesterday," Bane agreed, studying Chris. "Do you trust Jacqueline?"

Her brother slowly set his beer on the counter. "She hasn't given me a reason not to."

"We need to shore up our allies. This reeks of an impending coup, and it's vital that we know who we can trust. Jacqueline is the granddaughter of Margot Silva, wife of Thierry Baptiste. The Baptistes have always supported the Waevers, but it would be nice if you could nudge a new alliance along."

"Too bad this isn't like old times when parents would simply marry off their children to strengthen the bonds between the families," Chris joked. When Tally and Bane looked at each other and then turned to him, neither laughing, her brother paled. "Hang on a minute. No! Definitely not!"

"It's not such a bad idea when you think about it," Bane said.

"You're suggesting that I marry Jackie? That's going a bit too far, don't you think?" Her brother looked aghast. Tally smirked at him, sensing that he wasn't exactly against the idea.

"Bane's right, Chris. Think about it for a moment. Our generation is the first that hasn't used marriage to strengthen our families. Mom and Dad did it. And for better or worse, so did Bane's parents."

"Worse," Bane interjected.

"But I'm not ready to get hitched," Chris squeaked.

"Maybe just an engagement then," Tally reasoned. "Did you know that Donatelle Grossomm is dating Luke Ryan?" They both looked at her in surprise—clearly this was news.

"Shit. Alright," Chris said. "I'll propose. But it might be a *loooong* engagement." He gave Bane a friendly shove, nearly toppling him from his stool. "And don't think you're off the hook if I do this, Caron. Let's see. Who haven't you dated and scared out of their wits?" Chris pretended to ponder this, then slapped the kitchen island with his hand. "I don't think there's anyone left. Hell, the only woman who isn't afraid of you is Tally." He started laughing, and Bane choked on his beer. Tally hoped her laughter didn't sound too strained.

She cleared her throat. "That leaves us with the Sedges, and I don't see Orson's support wavering. Maybe we should have a party, like Mom and Dad used to have."

"A ball at the estate? It's been years," Chris said. "But it would be the perfect way to announce an engagement. Planning such a big event will give you and Jacqueline a chance to get to know each other better."

Tally didn't relish the thought of working closely with Jacqueline, but Chris seemed to be warming up to the idea of an engagement, so she feigned enthusiasm. Maybe they *would* find some neutral ground. "Sounds great, Chris," she said. "Especially since she's going to be my sister-in-law."

"Awesome," Chris stated emphatically. "I'll work on my proposal—I guess I should pop the question this week. And I'll need to find a jeweler."

Bane was smiling as he watched his friend, but Tally put her hand on her brother's arm. As much as she wanted to keep their family safe, she also didn't want her brother caught in a terrible marriage. "Chris, do you love her?"

He looked back and forth between them. Finally, he nodded. "Yeah, I do, Tally. I have for a while."

"Then I'm really happy for you. For both of you."

Bane clapped him on the back. "As soon as I set up an appointment with Jim Pierson for Tally, I'll text you with the name of my jeweler."

"Jim Pierson?" Tally asked. "Wasn't he the lawyer who got that governor off the hook for embezzlement, fraud, and all those other charges?"

"You think he's the right person to defend Tally?"

"This attack on your sister is politically motivated," Bane reasoned. "And Jim knows every dark and dirty crevice in D.C. Plus, he owes me a favor."

"I hope it's a big one," Chris put forth.

"Big enough." He pulled out his phone to send a text. Seconds later, his phone rang, and he accepted the call. "Jim. Thanks for calling back so quickly... Uh-huh... Yesterday..." Bane laughed. "No, no. Tomorrow's good." He stepped away to finish the call, and Tally and Chris watched, catching only bits of the conversation.

"No, in person... You're probably right... Yes. Excellent. How's the family? Mandy?"

Chris shook his head. "Thank God Bane's on our side."

"Right?" Tally said with a grin. She reached out for Chris's hand. "Hey, you don't have to ask Jacqueline to marry you, Chris. Not if you're not ready. Mom and Dad would never want you to get married simply to protect our family."

"I know, Talz. To be honest, tonight's not the first time I thought about it." She saw the excitement growing in his eyes and knew that he really did love Jacqueline. "I know that she's been standoffish; I think she just doesn't know how to act around you. And it's not because you're not like us; it's because Bane and I treat you like you are...like us, I mean."

"Uh-huh," Tally managed, not quite sure how to take that.

"Listen, I love you, sis. You could be a maliker or the strongest Fascina in existence or simply be the way you are, and it wouldn't make a difference to me. I would still think you are the smartest, most caring person I know. Jacqueline will see that, too."

"Then it'll be good to plan your engagement party with her."

"If she says yes," Bane quipped, returning to the kitchen and punching Chris in the arm.

So that's what it looks like when someone blanches, Tally mused, grinning at her brother. "She'd be a fool not to."

"Right," Chris said, glancing at the clock. "So, what did Pierson say?"

"He'll be here tomorrow by ten. Tally, he doesn't want you going any place where they can snatch you up. With multiple agencies involved, if they manage to take you into custody, Jim said it would be weeks before he'd find you."

"Looks like I'll have to go to the mattresses," she conceded, quoting one of her brother's favorite movies. "I'm off this week, anyway, so I'll just staycation here, I guess."

"Or Bane could slip you out," Chris said. "What? You didn't think that I knew about that? Come on. You two have been doing it for years." He grinned at them. "Don't worry. No one else knows. Well, except for mom."

"Mom knew?" Tally asked, astounded.

"Yeah. I kind of ratted you out. One day, I saw you guys go into the family room. I went in, and you weren't there. I went outside to see if you were on the terrace, and when I came back in, you were plopped back on the couch with a couple of new DVDs."

"What'd your mom say?" Bane asked.

"She told me to mind my own business and to never tell another soul. Funny how I've been reminiscing about Mom and Dad lately."

"You're going all sentimental on us," Tally teased.

"Shit, I gotta go. Jackie'll be back tomorrow. I need to get in gear." He hugged Tally, then shook Bane's hand. "Thanks for being my best friend, Bane. I guess it goes without saying that you'll be my best man, too."

"You haven't asked her yet, and she hasn't agreed, you dolt. But yeah, I'd be honored."

"Let's have dinner on Friday," Chris said. "My place. It can be a double date."

This time, Tally choked, and Bane turned to hide his grin.

"Careful that you don't come down with something," Chris worried, patting her back. "Bane, make her some tea—she needs a little TLC."

"On it," Bane promised.

"Don't forget to call me with all the gory details!" Tally called out as her brother slipped away. "What are you looking at?" she asked Bane as he stalked toward her from the other side of the kitchen.

"You heard your brother. He wants me to give you some tender loving care." He reached for her, and she went to step into his arms when another sudden shift of pressure popped in her ears. She immediately pulled open a cupboard door to separate them.

"Sorry, I didn't catch that," Chris said, a split second after he reappeared.

Tally walked over to him while Bane busied himself in the fridge. "Make sure to call me tomorrow and let me know how everything goes." Her twin nodded and then gave her a hug. "Good luck, Chris," she added. And when he slipped away, she crossed her arms and spun on her heel.

"I know. I know," Bane groaned. "We have to be careful. Feel like cleaning up here and then heading over to my place? I have ice cream."

"Can anyone other than you slip there?" Tally wanted to know.

"Just me. And now, you. Want to try it again?"

"Oh, most definitely! When we slip, uh, can we—"

"Absolutely not!" He started laughing. "Look, Tally. This connection between us, I want to make sure you understand everything that could happen, maybe *is* already happening."

"So, tell me."

"It would be easier at my place. I have these books that you could read."

Now it was Tally's turn to laugh. "Ah, Bane, you should have started with books."

Chapter Seventeen

Tally woke to sunlight streaming through the slits in Bane's bedroom blinds. She rolled over to cuddle up next to him and found an empty bed. Naked and with no idea where her clothes had gone, she walked over to his closet and found where he stowed his perfectly folded tees. She snagged one and a pair of white boxer briefs and headed to the master bath to shower. There was a little tray on the counter with a new toothbrush and her favorite brands of toothpaste, mascara, and eyeliner, as well as other basic toiletries. Thick white cotton towels were stacked high on the bench next to the shower, and inside, he had stocked one cubby with shampoo, conditioner, and soap, also her preferred brands. She shook her head and grinned. How could one man be so impossibly considerate?

Tally had never been one to dawdle in the shower, but this morning, she took her time, luxuriating in the steady pressure of the jets and rainfall showerhead. She turned on the steam and sat on the teak bench, inhaling the moist air, scented with subtle hints of eucalyptus.

When she was done, she buffed herself dry, pulled Bane's tee over her head and slid into his boxers. She whipped a comb through her wet hair, then tied it in a loose knot at her nape, and then went in search of him. On the way out, she noticed a small pile of clothes—her stuff from the day before, plus a pair of jeans, a T-shirt, and a pair of her socks and underwear. Bane must've slipped back to her house. "Too late," she said aloud, making her way down the hall to the kitchen.

He sat at the breakfast bar, hunched over a laptop, his muscular back beckoning her closer. When she wrapped her arms around him and rested her cheek on his shoulder, he startled.

"Ahem," Bane said loudly, coming into the kitchen from the hall that led to his office.

Tally jumped back, releasing the man she was hugging, thanking God that she hadn't started to reach lower. "I'm so sorry," she cried and stared at the man who rose from the stool.

"No need to apologize," he assured her. "Just don't tell my wife."

Tally flushed pink.

"Please excuse me, Ms. Waever. That was my feeble attempt to put you at ease. I'm Jim Pierson, your lawyer. And as your lawyer, I'm bound by attorney-client privilege. I'll never tell a soul."

Tally suddenly remembered what she was wearing and tugged at the tee, groaning when the hem didn't quite cover the boxers she sported. The smoldering look Bane was giving her was *not* helping. But she was made of sterner stuff, so she held out her hand. "Pleased to meet you, Mr. Pierson," she said gamely. Now that he was standing, she saw that he wasn't as tall as Bane and was perhaps fifteen years their senior. But he was a fit man, and attractive, too. "If you'll excuse me, I'll go put on something a little more appropriate."

He nodded to her and turned to address Bane as she moved out of the kitchen, hustling back to the bedroom, where she stuffed her legs into her jeans. She pulled her arms through her sleeves, wriggling into her bra without removing the T-shirt. She was tucking her hem into her waistband as she came back into the kitchen. Bane took one look at her and grinned.

"Breakfast?" he asked.

"Coffee, please," she begged, needing to jolt her system. Bane set a steaming mug before her, and she pulled over the little pitcher of creamer. She turned to her lawyer, and he nudged a plate of bagels, schmear, and lox her way.

"New York's finest," he said.

"Mmm, thank you! I'll pay you a king's ransom to bring some real pizza next time you're back in town."

"Is it possible that I've finally met a rational Chicagoan? One who doesn't wax poetic about deep dish?"

They shared a laugh as Bane scowled. "I'll not have you malign Chicago's greatest gift to humanity in my own home!"

"My sincerest apologies," Pierson stated, winking at Tally. "I had no idea it was such a sensitive subject."

"Just steer away from discussing licorice," she stage-whispered, and then took a bite of her bagel.

"There are some things that a lawyer should never be told, Ms. Waever."

"Tally, please," she said, after swallowing another bite.

"Then you must call me Jim. Now, before we get started, is there anything I should know? Is anyone else aware of your illicit relationship?"

Bane bristled, but Tally just smiled, liking Jim even more for his directness.

"Was it my entrance that tipped you off?"

"That, and your teasing," he confirmed. "No one else knows? Not even your brother?"

"We just recently, uh, *discovered* this thing between us ourselves," Tally admitted. "But how do you know it's considered illicit?"

"My clientele, exclusive as it is, is quite varied in its demographics. I know about malikers and how they come to be. Not to be indelicate, but you *are* being careful...?"

"That's not really—" Bane started.

"There's nothing to worry about," Tally told him. "We both agree that in light of current events, it's best to keep our relationship quiet. We plan to tell my brother, but not yet."

"My advice? The sooner, the better." He turned the screen of his laptop toward them. "Now, let's go over what I've found out about the investigation, Tally. Bane has told me he has some research to share that might be pertinent to your defense."

Tally swallowed. "I can't believe this is really happening."

"I'm afraid it is," Jim said.

Tally slumped in the high-backed stool, the half-eaten bagel and lox sitting heavily in the pit of her stomach.

"They'll put it before a grand jury," he said. "But there's no proof, and even more evidence supporting your altruism. An indictment will never be granted. You have many powerful people who owe their positions and wealth to you and your family. If and when this goes to a grand jury, you won't have to be there; I'll represent you."

"Thank you, Jim," she said. "I have a feeling there's more."

"There is," he said heavily. "One of your charities has been linked to a domestic terrorist group in California."

"What?" she cried. "Which one?"

"What do you know about BioGenX?"

"Never heard of them. Bane?"

"As their name implies, they're a genetics company in San Diego, and a subsidiary of WorldGen. Some of their research has been promising," Bane went on. "Potential applications and advancements in childhood leukemia, for example."

"I'm familiar with WorldGen. The Lumina Foundation awarded them a research grant," Tally said, remembering. "They discovered a new track to combat the disease. It was cutting edge at the time, but that was nearly ten years ago."

"I believe this is where your findings come in, Bane," Jim said.

"WorldGen contracted out to BioGenX to provide the raw materials for their research. What they didn't know was that the cells they were experimenting with were illegally sourced. BioGenX had set up a subsidiary called BGX. Both appear to have been dissolved. I called a friend of mine in the San Diego Order. There were reports of attacks on Fascina, including at least one attempted abduction, loosely linked to people on the BGX payroll. They were sampling the Fascina community down there, then using our genetic codes to treat cancerous cells.

"The National Order stepped in," Bane continued. "Cleaned up the mess, recovered the samples. What originally looked like a miracle cure turned out to have severe, life-threatening side effects."

"What were they thinking?" Tally wondered.

"The National Order," Bane explained, turning to address Jim, "is headquartered in San Francisco. They are not sure if any malikers were bred, but there was equipment in that BGX lab that had nothing to do with cultivating cells."

"Wait a second," Jim interjected. "You said BGX had been dissolved."

"On paper, yes. The lab was closed. A good number of people lost their jobs. But I dug deeper and found a money trail that pointed to another, smaller facility that opened in Oakland about four months prior to the closure in San Diego. That facility, doing business as XGen, continues to have a great influx of money and not from WorldGen. WorldGen does not list them on their SEC subsidiary filing. I'm waiting to hear from San Francisco to see if they have had any trouble in the Bay Area."

"What was the other equipment used for?" Tally asked.

"Bio-chemical research," Bane stated.

Jim whistled. "How much do you want to bet this is tied to the Pro-Registration movement? I would put money on XGen receiving funding through backdoor government channels."

"How does this translate to a domestic terrorism charge against me?" Tally asked.

"That's where it gets tricky," Jim replied. "There's no direct link, but a mutated strand of the common cold virus was released in an up-and-coming research lab in California's Modoc County, up near the Oregon border. Evidence was found that linked the outbreak to XGen. It's tenuous, but when it comes to DHS, they storm in first and ask questions last."

"Then the only thing they have on me is a grant that the Lumina Foundation gave to WorldGen, who then funneled funds to BGX for materials for their research? Is that enough to warrant an investigation, Jim?"

He shook his head. "No. And that's what worries me. Bane and I believe a top-level politician is orchestrating this. Unfortunately, DHS doesn't need tangible proof to accuse someone of domestic terrorism, nor do they need to go through the courts for warrants to hold you. Hell, they don't even have to arrest you, just take you in for questioning, and then you're gone. Even if they drop the charges and the investigation, your reputation is ruined."

Bane took her hand. "I won't let it come to that, Tally."

"There is some good news," Jim continued. "We're already ahead of them. They don't know you're even aware that there are investigations. We have a chance to spin this so that *they* are the ones looking like monsters." He turned to Bane. "See what else you can find out about XGen. And you, Tally..." he said, giving her a sober look. "You need to stay out of sight. No going to the hospital. No driving around Chicago. I think it's safer for you to stay here."

He looked at Bane. "I'm assuming you can move her about if need be?" Bane nodded. "Your own home and here. That's it."

"My brother is getting engaged. I have to plan the engagement party and—"

"The only thing you have to do is stay out of sight," Jim ordered, holding up his hand when she was about to argue. "You may not be Fascina, but you have your parents' genes. I don't want you taken, even for five seconds. Do you understand?"

"I can't just quit my life. I have responsibilities."

Jim tapped his pen on his hand, frowning. He looked at Bane. "You can keep her safe if she has to go out?" Bane nodded. "That might work. But no going anywhere without him, Tally."

"What about my brother?" Tally asked. "This has to be happening because someone wants him distracted so they can take over the C.O.F."

"Chris isn't my client," Jim said. "You are. But if we find out who's pulling the strings on your investigation, then there's sure to be a trail to Chicago. Someone here started the ball rolling. I would like to know who."

"I'll find out," Bane promised.

"In the meantime, you're going to release a statement, Tally—The Lumina Foundation is revoking the WorldGen grant and opening a civil suit against them. We want to be the ones to break the news about BioGenX. By the time we're done spinning this, the entire country will be clamoring to put you on a pedestal." He started packing up his laptop. "I've got to catch a flight back to New York, but I'll have my PR department send you your script this afternoon."

After Jim left, Bane pulled her into his arms and held her.

"I don't want to be put on a pedestal," she murmured. "It's a long way down if I fall."

He lifted her chin with his finger and gazed at her. "I'll be there to catch you. I promise."

He kissed her then, gently, but Tally was filled with a desperate need to be consumed by him, and she courted his tongue with her lips and teeth, ramping up the passion between them, feeling the heat grow and reveling in its fire.

Bane drew back. "We need to talk."

"Now?"

"Yes. It's vitally important."

She sighed. "Tell me."

"Well, it's just that I really liked what you had on this morning." He plucked the sleeve of her tee...his tee. "I can't help but wonder what you've got on under your jeans."

His comment wasn't at all where she thought he was going, and she grinned mischievously. "You'll just have to find out for yourself, won't you?" she teased, then gasped as he lifted her and hefted her over his shoulder, carrying her down the hall to his bedroom.

Chapter Eighteen

He sat through the Chicago Order Meeting, his gaze drawn again and again to the empty chair. Where was she? Chris had mentioned some excuse about a head cold. He wasn't buying it.

In all the years that he had known her, Natalia Waever had never been sick. There were the occasional headaches, but even those may have been convenient pretexts to escape having to spend time with her betters. At least he wouldn't have to put up with watching her and Caron pass little notes back and forth. They didn't think anyone saw, but he did, now that he knew what to look for. He saw everything. He'd tried once to discover what they'd written, but the pads had been removed. That was likely Bane's doing. The man excelled at covering his tracks.

Caron had hovered over her one time too many, and they'd shared lingering looks that were just a little too long when they caught one another's eye. Before, Natalia had always looked demurely away within the appropriate amount of time to make it acceptable behavior, but not so anymore. He'd been looking forward to this council meeting so that he could study them, but her unexpected absence had thwarted his plan.

He stared at the agenda, wondering if there would be time for him to haunt Natalia Waever's neighborhood again, perhaps stake out Nonna Lucia's in case she ventured out from her hidey-hole. They had just finished the last item and, impatient to leave, he waited for someone to make the motion to end the meeting. Finally, Chris Waever stood, drawing all eyes to the head table. Chris nodded to Bane, who then picked up his phone and texted someone.

"Before we adjourn, I need one more moment of your time," Chris began. The doors to the room opened, and a phalanx of servers entered, carrying champagne flutes and bottles of Cristal. After everyone had been served, Chris raised his glass to the room.

"I realize this is not on the agenda," he began, "but I have a special announcement." He turned and held out his hand to Jacqueline Silva. She rose to stand next to him. "I've asked this lovely and intelligent woman to marry me."

"And I said yes," the Silva bitch added.

"A toast," Chris declared, the happiness in his voice sounding authentic, "to my beautiful bride-to-be."

Everyone in the room took the obligatory sip of the expensive bubbly, including him. This was the final Waever betrayal. He managed to not choke on the champagne. A few Order members threw back the contents of their glasses at the unexpected news, no doubt those with eligible daughters. Chris Waever and Jacqueline Silva basked in the glow of the well-wishers, completely oblivious to the undercurrents that only he recognized. Sometimes it amazed him that the Waevers had maintained control over the Chicago Order for as long as they had.

And then he felt it, another's scrutiny bearing down on him. He couldn't tell because he was wearing those damn sunglasses again, but he swore that Bane Caron had been watching him. Curious. Maybe Chris Waever wasn't so stupid after all for allying himself with Caron.

As the council members began to disperse, he sidled up to where one of the Baptistes was inquiring after Natalia. Jacqueline was fast to cover her impatience at the mention of Chris's sister, but not fast enough. She was jealous, and his mind immediately began to calculate how he could use the information to his benefit. Maybe that was why Natalia wasn't present. Not wanting to draw attention to himself, he offered a completely believable, heartfelt congratulations before moving on. At the door, he stopped, feeling that penetrating gaze on his back. He turned, but Caron was nowhere to be seen.

• • •

Tally put the final touches on the hors d'oeuvres—artisan cheeses and breads, pâte on her favorite dried fig toasts and topped with bits of raw honeycomb, exotic fruit, crudités, and a few hot appetizers, including the mini-beef Wellingtons that Bane and her brother loved. She'd made sure to stock top-shelf liquor for cocktails. Red and white wines, microbrews, and Cristal finished off the bar. Bane had shopped for everything on her list, right down to the pretty cocktail napkins and gorgonzola-stuffed olives. She stepped down the hall to the powder room and then turned on the LED votive candles that she had placed on the counter and window ledge. Retracing her steps, she continued to light votives, dimming the lamps throughout Bane's home until the space was diffused with a warm, romantic light.

When Tally had offered to host an intimate engagement party in her home, Chris had suggested that perhaps Bane's place would be better. No sense inviting people into her house and then having to greet each one outside so that they could find her porch. Besides, Tally always enjoyed playing hostess at Bane's place. She checked the clock; he should be getting back any moment. As if on cue, the elevator doors in the private foyer dinged. Bane and Chris, with Jacqueline on his arm, entered. Tally smiled at them, hugging her brother and his fiancée.

"Congratulations! I'm so happy for you both." And when she said it, she found that she meant it. Jacqueline was studying her, perhaps listening for some underpinning that would tell her that Tally wasn't completely pleased. "Jacqueline, come in. Can I get you a glass of champagne? Something stronger?"

"I'll have some bubbly now and save the stronger stuff for when my family arrives," she said, laughing nervously, then looking stricken, no doubt remembering the loss of Tally's parents.

But Tally laughed, then commiserated with her about family, throwing a knowing look in the direction of her brother, and Jacqueline seemed to relax.

"Have you and Chris set a date yet?" Tally asked, handing her future sister-in-law a flute of champagne.

"Not yet. But I think a spring wedding would be nice. Sometime after the last freeze, just to be safe. You never know when it comes to Chicago weather." Jacqueline took a nervous sip. "Uh, Natalia, I wanted to say... I mean... I know we haven't always seen eye to eye, and I just want to tell you that I appreciate your support of our engagement."

"Support? Oh, Jaqueline, I'm truly happy for you and my brother."

"Really?"

"Absolutely."

"Then, do you think you could just call me Jackie?"

"If you call me Tally, it's a deal." She topped off their champagne, and they toasted. "By the way, has Chris mentioned—"

"The engagement party?" Jackie finished. "I love the idea of having it at Rosegate, but I don't know that I have the time to arrange everything so quickly. He wants to have it on the twelfth. That's less than a month from now."

Tally shook her head and frowned at her brother, where he was pouring himself a drink. "Chris asked me to plan the party. Didn't he tell you?"

"He didn't mention that, no."

"That's my brother for you." She and Jackie smiled at each other. "If you would rather I didn't handle the arrangements, I understand."

"Actually, I'm grateful. And I'll help, of course. Plus, now I can tell my mom that she doesn't need to worry."

"I'm sure we could use her help—oh, I see," Tally said when Jackie pulled a face. "She'll try to take over."

"Not just my mom—my tías, too. But if I tell them that you're the official hostess, like Bane is tonight..."

"Got it. And don't worry, I'll give them enough to do so that they feel included." The elevator doors chimed and multiple female voices, *oohing* and *ahhing*, sounded in the foyer. Tally nodded toward the alcohol, and Jackie laughed.

Jackie touched her arm, stopping Tally as she went to greet the arriving guests. "I think I might like having you as a sister."

"Me, too." Then she was off, helping Bane with his host duties.

Jackie's family was a close-knit group, but they went out of their way to make Tally feel comfortable and welcome. It wasn't always that way. Most families didn't know how to deal with her and her non-Fascina status. By the end of the evening, she had made at least five promises to send various recipes to the aunts, including her miniature beef Wellies.

Only the immediate members of the Silva and Baptiste families had been invited to the get-together—all twenty-three of them. Filling up the church would be interesting, Tally mused. She and Chris had very few relations. But they could count on their adopted-uncle Orson and the rest of the Sedge clan. She could add Marc and Ryan, and Michelle-plus-one to the list. Her mind switched gears, imagining the engagement party. Perhaps Nonna Lucia's could cater.

"What are you thinking about?" Bane asked, coming up behind her and setting a friendly-but-not-in-a-boyfriend-way hand on her shoulder. Regardless, the heat of his touch shot straight to her toes.

"You," she answered with a friendly-non-girlfriend sort of smile on her lips. He turned his back to everyone and gave her a look that seared her insides.

"The party is wrapping up," Chris said, coming over and slapping Bane on his shoulder. "Thanks, man. This was great. And Tally, Jackie is so relieved that you're planning the engagement party."

Tally smiled but rolled her eyes at her brother. "You forgot to tell her."

"My bad," he replied, and put his arm around Jackie's waist when she joined them.

"Everyone's gathering their coats to leave," she said. "Should I wait for you, or get a ride with my mom?"

"Me, please," Chris answered with an enthusiasm Tally hadn't seen before.

"I was just headed to the foyer with Bane to say goodbye to everyone," Tally said, and Bane held out his arm to her. Chris mimicked the old-fashioned gesture with Jackie. "Your family is great, especially your Aunt Ixi."

"She's not only my favorite aunt, she's my godmother as well. I bet she asked you to call her Tía Ixi." Tally laughed and nodded. "It's a sign that she likes you. And since you're almost family, I must warn you: *mi familia es su familia* now, and that's as good as blood related. Tía Ixi's approval of you holds a lot of weight. She can sense things about people, like if they have a good heart."

"That's so nice," Tally replied. "I think I might like having a big extended family."

Jackie grinned. "Tell me that again in a couple of years, after you see all the drama that comes with it."

• • •

Chris and Jackie hung back to help straighten up, but Tally could see that they had other things on their minds. "Bane and I can handle the rest. Why don't you two take off."

"You're staying here tonight, right?" Chris asked. "Bane filled me in on what Pierson said." At Jackie's confused look, he looked to Tally for permission, and she nodded. "Tally has a stalker. Until we figure out who, she'll be spending a lot of time here. And staying away from the hospital."

"That's terrible," Jackie said. "Chris told me how much you enjoy coordinating the volunteer program and running Lumina Foundation. I don't know what I would do if I wasn't able to do the work I love."

"I'll miss it, true," Tally replied. "But I have so much vacation time accrued that I could probably take an entire year off. Besides, now I can work full-time on your engagement party." It was the cover story they'd come up with, half-true. Of the federal investigations, they were keeping quiet. "Chris," Tally started, "I think you should tell Jackie everything. A different perspective could prove valuable."

"I'm glad you said that, Talz," her brother admitted. "I wasn't sure if you wanted me telling anyone."

"Our family is her family," she said, and winked at Jackie.

"And all of the drama that comes with it," Jackie added. "Just make sure to let me know what I can do to help?"

"You might want to run for the hills after talking to Chris."

The affianced couple stepped into the elevator. "Oh, Jackie! Before I forget... I was thinking about the engagement party and wondered if you liked Italian food?"

"Nonna Lucia's?" Jackie asked on a sigh.

Tally grinned. "I'll call you tomorrow."

The elevator doors closed, and Tally and Bane were alone.

"They were all really quite nice."

"I like Jackie's family," Bane said at the same time, taking the empty plates she was clearing up from her hands and setting them back down on the end table.

"Let's leave the rest for tomorrow," he said, drawing her toward the couch and making her sit. He walked over to the bar. "What can I get you?"

"What's left?" she asked. Except for that first glass of champagne, she'd barely had anything to eat or drink.

"Bourbon," he said, holding up a bottle of Eagle Rare.

"That'll do nicely."

"You seem to be getting along with Jackie."

"I never disliked her, you know," Tally insisted, taking the rocks glass, then tucking herself next to him when he sat. "I always got the feeling that she was looking down on me."

"I think it may have been more along the lines of Jackie not knowing how to handle your close relationship with your brother. Even before I knew you had gifts, I was in awe of your twin-sense. You two are kind of scary sometimes, the way you think alike and finish one another's sentences." He took a sip of bourbon. "It's not as bad as it used to be when you were younger. Going to different colleges probably helped with that."

"Was it hard for you, hanging around us?"

He laughed. "For me? No way! I can't even put into words how lucky I was that your parents took me in, that you and Chris were—are—such great friends to me. I don't really talk about it much, but I wouldn't have survived my father had I stayed there. That last time...he almost killed me. I didn't realize it then, but he not only broke my arm, he ruptured my spleen. I was bleeding inside, and your mom healed me."

"I'm sorry that happened to you, Bane." She sensed something shift inside him, almost as if he had cringed, but it was gone a second later. She had noticed it before and was about to ask him what was wrong, but he downed his bourbon, set aside the glass, then pressed her into the deep cushions of his couch.

"Have I told you how beautiful you are tonight?" he rumbled. "Dim lights," he instructed his smart home system. "Music on—playlist fourteen."

"Playlist fourteen?"

"Something I put together especially for you. For an occasion like this."

She smiled up at him. "You're such a romantic."

"You've no idea," he murmured, then dipped his head to ply her with kisses warmed with good bourbon. As things grew heated, he whispered in her ear, "Don't you dare get rid of our clothes." He nibbled on her earlobe, then traced his tongue down her neck. "I've been thinking about peeling this tiny scrap of a dress off you all night." He lifted her arm, then pulled the tab of the hidden zipper that ran down one side. Gently nudging the spaghetti straps off her shoulders, he glided his hand lower to fondle her breast in lazy circles. Propped up on one elbow, he watched as her nipple hardened under his teasing fingers.

Tally verily hummed, and he wasted no more time and set his mouth to her breast while sliding the silken fabric down her body. She hadn't worn a bra, an advantage to having a slight figure, but she'd picked out an especially sexy pair of panties for the night. She arched her back and lifted her hips as Bane tugged the dress down her body and past her knees. Upon noting the tiny triangle of lace that covered her, he swallowed, then slid off the couch to kneel on the floor.

"Scoot up a little," he told her. "I want you to watch me go down on you." If his words had incited her, his kissing and licking ignited a conflagration. His fingers traced and teased circles on her thighs, over them and in between, then he hooked one fingertip into the crotch of her panties, and stroked, lightly, and nowhere near where she needed him most.

Tally moaned and drew up her knee, settling her calf on the back of his couch to better offer herself to him. Propped up on thick cushions, she had a perfect view of what he was doing. Watching him lick her, using broad strokes of his tongue, sucking at her through the lace, was a sensual experience bar none. And when, looking up at her, he sucked on her clitoris, pulling it and the lace between his lips, she came right then and there.

He leaned back, waiting and watching as she caught her breath. Her climax had been brutally short-lived, but Bane wasted no time. "Keep watching me," he said, and she gasped when with one hand he tore off her thong, stuffing the bit of lace in the pocket of his dress pants. He pressed her thighs wide, then went down on her in earnest.

Tally clenched the cushions, bracing herself for the shock of his tongue on her still-sensitive bud, but he avoided her there, feasting elsewhere as the intense pleasure built up once again. And when he finally pulled at her clitoris, drawing her into his mouth and sucking, she cried out. "Oh, Bane!" she gasped when his tongue plunged inside her, and she threw her arm over her face. He lifted away, and she nearly growled, thinking he was going to stop. But he was staring at her writhing hips, his own chest heaving, his arousal straining against his dress pants. Then, he pulled her so that her ass rested at the very edge of his couch.

He smiled. "I'm not finished yet, so why aren't you watching?"

Her eyes shot down to that space between her legs as Bane ran his fingers along her seam. "You're so wet for me, Tally." Then he slid his fingers home, thrusting his hand forward again and again. Her hips bucked as they strove to meet his stabbing fingers, pressing ineffectually against his knuckles as they bumped against her, but always, always missing that essential spot. He kept going, and when she thought she would fracture, he sensed it, and eased off, pulling her away from the edge she craved.

"Please," she begged, not recognizing her own voice.

He played her for a few more minutes, then, with his thumb and forefinger, he plucked at her clitoris, pinching it gently and stroking his tiny, little strokes.

She screamed his name. "Quit teasing me!"

So close to fracturing, she watched as he unbuttoned his trousers, ripping them down, along with his boxers, in one fluid movement. With a powerful thrust, he impaled her with his cock, pumping into her hard and deep. Another thrust and another, and Tally shattered. He continued, brutally and beautifully, grabbing her hips and slamming against her. He withdrew, then plunged again, and Tally's second orgasm transmuted into a third, devastating her.

Bane tensed, then stabbed impossibly deeper as he, too, climaxed, his semen spilling into her as they rode out the waves of pleasure together.

He fell back on his heels, pulling her sated body down to the floor with him. He grabbed a few of the plush pillows from the couch, placed them on the thick rug, and then guided her down so that they lay sprawled on the floor. She set her hand on his chest, watching it rise and fall as his breathing slowly returned to normal.

"I love you, Tally," he said, his deep voice vibrating through her core.

"I love you too, Bane," she answered back. When she felt his pain spike, like a bee sting, she propped herself up to get a good look at him. "What was that?"

"What was what?"

"Don't. I can sense that you are hurting. It happened before, and it just happened again, when I said I love you." And this time, she saw the flicker in his eyes, like he was trying to remain expressionless, but inside he was wincing. "There! I am *not* imagining it. Tell me what's wrong, or—"

"Fine," he said, rolling over to his back and resting his arm on his forehead. "I hate it when you say it."

"That I love you?" she asked, not bothering to hide her confusion.

"No, not that. When you say that you love *Bane*."

Tally sat up and leaned back against the couch, pulling a pillow into her lap. No way was she going to have this conversation naked and without some coverage. He stared at the pillow, then up at her face, and raised an eyebrow.

"Shut up," she scolded, hitting him with the cushion, then covering herself again. "I never knew. I mean, I guess I never thought about it. You always referred to yourself that way, from the very beginning. My mom always called you Braeden, but... Oh hell, Bane, why didn't you say something sooner? Damn it! I just said it again. Geez, Chris and I... We would've made sure no one called you that. All these years, and we never guessed."

He groaned and propped himself up. "Tally, I don't care that other people call me Bane. I welcome it," he explained. "If it makes them wary around me to be reminded of who my father was, good. I've cultivated my ruthless image for years." He took a deep breath. "And I don't care when you and Chris call me Bane. It's just not what I want to hear when you profess your love."

She smiled softly at him then. "You're the sweetest man in the entire world."

"See, now you know why I didn't tell you. You think I'm a doofus."

Tally shook her head. She took his hand and placed it over her heart, then did the same to him. "Look at me," she ordered when he started to turn away. "I love you, Braeden." His gaze shot to hers with a laser focus. "I love *you*, Braeden." She allowed herself to slip, just a little, and he went with her. Their auras sparked and sizzled around them, and she pushed all the love she felt for him outward, letting him absorb the intensity of her emotions. In return, his love for her soaked into her body through her very pores, her breath, everywhere, and as she pulled back, she was astounded by the depth of his feelings for her.

She tossed the pillow away and straddled him, played with him until he was hard again, and then lowered herself down his length. She began to ride him then. "Braeden," she moaned. "Braeden." Caught up in the emotions swirling around them, she allowed herself to slip again, and his eyes widened. He followed her there, to that place where their essences misted, surrounding her—and she, him—until they were something different. "Braeden," she said again, but not really, as there were no words in that suspended place they occupied. She heard him say her name, felt him say it, because she had said it as well. They were one. Combined. There was only love. And passion. And an all-consuming pleasure. She came, then felt herself fracture. Felt him fracture. And in the fracturing, they fell apart and back into their own selves.

Sweat glistened off their bodies as they held onto one another.

"Tally," he whispered with an edge of worry in his tone. "You... We shouldn't have... I should have warned you. I just couldn't stop. I'm—"

"You better not say that you're sorry," she warned.

A harsh laugh erupted from him. "No. I'm not sorry for the bonding...I could never be sorry for that. I should have told you the consequences, though, before we did what we did. I should've said something so that you could have made an informed choice."

"Choice? I had no choice, Braeden. You could tell me that loving you could cost me my life, and I would not choose otherwise." He winced at that. "Wait. What did you mean, *bonding*?"

"Uh..." he stammered, scooting over and pulling on his boxers. "I started telling you before...about slipping while making love...about—"

"Braeden, are you telling me that we just...? I mean, my parents did...my mom told me once that she and my father were bound together." He stood suddenly, then walked into his bedroom. She grabbed the throw from his couch, wrapped it around herself, and followed him. He came out of his closet and tossed one of his T-shirts to her. He grabbed another and pulled it on, looking hotter than she ever could in his clothes, then followed up with joggers. He gave a pair to her as well, then took her by the hands and led her to the bed. Before he sat, he stopped, reconsidered, then led her back into the living room. One look at the couch and the pillows strewn about the floor had him drawing her to the two overstuffed chairs near the fireplace. As she sat, the logs in the hearth caught fire with a big *whoomph*.

She would have to try that little trick later, she thought as he went to refresh their bourbons.

"When Mallory...when your mom died," he started, "it was more than the poison that killed her. It's always been true that she also died from a broken heart." He swallowed. "Toward the end, she gave me more of her books. One was an old text about 'binding love,' and it stated that there are three levels, or phases, that lovers must achieve before they can be bound." He took a generous swallow of bourbon and stared at the flames.

"And..." Tally prompted, swallowing some of her own drink, feeling the mellow liquid fire slide down her throat, giving her insides false warmth. "What are these three phases?"

"When we slipped together, we completed the pragmalia stage, or deep, longstanding love. It comes from the Greek for—"

"Thing," Tally inserted. "I remember my lessons on ancient languages. So, we have two more phases to go. What are they?" Bane was shaking his head. "Uh-oh."

"Yeah," he said with a bleak expression. "Philosi, the love of family and friendship. We've had that phase down forever."

"And?" she asked, almost afraid, yet also strangely excited by the notion that she and Bane were bound together.

"Erosa."

"Oh," she said, feeling her face grow hot. "No problem there." The grin he gave her almost had her scrambling into his lap. "So. Pragmalia. We're now a...a thing."

"Thing, yes. But as in something that is done. A deed, or fact. A *fait accompli*. The final tying together of two souls—*agapia*."

"Before you say anything else," she began, "I want you to know something." He stared at her as if he were a criminal and she was the judge about to pass sentence. She took his rocks glass and set it on the side table. Then, holding his hands in hers, she gazed up into his worried face. "You said you weren't sorry for the bonding. I'm not either. I have loved you as Bane my whole life, and to be tied to Braeden, to you, all of you, until the end of my days... I could not imagine a more perfect life."

He pulled her into his lap, and she went willingly, and he held her tight, tucked under his chin and pressed against his chest. And Tally, for the first time in her life, even though everything around her might be destroyed the next day, felt complete. Because she knew, now that they were bound together, he would do everything in his power to keep her safe. Just as she would do the same for him.

"There's more I have to tell you," he whispered into her hair. "Certain consequences. Like not being able to be away from each other for too long. And—"

Across the room, his phone buzzed where he'd set it on the coffee table. Hers went off where she'd left it in the kitchen. Text messages. His phone rang next. "That's Chris's ringtone, isn't it?" And he nodded, as she climbed off his lap to retrieve it for him.

He answered, "What's up, Chris? No. Still awake. Let me put you on speaker."

"Hi, Talz."

"Hey, Chris. Shouldn't you be celebrating with Jackie?"

"Hang on," her brother said. "You're on speakerphone, too."

"Hi, Tally... Bane. Thanks again for tonight," Jackie's voice came through. "For everything."

"Our pleasure," Bane said, and Tally lifted her eyebrows at him, smiling at the pronoun. He shrugged, then mouthed, *oops*. "What's going on? Because I know you didn't call this late to thank me and Tally again?" he asked, getting straight to business.

"It's probably nothing," Jackie answered, "but Chris was telling me about Tally's stalker, and the rose, and it reminded me about something my tía said tonight about Bane's father."

She stopped talking, and Tally could practically hear Jackie's brain trying to come up with an easy way to say something horrible.

"There's nothing you could say that I probably don't already know," Bane encouraged. "And even if I don't, I won't be surprised."

"Go ahead," Chris whispered.

"Tía was saying how much she liked your place, that it didn't match her impression of you. And then, how you were so nice and welcoming to our family and that I would have to make sure you knew that she considers you to be Chris's hermano." There was a pause, then she added in a rush, "And then she made the evil eye and said how nice it was that you weren't like Sebastian's other children."

"Bane?" Chris asked.

"She's ninety-four years old," Jackie excused. "It could mean nothing. She likes to tell stories, but she never gossips, not meanly, anyway."

"No, it's fine," Bane said too quickly, and Tally felt the tension rolling off him. "Really."

"I'm sorry; Chris and I just thought you should know."

"No apologies are necessary. My father was a bastard. Like I said before, I'm never surprised by anything that he did."

"Okay. Well, goodnight," Jackie said, and Chris echoed her.

"Night," Tally said.

"And Jackie," Bane added, "thank you for telling me. You guys get some rest."

He ended the call and tossed his phone away like it was diseased. He leaned his head back and closed his eyes. She sat across from him, soaking in the heat from the fire and sipping her bourbon, waiting patiently.

"I knew that he had mistresses," he said finally, his eyes opening and looking at her. "My mother hinted as much. You confirmed it with what you told me about how he coveted your mom. It's no stretch of the imagination that he got more than that one woman in California pregnant. It would explain the missing money."

"Money?" Tally asked.

"After he was sent to The Null, and my mother censured, I took over the management of the estate. I gave most of it to charity. My mother retained the house and some real estate investments. As bad as she was, she'd suffered enough of his abuse, and I didn't want to leave her destitute."

Tally nodded, refilling his glass for him.

"Good ol' dad was involved in a lot of shady dealings. It took more than two years to sort through everything. My contacts in D.C. helped me to protect Giselle, and by cooperating with the IRS, I was able to separate most of the estate from the not-so-legal enterprises. Besides, they were ecstatic about the arrests they were able to make.

"But there was one money trail I could never track to its endpoint. It would've been chump change to Sebastian, a few million here and there, and though I disclosed it, the IRS decided it wasn't worth pursuing."

"You think he set up a fund for another child?"

"Maybe. And maybe more than one."

"What are you going to do?" Tally asked.

"I need to visit Giselle again." He stared at the fire.

"I hate to agree, but you're right," Tally said. "What can I do to help?"

"Stay here," he said, then quickly outlined his plan.

Tally didn't like it. It was much too risky. But she needed to disappear for a bit, and staying at his place would do the trick. And at least this way, if he needed her to rescue him, she would be nearby.

Chapter Nineteen

"You have somewhere to be, Sis?" Chris asked, when she looked at the clock for the hundredth time. She scowled at him as he raised his hands in surrender. "Look, I get it. You're going stir-crazy cooped up in here, especially with Bane gone."

"Why would you say that?" she demanded, then immediately felt bad that she'd snapped. What was wrong with her? Chris had been hanging out with her for the last hour, patiently listening as she gave him the lowdown on what she'd heard from her lawyer. He took another bite of one of the breakfast burritos he'd brought over. What Tally had been able to swallow now sat in her gut like a pile of rocks.

"I only meant that with you not being able to leave, and having no one to talk to..." Chris began, "well, it must be really hard. You at least had Bane here for company before he left, and TV binges can only take you so far."

"Bane's gonna kill me when he sees how many movies I've charged to his account. I just want to get back to my normal routine." She sighed. She also wanted her brother to eat his egg burrito and leave, but she didn't say that part out loud.

"So, what else did Pierson have to say?" Chris asked, drawing them back to the reason for his visit.

"He thought it strange that some of his contacts didn't even realize the investigations were running. Not good, considering they're the ones supposedly in charge. The alarm's been pulled, and the backpedaling has already begun."

"Does he know who started the ball rolling?"

"Not yet, but he suspects the Bureau. DHS and Justice have called off their dogs from what they now consider a bona fide witch hunt. Check out these letters that were sent to Pierson." She brought up the images on her phone to show her brother.

He whistled, scrolling through them. "Damn... Stinton is the head of Homeland Security, and he's written a letter in support of you."

"I know!" she exclaimed. "Jim says to expect one from the White House. Right now, it looks like only the FBI is continuing with their investigation. Someone has a lot of clout if they can control the director."

"Or has major dirt on them," Chris finished, then took the last gulp of his coffee. "Has Bane contacted you yet? It's been nearly a week."

Tally shook her head.

"He'll want to be updated on Pierson's progress. Maybe I should check in with his mother."

"That would be a really bad idea, Chris," Tally cautioned. "If Giselle Caron is in any way involved in this attack on our family, putting yourself within her grasp is not wise. Bane would tell you the same."

"I know, but that last time he visited her was bad. I'll give it a few more days, then check with Orson to see if he would be willing to come with me." Her brother kissed her forehead, then reached down and lifted the leg of her yoga pants. "Just looking for your ankle bracelet," he joked, making light of her self-imposed house arrest.

She slapped his hand away, laughing. "Thank God Bane has a workout room here," she said, shooing him toward the elevator. "I'm kicking you out now so I can finish my yoga."

"Alright already, Talz. I'll see you in a few days."

Tally had completely forgotten that they were having lunch at the end of the week to discuss the engagement party. Jackie would be coming with her mom and bringing the food.

"Hey, if you're worried about Bane, don't be," Chris assured her. "He knows all of Giselle's tricks. But if he's not back, we'll postpone."

"Just promise me you won't go there by yourself."

"Hand to heart, sis." And with that, he departed.

Tally put her brother's mug in the dishwasher. She rinsed out hers and did the same, then wrapped up the leftovers, stowing them in the fridge. Then, with studious patience, she wiped down the counters. She walked down the hall to the home gym, resisting the urge to check on Bane in his bedroom. Rather, that small percentage of Bane supine in his bed. This time, when he'd gone to his mother's home, he'd shaded, leaving about ten percent of his essence in his penthouse.

The first two days alone in his place, Tally had spent nearly every moment checking on the ephemeral ghost of his form. She'd lined up pillows in the center of his bed, fearful of rolling into him and disturbing his aura. On the third morning, she'd woken to find his hand resting on hers. She'd turned over her palm, her fingers moving through his essence, feeling him and knowing he was well, but strained.

On the fourth morning, the same. She'd allowed herself to slip, just a little, mingling with him and willing him her strength and love. She did so again yesterday, but felt his increasingly high level of stress. Then last night, everything changed.

Even his resting form appeared somehow less. She slipped for about five minutes, her hand in his, but barely felt his response. And what she did feel was pain, but that he wanted her to have patience. She could hear his voice in her mind as clearly as if he stood next to her. "Not yet." And when she tried to give of herself to him, to bolster his strength, he repelled it.

She'd been interrupted this morning by her brother's arrival and so hadn't been able to check in on him. "To hell with yoga," she said angrily, turning herself around and marching into his bedroom to sit vigil. She dragged over the lounge chair from the corner, pulling it right up to the bed, and stared at the inconsistent shimmer of his form. After what felt like an eternity, she got up and paced, stopping now and then to hover over him and examine his expression in repose.

"Not yet?" she yelled. "Could you be any more vague? Damn it, Bane!"

She plopped into the chair and studied his bedroom. The space was a perfect combination of comfort and good taste, like a modern luxury hotel room. Except the artwork on the walls was original, and he had framed photographs set out on his bureau and nightstands. Most of the photos were of her family.

Tally picked up the picture frame that he kept next to his bed. It captured one of those rare moments when he was laughing—Bane, Chris, and her mom and dad in the middle of a snowball fight. Everyone was busy trying to dodge her brother's missiles, everyone but Bane. He stood there, frozen in time as he packed snow with bare hands, staring straight at the camera and grinning. Tally remembered the moment, for she was behind the camera, and was so happy to see him enjoying himself. She'd snapped the picture seconds before getting hit in the head by her brother's snowball. It hadn't hurt—her winter coat had a thick hood—but her parents and Bane ganged up on Chris, pummeling him for taking a cheap shot. Later, her mom had made hot cocoa with marshmallows that she'd sorted from a box of Lucky Charms cereal, while her dad had secretly laced the mugs with a thimble-full of Irish whiskey. Their teenaged selves had thought they were so cool. She held the frame to her chest, closing her eyes and reminiscing about that day.

Tally woke with a start. The bright, sunny, east-facing room of late-morning was gone, replaced with the dim light of dusk. There was a crick in her neck from napping upright. Her eyes went straight to Bane. Something was different. She flicked on the bedside lamp, perching herself on the very edge of the mattress to try to figure out what she had seen, but Bane looked just as he had before she'd fallen asleep.

"I need some caffeine. Be right back." She leaned over to pick up the photo that had slid to the floor and glanced over at Bane as she placed the frame on the nightstand. The difference was immediately visible—from the side, Bane's split appeared far less than it had been. She ran to the other side of the bed and crawled up next to him, stretching out along his length. She set her hand over his and tried to draw some part of his consciousness to her mind. Nothing. His aura was an empty husk.

"Bane!" she cried. "Oh God, please let him still be there." She set her hand over his heart, allowed herself to slip just a little. "Thank you," she said, sensing the struggling beat of his heart. What was left of him was so weak, she doubted he would be able to return. She couldn't imagine the strength it took to maintain the split.

"How do I get you back? Think, Tally. Bane is somehow connected. And if there's a connection..." She stared at him, wondering if what she wanted to attempt was even possible. "No way to know until I try." She stared at his profile. "Hang on, sweetie, I'm coming to get you."

She closed her eyes, her hand still over the space where his heart would be, and allowed herself to slip, a little at first, then more, until they occupied the same space. Her mind's eye looked for him, his essence, and she sensed it—a trail no thicker than an atom. She followed it, half-afraid that she might somehow break the chain. And then she was with him, almost all of him. She pulled herself together, coming back in a dark cell, one that smelled of rot and decay. Bane lay unconscious on the floor, beaten within an inch of his life.

Tally dropped down next to him, willing him to heal, sending her strength into his body. "What did she do to you?" she whispered to the cold dark, placing her hands on him and searching for his injuries. He was hooked up to an IV, and she carefully removed the port they'd placed in his arm. She searched deeper, triaging the damage. His right lung was bruised. His kidney ruptured and bleeding. He'd been starved. Broken ribs. Fractured ankle and smashed fingers. A concussion. His left eye was damaged, and his shoulder dislocated. There was something else, two small puncture wounds, their insignificance somehow making them important.

Tally kept healing him, knowing she would have to pay an awful price later. To give him the strength to return with her, she kept at it, pausing now and then to feel for his pulse. He was knitting back together faster than she thought possible, but she was starting to feel the effects, and was forced to stop and rest more and more often.

She heard voices, then lights flickered on outside of the cell. "If you can hear me, Bane, you have to slip with me now." The voices were getting closer. Tally took him up in her arms, and let herself disperse, surrounding his prone body with her essence. The sound of keys jingled outside the cell's door, then Bane caught hold of her. *Hang on to me. We're going home.* She sought out the trail, followed it, then came back to herself, with a damaged but blessedly more substantial Bane at her side. According to his alarm clock, she'd been gone for hours.

She rested, afraid at first to move. Finally catching her breath, she rolled to face him, holding him in her arms and giving him what strength she had left before yielding to exhaustion.

When she woke, less than an hour had passed. She expected to feel ill, pain, something. But she felt fine. Bane was no longer unconscious, but asleep. And his breath was steady and strong. His clothes were a mess of blood and vomit and who knew what else. She willed the offending garments away as she walked to the kitchen for a large bowl, and then grabbed clean sheets from the linen closet.

In the bathroom, she filled the bowl with warm, soapy water, and loaded up her arms with thick terry washcloths and towels to bathe and dry him. She took her time, assessing and cataloguing his already healing injuries as she washed away the proof of what had been done. She rolled him to his side and stared at two dirty scraps of gauze that had been crudely taped to his skin, one at the small of his back, the other on his hip. She removed the bandages and threw them across the room as if they were diseased. She must have healed the wounds, for his skin was unmarked. After scrubbing him clean, she ran her hand over the tattoo, some Nordic design, that graced his shoulders and back, now free of the dirt and grime of his captivity. When he woke, she wanted no reminders of that cell.

Changing the sheets had been as easy as removing his clothes, and she gently covered him with the top sheet and a light, downy blanket. Then she turned off the lamp and headed to the shower to wash. When she returned, it was dark outside, but Chicago's ever-present light-pollution flooded the room, lending it a soft orange glow. She climbed onto his high bed and snuggled up against him. Questions warred in her mind. How could his mother hurt him so badly? Was she trying to kill him? And why, after Tally had healed him, had she not fallen ill?

Next to her, Bane shifted, turning and pulling her up against him before falling back into a deep sleep. Tally stared out his window at the flickering lights of the city and the vast darkness of the lake that waited beyond. She dozed on and off, finally rousing herself when Bane rolled over again. His clock read 6:22 a.m., and she quietly moved off his bed, padding barefoot into his kitchen. Her stomach growled, reminding her that she hadn't eaten since the previous morning. She prepped fixings for omelets, brewed coffee, and sliced some melon and strawberries. The light in the bedroom flicked on just as she finished cooking, and she set everything on a tray and carried it down the hall.

Bane had propped himself up on his pillows, and he scooched over to make room for the tray of food. She set it on the bed, then sat in the chair she'd pulled over. "Are you okay?" Her words were clipped.

"I am, thanks to you."

"Can you handle solid food?" she asked tersely.

He nodded.

"Coffee?"

"Please."

She poured him a cup, dressed it the way he liked, with a drop of cream and a sprinkle of raw sugar. "Shoulder?"

"Sore, but it was dislocated." He reached for his fork and winced, and she batted—albeit, gently—his hand away.

"I got it," she growled. She was furious with him, and she stopped to wrangle with the emotion.

He took his fork from her clenched fist and then calmly cut off a bite-sized piece of omelet. He closed his eyes, savoring the taste. Just how many days had he gone without food?

The anger inside her ballooned. Bane was watching her closely now. Tally stabbed her fork into a strawberry and ate it. She took a rather large bite of her own omelet, then swallowed a good amount of coffee. It was really too hot for more than a sip, but she didn't care. It scorched a path over her tongue and down her throat, making her eyes water. She ignored the burn and shoveled another bite of fruit into her mouth. If she kept eating and drinking, she wouldn't be able to talk. And if she couldn't talk, she couldn't yell, and they wouldn't end up fighting.

She found it impossible to look at him, and so she stared at her increasingly empty plate. Bane reached out and touched her arm, and she bolted back in the chair, sloshing her mug. She stood, grabbed her dish from the tray, and stalked out of his room and to the kitchen. It took everything in her to not smash the plate in the sink. Bane hadn't followed her. He couldn't. He physically couldn't.

She grabbed the omelet pan and started scouring away the few bits of cooked-on egg. "You almost died, you asshole," she said under her breath. "Died and left me here alone. Without you." She rinsed off her plate and slammed open the dishwasher door a little too hard. The dirty glasses, plates, and utensils rattled and clinked. She shoved her plate in the bottom rack, cracking it against a bowl, and it broke in her hand.

"Shit!" she yelped, dropping the shards and holding her hand while rushing to the sink, peppering the dishwasher, floor, and counter with drops of blood. She elbowed the cold water on and held her lacerated palm under the tap, watching the dark-scarlet blood swirl with the water as the liquids circled the drain. With each pulse of her heart, there was less and less red, until finally, the water ran clear. Her hand shook as she examined the cut, watching as her skin mended itself until all that remained was a thin, red scar. And that mark, she guessed, would soon be gone.

She turned around and sank to the floor, beginning to understand a little more about the bonding. If he died, so would she, because like her mother, she wouldn't want to live without him. And that, more than anything, scared the crap out of her. But this anger, this was something new. She'd heard of the expression "seeing red," and not until she deliberately slammed her plate into the dishwasher did she understand what that meant. Even now, the tendrils of her ire were woven through her system, anger she'd been tamping down over the last week.

She sat there by herself, trying to calm her breath. She needed answers, but didn't want Bane to see her in this state. Of course, he probably wouldn't give her a choice and was most likely getting dressed to come find her. That thought, more than any other, had her shoving herself up from the floor. She poured herself a glass of water, gulped it down, carefully set it on the counter, and then turned and stalked toward the bedroom.

"Lie back down," she ordered, managing to keep her voice level. An amazing feat, since all she wanted to do was shout at him when he moved to sit on the edge of the bed, trying to steady himself and not keel over.

"Are you crazy? I said to lie back down! You'll only hurt yourself more, and I'm not sure I want to heal you again." Okay, that was mean. "Don't you dare smirk at me, Bane," she yelled, when his eyebrow lifted and the corner of his mouth twitched.

But he did as commanded, and she pulled the sheet and blankets back up over him. She paced, then finally settled herself at the foot of the bed.

"There's blood on your shirt."

"Maybe it's yours! You ever consider that?" She was being a bitch, but it felt right.

"It's fresh," he said calmly. "I heard something crash."

"I'll replace the damn plate, don't worry." She stared at the ceiling, willing her emotions contained.

"It's not the dishes I care about, Tally."

She was about to make a scathing remark and ended up taking a deep breath instead. "I was careless and cut my palm."

"That's a lot of blood on your shirt. Can I see?" He held out his hand to her.

"No, Bane, you can't see. You can't see because it's gone. Healed. Want to explain that to me? How I bled all over your kitchen, and there's not even a scar? Well?"

He leaned back, closed his eyes, and she could tell he was losing his patience. She didn't care. Finally, he looked at her again, sat up a little, and tried to adjust his pillows. Tally crawled up next to him and did it for him. She sat back, her legs crisscrossed, and this time, he took her hand and traced his finger in the exact location of where she'd cut herself. "How did you know it was there?" she asked, a touch more softly.

"I just did."

"What's going on, Bane? What's happening to me, to us?"

"Let's start with why you're so angry. Can you pinpoint the reason?"

Tally shook her head, then her eyes opened wide. "You were dying, Bane! You jerk! You can't just die!"

"Tally, please come here." He held out his arms, and she reluctantly settled next to him. And in doing so, feeling his steady heartbeat, the warmth of his arms, some of the anger dissipated.

"It's like you're soaking it up," she whispered, feeling the physical ebbing of her ire.

"I didn't know all of this would happen so fast, or I would have explained before I left."

"Just spit it out already," she ordered, apparently not completely over being pissed.

"There are certain benefits to bonding," he started. "More than just the deepest level of love for one another." He took her hand and then kissed her palm. "We're stronger together. My gifts enhance yours and vice versa.

Your hand mended on that combined strength. It's also why I'm not dead right now. Why, I think, that by this evening, I'll be completely better."

"You're not a healer, though," she said.

"No, I can't heal other people like you can. But I've never been sick, and my body has always been quick to recover. When we were younger, and my dad hit me, I think being around you must have helped, though neither of us knew it at the time."

Tally traced lazy circles on his chest, her anger moving farther and farther into the recesses of her mind. "Are you really going to be okay?" she asked, needing him to say it.

"I am. I promise." He kissed the top of her head. "You're very sexy when you're mad."

"I wasn't mad. I was furious."

"About that..."

She looked up at him expectantly.

"Do you ever remember your mom and dad fighting?"

"Sure, it happened once in a while. My mom would get so angry with him, usually after one of his trips...oh, shit. They only fought when one of them was away from the other for an extended period of time. But my mom and dad never threw dishes just to break them. They weren't destructive. I *wanted* to smash things."

He nodded. "The longer we're together, the more that separation anger will ease because we'll become better able to control it. But how you felt this morning wasn't just because I was gone. It was that I was in danger. We're linked, Tally. And if one of us is vulnerable or being threatened, the other will sense it. Anger is a very powerful defense mechanism. Couples who have bonded go into a kind of survival mode, pure and simple. I didn't expect to be in danger—and before you ask, it wasn't Giselle; I'll explain in a second."

"That rage...it made me feel powerful, Bane."

"How did you find me?" he asked.

"I...you...you were disappearing before my eyes. I slipped into you. I saw how you were tethered to the rest of yourself, and I followed the trail. I brought us back the same way."

He was thoughtful for a moment. "I went to Giselle's. We talked. Perhaps honestly, for the first time. She said that she's not behind the threats against you, nor is she colluding to unseat your family."

"Do you believe her?"

"I want to. I don't think she's directly involved, but someone is using her. She didn't realize it until I told her about the investigation. She got this strange look in her eyes. It was when I left her house that I was taken. I didn't see it coming, Tally."

"How?" she asked gently.

"Tranq gun," he said wearily. "I came to in that cell. They kept me so drugged up that I couldn't slip back. And then they beat me while I was down. Fucking cowards. A cycle of drugs—putting me down; waking me up—and asking me questions, hitting me, and breaking things."

"They had you hooked up to an IV; I should have taken the drip bag, so you could analyze whatever it was that knocked you out."

"You got me back. That's all that matters." He took her hand and kissed her knuckles. "Hey, what're those?" He pointed to the bandages that she'd flung to the floor.

"They were on your back and hip... Right above your lumbar vertebrae and pelvic bone." She frowned.

"Tally? What is it? You know what it means, don't you?"

"They're the same spots needed for a spinal tap and a bone marrow test. Bane, the IV, the bandages, the port in your arm. They probably took more than your blood." She could feel the anger boiling inside him. "We'll find them," she promised.

"But I don't know where I was being held."

"And I just followed your trail. I didn't think to look around." She closed her eyes and concentrated on remembering the cell. "There were numbers on the door. Painted on with a stencil. It—the door—was oval-shaped, and you would have had to step over a threshold to pass through it, like a hatch."

"A ship," he guessed. "All that time, I thought the drugs were making me unsteady. Could've been waves."

"The walls were metal and riveted. Light-gray paint."

"Sounds military. There were no uniforms that I could remember, just standard camo-fatigues. So maybe a decommissioned ship." He sat up and held her tight. "My cell wasn't the only one. I heard others. Screaming. Some of them didn't sound completely human. It's why I didn't want to come back right away. I thought I could figure out where I'd been taken."

"We need to tell Chris." She stood and paced. "Crap."

"What?"

"He'll want to know how you escaped."

"I'll lie for now. But I think we need to let him in on your secret. And we need to figure out how to tell him about us. Eventually, he's going to sense that there's more than just friendship."

"We'll tell him, just not yet. He'll feel betrayed. Maybe not by me, but definitely by our mom. I have to think about this."

"Call him. Invite him and Jackie over for dinner."

Tally moaned.

"What?"

"If I don't get out of here, even for an hour, I think I might go crazy."

"I don't want to risk you being taken, Tally. You think you were mad? I would go nuclear meltdown on that shit. And I don't think that I have that ability to locate you, like you did for me."

"I'm not completely helpless anymore. And considering how fast I heal now that we're bonded, tranqs probably won't work on me. Alcohol sure didn't while you were gone."

He lifted an eyebrow.

"I was alone and bored. And alone. And not reimbursing you. Be quiet," she said, chucking a pillow at him, which he caught, then sent back right to her head. She batted it away, only to find that he had a handful of her shirt. He gave a great tug, and she fell next to him on the bed. He rolled on top of her, wincing only a little, but grinning.

"How bored?" he asked.

"Very. At least six-bottles-of-your-best-wine-bored." She felt him, the hard ridge of his cock pressing against her. "Hmm."

"Yes?"

"It's good to know they didn't—"

"Don't say it," he begged.

"—break everything." And she started laughing. But then, he was kissing her lips, her neck, her collarbone...she lost herself to the feel of his tongue and lips and teeth as they cruised over her skin. And this time when they came together, it was Bane who initiated the slip.

Chapter Twenty

Tally was in his kitchen, pulling glasses out of the cupboard in preparation for the late-night arrival of Chris and Jackie. She'd found the decks of cards and had placed them on the table along with several bowls of snacks, one of them filled with Red Vines and strings of black licorice.

Bane plucked out a few of the long black laces from the bowl and stalked toward her. "I calculate that we have about thirty minutes."

"What're you planning to do with those?" she asked, edging past him and then bolting to the bedroom. He flicked his wrist, and the black licorice whipped out and snapped at her legs. She laughed wildly, and he chased her to where she dove onto the bed, then proceeded to chuck pillows at him until she was out of ammunition.

He pulled the long strands of candy taut, holding them out before her. "I think we need to test their tensile strength," he suggested. She shrieked, laughing, and he jumped onto the bed to join her. He pinned her wrists together, winding the licorice around and around them, and then proceeded to kiss her senseless. He pulled away and grinned at her.

"Hey, these are really strong."

"But no match for your teeth," he reminded, and they nibbled on the sugary bindings until their lips met. "Later, we can get more creative."

"I'll never look at licorice the same," she said with a giggle.

His phone chose that moment to buzz. "Hold that thought," he said as he opened an app, entered a code, then got out of bed, pulling Tally with him. "Chris and Jackie are early—they just pulled into the garage."

She kissed him again, long and slow this time, and then sashayed away, dropping bits of licorice in her wake. He followed her from his bedroom but headed to the kitchen in time to see the elevator doors open and Chris and Jackie tumble out, grinning—Jackie's lipstick was smeared, and there were traces of it on Chris's mouth.

"Help yourself," Bane called out to them, indicating the wet bar where wine, beer, and liquor were ready and waiting.

Tally came from the hallway that led to the guest room and smiled.

"Ooh! Licorice," Jackie crooned, picking up a Red Vine. "My favorite." Tally and Chris burst out laughing, and Bane scowled. "What's wrong, Bane? Don't you like licorice?"

"Now you've done it," Chris said. And over a game of President, Bane explained the differences between licorice and the strawberry-flavored rope she was nibbling on. He kept an eye on Tally seated across from him, especially when she began braiding the black laces and then timing how long it took her to pull hard enough to break them.

It was nearly two in the morning when they decided to call it quits, and while Bane and Chris straightened up, Jackie asked Tally to show her to the bathroom. They were gone for almost ten minutes.

"You and Jackie seem to be connecting," he commented when he and Tally were finally alone. "Dare I ask what you talked about?"

"She wants us to be careful," Tally answered. "Her love antennae are tuned in to romance."

"She said that?" he asked. "Love antennae?"

Tally wiggled her index fingers near her forehead.

"You look like a deranged alien," Bane said, and chuckled. "What did you say to her?"

"I didn't tell her anything, and she didn't ask. But she said that it was only natural, seeing as how we're thrown together. She won't say anything to Chris but advised telling him if things start turning serious. She doesn't want him hurt—personally or politically."

"She's fine with us having a relationship? Huh, I didn't expect that."

"Me, either. But then I remembered that one of her tías married outside of the Fascina community."

"I'd forgotten. When should we talk to your brother? Because things are definitely serious."

"Let's wait until after the engagement party."

Bane nodded, then scooped her up and carried her to his bedroom.

"Aren't you tired?" she asked, throwing her arms around his neck.

"I have exactly one week before I have to tell my best friend that I'm eternally bound to his twin sister, and I have no idea how he'll handle the news. I'd better make love to you now, and as much as I can, in case he decides to castrate me."

• • •

"It's time to call the FBI's bluff," Pierson agreed on the videocall. "Tally can't be indefinitely penned up at your place, like she's in some WITSEC safe house."

"Good. I'll let you know how it goes," Bane said. "And thanks for everything, Jim." He hit END CALL on his screen, then straightened his desk. He locked his office door, then took the elevator to the garage. Traffic was light, and he stepped into his penthouse a half hour later.

Tally was at the kitchen counter and smiled as he walked over. "I just hung up with Jim," she said, closing her laptop. "He said that it was finally time for me to come out of hiding."

"I spoke to him as well. The investigations have been dropped. Even the feds have gone silent. But I want to be sure. I don't want anyone grabbing you up. And I have a plan." He held out his palm to reveal a capsule. "It's a new tracker. From my lab."

"I'm supposed to swallow that?" she asked, eyeing the device dubiously.

• • •

Reiss didn't like the way the colonel was drumming his fingers on his desk, and said hastily, "The order to end the investigation came from the top. We can't go near—"

"You feds mucked it up. Time to let the professionals take over." He pressed a button on his desk phone.

"Yes, Colonel?" asked one of his adjuncts, having just stepped into the room.

"Assemble a team. Three men. Eighteen hundred hours. We finish her tonight."

Reiss was too late to stop Lima from arguing.

"You don't have jurisdiction," his partner complained.

"I don't need it, you idiot." He stood, and more of his men crowded into the small room. "Now, you and Reiss can quietly leave, or we can show you out. We're taking over."

Lima glared at the man, and Reiss worried that he didn't see the immediate threat. Now was not the time for a confrontation—they were outmanned and outgunned. "We're leaving. She's all yours," Reiss conceded, dragging Lima from the cramped quarters before he could blurt out anything else.

They made it down the hall and into the elevator. When the doors closed, Reiss drew his weapon and chambered a round.

Lima stared at him, then did the same. "Those guys give me the creeps," he finally admitted. "I guess we should be glad we're out of this mess. The less we know…"

The elevator doors opened to an eerily vacant lobby. "You're a fool if you think it's that easy. That man just called a hit on a prominent Chicagoan. We're not only witnesses, we're loose ends." Instead of walking out the main entrance, Reiss backtracked to the staircase, knowing it would lead to an emergency exit in the alley behind. Lima had his back and was looking toward the elevators through the gap he left in the door.

"Four men. Street clothes, but packing," he whispered. "They went out the front."

"Let's go," Reiss urged, tapping his phone screen. "Watch for them when we come out on the other side of the block. I just ordered a pick-up—I would bet my pension that our current ride is compromised."

• • •

Without even looking up at the window above Nonna Lucia's, Tally could feel Bane's gaze on her as she stepped out of her car where she'd parked across the street from the restaurant. Bane owned the building and had converted the upstairs into an apartment, which was conveniently empty. Chris was inside, she knew, sitting at the bar and keeping an eye on the patrons. Jackie waited near the main entrance and waved to Tally. Her phone was in her hands as if she was texting someone. But Tally knew that she was only feigning the thumb-typing. She had her phone's camera focused directly on Tally and was videotaping the moment for posterity. If someone in the government thought it was acceptable to snatch a civilian off the streets in the United States, in daylight, in front of witnesses, they would soon find themselves on trial on social media.

Tally locked her door, then walked around the front end of her Audi. She waited for a car to pass, then stepped into the street. Nothing seemed out of the ordinary, and then she remembered that she'd left her purse on the passenger seat. She held up a finger to Jackie to let her know it would be another second.

She unlocked the passenger side's door, ducked into the car and was reaching for her purse when the hair on the back of her neck stood on end. She slid her hand into her pocket and grabbed the tracker…something bad was about to go down. She swallowed it just as a dark sedan came around the corner. The engine roared, and Tally breathed a sigh of relief when they didn't slow down. It was just some jerk driving too fast in a residential neighborhood.

At the last second, he swerved right into her. She dove into her car, tucking her legs in as the sedan barreled into the rear fender. After taking the impact from the car's bucket seat, she bounced into the front console, the stick of her pretty sports car jabbing hard into her ribs. It was a surreal moment as she watched the headlight and grill of the sedan scrape by, demolishing the passenger side of her Audi as it plowed forward, catching the open door and ripping it from its hinges. It flew up, then came crashing down through the windshield. Tally turned her face toward the seat and covered her head with her arms as safety glass rained down upon her.

The screeching was terrific as the sedan skinned her car down to its chassis, careening forward and rending the metal, fiberglass, and safety glass into chunks of deadly flying debris. Tally could hear Jackie screaming in the distance. Or maybe it was her. And then it was over, and all she could hear was the sound of the sedan revving its engine as it sped off.

She was missing a shoe.

At least she could still feel her feet, but her neck could no longer support the weight of her aching head, and she dropped her face to the leather seat.

Someone wrenched open the driver's side door, and she thought she heard Bane's voice. She wanted to touch the hand that was pushing her hair out of her face but couldn't move her arm. Something warm and wet was pooling under her cheek.

"Don't move, Tally," Bane ordered, sounding helpless.

"My shoe…"

"Shh, I'll buy you new shoes."

Her brother and Jackie were talking behind him, and then, as dusk descended on the maple tree-lined street, the air was filled with strobing light in red and white and blue. A blanket was laid over her head and body, and Tally wanted to scream that she was still alive. The night was filled with the sound of rending metal, and pellets of glass rained down upon her as the firefighters peeled back what remained of her windshield. The blanket was lifted away, and she smiled up at an incredibly hot fireman—she'd always had a thing for firemen, and chefs, and baseball players. The men above her grinned, and…oh shit, did she just say that out loud?

She tried to look at Bane for confirmation, but when she started turning her head, the cutest of the firefighters told her not to move.

"Miss…?"

"Her name is Natalia, Natalia Waever," Bane said.

"Miss Waever, we need you to hold still. We're going to put a cervical collar around your neck for support, then we'll get this door off you and get you out of here."

"Okay..." She closed her eyes as more emergency vehicles arrived. The smell of exhaust was making her sick. The wrenching noise seemed muted, as were the voices, everything sounding as if she were underwater. It was the searing pain in her arm as they lifted the door away that made her pass out.

"Hey, there," a very attractive EMT said to her, staring at her face, flashing a penlight in her eyes. "Back with us. That's good. We'll get you to the hospital in no time at all."

She tried to nod, but her head was immobilized. Ah, collared. Now she understood.

"There are a couple of people here who want to see you before we go."

He climbed out of the ambulance, and a moment later, his face was replaced with her brother's. "They said there's no room for us in the rig, so we'll have to meet you at the hospital. You're going to be alright, Talz. I promise."

Bane climbed up next, but she was so tired. She thought he took her hand, and she might've squeezed back, but she couldn't tell. Everything felt numb.

"Really need to get going, sir," the EMT said. "We gave her something for the pain, so she'll be out soon."

Bane said something to her, but she couldn't make out his words. Then, he ducked out of the ambulance. The good-looking EMT climbed in, and Tally drifted away to the sound of wailing sirens.

She came to with a jolt, and it took her a moment to recall where she was. The handsome EMT was slumped on the floor, his chin resting on his chest. Then, the wailing of sirens started up again, and the ambulance lurched forward.

A face loomed over her, only it wasn't either of the EMTs. This man was brutal looking. There was a long scrape down the side of his face, and Tally had a flashback of the accident—he was the driver who hit her car. "Good to see you again," he said coldly, then he touched his ear and spoke. "We got her...no, alive...not badly injured...Roger...a viable subject. Copy that." He sneered down at her. "It's your lucky day—we've got new orders now."

He laughed, a sinister-sounding bark, then traced his finger along her IV, starting where it was taped in place on the back of her hand, following the plastic tubing all the way to where the new bag hung. Then he grinned down at her, producing a syringe and shooting its contents into the IV port. "Nighty night, princess."

Just before everything went dark, Tally heard, for the second time that night, the metal-wrenching sound of a car crash.

• • •

Bane paced. "I need to see her..." He was about to slip into Tally's childhood bedroom, when Jackie set a gentle hand on his arm.

"Chris will be down in a minute," she promised. "Your tracker worked, and you and Chris got to her in time."

Bane nearly howled his frustration. She'd been in that rig for nearly thirty minutes. If he hadn't been constantly checking the tracking beacon on his app, he might've missed that the ambulance was headed south on the Dan Ryan, miles past the exit to the hospital.

"Tally's strong," Jackie repeated to him for what seemed like the hundredth time. "You saw her. She was awake and talking."

"But they got away, Jackie. Someone slipped them away. You know what that means?"

"A Fascina is involved. Did you at least get a look at him?"

Bane shook his head. "And the driver died in the crash. Damn it, we still don't have any leads."

Suddenly, outside the thick oak door of the office, they heard shouting. Chris's staff had been with his family for generations and were fiercely protective of the Waever twins. Bane strode to the door and yanked it open. In the vast foyer, a man stood arguing with Chris, then unbelievably, another person arrived. And another. And again, until Bane and Chris faced six unexpected guests. Guests who had managed to bypass the security wards—something no one had ever done before.

He readied himself for an attack but then recognized one of the intruders. She stepped forward, holding out her hand to Chris. He shook it warily. She turned her gray eyes on Bane, but her warm smile did nothing to ease the cold calculation in her eyes.

"Braeden Caron," she said, holding out her hand, "I've heard quite a bit about you. We've not met. I'm—"

"Janine Almarque," he finished, taking her hand and stooping slightly to kiss her knuckles, all according to proper protocol.

She showed neither annoyance nor surprise. "Our meeting is long overdue."

When and how had he come to be within her radar?

At his loss for words, her expression turned wry. "Yes. Most would agree it's better to not catch my attention."

"Now, Janine, let him alone," a man who Bane did not recognize said, stepping forward. "You know it's not polite to read people without their permission." She laughed at that, and the man shook his head at her as if they were sharing some private joke, then held out his hand first to Chris and then to Bane. "Frederick Stiles, National Order Co-Chair. You're wondering how we were able to breach your security. I'm afraid that was my doing. I would be happy to—"

Janine cleared her throat. "I'm assuming the dining room is still this way," she stated, walking past the group. "Unless you've remodeled since I was here last."

Chris caught up with her. "Just modern plumbing and electricity," he said sarcastically, and Bane readied himself for the backlash his insult would cause.

Janine Almarque grinned. "I see that you inherited your sense of humor from your father's side of the family."

"You've been to Rosegate before?" Chris asked.

"Yes. Long before you and your sister were born. There were plans to induct your mother into the National Order, but when your father was murdered, Mallory filled his seat in Chicago. Shame, that." She glanced at Bane to gauge his reaction, but he met her gaze, unfazed. He'd long since divested himself of his father's legacy.

"We've been keeping tabs on your chapter for a number of years," Frederick noted as they entered the dining room.

Chris pulled out a chair for Janine, then took a seat next to Jackie while Frederick found a place for himself.

The four others positioned themselves behind the two—bodyguards, Bane guessed. He suddenly realized that they were waiting for him to sit. He pulled out the chair at the other end of the table, opposite Chris. "We've urgent matters to which to attend, so if you don't mind telling us what this unexpected visit is—"

"Yes, yes, we know all about your urgent matters," Janine said, her voice tight and angry. "Give us five minutes to tell you some backstory, and then we can discuss how we might be able to assist each other."

Chris nodded; but Bane made a point of checking the time.

"I mentioned how we've been keeping a closer eye on Chicago—actually, all the major chapters. Two years ago, a number of smaller orders in what we call the unprotected regions were upended. New leadership was put in place, leadership that does not cooperate with the National Order. Next to fall were several mid-sized groups—Atlantic City, Austin, even Sacramento. Chicago has always had strong leadership, thanks to your family, Chris."

"I don't mean to be rude, but tick tock," Bane said, standing again.

"We know about the investigations into Natalia Waever's activities. Well done, putting a stop to that," Frederick said, then turned to regard Chris. "The current Chicago leadership must remain in control. You've done an excellent job thwarting those who would like to bring you down." He nodded to Jackie. "The union of your families is a brilliant move."

"I happen to love Jacqueline," Chris interjected.

"Even better," Janine remarked with an amused smile.

"This attempted murder—you weren't the only person filming the accident, Ms. Silva—and the subsequent abduction of your sister cannot go unchallenged," Frederick went on. "Yes, we are aware of that. To take a member of a leading family, even if that member has no Fascina abilities, is an attack that merits an immediate response. A closing of ranks, so to speak."

Shit, Bane thought, clearing his mind of everything Tally could do, but it was too late. A flicker of a frown passed through Janine's eyes, but she remained silent. He did the only thing he could and projected two clear thoughts: *I love her. No one else knows.* She pursed her lips. He hoped it was enough.

"Your sister was lucky," Frederick went on. "Others have disappeared."

"You were aware that this was happening and didn't warn the orders?" Chris accused, rising from his chair. "They tried to run down my sister in broad daylight. And when they *missed*, they took her, injuring two paramedics in the process. These people are working beyond any government control. And just why do you think they wanted Tally?"

"Chris," Bane warned.

"What?" he shouted at his friend, then looked at the people gathered in his dining room. "It doesn't matter that she has no powers. Tally's DNA is the same as mine. What about the others? If they're even still alive," he demanded of Janine. "What kind of monsters do you think they'll breed with—"

"What are you saying?" Janine asked, aghast, also rising to her feet and bringing Fredrick to his so that everyone was standing.

"Come on," Bane said incredulously. "Surely you know? Or do you only record the Fascina who've been taken and leave the non-Fascina to fend for themselves?"

Chris barked a grizzly laugh. "They have no idea, Bane. Look at them. They're so caught up in their politics and courtesies that they're blind to what is happening at the local level."

"We're not your enemy," Frederick said. "You don't know what we've been doing. What we've accomplished."

"That's right. We don't," Chris spat. "The national meetings that we've attended tell us nothing. Just a reason for you all to have the serfs stop by to pay homage. How many have fallen while you stood by and did nothing?"

Bane felt the pressure in the room expand, and he whipped his head toward Janine. Chris gripped the back of his chair and managed to not be forced back by the rage and grief she let loose. Bane gritted his teeth, let her emotions flow around and through him, understanding coming into his mind. Then Chris gathered his own rage and hurled it back.

Bane was about to ask who was taken, when Jackie broke the stalemate. "Your granddaughter," she said to Janine. The two words broke the woman's hold over everyone, and she seemed to shrink a little. Frederick held out her chair for her to sit again. Chris checked his temper.

"What did you mean by monsters?" Janine asked softly.

Chris grabbed a rocks glass and poured three fingers of his best scotch, and then slid the glass across the table to Janine. He picked up more glasses and set them in the center of the table, poured himself a drink, then set down the decanter with a decisive rap. "Self-serve," Chris stated, and Frederick reached for a glass.

They waited while Janine took a drink. "If you know about the investigations into Tally," Chris started, "then you know about the experiments that BGX was performing. But it's worse than that. Someone is breeding malikers and using them to wreak havoc on our communities and destabilize our relationship with the Norms."

"You're sure? We've heard about the murders here," Janine said. "They seemed too organized for a maliker."

"They are," Bane agreed. "Chicago has more than one problem right now. But recently, a maliker was taken into custody. On the surface, it appears that he brutally murdered a Fascina woman, but he was whisked away by the feds. And Chicago isn't alone. Malikers are popping up in other cities where registration isn't required. It doesn't take a genius to figure out how or why."

"But you think it goes deeper," Janine said.

"I do," Bane continued. "Whoever is behind this is trying to weaponize the poor creatures, trying to make them controllable. A covert military group, sanctioned or not, is breeding killers. And they're also trying to find out our secrets. And if they know what we can do…"

"They can control our communities…control us," Frederick finished. "Janine?"

"We don't know where to start looking," she said.

"I have an idea about that," Bane provided.

Chapter Twenty-one

As Tally had never actually made it to the hospital—thankfully, Bane had slipped her straight to Rosegate—she'd been able to hide the extent of her injuries, and more importantly, the rapidity of her healing. Bane and Chris had forced the ambulance off the road, and whatever drug they had given her had quickly worn off once the IV was removed.

The driver had been killed on impact. But the brutal man inside the rig had managed to elude even Bane. Tally had been out cold, so had not seen who had slipped the man away.

Haneluk had gotten word to them that agents Reiss and Beans were on an undetermined leave of absence, and that the FBI had apologized to Mayor Greene for their interference in the governance of Chicago. No apology was issued to Tally, but Jim Pierson had said to not expect one.

Marc had prescribed rest, and Chris had insisted she stay with him for at least a week. It had been five days, and Tally was bored. She sported a sling, feigning a sore arm, and several bandages that hid how quickly her cuts had healed.

Chris wasn't home yet, and Tally left her bedroom suite. As she made her way down to the main level, she ran her hand over the polished wood of the curved banister. She'd always loved Rosegate, but she missed her own house. It was time to go home.

As she walked into the living room where she could pour herself a glass of wine, she texted Bane that she would be packed and ready to be picked up by seven. He texted back that he was already on his way. Chris had invited him over for pizza.

"Join me by the fire, Natalia."

Tally whipped around to find an older woman ensconced in one of the deep leather chairs near the hearth.

"We've yet to meet, something I've long wanted to remedy. I'm Janine Almarque." She made a beckoning motion with her hand toward the opposite chair. "Don't worry. I won't bite."

Despite the woman's promise, Tally warily approached the head of the National Order, putting up the falsehoods in her mind like she always did to prevent another from reading the truth. Janine had a fire going in the hearth, and suddenly chilled, Tally added more logs until it was blazing. "My apologies, Ms. Almarque. Had I known you were here, I would've come down sooner."

"The staff isn't cognizant of my arrival." She smiled. "One of the perks of being me is that I can come and go as I please."

"That must be nice," Tally started, carefully keeping her thoughts bland. "Can I get you anything?"

Janine lifted her hand, revealing a rocks glass filled with bourbon. "I have this, and the fire is lovely. My bones are no longer used to these Midwest cold snaps. Too many years in California."

Tally finally sat down in the deep armchair across from Janine. And waited.

"Your grandmother and I were great friends. Did you know that?"

Tally shook her head.

"We were very close and both very much in love with your grandfather." Janine's almost-avian features softened at the memory, and Tally could picture her as a beautiful young woman in love. "My parents had bigger plans for me than sitting on the Chicago Order. In those early days of the National Assembly, alliances were everything. I married for duty. Your grandmother married for love. It was for the best, for I suspected that he loved your grandmother more." Janine was silent for a moment, deep in some remembrance, a wistful smile gracing her thin lips.

"I was your mother's godmother. Bet you didn't know that either."

Tally hadn't and shook her head.

"I have some photos that I'll send to you. Pictures that your grandmother sent to me after your mother was born. All those years, and we kept in touch despite the distance."

"I would like that, seeing pictures of my mom when she was young. I always thought that she took after her father more than her mother."

"She did. And you lost Mallory much too soon. You and your brother resemble her side of the family, but you, Tally, you remind me of your grandmother. She was a powerful woman. Spirited. Your mother inherited much from her. Mother to daughter, mother to daughter, again and again. It's like that for the strongest of the Fascina women. But you already knew that."

"Except with twins..." Tally trailed off.

Janine pinned her with her eagle eye. "Mallory Waever protected you well, my dear."

"I don't know what you mean."

"Hmm. Your brother's engagement with Jacqueline Silva reminds me of the making of old alliances. He's done well. Chicago will remain strong, protected, and free for our kind. But you, your match will be a brilliant one, won't it?" Janine began to laugh, though to Tally's ears, it sounded like cackling crows.

"We've been keeping an eye on Braeden Caron," she added. "He's meant for more, not just for the Chicago Order. Maybe even more than our national level, thanks to the contacts that he's cultivated around the globe. There are many Fascina leaders who already respect him. He'll need a strong partner."

"Why are you telling me this?"

"It may not yet be obvious to the others, but I sense that you love him. And Braeden... He let it slip that he returns the sentiment."

"And you want me to walk away so he can make some alliance?"

"You misunderstand, Natalia." She gave Tally another shrewd look. "Tell me, how are you feeling? You look remarkably healthy for a woman who was hit by a car and nearly killed."

"I wasn't hit. My car was. Cuts and bruises, only."

Janine held up her hand. "Perfectly plausible. But a lie." She leaned forward in her chair and stared into Tally's eyes. "Want to know what gave you away?"

Tally remained silent.

"Your thoughts. They're too perfect. Too ordered. Everything precise and practiced. A brilliant façade. I've never seen better. Your grandmother would've been proud." She paused, as if waiting for Tally to agree.

When Tally refused to comment, Janine smiled as if she had won. "No denial, I see. But no confirmation either. Fine. I won't out you. And that's because I loved your grandmother like she was my own sister. And when your mother was murdered—" There were tears in her eyes.

"Yes," Tally said, wresting control of the conversation, "when my mother was murdered. But she had time to prepare. Time to safeguard her children. And knowing my grandmother as well as you did, then you know she had a sense for prediction, a gift my mother inherited. Mallory Waever would have figured out a way to warn her children, to counsel them."

"By that same reasoning, one would imagine that for your mother to so successfully *protect* you, she would perhaps have sought out the sage advice of a beloved godmother." Janine lifted an eyebrow. "Don't be too angry with her for the predicament she's put you in. There are still those, even among your generation, who fear children with immeasurable abilities. Parents will go to great lengths to protect and shield these children. Bane would know something about that, though in his case, it might work both ways."

Janine rose from her chair, standing straight and shaking off her old-woman mien. She winked at Tally. "I like you, Natalia. But know this—the National Order is not finished with you, nor with Braeden. If our kind is going to survive what is coming, we need your youth and your strength to fortify our ranks."

"And if we have our own plans? Our own dreams?"

Janine smiled indulgently, as one would to a young child. But before Tally could utter another word, the formidable woman slipped away. Tally sat back down and stared at the fire. A few minutes later, a large, flat box appeared in the place where Janine had sat. Tally reached for it, removed the lid, and folded back the tissue paper. A leather-bound photo album sat nestled in the box. A black-and-white photograph graced its cover—two women hugging each other and leaning back, laughing at some joke they had just shared. Her grandmother and Janine, dressed in wide-bottomed pants, daring for the time period. And they were beautiful.

"What's that?" Bane asked, coming up behind her.

"A gift...or a threat. I haven't decided which yet."

Chapter Twenty-two

The fight against whomever was abducting Fascina had just begun, but it appeared as if the usually ineffectual National Order finally had a fire lit under them. After revealing that he had discovered that their missing people were most likely on a ship, Bane had been called to San Francisco. Declining the invitation was not an option. He and Chris had long ago talked about this eventuality—the N.O.F. wanting to tap Chicago leadership as a resource. It was why Bane had tried so hard to remain under their radar.

Tally closed her email inbox. It was almost six o'clock, and Bane would be picking her up in a few minutes. She shut down her computer and straightened her desk. There was a soft knock on her office door, and Bane entered.

"Ready?" He looked like he hadn't slept in days. The stubble on his face only made him more attractive. He rubbed his shoulder and stretched his neck as if trying to release the tension.

"Almost," she said. "I just need to finish a couple of things. Why don't you take a load off?"

He nodded and sat heavily in one of the chairs.

After locking her desk drawers and loading up her satchel with the papers she would work on at home, Tally walked around her desk and stood behind him. While she massaged his shoulders, she concentrated on healing his weariness. He groaned in pleasure when she found a knot at the base of his neck and began to gently work out the tension. "Slipping back and forth across the continent is taking its toll on you," she said. "You could stay the night in San Francisco once in a while."

He reached up and stilled her hands. "I would miss you too much. Besides, I'm not sure it would be wise to test the limits of our bond yet."

She leaned forward to kiss his ear, neck, and cheek, loving how his whiskers felt against her skin. He kissed her back with a longing that echoed in her breast.

In the weeks since the attempt on her life, they had seen each other nearly every day. Only, every moment had included Chris, Jackie, and on some occasions, when they needed his guidance, Orson. The poor man had been shocked to hear about the abductions.

"I would miss you too, Braeden. We'll find time to be alone tonight, no matter what." She cupped his cheek, and he turned to kiss her palm.

"I'll hold you to that. Hey, what's this?" he asked, picking up some papers that had fallen off her desk.

"My assistant dropped them off before she left. She said it was nothing urgent, so I—is that from Shareff?" Together they looked at the copy of the check written out to the Lumina Foundation and the tax donation letter.

"Ten thousand," Bane said thoughtfully.

"Not too extravagant, but not a pittance, either."

"I wonder where Adrian got the money. He doesn't work, and from what I've heard, his father cut his living allowance. The family made a few bad investments, and the old man has reached out to a friend's financial firm to manage what's left of their estate."

"Is it that bad?"

"Nothing that can't be fixed in a generation, if they're smart about it."

"And you know so much about this because..."

Bane shrugged.

"Never mind," Tally said, shaking her head.

"I guess we should get going," he said, setting the papers on her desk. The exhaustion had seeped back into his voice.

"What's going on, Bane? You sound more tired than usual."

"This thing with the National Order has me off, that's all," he explained. "I don't like not having options."

She sensed that there was more to it. "Couldn't you just tell them no?"

He chuckled. "You've met Janine—what do you think?" He pulled her into his arms. "It'll all work out. Come on, let's go see your brother."

"Not until tomorrow," she said happily. "I told you we would find time for us tonight. Chris has an early date with Jackie and her family."

"This is the best news I've had all day. Your place or mine?"

"Mine, if you don't mind. I have an itch to cook for you. You can tell me about Janine and San Francisco while I make dinner." She grabbed her coat, purse, and laptop satchel. It wasn't long before they were driving down her alley and pulling into her garage.

They said hi to Michelle, who was in the backyard harvesting the last tomatoes of the season. She gave Tally a bowlful, and they wished each other a good night. Inside, Bane mixed Negronis as Tally made up a tray of olives, pecorino, and soppressata with olive oil and sliced crusty bread. Then she ran up to her room to change.

"What's the news?" Tally asked, coming back down. Bane was on the couch with his head back and his eyelids closed. She quieted and was about to cover him with a throw when he opened his eyes. "Why don't you rest? We can eat later."

"No, no. I'm fine, really. If I do, I'm liable to sleep through the entire weekend when I would much rather talk to you." He sat up, and she settled next to him. "We found a money trail to follow," Bane started, pausing to nosh on the antipasti. "And tracked it to a half-dozen labs."

Tally whistled.

"A couple were legit—labs dedicated to finding cures to illnesses suffered by the Norm community. But four"—he downed his Negroni, and Tally pushed a Nebbiolo she had opened toward him—"were using Fascina blood and cell samples. It looks like they were trying to determine how to infuse Fascina powers into Norm DNA. The results were disastrous. It's right out of a mutant comic book."

He stood and pulled her up from the couch. They transferred the food and wine to the kitchen island so Tally could start cooking. "Military applications?" she asked when Bane was settled on a stool.

He nodded. "We caught a break. One phone call from Janine, and we were given a name—General Canfield, retired and living in Maine. Another call, and we had an appointment to visit him in his home. Canfield was impressively forthcoming for retired military, and he outlined a 1990s' program that'd been scrapped due to the less-than-desirable results. The program, funded by the military, had been co-sponsored by several high-ranking Fascina families—no surprise that my father was involved."

"Oh, no."

"Oh, yes. But no one on the National Order seemed to care, which makes me think that they already knew. Canfield wasn't pleased that the program, or an unsanctioned version of it, was up and running."

"So maybe not exactly military," Tally deduced, "but some group working outside of proper channels. You're right. It does sound like *X-Men*, with a little *Bourne* thrown in for good measure."

Tally took a break from stirring the risotto to run her fingers through his dark locks, twisting them up, around, and back. "There. That's better."

"I am *not* going as Wolverine for Halloween!" he insisted, but chuckled.

She indulged in a quick kiss before getting back to the risotto. After she poured more stock into the Arborio rice, she gave it a good minute's worth of gentle stirring, then brushed clean the wild mushrooms that she had stored in a paper bag. Bane watched her as she went back and forth between the two tasks. She started the diced pancetta on low heat to slowly crisp, occasionally flipping them with short tosses of the sauté pan.

"Can I do anything other than sit here, eat, and watch you cook?"

"You could answer my phone."

"Your ph—" Her phone rang. He shook his head and laughed. "Hey, Chris. Putting you on speaker."

"Jackie's family had to bail—something about a grandkid and a last-minute entry into a talent show. We're wondering if you want to meet us for dinner."

"Tally's cooking risotto."

"I made enough for all of us," she called out over the spitting pancetta.

"Hang on a sec..." Chris replied, while Tally set out plates and salad forks and pushed them toward Bane. "Jackie wants to know if she can bring anything...like the huge Caesar salad that she already made."

"Uh, perfect," Bane replied, smirking at Tally and shaking his head.

"Great. See you in a few."

Bane hung up, then pointed to the salad plates. "How'd you know?"

"No prescient powers for me, other than knowing when Chris needs to connect. Jackie had mentioned that she was making salad for her family get-together."

"Think we have time for a quick—"

She threw a damp kitchen towel at him.

"I was going to say conversation," he protested, tossing the towel back at her. "I managed to mostly avoid Janine, but she thinks it's crucial, especially now, for us to out ourselves."

"I hope you told her that it's none of her business." She frowned when he remained silent. "Shit!" She had forgotten to stir the risotto and add more stock. "It's good," she said, more to herself, then glanced at the clock. "We have a few minutes before they get here, so spill."

"Janine's not entirely wrong, Tally. But I convinced her to let us make the announcement after the engagement party. Look, I know you're worried about how Chris will take the news."

"I was." She tasted the rice. It still had another round of stock and stirring to go, but it was glistening beautifully. She added the trio of shiitakes, criminis, and porcinis and then a pinch of salt. "Chris is seriously happy right now. I'm convinced he'd want the same for you and me. I'm just worried that he'll feel that he has to share his Chicago Order responsibilities with me, once he finds out that I'm Fascina."

"Would that be so bad?"

"For one thing, I don't want him giving me co-control because he feels duty-bound to do so, especially as he's so phenomenally good at herding the cats. And for another, I can't imagine quitting the hospital. Are you going to finally spill?" Tally asked when Bane made a face.

"Chris might not be the problem," he said. "Janine made it clear that it's time that someone from Chicago be installed at the national level."

"You."

"Not just me. Both of us. They've never had a national liaison to the Norms, and she sees your success with the mayor as something that could be a model for the entire Fascina community."

"So that's what's been bothering you. They're trying to tap 'us.'" He nodded. "And if I decline the offer..."

"I don't know. No one ever has before. Said 'no thanks,' I mean. I guess we'll cross that bridge when we come to it. That looks delicious, by the way. Smells even better."

Tally dipped a spoon in, then held it out for him to sample. There was a change in the room's pressure, and Chris and Jackie appeared—just as Tally was pulling the spoon from Bane's lips. It was a miracle that her brother missed their smoldering looks.

"Just set that on the island," Tally told Chris. Jackie poured more wine into Tally's glass and handed it to her with a shrewd look. Then she poured two more, emptying the bottle. Chris was already opening the next while chewing on a piece of the pecorino and bread.

"Thanks for letting us crash," he said, ignoring his phone when it chimed. "Janine. She won't let up. She really wants you, Bane. I keep telling her that it's your decision."

"It's not such a bad idea," Jackie put in. "I mean, they want someone from Chicago. So why not send someone you trust? And it's not like you would have to move there, Bane. You could still be based here. I think the Norms call it teleworking," she joked.

"I could always propose that Orson join," Chris said. "He would think it was a real honor. And I trust him."

If Tally hadn't been holding out salad tongs to Jackie, she might have missed the frown that flitted in her eyes before she asked, "As much as Bane?"

Chris shook his head. "What's your opinion on all of this, Tally?"

"I think we should discuss it after dinner. The risotto is done," she announced, but at the same time wondered if Jackie had something against Orson. Or was she trying to get Bane out of the picture?

Tally scooped up generous portions of the glossy rice, then grabbed the bowl of pancetta cracklings and a ramakin of shaved parmigiano-reggiano. They ate and talked about their new relationship with the suddenly active National Order.

"There's really no choice, is there?" Bane asked. "We're the first new blood they're bringing into the fold. Better to make our mark and get settled in before other cities are invited."

"Sounds like you've decided," Chris said. "What's the time commitment? Still four days a month?"

He shook his head. "Four full weeks to start, then it'll go to two a month, then one after the first of the year. They're finally modernizing and want me on board. They've decided to leave the nineties."

"Now that you mentioned it," Chris said, "I haven't received a fax from them in months."

"You're kidding, right?" Jackie asked.

"Sadly, no. If you accept, when will you start?"

"Next month. They know I have my hands full with my various ventures. Not to mention planning my best friend's bachelor party."

Tally slanted a look at Jackie. A slow, mischievous smile formed on her friend's lips. And then, Jackie winked.

Tally cleared their dishes, and Jackie got up to help. "Have you told Chris about your bachelorette trip?" she whispered to her soon-to-be sister-in-law.

"I have. What about you?"

Tally gave her a quizzical look, to which Jackie immediately rolled her eyes. "Fine. I haven't mentioned it to Bane yet. I was waiting for him to get back from his latest trip. Jackie..."

"Don't worry. No one else can see your connection. I didn't notice until it was brought to my attention. It was Tía Ixi who saw it—something about your auras and yin and yang." Jackie laughed. "My South American tía stealing from Asian culture, imagine! Don't worry, though. She won't say anything to anyone else. She only mentioned it to me because she assumed that I knew. I won't say a word, I promise. But you really should tell your brother."

"We will. We're waiting until after your engagement party."

"That's cool. I'm not lying to him, but it'll start feeling that way. After the party is soon enough, I guess."

But Tally was more interested in Jackie's impression of Orson Sedge. He was the closest thing to a surrogate parental-figure that she and Chris had, and Tally hoped that there wasn't any bad blood between the Sedges and Silvas. She was stopped from asking when Chris came over with a box that Tally hadn't noticed when they'd slipped in. "Cannoli!" She hugged her brother.

Jackie nudged him.

"You know," Chris conspired, "Bane's not going to like not having you close for an entire weekend."

"He's not going to—? Why wouldn't he—?" she gulped.

"Because you won't be here to order from Nonna Lucia's and make him more money. Geez, Tally, what's up with you? Don't worry, I've got you covered. Watch and learn." He walked over to Bane, throwing his arm around his friend's shoulder. "So, where are we going for my bachelor party? Or is it a secret?" he asked. "Jackie and Tally told me where the bachelorette trip is happening. I think it's only fair that they get to know where we'll be."

"Switzerland," Bane stated. "Ski trip. Wait. What do you mean, 'bachelorette trip?'" His eyes homed in on her, and she hastily turned her back on him to load the dishwasher.

"Uh, yeah," Jackie interjected. "We're going to our family's estate off French Guiana. It's owned by the Baptiste side of the family. A little coastal island all to ourselves. But, ah, don't try to find it on Google maps. It's been shrouded."

"An entire island?" Bane asked.

She nodded. "It's not that big. Smaller than La Mère—that's another little islet. Tally won't have to fly in. I'll slip her directly there. The isolation of the place is its strongest defense. The Silvas and Baptistes have more than a few complexes that are off the grid, but Île de Lune happens to have pristine beaches. It's the same weekend that you're going to Switzerland. Tally and I could go early and—"

"Sounds great," Bane said.

"You don't have to worry, Bane. It's completely safe," she argued. "Chris checked it out. We wouldn't even—hang on, what?"

"Sounds great," he repeated. "You'll have to stock the place ahead of time, right? With your permission, I'll go with you and make sure everything is secure."

Tally looked back and forth between the two. Bane had crossed his arms over his chest. Allowing an outsider into a family's bolt-hole was unheard of. It wasn't until you were officially married into a family that the location of such a place was shared. The Silvas had been extraordinarily flexible in allowing Chris to go there before the wedding, and Tally later. It was a sign of just how much they had been accepted into the family.

Jackie stood before Bane and narrowed her eyes. He'd outmaneuvered her. Her family would never allow such an intrusion, and he knew it. It would force Tally to have to make a choice between publicly disrespecting Bane or insulting Jackie and her family. That left one option—cancellation of the weekend. Bane was a master in the art of the Fascina community's unwritten laws of propriety, rules established generations ago that surprisingly were still in use to this very day. As modern a man as Bane was, he could have been plucked from the pages of a Regency romance novel, so studied was his adherence to the arcane Fascina etiquette. Chris waited with bated breath for Jackie to respond. Tally wasn't so patient and was about to order Bane to rescind his offer of help.

But Jackie turned out to be made of sterner stuff, and she straightened her shoulders, then crossed her arms over her chest, miming Bane. "Not a problem," she parried, and a little of Bane's smug resolve faded away. Jackie pulled her phone from her pocket and sent a quick text. A moment later, her phone chimed, and she smiled. "Tía Ixi expects you for dinner tomorrow at seven. She said that you don't need to bring anything."

And thrust.

Chris began laughing, and Tally hid her grin behind a kitchen towel. She'd never before seen Bane outwitted at his own game and was soon laughing at his expense, along with her brother. Jackie's phone pinged again, and she grinned as she read the message. "Tía wants you to bring something after all—Tally."

"Uncle," Bane surrendered as Tally choked.

"Don't you mean *tío*?" Chris quipped, then drew Jackie into his arms. "I love you more and more every day. That was epic."

Tally came around the kitchen island with the pastry box and four plates. She doled out the cannoli, and they discussed the two disparate trips. After Chris and Jackie slipped away, she sat on the couch with Bane.

"It was Jackie's tía who tipped her off that you and I are connected," Tally warned, after telling Bane about Tía Ixi's observation. "I guess we'll find out tomorrow how much she knows."

"Are we still in agreement? We tell Chris after the engagement party?"

"The timing is good…right before our trips. Chris won't be able to stay mad at you for long. He loves to ski. By the way, who else is going?"

"Jackie's two cousins. And Marc and Ryan."

"Marc and Ryan?"

"It's Marc's parents' lodge. Plus, he's a good friend to all of us."

They both sat silent for a moment, then Tally turned to him. "I finished reading the books you lent me. That anger we felt when forcefully separated…it helped me to heal faster than I normally would after the wreck."

"I know. I went a little crazy that night, forcing the ambulance off the road."

She touched his cheek. "They were paid mercenaries, and the same people who took you." Her temper hitched up a notch at the thought. For just an instant, her eyes bored into his, and he met her wrath with a fierce gaze of his own. "You know, the residual effects of my abduction haven't completely worn off. I read that it might take a month. I also read that making love during this period would be amazing and would further cement our connection." She leaned in and gave him a savage kiss.

Bane pulled back, touching his lip where she'd broken the skin. "Then I guess we'd better get this out of our systems."

Tally grinned and got to work on just that.

Chapter Twenty-three

Tally smoothed the sheer midnight-blue silk of her gown one last time. She turned to check that the draped fabric fell naturally down her back. The skirts, as she did a quick spin, swirled out perfectly, as many of the gowns that the women wore tonight would. Her hair was piled in a loose updo—one secure enough to withstand the rigors of ballroom dancing. She gazed about the bathroom that once belonged to her parents, remembering with nostalgia the nights she'd watched her mother getting ready.

Finally, she plucked an earring from her mother's jewelry box, a collection of gems that would rival any royal family's. The fat, pear-shaped diamond bobbed gently in time with its twin already dangling from her other ear. From the hall came the *click clack* of heels approaching on the marble floor. Jackie. "I'm in here," Tally called out.

"This place is huge," Jackie exclaimed, and not for the first time.

"You'll get used to it," Tally said warmly. "You'll put your stamp on this house and make it a home again."

"You really feel that way, don't you?"

"Of course."

"I was worried that you might be upset knowing that I'll be taking over your mom's rooms one day."

"Jackie, my mom would love you. How could she not?"

"But you didn't always feel that way. And I wasn't exactly nice to you," Jackie stated, looking at her reflection and turning at her hips and waist to watch how her dress managed the movement. "You know, I used to watch you in high school. I was two years behind you. Even then, you were a legend—the non-Fascina who knew more about our history than any student there, and even some of the teachers. And the three of you together, come on. You, Chris, and Bane were a force to be reckoned with. When Chris and I started dating, it wasn't that I was jealous... More like, wary. As if I was trespassing into your secret club."

"But I also misread you," Tally admitted. "I wasn't exactly approachable—too many walls. Growing up in this community; I never had any girlfriends, Fascina or otherwise. I'm so happy that we got over being foolish." She reached under one of the hand towels and handed Jackie a flat, velvet covered box. "An engagement present, from me and, well, my mom." She watched as Jackie opened the lid.

Jet-black onyx beads and diamonds gleamed in the bright lighting of the bathroom suite. "It was one of her favorites," Tally explained, holding out her hand to take the rope of gems. "Here, let me. That's a black diamond," she said, centering the fat stone that dropped to just the top of Jackie's breastbone. "It was part of another necklace that belonged to my father's great-grandmother. The necklace was damaged, and some of the stones were passed to other family members. But my dad had this made for my mom. The two princess-cut diamonds on either side of the pendant are as near as identical as can be. They had just found out that—"

"Your mom was pregnant with twins," Jackie finished, her eyes glistening. She brushed her fingers over the large stone and closed her eyes. "So much joy over the years...some pain, but yes, this stone is wholesome and good. I can get a sense of the women who wore it over the centuries." She opened her eyes. "You've never worn it."

Tally shook her head. "It wasn't meant for me. And thank you," Tally said, acknowledging the great gift that Jackie had just given her—the revelation of one of her powers.

Jackie grinned. "I would say that we should hug."

"But we don't want to mess up our gowns." They laughed. "I'm so glad that we're friends."

"Just you wait," Jackie warned. "Soon we'll be sisters, and then it really gets fun. Come on, Chris and Bane will be waiting for us."

As they walked from the wing that housed the family's private rooms, strands of "Pachelbel's Canon in D" filtered through the corridors, growing louder as they approached the front hall, much like the crescendo nature of the composition itself. Ahead, her brother, Chris, stood in the foyer, greeting the early arrivals. Orson and his wife were numbered among them. Tally's breath hitched when Bane stepped into view, his tuxedo fitting him like a glove—it was a sin that he looked that scrumptious. She closed her mouth and snuck a glance at Jackie to see if she'd been caught ogling. Jackie's mouth was open, and she was staring at Chris with what had to have been the same expression Tally had just worn. Her soon-to-be sister-in-law looked at her, and they both broke into a fit of giggles.

"We are definitely in trouble tonight," Jackie predicted. And when they looked back at Chris and Bane and saw that the men were staring at them, mouths open, their giggling turned to laughter. Chris broke away to escort them to the entrance, while Bane hung back, chatting with Orson and the newly arrived Adrian Shareff. When Tally had first seen the guest list, she wondered at his inclusion, but then Bane had reminded everyone that Fascina tradition required that they include everyone on the Chicago Order's roll call. This event wasn't like the actual wedding, when only their closest friends and relatives would be included in the private ceremony. Tonight, if they omitted any of the families, even the minor ones, it would be interpreted as politically motivated.

Engagement celebrations in their community were just as important as wedding ceremonies. Even more so because they sometimes established a new alliance between previously unattached families. The Silvas and Baptistes, along with Tally, Chris, and Bane, would all be on alert, listening for any comments about the union of their families, innocuous or otherwise.

Tally smiled, then held out her arms to hug June Sedge and buss the woman's cheek. She did the same to their daughter, Amy. "What a lovely gown," she told the young woman. Tally didn't know why, but she still thought of Orson's daughter as a teenager.

"Thank you," Amy enthused, then whispered, "I was able to choose my own dress for once. Papa even said that I could have a glass of champagne tonight. He's in denial that I'm twenty-one and about to graduate from college."

"Well, I won't tattle if I see you having more than one."

Amy giggled, and Tally got the feeling that she might have had a nip of something stronger already. Her gown was definitely more sophisticated than the flouncy getups her parents had made her wear in the past, but the tight, sheath-like skirt would ensure that she would be unable to join in most of the dancing.

"You look as lovely as ever," Orson exclaimed, and leaned in to kiss Tally's cheek. Behind him, Adrian Shareff moved a step closer, and Tally suddenly felt queasy. "Are you unwell, my dear?" Orson asked, taking her hand.

"Not at all," she said brightly.

"You probably haven't eaten all day," Bane admonished, coming to stand next to her. His proximity had the immediate effect of quelling the roiling in her stomach.

"Of course, he's right as usual," Tally admitted, winking at Orson, who smiled indulgently at her.

"You should skip away to the kitchen after receiving the guests," Orson recommended. "We'll cover for you in case anyone asks."

"I might just do that," Tally quasi-promised, nodding to him as he stepped away to congratulate Jackie and Chris. "Shareff," she managed to politely say. "Welcome."

"B-beautiful," he stammered. "I mean you look as beautiful as ever. Bane," he barely acknowledged, too preoccupied with the deep vee-cut of Tally's gown. He reached out as if he wanted to straighten the jeweled necklace that dropped low to her cleavage, but she turned slightly to acknowledge the people behind him. "Did you get the check?" he asked suddenly.

"We did," Tally acknowledged. "But now is certainly not the time to—"

"If you expect more, you'll have to meet with me."

She wasn't sure what he was up to, but thankfully, Orson had moved on, and Chris and Jackie were free to greet him.

She smiled at the brunette who was next in line, thinking she was Adrian's plus-one, but the woman hooked her arm into the crook of the man next to her.

"Tally," Bane introduced, "this is Emily Sykes from the National Order, and her husband, Jasper. I'm glad you could make it."

"Wow. What a dress!" Emily exclaimed upon meeting Tally. "Bane, how long has it been? Four, five days?"

"At least a week. Good to see you, Em. You as well, Jasper."

Emily peeked into the ballroom. "Nice. Chris really went old school. Waltzing?"

"Of course," Bane answered, and Tally felt his fingers trace up her back. The Fascina, along with their adherence to protocol, loved a good waltz. Tally couldn't wait to be spun around the floor in Bane's arms.

As the arriving guests filed past, Tally played her part, smiling and kissing cheeks and sharing niceties, until finally, there were no more people to greet. Chris looked a little stretched, but Jackie was as poised as ever. "Shall we head in?"

Tally walked, her arm resting on Bane's, through the guests clustered about the dance floor. The quartet eased off their playing as Tally took her place before a standing microphone. She looked out at the expectant faces—Silvas, Sedges, Baptistes, Fortunas, Ryans, Prestons, Grossomms, all of Chicago's head families represented, along with their offshoots, and the many minor families. She smiled at the Garban family, and, remembering

Joseph's kindness at the hospital, made a mental note to sing his praise to his parents.

She ignored Shareff's unwelcome examination of her, focusing instead on Emily and Jasper, a welcome addition to the crowd. Their presence marked the approval of her brother's engagement by the National Order.

Thus, with confidence, she began her speech, thanking everyone for coming to the celebration, running through her practiced lines not as if she were orating, but rather, having a conversation with everyone in the room. She quickly came to the point of the celebration, earning approving smiles and nods from the attendees—they wanted to drink and eat and dance, not listen to speeches. And as she introduced her brother and Jackie, all eyes turned away from her, finally, and settled on the obviously happy couple as they entered the ballroom, now officially recognized as affianced. Chris and Jackie took center stage—or dance floor—accepting the congratulations from the community.

Tally stepped back as the orchestra played the first waltz, a simple composition to give everyone a chance to warm up and remember the steps. It had been years since a get-together such as this had been held, and she backed up against the wall to take in the scene. The ballroom was beautiful, absent even of the agitated undercurrents that had been eddying under the surface of the Chicago Order. She smiled. In another century, standing where she was on the edge of the room and watching the revelers, she would have been labeled a wallflower. Except she wasn't, not really, and she sensed him approach. Bane.

He kept a respectable distance, acting as her escort, as he'd done countless times before. Their dinner with Tía Ixi had gone as suspected. It was an interrogation, a required approval process that would protect the Baptiste family and the secrecy of Île de Luna. It wasn't until they were taking their leave that the wise woman reached out and placed her hands on their heads, giving them her blessing. But it was what she'd said to Tally when Bane had gone to get the car that remained fixed in Tally's thoughts: *"The time will come when you'll only be able to trust your heart, even when your mind tells you to do the opposite. If you can manage to do that, you might just live a long, love-filled life."* It had been a warning of sorts. A promise of trouble on the horizon. But Tally and Bane already realized their path would not be an easy one. There was still a murderer in the city, and the people behind the threat to Chris's leadership had not been uncovered. Not to mention that she still had a stalker to contend with. Oh, and she would need to out herself as both a powerful Fascina and Bane's bondmate. She sighed.

Bane leaned against the wall. "I don't know how your father handled it, being bonded to a beautiful woman and having other men pay her compliments. I've never been a jealous man, but I wanted to break Shareff's wrist for almost touching you." He held out a glass of champagne but then frowned. "Hey, how are you feeling?"

"I thought I was getting a migraine earlier, but it's gone. Must be because I'm standing so close to you. Another happy side effect," she murmured behind the rim of her coupe. A server offered them a prosciutto-wrapped scallop, and Tally's middle churned. She'd never liked them, but with an empty stomach, the smell made her feel ill.

"I should check on Frank. Want to come with me? Maybe grab a bite in the kitchen?"

"Sure. I could use a break from smiling," she said and gave him the most exaggerated, maniacal grin she could summon. She followed Bane through one of the service corridors. The catering staff stiffened in their preparation at a perceived trespass into their territory, but recognized Tally and Bane and went back to the controlled chaos of their duties. He led her deeper into the house to the main kitchen where Chef Frank was directing his line cooks like a maestro.

While Bane went to converse with Frank about some detail, Tally plucked a piece of bread off the counter and pilfered a thin slice of Camembert to put on top. When Bane finished, he escorted her into the dining room.

Kathy had everything in hand and was expertly directing the staff, much like her husband in the kitchen. "Can I get anything for either of you?" she asked.

"We just came to see if we could help, but everything looks beautiful," Tally said, as a host of servers descended to place food into the gleaming silver chafing dishes. Tally went to the dessert buffet and snagged a mini cannoli from the arrangement, taking care that the powdered sugar didn't dust her dress.

"Your gown is spectacular," Kathy exclaimed. "The skirts remind me of those old-time movies with Ginger Rogers. Please tell me you plan on dancing."

"Most definitely," she replied, and Kathy followed her gaze when she glanced over at Bane.

"There's something supremely sexy about a man in a tux who can dance. Don't let Frank know that I told you this, but last year, he signed us up for ballroom dance lessons for my birthday. I think he enjoyed it more than I did. He's so graceful. I felt like a princess, whirling around the floor in his arms."

"Bane and Chris are both excellent dancers. At least they are now," Tally joked. "When we were kids, they smashed each and every one of my toes during our lessons."

"Everything looks perfect," Bane told Kathy, approaching. "Frank said you and the staff will be finished setting up in the next half hour. Chris's kitchen staff will take over then, making sure the Sternos stay lit and the food replenished."

"This has been one of the easiest catering gigs we've ever had. Frank couldn't stop exclaiming over Chris's kitchen. It's got everything a chef and caterer could need," Kathy said.

"My parents used to have functions here every month," Tally explained. "And their parents before them. It's good to see this place filled up again."

"Well, I should get back to it. Frank and I are looking forward to our early weekend night—unheard of in the restaurant industry," Kathy exclaimed.

"Do you have plans?" Bane asked. Because of the catering job, Nonna Lucia's was closed for the night.

"Frank said it was a surprise, but maybe he'll add dancing to the agenda." She winked at Tally, then bounced away.

"You ready?" Bane asked, holding out his arm to her. They left the dining room and walked down the hallway that would lead them to the ballroom's outer vestibule. As they passed within, Tally felt the ward on the space that would deter any non-Fascina from entering without an escort. She and Bane walked in and stopped to admire the dancers swirling across the floor.

"You were right," he said. "It's great to see this place filled up again."

"I wonder if that wasn't part of the problem," Tally mused, and Bane turned to her. "Chicago's leading family always, and I mean *always*, entertained. Dinner parties. Holiday celebrations. Hosting engagement parties. Most of it stopped when Dad died, then later, all of it ended with Mom's passing. The Chicago Order used to be such a tight-knit community. Even the families who didn't get along behaved themselves at the events."

Bane stared at the people milling about with fresh eyes. "You're onto something with that, Tally. We'll have to talk to Chris and Jackie about more community engagement." He pulled her hand, drawing her toward the dance floor, and they joined in with the others. The music ended, and another tune was struck up, followed by a light waltz.

Tally danced with her brother, then Orson, and when the music changed again, she saw Adrian Shareff home in on her. But Bane made it to her first and swung her out of the man's reach. When the orchestra stopped playing to take a well-deserved break, a DJ brought a little contemporary flair to the night, starting with classic club music, each song merging into the next. Finally, her brother and Jackie got up on the stage and took the mic. They thanked everyone again for attending and celebrating with them, then announced that the buffet was ready in the dining room. Nearly half the room followed them out, leaving Bane and Tally, along with a dozen or so other couples.

"Let's get something to drink," Tally said, noticing how Orson was at the bar and in a heated discussion with Rene Grossomm and his father, Jean-Christophe. Their wives stood nearby, looking as uncomfortable as Rene's date. She stormed off when Jean-Christophe and Orson shook hands.

When Rene saw them approach, his features instantly shifted into a practiced smile. "Natalia," he said, drawing out her name. "You look as pretty as ever. You must spin for us," he suggested, and she ignored his twirling finger. "Your gown looks as if it could float away on its own. Stunning, isn't it, Bane?"

Orson looked even more uncomfortable than his wife. But Tally had dealt with Rene's backhanded compliments before, and she was adept at turning his hidden insults back at him. She smiled at Jean-Christophe and his wife, Margot. "So lovely to see you both," she said, snubbing Rene by following Fascina protocol and greeting the elders of the family.

"Chris and Jackie have outdone themselves with this party," Margot enthused. "Jean-Christophe and I used to love coming here when your parents were alive." She paused and covered her mouth, as if she shouldn't have mentioned Tally's parents.

"It was a lovely time then," Tally said, putting Margot at ease. "Chris and Bane and I used to sneak up to the gallery to watch you all dance. I know my parents would approve of Rosegate being opened up to the community again."

"Oh, I'm so happy you said that. Those celebrations, they made us stronger somehow. And it's been ages since there's been a proper event like this, one where we could all waltz in the Fascina tradition."

"Now, Mother," Rene cautioned, "don't forget that Natalia isn't…"

She really hated the way he let the words trail off and how he made his mother look foolish. She was a nice woman and deserved better. "I'm looking forward to more dancing," Tally said, briefly clasping Margot's hand. "And I know that my brother and Jackie will want to have more of these celebrations. Who knows?" she added, flashing an innocent smile at Rene. "Maybe you can host one for your son's next engagement party."

Rene turned deep red, drained his cocktail, and set it on the bar with a loud crack. He'd been married twice already. The word in the community was that he was a terrible husband, both in temperament and in bed.

Oblivious to her son's discomfiture, Margot nodded enthusiastically. "Oh my, that would be splendid, wouldn't it, Jean-Christophe?" Her husband grumbled a reply about their son, something Tally didn't catch.

Rene looked at his watch, then at Bane. "I hope your caterer brought enough food." He stalked away in the direction his date had gone.

Orson checked his watch, looking somewhat uneasy. "I suppose we should grab something to eat, June. Have you seen our daughter?" His wife shook her head, smiled apologetically at Tally, then followed Orson from the ballroom. Jean-Christophe went after them, but Margot stayed back.

"I'm sorry about Rene. He takes after his father and is a little rough in the social niceties." She stared after her husband for a moment. "Did you mean it, Natalia, about having more celebrations here?"

"I did," Tally replied.

"Good. It's just the thing to get the Chicago Order's act together." And with that, Margot departed, leaving Tally and Bane to ponder over her final statement.

"You handled Rene impeccably, as usual," Bane stated, giving her a glass of champagne and then clinking his coupe to hers.

"What are we toasting?"

"My restraint," he said and laughed. "And the fact that I can count on you to manage Rene so that there's no need for me to punch him. Although, I was sorely tempted."

They sipped their champagne, then Tally held up her glass in another toast. "To my restraint as well. I already punched him on the playground when we were kids, so I know firsthand how satisfying it can be."

"To us, then," Bane said, giving her a dashing smile and letting her know he meant his toast on a much deeper level.

"To us," Tally echoed. Girlish laughter drew Tally's attention away, and she watched as Amy Sedge left the ballroom, headed toward the ladies' lounge. "Let's go check on the food again before the musicians return."

"Good idea," Bane said, holding out his arm. He escorted her into the dining room to find the buffet crowded with revelers. "Kitchen?" Bane suggested, and Tally nodded.

Feeling the weight of someone's stare, Tally checked behind them. Everyone seemed more interested in the food. "That's strange," she noted, pointing to Amy Sedge. "I thought I just saw her in the ballroom, walking in the opposite direction."

Bane looked back. "Poor woman. She's been trapped in a conversation with Rene Grossomm. Come on. Let's grab something to eat before heading back into the fray."

Chapter Twenty-four

"Thank you for organizing everything, Tally," Jackie enthused, giving her a hug. Her extended family had just departed, as had nearly half of the guests. Not only had the engagement party been a success, but they'd gleaned useful insights on the political undercurrents running through the Chicago Order.

Bane and Chris came over to where they were chatting and handed them each a glass of champagne. "How are the musicians holding up?" she asked, after noting that Bane had just been conversing with the director. It was well after midnight, and they had stopped playing, but weren't striking their gear and instruments.

"They're happy. Providing them with excellent food was essential. Dennis, the director, told me that he's given out over a dozen business cards with promises for future bookings."

"One of those from my parents, no doubt," Jackie said. "Hey, before we mingle again, we're still on tomorrow for brunch and a recap?"

"I already set my alarm for eleven," Tally replied. "We'll come back here and help you two finish off the leftovers."

"There aren't any," Chris said. "So I'm making my famous chicken waffles."

"I know dancing works up an appetite, but all of the food is gone?" Tally asked.

Chris laughed. "Not quite. Except for the dessert buffet and some late night fare, Jackie had the catering service send the surplus to one of the local shelters." Her brother held out his arm to his fiancée. "Tomorrow, I want to discuss that interaction you two saw between Jean-Christophe and Orson. Both families left early."

"I saw Amy dancing with Adrian about an hour ago. But I think they've gone, too. Rene's date is still here," Bane said, nodding toward the woman talking to another group across the room.

"We'll go cozy up to her," Jackie suggested. "Maybe she can tell us what happened between the Sedges and the Grossomms."

"Good luck," Tally offered as they swept away.

"They'll need it," Bane commented. "I tried earlier, and she was tight-lipped."

"She's had a couple hours and a few cocktails. Maybe that will help." On the dais, the musicians were taking their seats and retuning their instruments.

"Come on," Bane said in a lowered voice. "There's something I want to share with you, but not here. Too many prying eyes."

She followed him out of the ballroom. They crossed the now empty and dark dining room and through the paneled exit to the service corridor. "Ready?" Bane asked, taking her hand. He knew the house as well as she, and he opened the hidden door leading to the gallery above the ballroom, a place that had been closed off for years and used for storage. From the floor below, stained glass panels lined the entire gallery, closing off the space from view. The art nouveau windows sat in grooved tracks and, backlit, provided a brilliant turn-of-the-century art gallery to the guests below. If desired, they could be slid aside in neat vertical stacks of three, thus opening the gallery to the main floor.

Bane grabbed her hand and pulled her to the north end where, if someone managed to venture up into the space, they would be hidden from view. Before them sat a linen-covered table. Two silver domes covered expensive antique dinner plates, sterling utensils gleamed atop pristine napkins, and a spray of violets cascaded over a crystal bud vase. "My favorite flowers."

He smiled and held out her chair. "I knew you wouldn't take the time to eat. I figure that we have about twenty minutes before our absence is noted and considered rude."

He'd thought of everything, and her eyes shone as he took her napkin and placed it in her lap. "Almost forgot," he said, and the votive candles caught fire, lending a luminous ambiance to the already intimate tableau. He lifted the lid off her plate with a flourish, exposing a grilled cheese sandwich. And not just any grilled cheese, but one made from crusty Italian bread with a mix of Gruyère and cheddar.

"My favorite comfort food," Tally admired, breaking off a piece and watching the cheese stretch. "I love you, Braeden."

"Lucky for me that I know the way to your heart is food," he teased.

She touched his wrist when they finished. "Thank you for this."

"My pleasure. Come on, we should head back."

She nodded, and he angled his lips to hers and gave her a sweet kiss that warmed her to her toes. "In case anyone has noted our absence, you go first," she said. "I'll walk around to the other side and come out on the far end of the ballroom."

He nodded, kissed her one more time, then let her go.

Softer strands of another song floated up from below, and Tally sashayed and spun her way to the other side of the gallery. She passed by the windows facing the lake and slowed to stare at the cloudless sky, the moon having already passed. She could only make out a few of the constellations. Andromeda, Pisces—before its stars were lost to light pollution—and Cassiopeia. Perseus, on his way to rescue her, was somewhere above the estate and not yet visible from the window. Tally's gaze swept along the darkened shoreline, south to where the aura of the city drowned out even Orion's belt.

Across the expansive lawn behind Rosegate, something unseen, cold and evil, stared back at her, and she shivered. She stepped back from the broad window and hastened to the door that would return her to the others. When she entered the ballroom, Bane, Chris, and Jackie were walking with another couple toward the foyer, and she caught up with them. With the last of the guests were finally gone, she grabbed Bane's wrist and checked the time—1:40 a.m.

"I'll get Tally home," Bane said.

"Your home, you mean," Chris corrected.

"Yeah, I guess I'm used to having your sister around as a roommate." He turned to her and caught her stifling a yawn. "You ready?"

"See you tomorrow," she said, then Bane slipped them away. They arrived in his bedroom and his lips came down on hers in a demanding kiss.

"I've wanted you to do that all night," Tally confessed after he pulled back.

"Not as much as I've wanted to do this." He turned them toward the windows and a view of the vast lake from another part of the city. In the dim light, Tally could just make out their reflections in the glass. She watched him slide his finger under the silk holding her dress on her right shoulder, pushing it down, then letting it fall. Her breast, now bare, ached for his touch, and her nipple puckered in anticipation. She lifted her gaze, and he met her eyes in the reflection.

He kissed her neck, still watching her in the window as his hand massaged her breast. And then he drew the silk off her left shoulder. Her head fell back, but she continued to observe him through lowered lids as he played with her. She pressed herself back against him, against the hard ridge of his erection.

Finding her gown's hidden zipper, Bane slowly drew down the tab and, with his other hand, held her skirts pressed to her middle so that the sheath couldn't slither to the floor. All the while, he watched their reflection as he nibbled and nipped her earlobe.

He slid his hand up her middle, away from the silk. The released fabric hung on her hips, and Tally waited, her breath coming faster.

Behind her, Bane eased his pelvis away, just long enough for the silk to whisper down her legs. He groaned upon seeing the tiny scrap of lace that covered her and brought her up against him once more.

Tally gasped at how hard he was, his cock fitting perfectly against her.

They watched each other. Her breath was coming in pants as his palm skated back down her stomach and lower, until his long fingers slid inside the band of her panties.

"Yes," she moaned when he fingered her. "Braeden, yes!" And he thrust first one, then another long digit into her. His other hand left off rolling her nipple to undo his trousers. He struggled to release the cummerbund before grappling with his waistband. She could've whisked his clothing away, but she wanted to see him take her—she completely naked, and he still in his tux, looking as sexy as hell. His harsh breathing washed over her ear as his arm slid lower, belting her below her navel to hitch her high up onto her toes. She nearly pitched forward as he stabbed up and deeply into her, but he wrapped the length of her hair around and around his hand before gently palming the back of her skull, exerting just enough pull to hold her steady.

He withdrew, though not completely, and stabbed up again, taking her from behind. Their eyes met again in the glass. She'd never seen him this intense before, not while making love, and when the darkness in his eyes flashed at her, she knew she was at his mercy. She couldn't wait to find out what he would do to her, how he would use her body.

Another slow withdrawal and thrust had her gasping, and the corner of his mouth tilted up. It wasn't enough, and Tally moaned her dissatisfaction. But he refused to give her more than the tortuous retreat and patient invasion. Her thighs quivered from the strain of being on tiptoe, and she mewled. Finally, she begged. "Please, Braeden." And when he thrust up into her again, she ground back against his hips, arching her entire body as she strained to feel more of him. He pulled back again, thrust forward mercilessly, and finally, she felt him high inside her. She craved so much more. "Braeden."

On the next thrust, he lifted her a little and moved them closer to the window. "Hands on the ledge," he ordered, and she complied. She was skewered by his cock, held before him, unable to do anything but press her ass back against his hips when he seated himself inside her again. He untangled his hand from her hair to hold her hips steady as he continued to drive into her. Only now, when he flexed his hips forward, his retreat was not lazy like before, but swift and complete, and his return just as masterful. He pounded into her, over and over. And when his hands left her hips, she braced herself. Her entire body was aquiver with the strain of the unfulfilled climax that burgeoned inside her.

Suddenly, he spanked her, hard, on her backside, and she gasped. Her eyes flew to his searing gaze reflected back at her. He continued to thrust, and she watched as his open palm came up again, a foot from her stinging cheek, waiting.

"Please," she begged him, watching him, yearning for the surprise of the smack. And then he did it. Fast. A blur. "Yesss," she moaned. And another. And another. And then the warm, soothing pressure of his palm against her burning skin. His fingers reached around to brace her for his onslaught. The spanks had revved him, and she saw in their reflection that his control was unraveling.

All she wanted was for him to come inside her, to feel that wild pumping, knowing that seeing Bane undone would be enough to push her over the edge. She braced herself, concentrated on the feel of him sliding in and out, the teasing sensation of the starched fabric of his dress shirt on her skin. His hand on her ass, massaging in circles, closer to her...

Her head whipped up—she'd been wrong. He was still very much in control. He smiled as he plundered her with his cock, and then pressed his thumb gently against that other opening, sliding past, taking up the juices from where they were joined, then dragging back up and over and down again until her seam was slippery. She gasped at the pressure, groaned when he pushed in, just a little, invading and stretching, retreating as he had done before he had started the relentless flex of his hips. He pressed in a little more, smiling at her, pulling his thumb away, then making that tiny invasion again, over and over, in time with his thrusts.

His eyes shifted from her face to watch what he was doing, and Tally felt herself coil tight inside, like a spring winding and winding, until she was certain she would be sprung and useless. He pulled out. "Don't stop, Braeden. Please. I need... I need—"

He thrusted up into her again, bringing her to her toes once more. She was just able to press her forearms to the glass, and she turned her cheek to the cold surface, so opposite to the heat being generated in her body.

"*Ooh.* Right. There," she instructed, panting with each word.

"More?"

"Yes. Harder."

And then he plundered her in earnest. Her climax ripped through her, and she screamed. When her strength gave out, he lowered her to the thick rug, the wool abrasive and tantalizing against the bare skin of her breasts and stomach. Behind her, he positioned her legs, spreading them wide by hitching up one knee, and he entered her again, covering her entire body. He lifted up onto his hands, and pounded harder and harder into her, hips slapping against her ass. The exquisite tension built again until she fractured in a slow wave of clenching that took over her body. He stiffened, pressed deep inside, his hips spasming with each pulse of his orgasm. And then he collapsed in a heap on top of her, shuddering. They stayed that way, catching their breaths, until he slipped them into his bed. Tally used her gifts to cover them, removing his clothes along the way.

He mumbled something, sliding off her and spooning her from behind. Then his soft snore rustled the hair at her nape. The drag of exhaustion pulled her deeper into the pillow-top mattress, and soon, she was asleep as well.

• • •

He would kill whoever was calling him at this hour, Bane thought, nuzzling his face closer to Tally's neck. The buzzing continued, and he levered his eyes open. Across the room, his laptop sat open on his dresser. The screen was lit up, and message notifications were popping up in rapid succession, clamoring for his attention. In the other room, his phone beeped, then squealed. He shot up in bed.

He knew what that alarm meant, and though he hated doing it, he nudged Tally awake. She blinked up at him and smiled, and then she saw his expression.

"Something's happening," Bane said, striding across the room to his laptop. Detection alarms at Tally's home had been activated—someone had breached the warding. "Is Michelle still visiting her family in Florida?"

"Yes," Tally replied, getting up and going to the living room. "Only Dusty has been there, and you and I when we've slipped in to feed her."

Bane glanced at the clock. 4:11 a.m. He pulled on jeans and a T-shirt. Tally was clothed when he went to join her, and she tossed his phone to him. At the same moment, they looked up. Even from the height of Bane's penthouse, there was no mistaking the meaning of the intermittent red-and-blue strobing that washed faintly across the surface of the vaulted ceiling. Down below on the street, no less than four police cruisers were parked out front. Her phone rang as she held it, and she nearly dropped it in her surprise. She scrambled to flip it over and hit the accept button. "Barney?" she answered. "What's going on?"

Bane's phone pinged that he had another message.

"I'm putting you on speakerphone, Barney."

"Are you with Bane?"

"Yes."

"Good. Stay there. I've got patrol watching his six."

"What's going on?" Tally demanded again.

But Bane knew. He'd read the text alerts.

"Amy Sedge is missing. There was an attack on someone's home. A family by the name of Fortuna. One of yours. Their house was damaged. Looks like arson."

"I have to call Chris and Jackie," Tally said.

"Just stay put. Bane, don't let her out of your sight. I've gotta go."

Tally hung up and started dialing.

"They're safe," Bane assured her. "Chris just left me a message. But someone broke into Jackie's aunt's home."

"Was Tía Ixi hurt?"

He shook his head. "Angela was staying with her and got her out of the house and into the main family compound." She stared at the strobing red and blue below. "Tally, someone breached the protections on your house. I need to check it out. If it's the same people..."

"You're not going without me!"

"Of course not. We'll slip into the apartment above Nonna Lucia's, then use the alleys to get closer. Check out the perimeter. You're sure Michelle is away?"

She nodded. "I'm supposed to pick her up at Midway next Thursday."

"Grab your jacket," he said, and they slipped into the empty apartment. Bane led them out onto the back deck, then down into the dark alley. They skirted the dumpsters and city garbage cans with their rat-chewed plastic lids. Three buildings down, they squeezed through a narrow break between the brick buildings, a passage barely wide enough to fit his shoulders and running in the direction opposite of the park. He stopped at the end, looking up and down the street. Not even a street sweeper prowled the neighborhood. "I think we should approach from your alley," he whispered.

They kept out of the circles of light cast by the streetlamps, entering the alley behind her house from the end of the block. Slowly, they crept to her garage. Tally was about to open the gate when Bane stopped her. He held his finger to his lips, listening to the rustling noises coming from the garden. He entered the code to her gate and then eased it open. A dark shape darted out, and Tally squeaked. "Dusty!" she hissed. "You scared me to death."

Dusty poked his head from between two garbage bins and glared at them. Tally patted her thighs, and he streaked across the alley and jumped into her arms.

Bane pulled at the gate, and then their world was rent apart as the front of Tally's home exploded. He spun around and grabbed Tally, who somehow managed to keep hold of the hefty cat as the back of her house went next, taking the garage with it. He could feel the heat from the explosion even as they arrived in his penthouse, both of them slamming into the wall of his living room. Dusty flew from Tally's arms and streaked across the floor to hide under a table.

"Tally! You're hurt!" he yelled when he saw her blood-covered hands.

"It's not my blood," she shouted back. They whipped around to stare at Dusty, who crouched even farther away, hissing at them. As they drew closer, they saw that his fur was soaked with blood, but he otherwise appeared whole. Spitting angry, but undamaged.

Tally started for Michelle's cat just as Bane felt his legs give. He dropped to his knees with a great thud.

"Braeden!" She caught him as he pitched forward.

"My...back."

She guided him gently forward to his stomach. "Oh, sweetheart, you're all ripped up."

He couldn't argue. Literally couldn't.

"Hold on, baby. I've got you. Hold on."

He felt suddenly cold but relaxed in her arms and somehow managed to maintain consciousness. She'd willed his coat and shirt off him. They were a shredded, blood-soaked mess. No wonder he was cold. But then a wonderful warming sensation spread across his back. As the heat grew, a terrible itch began.

"You're doing great, Braeden. Just a little longer."

He gritted his teeth as the itch became unbearable, and just before he thought he couldn't take any more, even opened his mouth to beg her to stop, the pain and itch disappeared. He tried to sit up, but lacked the strength.

"Stay there," she urged, kneeling over his torso. "You lost a lot of blood. But our bond, your body is already replenishing itself. You should be...should be..." She fell back on her butt, her face ashen and her breath shallow. She shook her head at him when he tried to rise. "I just need a minute," she panted.

He was close enough to the sofa to be able to hook the throw with his fingers, and he drew it up, then pulled her down next to him. She turned and snuggled into him, his chest beating steadily against her back. Thanks to her, he was alive.

"I'm fine," he said, kissing her hair. "You just recover a few more minutes." In front of them, green eyes caught the light as Dusty stared out from under the furniture.

"He doesn't seem to be injured," Tally whispered. "I wonder whose blood is on him."

"I am *not* washing that beast," he said to amuse the love of his life, giving her just another moment before they would have to get up and deal with whatever was happening. Against his chest, her body quivered with a silent laugh. "Do you need to sleep?"

"No... I'm just a little woozy." She pushed herself up. Dusty, determining that they no longer posed a threat to his well-being, padded over to investigate them. "Turn around. Let me check your back."

He did as ordered and felt her hands run over his skin, wiping more decisively in one area under his shoulder blade. He stared at the floor next to his clothes. Blood-coated bits of glass, splinters of wood, and a long, jagged piece of metal lay discarded in a pile. "Fuck, that's a lot of shrapnel. How ripped up is my back?"

"It's beautiful. Good as new, but..."

"But what?"

"Uh, your tattoos are gone."

He got to his feet. "You don't think—" he started, drawing Tally up from the floor.

"I don't know." She turned around, shrugging out of her coat, then pulling up her shirt. If he hadn't known what to look for, he would've thought the dark shapes across her shoulders were tricks of light and shadow. Before his very eyes, the marks dissolved, leaving her back a canvas of flawless skin.

He ran his hand over her shoulder blades and down her spine and sighed with relief that she wasn't hurt. She'd suffered for what she took into herself when she'd healed him. Tally's phone rang, and she picked it up on the first tone, putting the device on speaker.

"Hello."

"Good. If you're answering, you're still safe. Where are you?"

"With Bane," she replied. "What's going on, Barney?"

"Tally, I don't know how to say this, but your house..."

"What about my house?"

"I'm sorry, Tally. There was another explosion." There was a pause on the line. "Can you tell me if Michelle was home?"

"She's still with her family in Florida." Bane gave her a questioning look, and she held her finger to her lips.

"Thank God for that."

"How bad is it?" she asked.

"It's bad. Your house... It's completely leveled. Look, I'm not dumb enough to tell you to stay put, but, please, stay with Bane or your brother. We'll talk tomorrow. I'm so sorry about your house."

"Thanks, Barney. Chris, Bane, Jackie, Michelle. We're all safe. That's what matters right now."

"Right. Like I said, stay with Bane."

"Night, Barney."

"You mean morning."

She hung up and stared at her phone.

"You didn't want him to know that you already knew about your house."

She looked down at Dusty, who was circling her legs. "No," she said, scooping the cat up into her arms and shoving him at Bane. The cat's hair was matted. "This blood isn't from me or you. And it's certainly not Dusty's."

"They must've found someone's remains in the rubble."

Tally nodded. "That was my guess as well. Barney was ruling out Michelle as a victim. I hope it wasn't Amy—the news would kill Orson."

"You know what else this means? Barney wants us to stay together—for alibis," Bane deduced.

"Probably," she said. "You two go get cleaned up in the shower. I'll take care of this mess."

"I'll make it quick," he said, indicating the cat. "We need to get over to Rosegate. Are you sure you're recovered? If I feel this good already, then you must have expended—"

"I'm good. I don't like that Chris hasn't called. It's not like him." She looked at the bloody detritus on the floor. "Go on, give Dusty a quick bath, then clean yourself up."

"I hate to lose the rug, but if there's a body at your house, we'll need to dispose of it. Maybe shave Dusty."

The cat started struggling but calmed when Tally soothed him.

"I don't think we'll have to go to such extremes," she promised the cat. "Go, Bane. I've got this mess." She put her hands on his shoulders and turned and pushed him in the direction of the bathroom.

Bane dropped Dusty on the tiled floor of the shower and then stripped to his boxers. After arranging a pile of towels on the floor, he joined the cat and turned on the hot water. Surprisingly, the damn beast walked right into the spray and waited expectantly. Tally's organic herbal shampoo had to be good for the cat—it was natural, Bane reasoned. Dusty started purring while he lathered up his fur. He grabbed the hand sprayer and rinsed off the cat. Bane opened the glass door, and Dusty walked out, wet tail held snootily aloft. He plopped onto the piled towels, rolled a bit, then settled in to lick his fur.

Bane was showered and dried a few minutes later. He pulled on fresh clothes and then carried a clean shirt out to Tally. His shredded clothes sat in a neat pile, folded, and blood-free. The rug and blanket were pristine. So were her clothes. "Wow."

Tally shrugged. "I just focused on removing the item from everything that wasn't part of its makeup. It's what I do when I whisk away what you're wearing." She smiled at him. "What've you got there?" Upon realizing that it was a change of clothes from his closet, her face fell.

"I thought you might need something to wear since..." He set down the bundle, crossed the room, and folded her into his arms. "You're thinking that everyone's safe and that's what's important, and that your things are just things. But they are and they aren't. I'm sorry, Tally."

"Everything I owned...my clothes and shoes. My furniture. Oh, no. Michelle's belongings!" She stopped, her hand flying to her mouth in horror. "My mom's video. It was in my safe. It's supposed to be fireproof, but the explosion... What if—"

"I'm sure it's just buried—we can get it back later. For now, we really should go."

She nodded, but didn't move. Below them, the Chicago River passed peacefully under the bridges, bringing water into the city from Lake

Michigan. Then, she sought out his hand and, together, they slipped to Rosegate.

The mansion was eerily quiet.

Chapter Twenty-five

It was dark in her brother's home office. Too dark. Not a single light was on. Not the printer or phone. "Even the smoke detector light is off," Tally whispered. "Did Chris answer your texts?"

"No. And the backup batteries should be working," Bane whispered back.

They crept forward, listening at the door before venturing into the hallway. Emergency lighting had been installed in the residential wing decades ago, and the low-profile baseboard lights should have been casting a blue LED aura onto the floor.

"As much as I hate to do it, we should check the bedroom first. I swear," she whispered, "if Chris and Jackie are sleeping or…let's just say I'm gonna kill him if I see too much." She let Bane lead the way. They slunk down the corridor to the stairs that would take them up to the bedroom level.

He turned toward the main suite. The door was ajar, and again, no lighting.

Buzz.

Chris and Jackie were not in bed. Nor were they in the room.

Buzz. Their phones were on the nightstand, muted and lighting up with texts and calls. "How are their phones still working?" she whispered.

"I set wards on them," Bane said in a hushed voice. "Chris and Jackie wouldn't have left them willingly." He cocked his head at a noise in the hall and put his finger to his lips. They waited behind the door, hidden by shadows. Across the room, reflected back at them in an antique full-length mirror, the light from someone's flashlight app illuminated the opening of the door. A large form slipped into the room. A man, nearly as tall as her brother, but much thicker around the middle, made a beeline to the nightstand where the phones glowed with yet another message. Bane stepped forward, and the man flipped around and was thrown against the wall, his feet dangling two feet from the floor.

Tally checked the hall—empty—and then closed the door. She picked up the man's phone from where it had landed when it had flown from his hand and shined its flashlight into his eyes. He squirmed, his body and limbs pinned to the polished cherry paneling. Bane held him there, spread eagle. The bright LED beam did nothing for Jean-Christophe Grossomm's already pallid complexion.

"Where's my brother?" she hissed at him, and he gave her a look meant to kill.

"If I let him talk, he'll yell and alert the others," Bane reasoned in a low voice. "Better that I put him somewhere safe where he can't cause more mischief." At this pronouncement, Jean-Christophe turned a dangerous shade of purple.

"Wait," Tally said, holding the phone up until facial recognition unlocked the screen. "How careless of you," she whispered to him.

When Bane stalked forward, Jean-Christophe started breathing heavily through his nose, shaking his head back and forth in rapid, but tiny, motions. And then, he and Bane were gone.

A moment later, Bane reappeared. "Anything on his phone?"

"Just a text to meet back in the kitchen. No name—I don't recognize the number. Looks like they're being careful. Wait..."—she opened a folder—"ew, he's into some nasty fetish porn." She handed the phone to Bane, and he tucked it into his pocket after adding his own fingerprint to the settings app. "So where did you send him?" she asked. "Nowhere too comfortable, I hope."

"Just a place the national order told me about. They'll hold him there until one of us reports in to explain the detainment. No questions; no rush. Well, maybe a few questions."

"Nice," Tally remarked, grinning. They grabbed Chris's and Jackie's phones. Powered them off. Then retraced their steps. The entire wing was deserted. They were about to head down the stairs when they heard a terrible boom, one that rattled the entire mansion.

"The dining room?"

Bane nodded. "Let's use the service corridor." They backtracked to the bedrooms. At the end of the long hall, Bane opened the linen closet, and they stepped in. He closed the door behind them, then pressed one of the interior panels. It gave a muted click, and they groped their way up the narrow stairs leading to the attics. There was no emergency lighting here, but the dull predawn light filtered through a grimy window at the end of the corridor. On either side of them, doors ranged, all of them shut.

These were the rooms where, generations past, the servants had slept. In Tally's parents' time, they were emptied of staff and used for storage. Several had been opened up for play areas, and one was set up as an artist's atelier. Chris had plans to convert them to guest rooms, updating the plumbing and electrical along the way. His staff, a husband-and-wife team named Corbett, managed the housekeepers and kitchen and grounds staff. They lived in one of the guest cottages on the far edge of the estate. Everyone else lived off-site.

At the end of the hall, they entered what was once the common room, one where the servants could relax and unwind. She followed Bane as he crossed the space to open another panel. They stepped through, then made their way down a circuitous corridor where the two wings of the estate were married, passing more areas where discarded antiques were stored. When they passed groupings of retro furniture from the sixties and seventies, Tally sighed with nostalgia. The attics had once been their personal playground. A fortress one day; a pirate ship the next...whatever their childhood imaginations desired.

They were above the ballroom's gallery now, and so had just enough light from the evenly spaced windows that they could make their way to the exit, which would put them above the kitchens. Passing by the chimney, Bane signaled her to stop, and they leaned closer to a vent in the brick wall. They both listened, knowing that if anyone was in the kitchen, their voices would funnel up the channel that housed the old dumbwaiter.

"That last blast should've got us in," a man complained. Tally thought she recognized the voice. "And now your father has disappeared."

"Get a grip. I sent him to retrieve their phones. How did they get the block up so quickly? Probably that stupid Silva bitch." Tally looked at Bane and mouthed, *Rene.*

"I might know another way."

"Why didn't you say so earlier? You," Rene shouted to someone, "go to the cottage and bring back the Corbetts. Maybe some leverage will entice them to drop the ballroom ward."

A door slammed, and everything went silent. Bane eased away, and Tally followed. "We need to hustle. Whoever was with Rene might know about the service corridors."

They sprinted down the passage leading to the upper gallery. Heading to the side that was on the same wall as the main entrance to the ballroom, they stopped at one of the panels. Bane opened it an inch and peered through. Chris and Jackie were on one side of the room, sheltered behind a large, upended table. "Call to him, Tally. Use your secret twin-thing and try to let him know we're here."

It was a kind of magic, one that everyone attributed to their unique connection. But Tally, Bane, and Chris had always known the truth, even before it was believed that she was non-Fascina: she'd always been able to tell if he was near, and vice versa. Chris looked around the room, then whispered something to Jackie. Tally tried again, and Bane opened the panel a little more to reveal their presence. The relief on her brother's face was palpable.

Bane tapped his watch, then held up two fingers. Chris nodded. Even Bane couldn't slip into the ballroom. The block Jackie had created was just too strong. They turned to leave, and the floor bucked below their feet. Three of the stained-glass panels cracked in their frames, but the lead was flexible enough to hold the art. She and Bane lurched sideways, then regained their feet and raced to the hidden stairs that only three people in the world knew about, stairs that would bypass the service corridor and take them directly into the ballroom.

As much as she wanted to burst in, she thanked the stars that Bane was with her and was more cautious. He slid the wood paneling aside. Her brother was suspended in midair. He flew backward and then crashed against the wall before slamming to the floor, unmoving. Jackie took up a defensive stance in front of him and was generating some sort of shield that kept Rene and his men from moving forward. Only by using explosives had they been able to breach the ward.

"Go help Chris," Bane urged, and then raced to cover Jackie's flank. Two of Rene's men went flying back. Rene screamed, enraged.

Tally ran to her brother. His face and chest were a mess of lacerations and burns. She fell to his side, checked for a pulse in the gore that had been his neck. "No, no, no, no," she cried. "Chris!" But she felt it—a void where she once sensed his soul. Her brother was gone. "NO!" she yelled once more, searching for Bane to help her. But he was with Jackie, creating a shield around them, one that was blocking the bullets being fired at them.

"No, Chris!" Tally yelled at her brother's slack face. "I won't let you leave me. Not now. I won't allow it. Do you hear me, Chris?" Twenty feet away, Jackie and Bane continued fighting to keep the others at bay, steadily forcing them from the ballroom. She had to try to bring Chris back. Had to. She couldn't allow her twin to die, no matter what it might cost her. She wiped away the tears blinding her. "You are not leaving us, do you hear me? Mom, Dad, if you're around, you kick his ass back here—" Tally choked, unable to accept that her brother was dead.

Then she laid hands on him, imagining waves of energy flowing from her heart, up her shoulders and down, past her elbows and into her wrists. Farther, until her hands swelled with a power that she could channel through each finger. She imagined her strength pulsing into him, undoing the damage that had been wrought. Pushing her grief aside, she willed another surge from her heart, this one faster, sending it directly to the matching organ in her brother's chest, using the wave to kick-start the organ.

"Don't you dare leave me, Chris! Come back. Now!" Again, she charged him with her energy, watching through tear-blurred vision as the burns and gashes began to heal. Again. She pushed more of her strength into him, and she suddenly understood that it was her own life force flowing into Chris. Again. And again, and when she thought she had none left to give, she zapped him once more and fell forward.

"Please, Chris. Please come back. I need you. Please," she sobbed, a strangled noise as her own blood oozed from the echo of her brother's neck wound. "Don't go..." she murmured, her cheek resting on his chest. And then his lungs inflated as her brother gasped for breath. In his chest, she heard the staggered beat of his heart, one that grew stronger and stronger.

Somewhere behind her, a scream of desperate rage echoed through the ballroom, then a brilliant flash of light, followed by silence. A moment later, she was pulled off her brother. She came away limply, unable to muster the strength to move her limbs. Even her neck betrayed her, making her unable to turn her head to see who cradled her in their arms. A warm hand touched her cheek, turning her face. Braeden.

Devastation wracked her soul. This was her sacrifice. She'd finally given too much. "I'm sorry," she tried to tell him, but her voice had abandoned her. She wanted to remain with him, but was unable to stop herself from letting go.

• • •

"Tally, stay with me. Tally!" Bane brushed her hair off her forehead. He caressed her cheek. Beside him, Jackie was kneeling next to Chris, who blinked, then turned to stare at his sister. Bane watched as the realization that she was hurt came into his eyes.

"Jackie, I'm fine," he croaked, trying to roll to his side. "Help Tally!" His shout woke her from her shock at seeing her blood-soaked fiancé breathing, and she scrambled away.

"Let her go, Bane"—he was rocking her against him—"I need to check her. Go, get Marc. She needs a doctor." Jackie pulled Tally from his arms, laying her flat. Then she searched for Tally's pulse. In his chest, Bane felt his heart cramp as if he were having a heart attack. Tally was gone. Their bond forced him to feel her departure. Jackie wouldn't find a pulse.

An indescribable rage filled him when she began performing CPR. He started yelling at her to stop, but Chris had staggered to his knees and tackled him back.

"I'm still too weak to slip," he yelled. "Pull yourself together. Bane!"

He couldn't process what his friend was shouting; he couldn't make sense of anything through the red haze of his wrath, and worse, the blackness of his grief.

"Damn it, Bane!" Chris reached back and clocked him in the jaw. It wasn't much of a punch, given his weakened state, but it was enough. The agonizing fog receded, and he realized that Jackie was still trying to revive Tally. Compressions; breaths. Compressions; breaths. All the while ridiculously humming what sounded like a Bee Gees' song. When a figure entered the ballroom from the main entrance, Chris threw up an arm, needing the physical motion to throw the intruder back and against the wall. Upon seeing Orson, he let him drop.

"Bane, go get Marc. Tally needs a doctor," Jackie ordered.

But they didn't realize...he couldn't leave her, not if she was to have any chance at all. He shook his head. "I can help her more if I stay. Orson—"

"We can't find Amy," Orson lamented. "Have you seen her? There've been attacks, and... I came here to... But why is she here?" Orson asked, pointing at Tally.

Bane tossed a cell phone to Chris. "Marc's not answering. Chris, keep calling him." To Orson, "Slip to Dr. Changara's and tell him to come right away."

"But I can't just slip into someone's home. It's against—"

Bane scowled at him, positioning himself near Tally's head. "Chris?" he pleaded to Tally's brother who was just ending a call.

"I got through, Mark's on his way. Can you drop the warding, Jackie?"

"Let me," Bane said, gently nudging Jackie away so she could do as Chris asked. He took over the compressions, willing his strength into Tally's heart with each downward push.

"Are you a healer?" Jackie asked, after Chris and Orson had stepped a few feet away.

"I'm not, but you needed a break." He didn't have Tally's gift, but maybe some of her power transferred to him after the bonding.

"We're going to check on Rene and his men," Chris called back. "Make sure they can't cause any more damage."

"Bane, I know you love each other," Jackie whispered when Chris and Orson left the ballroom. "Talk to her. Call to her. Tell her to come back."

Bane didn't know if he could. He was too angry. At the realization, he let Jackie take over again. He leaned over Tally, kissed her forehead, her lips. Their broken bond made his anger spike, blaming her. She'd left him. He shook himself. He had to let go of his rage, so he kissed her again, then pressed his forehead to hers and began whispering to her, near-silently, so that Jackie couldn't hear. "You can't leave, Tally. Come back to me. I know you're around here somewhere. If you don't come back, I'm going to be so pissed at you." He pressed his cheek against hers and murmured in her ear. "I love you, Tally. Come back to me."

He lifted away and stared helplessly at Jackie.

She paused her compressions to check for a pulse, then immediately recommenced. "I'm not giving up on her and neither should you," she told Bane as Chris returned with Marc in tow. Marc raced across the ballroom, issuing orders.

"How many minutes?" he demanded, breaking out his portable defibrillator and attaching a sensor to her fingertip. He cut open her shirt, then peeled the backing off two pads and applied them to her chest and to her side.

"Fifteen at most," Bane replied.

"How many without compressions?"

"No more than one or two," Jackie answered, sounding out of breath.

"Bane, take over for Jackie after I check for a pulse," Marc ordered after staring at the red light on the defibrillator.

"Why aren't you shocking her?" Chris demanded.

"Because without a rhythm, there's nothing to shock," he said in a clinical voice. "Keep up the compressions, Bane." He grabbed a manual resuscitator and put it over Tally's face, showing Jackie how to squeeze it. "Chris, talk to her."

Tally's brother took up the spot where Bane had been, and then started calling to her, begging her to come back, threatening her, ordering her, then pleading again. It was all Bane could do to not smash his face in. The only reason Chris was alive was because Tally had healed him. And now she was dead. Bane gritted his teeth. He knew his emotions were getting the best of him because of the bonding, so he wrestled down his rage and tried to remember what Tally had once told him about how she healed. Something to do with her heart and her hands.

"I need to check for a pulse again." Jackie stopped squeezing, and Bane halted his compressions. He laid his hands flat over her sternum, closed his eyes, and focused inward. He tried imagining strength from his heart bunching up into a ball, forcing it to follow his arteries and nerves, believing that he could sense the energy traveling down his arm to his hand where his palm rested. He opened his eyes. Marc was preparing an epi.

Bane did it again. And again.

Marc held the syringe, the tip poised above Tally's heart. "This might not... I have to try."

Bane didn't take his hands away.

"You have to move."

Chris reached over to force Bane away, and they all heard a ping. The light on the defibrillator had turned green.

"Rhythm!" Marc shouted. "Bane, get out of the way, or I'll shock you along with Tally and leave you to recover on your own."

This time, Bane moved. "All clear," Marc shouted. He hit the button, and Tally's body bowed. On the machine, the heart monitor registered her heartbeat. After checking Tally's pulse at her neck, Marc nodded. "It's weak, but she's back." Outside, the wail of an ambulance pierced the dawn.

"I can get her to the hospital faster," Bane said.

"But we don't know what that will do to her heart in its current state. I'm afraid the slower route is safer." The Corbetts arrived, leading the EMTs. Marc surveyed the damage to the ballroom. "It looks like you and Chris have other things you need to settle here first. Besides, the paramedics know what they're doing."

"The last time she went in an ambulance..."

"I'll go with her, Bane," Jackie offered. "You can meet us there. Marc is right." She was already on a backboard, and an oxygen mask covered her beautiful face. "You and Chris need to take care of our guests, first. They might be unconscious now, but they'll—"

"I got it," he snapped, knowing she was right. He didn't want to be away from Tally, not when she needed his strength. "Fifteen minutes," he said, "or I'm joining you in the ambulance and I don't care who sees me do it." He followed as the gurney was rolled out of the ballroom. Chris stayed behind with a shaken Orson.

They loaded Tally into the ambulance as Jackie and Marc came out—she would ride up front and Marc in the back. Bane leaned down to kiss Tally's forehead. "I'll be with you soon," he whispered. "Hold on for me. I love you, Tally." With the lights on and sirens silent in the quiet, traffic-free streets, the rig was away. Bane turned on his heel and returned to Chris in the ballroom. There, he met the Corbetts.

"He went to his suite," Mrs. Corbett explained, wringing her hands with worry. "To get out of his pajamas and to grab a change of clothes for Jackie. He said to meet him there."

"Thanks," Bane said.

"Son, Tally is strong, and she'll pull through." Mr. Corbett stated.

Bane nodded and was about to slip away when he noticed that the lights at the mansion were on again. "The power—"

"I was on my way to the utility room when it came back on," Mr. Corbett said. "We'll have this cleaned up before you kids return."

"Be careful. We overheard them sending someone to your cottage."

"They never made it, and we didn't see anyone on the grounds. Likely, they heard the explosion and took off."

"Did you see anyone, Orson?" Bane asked, realizing the man was still there.

"No," he said a little too sharply. "I didn't see anyone. Why was Tally here? Aren't you supposed to protect her? Aren't you supposed to protect Chris?"

"Orson..." Bane started forward. The man was distraught.

"I have to find my daughter," he said, then slipped away.

"We'll do a thorough search of the grounds," Mr. Corbett promised.

"Just...be careful," Bane stated.

Mrs. Corbett crossed over to him and gave him a hug, patting him on the back. "You, too, dear. We love all of you kids. You boys bring our Tally home."

Bane slipped away before they saw the shine in his eyes. He found Chris in his office, a duffel bag in one hand. "We should talk before we go. There might be trouble."

"What happened to Rene and his men, Bane? Orson and I searched for them but couldn't find anyone."

"I'm not one hundred percent sure," Bane admitted. "I took Jean-Christophe to the N.O.F.'s holding facility. I think I sent Rene and the others there as well."

"You think?"

"I must have." His phone vibrated, and he scrolled through the notifications. "They made it there intact."

"Barney called—the phone woke us. We never had a chance to talk to him. Seconds later, the power went out. Rene's men barged into the bedroom, and there was just enough time to slip into the ballroom and strengthen the warding."

"Tally's house is gone," Bane said. "Blown to smithereens."

"She'll be devastated when she finds out."

"She knows," Bane divulged. "We were in the alley when it happened."

"Damn," Chris swore.

"There's more... We think the police found a body."

"Amy's?"

"Not sure."

"It will kill Orson if it is."

"There were other attacks tonight," Bane added. "The Fortunas. And Jackie's aunt. I texted her cousin, and everyone is safe."

Police sirens sounded in the distance. "Time to go," Chris said, and they slipped into Tally's office at the hospital. It was still too early for the administrative staff to be on duty, so no one saw them as they entered the reception area and made their way to the Emergency Room. Bane's insides were rioting, and when Chris's phone dinged, he nearly jumped out of his skin.

"Jackie says that they bypassed the ER. She stabilized in the ambulance, and Marc took her directly to one of the recovery suites. He punched the button on the elevator that would take them to the ninth floor. They've got her in one of the private VIP rooms."

"They should. We've given enough money to this place to at least be given that much courtesy." Shit, he was growing angrier. He needed to tamp it down. And fast.

"You okay?"

"Yeah. But I'm going to make them pay."

"Not without my help," Chris swore, and Bane gave him a curt nod.

Jackie was standing in the hall, waiting for them, and they entered the expansive suite together. Marc was there, as were the heads of neurology and cardiology, reviewing an EEG. "...normal activity, thank God."

"ECG is good. She has a strong heart."

"It was close," Marc explained, turning to them. "But she'll pull through. She's got some cracked ribs from the compressions, but that's to be expected. She needs rest right now, and will wake when her body is ready."

Bane stared at her pale face. She looked so tiny and vulnerable. Sensors were taped to her temples, and more wires and leads came from under the collar of her hospital gown, connecting her to more machines than Bane knew existed. A male nurse stood next to her bed, gently sponging away the dried blood on her neck and chest. His ID tag read Joseph Garban. Bane stared at the IV drip.

"Just fluids," Marc explained. "It's amazing, but other than Tally being unconscious, we might not even have known her heart had stopped." The other doctors nodded, gave some assurances to Chris, then excused themselves. "I'll be back in an hour to check on her."

The nurse finished adjusting the oxygen that flowed from the nasal cannula. "Ms. Waever is a fighter," he assured them.

Chris looked up at him. "Is your family safe, Joseph?" he asked. "Others were attacked this morning."

"They're fine, Mr. Waever. We're not powerful enough to be targets." He pulled up a blanket to cover Tally. "You all let me know if you need anything." Bane nodded to him as he stepped quietly out of the room.

Jackie urged Chris to sit on the loveseat, and he wrapped his arm around her shoulder. Bane took the chair nearer to the hospital bed. They were all silent, each praying in their own way for her to pull through. Then it was time to check their phones and begin giving assurances to those who needed them. Chris sent a blanket email to the Chicago Order's listserv, assuring everyone that Waever leadership remained strong. Then they all muted their devices. Marc came in again, as promised, but there was no change.

Barney barged in at one point, his face haggard. He told them to be ready for interviews the next day, giving them that much time, at least. The morning stretched into afternoon, and Bane refused to leave Tally's side. Chris ran out for coffee, and Jackie departed, seeking assurance that her family was safe the only way that would satisfy her, by seeing them healthy and hale in person. She returned with food from her mom and aunts and forced Bane to eat.

Bane finally convinced Chris and Jackie to go back to Rosegate and check on the Corbetts. He remained, sitting vigil over Tally, softly talking to her. At one point, he got up to wash his face in the en suite. When he came out of the bathroom, Orson was sitting by Tally's side. Bane immediately checked the monitors, the IV. He didn't trust anyone at this point, not even Orson. The man looked lost.

"Did you find Amy?" Bane asked.

Orson leaned forward and buried his face in his hands. His shoulders began to shake, but Bane didn't have it in him to console him, not with Tally lying there unconscious. Then he lifted his head—he'd been laughing, if one could call it that.

"Amy made a break for it. She texted us and said we couldn't force her to marry someone she didn't love. We think she's somewhere in the south of France."

"Amy was engaged?" Bane asked.

"Twice. Doesn't matter. It's all gone to hell." He stood and then placed one hand on Tally's forehead and one on her body before leaning down to whisper something in her ear. He shot up straight, as if shocked, and glared at Bane. The monitors hooked up to Tally screeched.

"What did you do to her?" Bane demanded.

"It doesn't concern you."

But Bane wasn't having it and stepped menacingly into Orson's space. To his credit, the man didn't cower. Then Tally's vitals settled back to normal. "Forgive me. I'm just—"

"Feeling guilty for bringing harm to her?" Orson hissed. "Well, you should. And I was only wishing her peace when she wakes. Now, if you'll excuse me."

Orson walked out of the room, leaving Bane to wonder after his strange behavior. His phone vibrated, and he answered Chris's text.

> She's still out. How's Rosegate?

> *Nothing that can't be fixed. Tally's house tho…*

Bane didn't text back. There was nothing he could say.

> *Barney's here. I won't be back til 4. Need anything?*

> I'm good. Orson showed up. Amy "was" engaged.

> ?

> I know

Barney says she's still missing

Tell him Orson said she's fine. She finally escaped

Later then

Ditto

His phone battery had less than five percent.

Bring a charger

K

"Hey, Tally," he whispered, kissing her cheek. "I'm here. Take all the time you need. Just come back." The monitors beeped steadily. "But I'm not going to lie…sooner would be better, love." He pulled the chair closer to the bed and took her hand in his. Before long, he nodded off, dreaming of them together. Then of the cat, Dusty. The damned animal was covered in blood again and yowling at him.

Bane shot up from the chair when Joseph burst into the room. Alarms were blaring. He pushed the chair back and got out of the way as Marc rushed in.

"It's not her heart," Joseph stated, sounding perplexed, drawing back the blanket to check her leads. The sheets under Tally were red with blood.

"Get out, Bane," Marc ordered. "Now!" Joseph pushed him toward the door. He went as far as the opposite wall, but refused to leave the room. "Call OB, Joseph."

The nurse gave up trying to get Bane out and picked up the phone. Minutes later, a doctor he'd never met entered. She took over.

Bane grew sick. Tally would never have expended herself to heal her brother had she known. His mind went numb.

When it was over, and Tally was cleaned up, her bed linens changed, and her monitors humming happily along as if nothing had happened, Bane realized that he was alone with Marc. His friend took him by the arm and led him to the couch. He felt too big for it. Too big for the room.

"Yours?" Marc asked, and he nodded. "You obviously didn't know."

"I don't think Tally did either," Bane mumbled. "She would never have...even for Chris...she wouldn't have."

"I don't know how Chris factors into this, but I do know what can happen if our laws about Fascina and non-Fascina are ignored. And I know that if it were discovered that you and Tally...she could be forced to have a hysterectomy."

Bane stood. "Hang on. You think I would let that happen?"

Marc stared at him.

"You don't understand. She..." Even now, he had to hide her true nature.

"I guessed a long time ago that Tally was in love with you—she would subject herself to that for you without hesitation." He glanced at the door. "Dr. Mazery is a close friend. And I think you know that you can trust Joseph. This won't be put on her chart. They love Tally. She's one of us."

"Thank you."

"I didn't do it for you." He scowled at Bane, then left.

"I love her, Marc," Bane said to an empty room. He collapsed back in the chair. "I love you, Tally." And still, she lay there. For the second time since the attack, his heart broke.

Jackie and Chris returned. Jackie forced him to eat, and Chris tried to get him to take a break.

Ignoring Chris, Bane suddenly realized something... Fewer than a dozen people knew how to find Tally's house, and a third of them were in this room. He started thinking again, and the running of scenarios through his mind helped to ease some of the rage that simmered under the surface.

"I don't care," Chris was saying, "you're going home tomorrow. You can shower and change and come back, but you're leaving this room. Even if it's only for an hour. You still have blood on you, for God's sake." His friend shoved a duffle bag at him. "Sweats and a clean shirt. And socks and sneakers, though my shoes might be too big for you. Some toiletries. Get changed. You're starting to smell."

Bane shoved the duffel back at him. "Don't tell me what to do. You're not my boss."

Chris threw the bag back. "What is with you?"

"Nothing. You're the one acting like an ass."

"Bullshit. One second, you're all concerned; the next, you're biting someone's head off."

"Guys," Jackie interrupted.

Bane bit back his retort, knowing that neither Jackie nor Chris were at fault. He was. He'd seen the signs, the unrest amongst the council members.

He was just so distracted by... "Fuck!" It was entirely his fault. If he'd just done his job protecting her. "Just go!"

"I am not leaving my sister," Chris yelled. "Have you completely lost it?"

"Don't you get it, Chris? I'm to bl—"

"Guys!" They both turned to Jackie. She gestured to Tally.

"Just stop fighting already," Tally grumbled sleepily.

Jackie shuffled back as Bane and Chris jostled each other to see who could get to her bedside faster. "I'll get Marc," she said, and went to the nurses' desk.

"Hey, Talz. You gave us quite a scare," Chris said, taking her hand. "Please don't do that again. I love you too much to lose you."

"Me, too," she said, her voice quiet. She turned to acknowledge Bane when he smoothed her hair back. "Love you too, Bane."

He pulled his hand away and averted his eyes from her face. She'd promised him that she'd never call him Bane when telling him she loved him. Marc entered the room, and Bane strode over to him, blocking him from Tally and Chris. "Something's wrong," he whispered. "Don't tell her about earlier. Not yet."

"I can't withhold—"

"Please, Marc, just examine her first."

Marc shouldered Bane out of the way to get to Tally's bedside. "Good to see you awake, my friend." He began the process of checking her vitals, shining a light in her eyes, having her track his finger, then making her wiggle her fingers and toes.

"How did I get here?" Tally asked.

"In an ambulance," Jackie blurted. "Marc and I rode with you. We wouldn't let you go alone. Not after last time." Tally frowned at her.

"I meant, what happened? Why am I in the hospital?"

Marc nodded to Bane. "Rosegate was attacked," Bane started. "You got caught in the crossfire."

"Your heart stopped," Marc said. "If it hadn't been for Jackie and Bane here, we wouldn't be talking right now."

"Jacqueline?" Tally asked, sounding incredulous.

"Anything for my future sister-in-law. You'd do the same for me." The crease on Tally's brow deepened as she watched her brother put his arm around Jackie's waist and pull her close.

"How are you feeling?" Marc asked. "Any pain?"

"Not really. Tired." Her hand slid to cover her abdomen, and Bane's chest clenched. She frowned as if trying to put something together and flicked her gaze to Bane. "Bit of a headache."

"We're almost done," Marc said. "Just one more question, and you can rest. Tell me, Tally, what's the last thing you remember?"

Bane caught Chris's eye, and he shook his head. They waited. "Uh," she pressed her fingers to her temples. "I...I was dancing, at the gala. Something happened to my dress. I can't seem to remember the rest."

"Don't let it worry you. It'll come back with time and rest," Marc promised.

"It ripped," Tally went on. "Bane helped me to...to..."

"Cover you up...with my jacket," Bane said, taking her hand. "Marc is right. You need to rest now." At his touch, she seemed to relax, but the confusion still lit her eyes.

"We'll give you something to help your headache, Tally," Marc promised. While he gave the instructions to Joseph, Chris and Jackie went into the hall. For the first time in two days, Bane stepped out of the room.

"...didn't understand why I was with you," Jackie was saying to Chris. "Bane, I don't think she knows Chris and I are engaged."

Marc joined them. "She's sleeping now."

"What's going on with my sister?"

"Retrograde amnesia," Marc explained, looking puzzled. "She doesn't have a concussion, she didn't suffer a seizure, nor has she been ill. What happened to her?" When no one replied, he swore. "Look, I can't help her if I don't know why her heart stopped."

Only Bane had the answer, and he was still in shock that she had taken things so far.

Marc shook his head in frustration. "Don't push her. She needs rest."

Bane swallowed, not wanting to ask the question that seared itself across his heart.

Chris asked instead. "Will she get her memories back? A lot has happened since that day. The car crash, the attack..." Chris seemed to have realized that he was saying things that probably shouldn't be said in mixed company, and he trailed off.

"I don't know," Marc said, then leveled his gaze at Bane. "But you should avoid talking about traumatic events with her until she does, or until she's stronger." Chris and Jackie continued to chat with Marc, and Bane headed back into the suite. He fell onto the couch and stared at Tally's sleeping face. She remembered nothing about what had happened between them.

Not even the love they shared. What would this do to her, to them, now that they were bound to one another? He leaned forward and buried his face in his hands. A few minutes passed when someone's hand rested on his shoulder.

Jackie sat on the couch next to him. "She'll remember, Bane. And even if she doesn't, she'll just fall in love with you all over again. What's in a person's heart doesn't disappear because their brain can't remember."

Bane could only hope.

The bonding was a symbiotic relationship in the purest sense. A codependency. That which would hurt her would eventually hurt him, and vice versa. And the more they were apart, the more their love remained unrequited, the angrier they would become.

Chris came in. "Seriously, Bane. You look like shit. If you won't go home, at least get some sleep here. That couch unfolds, you know."

He checked his watch, wondering where the time had gone. It was already after five. There was a soft rap on the door, and they all turned to see Michelle, Frank, and Kathy in the doorway. Michelle had flowers, and the Carilios were carrying various bags from Nonna Lucia's.

Bane went out into the hall to talk to them. He assured them that Tally was going to be fine, that she was sleeping. Then he suddenly remembered that Michelle was homeless. "Oh, I'm sorry. Tally will be so mad that I didn't think about where you can stay or—"

She handed him the flowers. "It's been taken care of," she assured him. "Jackie got my number from Chris. She had a car pick me up at the airport, and I'm staying in the apartment above the restaurant. Frank and Kathy are taking good care of me."

Despite her words to the contrary, Michelle looked like she was about to burst into tears. "Look, the apartment is yours for as long as you need. Rent free. And Tally has insurance. I know it can't replace your personal things, but you won't have to start over."

"It's not that," she said, swallowing and looking away. "Never mind. You take care of Tally, that's what's import—"

"Dusty!" he cut in. "We have Dusty! He's probably hungry. Hang on." He went inside the suite, gave the flowers to Jackie, then slipped to his place. A very hangry-looking cat was sitting on his kitchen counter. Bane didn't want to think about where Dusty had done his business. He just scooped the beast into his arms and returned to the hospital, coming back together in the en suite. Chris and Jackie gaped at him as he left Tally's room, carrying the enormous feline.

"Dusty!" Michelle cried, hugging the cat to her chest.

A nurse walked by and did a double take. "They're leaving," Bane intercepted. "I promise."

"Two minutes," she warned, then walked away at a brisk clip.

"Thank you, Bane. And give Tally our love."

Frank handed over the takeout bags. They hugged it out—something that was normally way outside Bane's comfort zone, but he found it strangely fortifying. Promising to check in again, the trio, plus Dusty, departed. He quickly reentered Tally's room and found that Chris had pulled a small, round table over to the couch and had moved the chair over.

Jackie took the bags and proceeded to set the table with the utensils, napkins, and plates. "Salad, entrées, and dessert. The soup must be for Tally." They turned when they heard Tally sigh and mumble something. "What did she say?"

Bane smiled for the first time in days. "To save a cannoli for her."

Chapter Twenty-six

Bane cocked his head hard to the left, then the right, trying without success to pop the knots in his neck. He was exhausted, as his best friend had just so unkindly pointed out. Again.

"—not doing anyone any good burning the candle the way you are. Is Janine asking anyone else for the same time commitment as you?"

"If you're worried that I'm not pulling my weight here in Chicago..." Bane let the words hang, hoping Chris would take the bait. He was itching for a fight. But Chris crossed his arms and smirked at him. "What?" Bane demanded.

"If you need a punching bag, you have several in your workout room."

Some of his tension released, and Bane finally sat, slumping in the chair across from where Chris waited. "Sorry. I'm just tired."

"Then tell her no, Bane."

"It's not that simple." Maybe he should tell his friend about Tally and the bonding. Or how Janine had him well and good by the balls. Not only was she holding his mother's welfare over Bane to get what she wanted, she'd threatened to out Tally to the C.O.F. It was blackmail, pure and simple. And Bane had no choice but to fall in line. To do so, without killing Tally and himself, he needed to do the near-impossible—break their bond.

He'd found some old writings about the three stages, that it was achievable, and only if the couple was newly bonded. But one had to go cold turkey. Anything less than fully committed would be devastating to Tally. To him.

If he was two thousand miles away, Tally could move on with her life. As could he. And who knew? Maybe one day they would find their way back to one another. She might get her memory back. Then they could tell Chris about everything. And he could figure out how to help his mother and tell Janine to fuck off once and for all.

He had managed to avoid Tally enough to know that she was better off than he. In the meantime, he would figure out what Janine had on his mother, and then clean up another one of his parents' messes.

"What a nightmare," Bane mumbled to himself. His phone buzzed, and he ignored it.

"Seriously," Chris started, "between your bad mood and Tally's—"

"What about Tally?" Bane interrupted.

"Yeah, Chris," came an annoyed voice from behind him, one that made Bane's gut clench, his heart ache, and his brain fire up all his synapses at once. "What about me?"

"No way," Chris said. "I am not refereeing here. Ever since Tally got hurt, you've been acting like assholes to each other." Chris stared pointedly at Bane, and he got the sense that his friend was laying most of the blame at his feet.

Bane's phone buzzed again. He still hadn't looked at her. He couldn't. He had to get away...immediately. "Shit. It's Janine again." Call him a coward, but he slipped away before Tally could walk into the room.

• • •

It was truly gone. Tally stared at the rubble that used to be her home. Even the garage. The only thing that had been recovered was her fireproof safe.

Chris had explained to her that the Grossomms had tried to take over the Chicago Order and oust her brother. No wonder her brain didn't want to remember.

Tally couldn't believe that the gala had been more than two months ago. And that she'd been injured in two separate attacks. "Three, if the night in the park is to be counted," she grumbled. But she'd talked to Barney, and he assured her that the stories weren't some elaborate ruse on her brother's part. It gave her a headache trying to remember. Chris and Bane—especially Bane—were hiding things from her. There was more to the story than some unsanctioned government plot to force Chicago's Fascina community into the registry.

Chicago was safe, for now. Bane had assured her of this in a brief moment when he'd deigned to talk to her. The National Order was finally giving their city, and others like it, its support. She hadn't been at all surprised when he revealed that he was now part of the N.O.F. He more than deserved the position.

So why was she so angry at him? At everyone?

After she was released from the hospital, she had assumed that she would move back to Rosegate. The place was big enough that she wouldn't be in the way—Chris and Jackie's engagement was a whole other issue that she needed to wrap her head around. But Chris had suggested that she continue to stay at Bane's place since some of her things were there already.

She sat on the park bench across from the double-lot that had once been her heart's work and tucked her chin deeper into the zipped-up collar of her coat. A brisk wind whipped through the city, a precursor to an early winter, and even the oak trees were losing their leaves in violent whirlwinds. She watched as that wind kicked up some of the ashes of what was once her beautiful garden. To her left and right and, she knew, somewhere at a discreet distance behind her, was the three-person detail appointed as her personal bodyguards. Again, Bane.

She shook her head. She had been staying at Bane's place. Much of her fall wardrobe was there. But her winter clothes were all gone—incinerated. The coat she wore was new, a gift from Jackie. Her makeup, toiletries, hair stuff, even her laptop and chargers were at Bane's. There was no doubt that she had been his guest. But when she went into the guest room, she got a weird sense that it hadn't been slept in. Bane and Chris did their best to explain why she was there and not in her own home. But there was more. She felt it in her gut. And when she pressed them, they finally revealed that one unresolved problem—a stalker.

Stalker, murders, coups, explosions, amnesia. No wonder she was so pissed.

She'd been able to remember that there was a murderer on the loose in Chicago. Orson had been the one to fill her in, purposely gliding over most of the gruesome details and admitting that the task force was at an impasse. He even went so far as suggesting that they reverify everyone's alibis, no matter the consequences, starting with the task force, Chris, and, of course, Bane. The latter he'd said as if it burned his tongue to say it, leaving Tally to wonder what Bane had done to anger the man. Was it related to why she was so pissed at him as well? Some residual emotion tied to a falling-out between friends?

So many damn unanswered questions.

A fierce whirlwind of ash and debris kicked up across the street.

Her brother and Bane insisted that she not go out alone because of her so-called stalker—it was hard to swallow. But then there was Bane—on a videochat, of course, because God forbid he ever be in the same room with her—showing her the mal de nuit rose. Chris and Bane had told her that the police had found a body in the ruins of her home. No way of knowing if it was related to her stalker, the attack, or even the killer. Or all three. It was unbelievable how messed up everything had become. But Barney had confirmed it—an unidentified woman, reduced to ash and charred bone fragments.

Fragments like her memory.

Tally watched as a couple walking their dog stopped to stare at the ruins. Their lab squatted and did his business next to the chain-link fencing that had been erected around the lot to keep people from getting hurt in the debris pile—the police tape had been removed a week ago. The couple didn't bother picking up after the lab. Who cared about a pile of dog crap next to the pile of shit that had once been her home?

Another, larger dust devil formed in the wasteland of her yard, heading toward the fence and the couple.

Tally felt the anger, her constant companion of late, rise up, and she tamped it down to a manageable level. It was by her side when she ate, showered, and dressed. It kept her company, nestled next to her heart while she slept, and rampaged in her dreams. She'd taken it out on the speed bag in Bane's home gym. And once, when she was alone and the rage threatened to consume her, she worked out on the heavy bag. After an hour, it had looked no worse for wear, pissing her off like nothing ever had in her life. She'd screamed at it, focusing an acute stream of rage at where it hung. And it had exploded. Tally had stood there, staring at the destruction, relishing the power she had unleashed. But the euphoria she had felt was short-lived, and she'd crashed.

She narrowed her eyes at the empty lot. At the neighboring house. Could she demolish it, like she had done to the bag?

She'd destroyed Bane's workout equipment only two days ago—though it felt like an eternity had passed. Bane had returned to his home, and found her curled up in a ball on his gym floor. He whispered her name, as if saying it caused him pain. She couldn't answer—she was near to catatonic. He sat next to her in the debris of ripped leather, grains, and bits of cloth that had once been the punching bag, heedless of his expensive, hand-tailored suit. He set his hand on her shoulder—a light touch only, and just enough to bring her back.

That was when he admitted that he knew that she was Fascina, and that she could heal, and more. Then he told her about the night that her home had been destroyed. How they had been there, in the alley, and how she had healed him afterward. Had cleaned the blood from his home. She closed her eyes, absorbing his words, unable to speak as he explained that it had been her brother who had died that night, and that she had been the one to bring him back, almost at the expense of her own life. Throughout his discourse, she sensed an underlying rage in his words and felt the echo of it in her heart. Her constant companion, loyal animal that it was, imbuing her with its strength.

Bane had continued a bit longer, explaining that no one else knew that which she had shared with him—the codicil to her mother's will. And near the end, when he removed the hand that had rested on her shoulder, she'd had an inexplicable urge to, and there was no other way to describe it, fuck him senseless. The sensation had left her shaking inside, weak in the knees, and that fact pissed her off more. Even now, sitting here in the cold, that shimmer of heat reared up again—it was a not unwelcome sensation. She barked a harsh laugh, and the couple with their Labrador sporting its cute pink bandana, seeing her watching them, hurried away without a visible speck of remorse for not cleaning up after their dog.

Tally looked inward, coaxing her wrathful friend back to a gentle simmer in the recesses of her heart. She might not remember the last months, but the fact that she had secretly loved Bane for years was something she could never forget. She had always believed that they could never be together, not when everyone believed her to be a non-Fascina. But now, he knew it had all been a lie, an intricate cover-up perpetrated by her mother. And he was rejecting her; it was the only explanation for his avoidance. Well, to hell with him and his brotherly love.

That day in his gym, when he had finished his story, they rose to their feet and, for a moment, he had held her by her arms before him. He'd pulled her closer, scowling, his face inches from hers. Then, he'd let her go and hurried to leave the room, almost as if he couldn't wait to put some distance between them. Just before he walked out the door, she gave him a lame apology for destroying his punching bag and making a mess of his gym. He had turned and shrugged, casual-like, then told her it was an easy enough trick for her to clean it up. Thanks to her memory loss, Bane knew about things she could do, things she didn't even realize herself. And more, she sensed.

At the time, Tally would've bet the family jewels that, despite his nonchalance, his parting gaze was filled with the same hunger that growled in her core. He had definitely almost kissed her before pulling away and telling her he was needed in San Francisco. He'd disappeared in front of her, and she had reached out as what made him Bane had faded before her. Her fingertips, for one brief second, not even, had slipped with him. The simultaneous pleasure and pain she'd felt had been acute.

Only one thing in the rubble still stood—the remains of the chimney stack, or about eight feet of it anyway. She thought of her brother and how he tiptoed around her and let the anger in her heart spark. The sad looks cast her way from Jackie added some much-needed fuel. Throw in the well-meaning, but increasingly unwanted, sympathy from Orson, and the furnace raged hot. She saved Bane for last and let her explosive thoughts find their target. Across the street, there was a loud crack, and the rest of the chimney crumbled to the ground. Yes, she could destroy, but with precision. The dust settled in less than a minute. No fuss, no muss. A cold and satisfied smile stole across her face.

Tally glanced at her phone. Scrolled to her last text message from Chris saying that Bane would be returning to Chicago at the end of the week. It was Friday, and he hadn't called or texted. Even if he wasn't interested in her, he didn't need to be so rude—they'd been friends for decades. She was determined to find out if she'd said or done something to offend him. Something she couldn't remember.

She got up, and her detail moved closer. "Ready to go, ma'am?" Clarice asked. Tally cringed at the address. She'd asked twice for the guards to call her by her first name, but they'd smiled politely and declined. She walked to the dark SUV that waited at the curb, missing her little A4 as she stared at the spot where it had been parked in what had once been a garage. "I don't suppose you would let me drive, Benjamin?"

"Good one, ma'am," he replied, climbing into the driver's seat while Dana opened the back door for her before walking around the vehicle to sit shotgun. Clarice slid into the seat next to her.

It was just as well, for she had so little energy. And as the Suburban pulled away from the curb, Tally made one request. "Can you loop around to the alley?"

"Certainly, ma'am," Benjamin replied. They didn't know that she was saying goodbye to the place she had so lovingly renovated. Or maybe they did, for when Benjamin turned down the alley, he slowed to a crawl and stopped so that she could survey the destruction one last time. Through the high, chain-link fence, she stared at the site, imagined the heavy machinery arriving in the next weeks to clear away the detritus. Then, the landscapers would come in the spring, with their piles of topsoil, the timbers for the community garden beds, and the equipment to build a playground in one section. She'd given the double-lot to the neighborhood, and an annuity to keep Michelle's first commission, a sustainable garden, in good repair for generations.

"I'm done now," Tally said, staring straight ahead and knowing that she would never want to return. She had bigger problems with which to deal. Number one on the list was taking control of her life again. She would begin by moving out of Bane's penthouse and back to Rosegate. Today.

• • •

"Hey," Jackie called, poking her head into Tally's room. "How's it going?"

Tally looked up from the vanity mirror and smiled. "I should be asking you that question. Not the other way around." Jackie dropped onto the other overstuffed chair and rested her chin in her hands. The only smooth transition during Tally's loss of memory had been the ease at which she had reestablished her new friendship with Jackie. Even Jackie's family had embraced her, and she adored Tía Ixi.

Sitting next to her, Jackie was unusually silent, and Tally raised an eyebrow, the lip liner she had chosen poised for application.

"Fine," Jackie said and laughed. "The night of our engagement party, you gave me this." She slid a flat jewelry case across the vanity. Tally opened it and touched the familiar diamonds that had once belonged to her mother. She turned the box so that it faced Jackie, then slid it back to her.

"The necklace suits you," she said. "That's why I must've picked it for you above all the other pieces. That, and my mother would want you to have something of hers."

"I sense a *but*," Jackie coaxed, patting her hand.

"Not about this," Tally said, a little exasperated. She pulled her hand away.

"Then what? You can tell me. I can see that you're hurting, and I want to help."

"Then stop being so nice."

Jackie's eyes widened. A moment later, she started laughing. "Oh, thank goodness."

"That was suspiciously easy," Tally said, but grinned.

"Can I level with you?"

"I wish someone would."

"Before you lost your memory, you and I started to get really close. And because of our rough start, we've always been honest with one another. Like sisters. I'm an only child, but I see how it is with my cousins. I've always wanted that, and with you, I finally had it."

"I feel lucky to have you in my life, Jackie."

"Really?"

"Of course. I may have forgotten everything, but I would be an idiot to not realize what a beautiful heart you have."

Jackie hugged her, then laughed at the pink smear on her arm from Tally's errant lip liner.

Tally handed her a tissue, then resumed putting on her makeup, hating that she had to depend on it more and more because she was so tired all the damned time. Not even Jackie's bachelorette trip to their secluded islet had helped. She needed concealer for the dark circles under her eyes, blush for her pale cheeks, even lipstick to fatten up her smile. She wouldn't have bothered if it had been any other night, but this was the first get-together since the attacks. The Chicago Order had lost a founding family with the treachery of the Grossomms, though no one but her brother, Jackie, and Bane knew the full extent.

Tonight would be a chance for the leading families to meet the new blood. At the urging of the National Order, they were hoping to induct two or three new families into the Chicago board. A distant relative of Bane's mother, Jasper Coyle, had been invited, as had Adrian Shareff. Carol Spearin and Toby Landruff rounded out the eligible parties.

"I'm almost done with my face," Tally said wryly.

"You don't need all that, Tally. You always look lovely." When Tally frowned, Jackie set her hand over hers. "Do you still feel awful?"

"It comes and goes." Much like Bane, she thought with rancor. He had greeted her pleasantly enough when he returned the day before, but then had made himself scarce, not even commenting on the fact that she had moved out of his place. It was weird that all she could think about in his absence was when she would see him again, and when she did, she couldn't help herself from sniping at him. It was the only time she found any energy. Tonight, she would control her emotions. She would stop wondering why he seemed to not even wish to be her friend anymore. Maybe it was because, all these years, he had thought it safe to be around her as they could never be together. And now that he knew she was Fascina after all, it had scared him. "Jerk," she mumbled under her breath.

Jackie laughed. "Thinking about Bane again?" At Tally's raised eyebrow, she added, "You asked for honesty."

"I promise to be good tonight."

"Chris will be relieved." She hesitated, then added, "He was so freaked out when you almost died, Tally—Bane, I mean. He refused to leave your side the entire time you were in the hospital. I promised him I wouldn't say any—"

"Are you two ready yet?" Chris asked, poking his head in the door. "Bane's downstairs in the game room, playing bartender. The pizza's here. Both deep dish and New York style."

"Yeah, right," Tally said and rolled her eyes at her brother. "Please tell me you at least ordered a couple of thin crust pies for those of us who don't think deep dish is manna from heaven."

"Better. Bane actually went to New York. So be nice."

"I'm always nice," she said a little too brightly, and Chris pinned her with a look. "Fine." She stood and felt her jeans drop low on her hips. She was still losing weight. Well, pizza from the Big Apple was her favorite, so maybe she would have an extra helping. They walked downstairs to the game room where Bane was pouring a glass of wine for June Sedge. Orson waved to them when they entered the room.

"Still know how to play eight ball, Tally?" he asked as she went to greet him.

"Of course. You taught me, after all. Partners?"

"Only if you're up to it."

"How about I let you know if I start feeling tired." She barely managed to temper her retort.

"I'll hold you to that promise," he said, then went to get a stick.

If Tally had to pick a favorite room in Rosegate, it would be the game room. There had always been a billiards table and a card table, an antique bar, and comfy furniture set around a large fireplace, but her parents had added an area for puzzles and board games.

Bane came around from the bar. Tonight would be self-serve, but he handed Tally a glass of wine. She eyed the pizza. "Victor's?" He nodded. "The usual toppings?"

"Yes. And extra cheese."

As conversations went, this was at least a start. She was about to say more when Chris and Jackie stepped in front of the fireplace. "Welcome back to Rosegate," Chris started. "Some of you, those not on the board, may be wondering why you were invited here tonight." Jasper Coyle and Carol Spearin exchanged nervous glances, and Tally wondered if Bane had noticed. "The Chicago Order is going to be restructured. We're reducing the size of the general council but increasing the number of board members. The Grossomms no longer have a seat at the table. And the Coyle seat has sat vacant for far too many years. We need new blood if we are going to survive and maintain our rights in Chicago. Now, I'm not going to give a big speech tonight. As we said when we invited you here, tonight's a casual evening. Pizza and pool."

"And pinot," Jackie finished. "We want to get to know you, and you, us, and then see if we're a good fit. For the existing families, we've operated much too separately of late. Chris and I intend to change that. Regular get-togethers, like tonight, are part of our plan to reconnect."

"That's it for speeches," Chris stated. "Grab a drink and a slice and make yourself comfortable."

For a moment, no one moved. Then Tally took Orson's arm and steered him to the pizza. "I don't know about you, but I'm starving." He gave her a searching once-over, and she waited for the inevitable comment about looking gaunt. But he didn't say a word. He just handed her a plate and then loaded one up with pizza for himself. They walked over to the billiards table and set their dishes and drinks on the highboy in the corner. Tally took a couple of bites, then sipped her wine before selecting a cue. Carol and Jasper stepped over to challenge them to a game. Across the room, Adrian and Toby were chatting with her brother and the Fortunas.

Tally and Orson let Jasper break as they waited their turn on the stools. In between shots, Orson leaned closer to her. "You still think this is a good idea?"

Tally nodded. "The families have drifted apart. You saw what happened with the Grossomms." After taking her turn, she returned to the highboy, snagging a bottle of wine along the way to refill their glasses.

Orson thanked her but looked thoughtful. "The damage to you and your home aside, it was a bold power play on their part," he finally got out. "I would never have agreed to the engagement between Amy and Rene had I known what they were up to. I thought it would give you another ally."

"I wondered about that," Tally said, sipping her wine. "I didn't think that Amy and Rene knew each other."

"June thought it was time," he said. "And it wasn't a bad match. Not the one we were promised, but that's no longer an option." Then, he went to take his shot, missing his target and dropping the eight ball. "Sorry, Tally. I guess my pool game has suffered from disuse."

"Not to worry. We'll get another chance to play."

"I think a game of darts might be more up my alley." He nodded politely, then moved to the bar to grab something stronger to drink.

Tally stared at his back, wondering why it seemed like he was lying about Amy's engagement. As much as June Sedge obviously adored her daughter, Tally couldn't imagine her giving up her control over Amy. Did the Grossomms have something on Orson? It was hard to believe.

Bane came over with a plate piled with four slices of pizza. He nudged it her way, offering her a slice after taking one off the top. They sat on stools and watched the room as they chewed. It was one of the benefits of people not knowing she was Fascina—they tended to forget she was around. "Do you recall if Amy was engaged to anyone other than Rene?" she asked.

"You know, Orson said something to me along the same lines when you were in the hospital. Why do you ask?"

"He mentioned it just now, and I think he was upset, though he tried to cover it up." She tipped her head toward June Sedge. "She's had a little too much to drink already. Maybe she could tell us. Or rather, you."

"I'll try."

Silence dragged. "How is San Francisco?" she asked, attempting to be polite.

"Tiring." He slid the plate with the last slice toward her.

"I've already had two."

"Two small slices. It's your favorite," he reasoned.

"Please tell me you're *not* counting my calories," Tally complained, her ire ticking up a notch. "Look, Bane," she whispered. "I'm doing the best I can. I try to eat. I just have no appetite. Wait. Is that why you went to New York? To get my favorite pizza? Did Chris say something?"

"You've lost weight," he shot back under his breath. "It's not healthy, and you're never going to get better if you don't start eating more."

"I'm not sick, and— Actually, it's none of your business, is it?" she asked brightly and with a completely fake smile. Shareff came over with, thankfully, another bottle of wine. She held out her glass to him; she would need it if she was going to get through this night without murdering Bane.

"Looks like you lost your partner," Shareff noted, pouring.

"She already has a new one," Bane pointed out.

"I accept if you're offering," Tally said to Shareff at the same time.

Bane got up and took her arm. Leaning in, he whispered, "You will always be my business, Tally." Then he stalked away.

"What's up with Mr. Dark and Dangerous?" Shareff asked. "Other than his usual angst."

"He does play the part rather perfectly, doesn't he?" Tally replied, loud enough that a few people heard her. She smiled at Bane while he only glowered back from a chair near the fire. She watched as a couple of guests tried to engage him, but he seemed intent on ignoring the world. Finally, he pulled out his phone and began texting. Almost immediately, it dinged, and he smiled, reading the reply. A surge of jealousy streaked through Tally. She wanted to walk over to him and smash his phone, then throw the remnants into the fireplace.

But, as he was ignoring her, Tally did the same to him. She focused on the game before her.

"No way you can make that shot," Carol bet.

Tally walked around the table, studying the green six ball from various angles. It was the last shot she and Shareff needed before going after the eight ball. Her only play involved a difficult-but-not-impossible bank shot. "What do you think, Orson?" she said a little louder so that he could hear her from the bar. When there was no answer, she turned to discover that he and June had left the room.

"No coaching," Jasper joked.

"She's got this," Shareff assured them, rubbing her shoulders as if she were a prizefighter and he was her manager. "Right, Tally?"

It was completely innocent, but she cringed inside. She barely stopped herself from slapping his hands away. When her eyes fell on Bane, she instantly regretted meeting his gaze. There was more than anger in his expression...there was a proprietary need. What the hell? She eased away from Shareff, turned her back on Bane, and leaned over the end of the pool table. She knew how she looked, stretched as she was across the felt to reach the cue ball, but she didn't care. She wanted the shot.

One bank. Two. Between the nine and eleven balls. Contact. Sunk. She straightened, backed up, and bumped into Shareff's chest. His arms came around her waist as she ricocheted away when his too-warm palms touched her exposed midriff. Tally turned and gently removed his hands, but high-fived him for form's sake. Bane was no longer seated by the fire, but stalking from the room. The door slammed shut. The game was over.

"Rematch?" Shareff offered.

"Not for me," Jasper replied. "I have an early day tomorrow. Carol?"

"I'm ready to take off, too. You can still give me a lift?"

Jasper nodded.

"Great game, Tally. Adrian," Carol finished, his name spoken a little more coolly.

Tally looked around and saw that everyone was leaving. Chris and Jackie must've gone to see them out. Shareff was hanging back, and though Tally didn't feel threatened, she wished he would just go. She walked over to the table where the pizza boxes were stacked and began marrying the leftover slices into one container. He followed and stood across the buffet table from her.

Honestly, she thought, he could help by picking up a stray plate or glass, but no, he just stood there staring at her. He reached out to take her hand, and she drew back before he could.

"What are you up to?"

"I don't know what you mean."

She rolled her eyes. "Pool is the only game I'm ever going to play with you, Shareff."

"I'm not trying to play any games."

"Oh, come off it." She scanned the hallway, hoping for Chris or Jackie to show up. Not because she was afraid, but because their presence would help her to curb her tongue. In the moment she looked away, he had come around the table, cornering her.

"Back off," she warned. He stayed put. "Look, you've treated me with nothing but condescension since we met. So, whatever it is you think you're proving right now—"

"That was before," he said, coming a little closer.

"Before what? Before my brother offered you a seat on the board. You know, he hasn't made up his mind yet." Her back was pressed against the wall. "What do you think he would do if he saw you right at this moment?" She readied her knee to slam up at his balls if he touched her.

"I'm just trying to protect you, is all. Besides, you owe me for the ten grand that I doled out to your little charity." He reached out to caress her hair, and she smacked his hand away. His leer morphed into a snarl.

"Ungrateful bitch. You have no idea the things I've done to protect you. Your brother's fiancée is going to grow weary of having you around, and Chris'll be quick to fob you off on someone else. Better me than a man you don't even know."

He leaned in to kiss her, and Tally shoved him away. "You're crazy. Now back off before I'm forced to hurt you. You know I can."

He smiled slyly. "Maybe, but I think I might enjoy that. And then you can make me feel all better again." There was a noise in the hallway, and he took a step away. Then another. "This has been a fun night, Natalia. I look forward to *partnering* with you again." He walked away, leaving her alone in the room.

Tally picked up her glass and finished her wine. Could Adrian Shareff be anymore disgusting? "Maybe he's a masochist," she commented to the empty room. "As if I would ever help him to feel better." She stared at the flames. "Oh shit. He knows about me. But how? Unless he was—"

"Are you talking to yourself?"

She jumped in surprise. "Geez, Orson, you scared me. I thought you had left."

"Well, yes. But I came back after getting June settled for the night. More wine?" he asked, holding out a full glass to her.

"Sure, thanks," Tally said. She really didn't want another drink, but he seemed so sad lately. And he came back, saving her from having to deal with Shareff. She set the glass on the side table while Orson added another log to the fire. "How are you doing, Orson?"

"What do you mean, Natalia?"

"You just seem, I don't know, out of sorts."

"Yes, well, I've recently suffered a loss."

"Amy will come back home. She loves you and June too much to stay away for long."

"Yes. Amy. She has always been a source of worry."

He probably missed his daughter and needed to talk to someone who was around the same age as her. This was going to be a long night. Tally inwardly sighed. She looked toward the door, hoping that Chris and Jackie would return.

Orson sat in the same chair that Bane had occupied. "Your brother and Jackie were on their way back here, but I told them I would help you clean up. They seemed quite happy to run off to bed. Quite the lovebirds, aren't they?"

He was staring at her a little too intently, so Tally picked up the glass of wine, taking a sip, then holding it to have something to do with her hands. She kicked off her shoes to tuck her feet under her and then leaned back into the deep chair. "How is—"

"You've—" Orson started at the same time. "You go ahead."

"I was just going to ask after Amy. How is she doing?"

"From all accounts, she's having the time of her life." He frowned into his glass, and Tally took a sip of wine. "I'm afraid we learned too late that we were overprotective of her. Such a disappointment. Her entire life, we groomed her to marry another, and then he broke the engagement. Amy saw it as a free pass to escape our control."

"I didn't know she was engaged. Before Rene, I mean," Tally said, intrigued. The young woman she knew was as shy as she was awkward.

"No. I suppose you didn't." Orson sighed.

Tally took another sip of wine.

"You know, I'm not *really* your uncle. You remember, don't you? It was your father's brother who married June first. He suffered an early death, leaving her all alone. I met her years later, and as she was already considered your aunt by marriage, I assumed the role of uncle. Your parents were happy with the arrangement. The Sedges were on the board already, and we were all very close."

Tally listened. She'd known he wasn't her uncle, by blood or marriage, but it had never mattered. After her parents had been killed, he'd always been there. But there was something in the way he was reminiscing that made her anxious. She took another sip of wine, then felt a prick of pain in her temple that usually warned her of a migraine. Maybe she had simply imbibed too much. She set the glass on the table, slightly less than half-full. Her knee hit the edge, and the glass wobbled, but Orson steadied it.

He *tsked*. "That's going to leave a mark."

"Well, Orson, it's been a long day. I guess we should..."

He leaned back, ignoring the hint that she wanted him to leave. "It was your father who had agreed to the marriage. We spoke about it the week before he was killed." Orson swirled his wine, and Tally couldn't help but stare at the eddying liquid. "He never had a chance to put it in writing, or your mother would have known. She would have made sure the contract was upheld before she died."

Tally shook her head, trying to clear it and understand what he was saying. "You don't mean my brother and Amy?"

"Of course I do," Orson snapped. "They were promised."

"But she's too young for him."

"She's only a few years younger than the whore he's engaged to now."

"I'm sorry, Orson, but I must have misheard what you just said."

His expression told her otherwise.

"Jackie is my future sister-in-law, and I insist that you refer to her with respect. I'm sorry things didn't work out for Amy, but she and Chris would never have made a good match. He's—"

"As if June and I were. It's not about being a good fit, Natalia. It's not about love. It's about power and alliances. If Amy had been a boy, he would've been matched with you, despite the fact that you're a Non. I would have overlooked your abnormality if only to strengthen the bond between our families. We would have kept you safe while trying to breed you—you know, it's not a guarantee that a maliker will be the issue when mating. But it's too late now."

Tally felt sick. "I think you should leave, Orson." She swayed when she stood.

"But we still need to clean up, Natalia." He caught her as the room reeled and scooped her into his arms. "And I'm an expert at cleaning up."

Chapter Twenty-seven

"I'm not asking again, Mother."

Giselle Coyle-Caron crossed her arms and refused to answer. "I have no idea what you are talking about, Bane. I have done nothing wrong. Not today. Not yesterday. Not even fifteen years ago."

"You're really good, you know. Anyone looking at your face would believe you. But not me. I see it in your eyes." His mother's security team was coming up behind him, and he smiled. Giselle's eyes widened as all three of them were frozen in place. "I'm done covering for you. You've screwed up my life long enough. You and Janine can play your games without me. I'm through with protecting you."

"Protecting me?" She gave him a scathing look. "Is that what you think you're doing?"

She continued to harangue him, but he had tuned her out and was walking away. He would never set foot in this house again. He'd once held out hope that they might reconcile one day. No longer.

Bane felt lighter than he had in weeks as he strode out through her foyer. He had made up his mind. He would tell Tally everything. He would tell the N.O.F. to go to hell. And as for Giselle? She could rot in one of their holding cells for all he cared.

"Don't you *dare* walk out on me, Bane!"

Without even turning, he flipped her the bird. Damn, that felt good.

"Wait! I'll answer your questions," she shouted after him.

But it no longer mattered, and he pulled on the handle of her front door, ready to face the consequences of his decision.

"Please, *Braeden*."

He stopped and slowly turned, waiting and wary.

"What's the worst thing one Fascina can do to another?" she asked him. "Worse than murder, even?"

"Worse than murder? Nothing."

"No, for a Fascina...think!"

"Steal their powers? You did that?" he asked unbelievably. His mother didn't have that kind of strength.

"Yes," she said. "And no. It's complicated."

"It always is with you." The urge to leave was suddenly intense.

"Come back. Let's talk. I promise, no more games. I'll send my men away."

• • •

"Put me down, Orson," she ordered, but her voice was as weak as her arms were feeble.

"Certainly." He set her on the edge of the pool table, and when she tried to slide off, he pinned her against it with his bulk. "Here, have another sip of wine." He grabbed her jaw and tipped her glass to her lips. Tally sputtered but was helpless to stop some of the wine from going down her throat. She coughed, spraying her shirt with pinot.

"Such a messy girl," he said, pouting.

"What did you give me?" she tried shouting, and then felt a dulling of her voice.

"Just something to calm you. Did you know that it is very easy for some Fascina to seal a room? No one can get to you. No one can hear you. And when the time comes, you can scream all you want."

"I insist that you—"

He squeezed her neck. "Hush! I'm thinking about how to start. The other ones never talked back. I didn't let them. But that sort of manipulation never worked with you." He stepped back to unbutton his jacket. "Maybe a little more wine first?"

Tally rolled to the side and off the table. Her knees hit first, and the painful jolt gave her a boost of energy. She started scrambling toward the door, but Orson grabbed her by her hair and threw her against the side of the pool table, cracking her shoulder against the wood paneling. She dropped to her stomach and squirmed under the table to get away from him. He let her. And she watched his feet as he placed himself between her and the door.

"Imagine my surprise when your brother assigned me to the very task force ordered to investigate the murders. Your friend, Detective Haneluk, sent me everything they had on...well...me."

It wasn't possible. Tally took a deep breath and screamed for Chris as loud as she could. Her cry echoed back at her. Orson grabbed her ankles and dragged her from under the table.

"You might not have any powers, but you've been immune to my persuasion. It's why I had to resort to drugging you. It's meant to dampen a Fascina's powers—weaken them—but I imagine it'll work on a Non."

She kicked at him, her bare feet ineffectual. Drugs didn't work on her for long; she needed to stall for time so that they could wear off.

"Enough of that." He kicked her in her stomach, knocking the wind out of her before dragging her up again and hefting her back onto the table.

"I've been waiting for years to have you. It started with a simple desire, but it's grown into so much more. I even sent you that rose. More elegant than that posy of violets someone sent you."

"In the park...the mal de nuit," she slurred.

"Not quite..." He reached into his sports coat and extracted a slightly crushed rose. Then he flicked it at her face, again and again, each time slapping a little harder, until he took the bloom and smashed it into her nose and mouth. "No. More. Interrupting."

He threw the destroyed rose aside. "I like to call them 'Tal de nuit.' Get it? For Na*talia*?"

Tally spit out the choking petals.

He took a handkerchief from his pocket and held it to her nose. "Blow. Blow!" he shouted, when she didn't at first obey. "That's better."

"Please, Orson, I—"

He gagged her with the handkerchief, then grabbed her neck and squeezed. "I'm not done talking."

Tears ran down Tally's face as she struggled to breathe.

"Now, where was I?" He let go of her neck. "Ah, yes...I'm always cleaning up after you. Just like I cleaned up after Bane when he carelessly left those men in the park that night." He grinned. "Don't look so shocked, Natalia. I was watching over you even then. They were quite easy to dispose of...after I played with them, that is."

She tried to push him away, but he grabbed her wrist and gave it a vicious twist. Tally gave a muffled cry.

"Oh, that's nice," he crooned. "You only have yourself to blame, my Tal de nuit. Getting yourself mixed up with that man." Orson made a disgusted face. "You allowed that filth to sully you. But I cleaned up that little disgraceful mess when you were still in the hospital, not that you can remember any of it. I've been taking care of things for you for a while now, watching you mature into a woman, waiting for the day that we could be together. And now, you're tainted...ruined. You're no longer worthy of my devotion. No, Natalia, you're just like the others. And so you'll get what I gave them."

She tried to get up, and he backhanded her, knocking her head against the felt-covered slate. "This is not the ideal location for us, but it will have to do. Actually, now that I think about it, it's quite poetic. Just imagine, Tally, who will be blamed for your death."

Her leaden arms swatted ineffectually at his hands as he yanked down her jeans. "You really tarted up yourself tonight, wearing all this makeup and showing off your body. Do you think they'll suspect Adrian? Perhaps your brother? No, probably not." He spread her knees. "No, I'm pretty sure Bane's life as he knows it will be over when they find you tomorrow. I was surprised when they didn't arrest him after I killed that little harlot who was his date at the gala."

He slapped her, then escalated to punching, growing more and more excited. "I'm usually much more patient," he explained breathlessly. "But I've never done this when other people were in the home. A dog, once, but that proved to be a mistake. This, though...it's exhilarating."

She spat at him, and he responded with a gleeful laugh, then reached down to undo his pants. She tried to summon her strength to repel him. Hell, she could destroy things with her thoughts. But her powers refused to obey her. Orson grabbed her thighs and pulled her closer to the edge of the table. She could barely move and, helpless, she turned away. She'd been a fool to be so angry with Bane. If only he were here now. Her eyes focused... The cue ball was mere inches from her fingers.

• • •

"It was Mallory Waever's idea," Giselle began, and Bane started to get up, not wanting to hear more of her lies, but she touched his arm. "I'm not blaming her. I just need you to understand how far back this goes. Back to when we were starting college."

"Go on," Bane said, even more anxious to leave.

"We told each other everything. Young women sharing our crushes, our dreams. As Mallory grew older, it became clear to us that she was more powerful than I. Her family had more money. She was expected to marry well. Our circles receded from one another. But it didn't matter...we were best friends. And she told me that she could help me."

"How?" Bane demanded, wanting Giselle to finish her story.

"She knew I was working in this very house, that I needed the money for college. She would visit while I was off duty, and we would lay on my bed and talk about our futures. Your father always had a thing for young, pretty women. I must have caught his eye. One day, when Mallory was visiting, he came to my room. I don't know why, but I made her hide in my closet. Sebastian Caron was interested in me. But if he ever laid eyes on Mallory...

"I went with him. I thought...I don't know what I thought. He said...he lied."

"Are you telling me that my father raped you?" Bane demanded.

"No! No. It was consensual. I wanted to be with him. But idiot that I was, I believed his promises."

"You were young," Bane allowed. "And he took advantage."

"Maybe we both did," she said, but she smiled at some memory. "I went back to my room, and Mallory was still there. Waiting for me. I was over the moon in love with Sebastian Caron, and she stood there and shook her head sadly. She had the gift of sight."

"I know," Bane admitted, checking the time on his phone. "Look, I really have to go."

"Five more minutes, please."

He nodded as unexplainable fear crept up his neck.

"Mallory saw that I would never be with Sebastian because I wasn't powerful enough. So, she siphoned some of his power away and gave it to me."

"Then Janine actually has nothing on you," Bane said.

Giselle looked away.

"What did you do?"

"I did it to protect you, Braeden. To save you."

"I find that hard to believe."

"You don't know how he was. How he needed to control everything...everyone. But Mallory gave me more than some of his powers—she inadvertently gave me some of hers. There have been moments in my life when I think she did it on purpose."

"Siphoning," Bane guessed. "And you used it."

"Yes," she admitted. "Our marriage was tumultuous at best, but no matter how much Sebastian cheated, he always came back to me. Always wanted me. After you were born, he no longer could claim sole possession of me, and he hated you for it. Even as a baby. He would see me nursing you and fly into a rage. I found him next to your crib one night, you crying and squirming as he held you suspended in front of him. Your lips were turning blue. That was the first time that I took some of his power. Enough that he couldn't hurt you. And when it seemed that you had no true power of your own, I took a little more. Each day. A tiny bit. All to protect you."

"I hid my gifts from him. From you."

"I know that now. I wanted to find out what you could do, so each time you visited, I tried to contain you. You always escaped. And when you held my men suspended, I saw finally that you are stronger than he ever was."

"Did Mallory Waever know?"

"Yes. Eventually. But she caught him once, in her bedroom, staring at her and Torbin, a shadow only. She knew him for the monster he was."

"Why didn't you leave him?" Bane demanded. "I was just a child. You let him beat me."

She shook her head, tears welling. "I couldn't leave. As long as I was here, he couldn't discover what I had been doing. It was the only way to keep him from killing us outright."

And he suddenly saw the real Giselle—a deeply flawed, vain woman who had committed the worst Fascina crime, all to protect her child. But a woman who refused to be a victim.

"You can do it, can't you? Shadow?" His surprised silence was answer enough. "Never tell anyone about it, Braeden."

"I'm not stupid."

"Good. It only causes scandal. The Sedge family barely recovered after it was discovered that one of their ancestors had used his power to steal and become rich. They lost their control of the C.O.F. to the Waever family. It took decades for them to recover their respectability."

Tally's words about the killer being in two places at once suddenly came back to Bane. Shadowing was inherited. Maybe she did see Amy Sedge in two locations at the engagement party. As the pieces fell together, he swallowed at the implications.

"Do whatever you need to do, Braeden. Leave Janine to me. And whatever is happening with you"—she waved her hand near his face—"is terrible for your complexion."

He laughed then. "Thank you, Giselle. For everything." And he slipped away.

• • •

Tally waited until Orson climbed on top of her and swung up her arm, letting the weight of the ball propel her hand. There was a fleshy *crack* as the white orb connected with the spot just above his ear. He howled, holding the side of his head, and blood dripped from between his fingers. He backed away, and Tally pushed herself up and slid off the billiards table. Her legs didn't want to work, so she held onto its edge, scrambling to the opposite side.

Orson lifted his other arm and swept the table sideways; again, and Tally flew across the room. The back of her head slammed into the oak paneling, and she saw stars. Orson stalked, strobe light-like, toward her. He was steps away from where she was pinned to the wall, bruised and bleeding. Broken.

A dark fog descended around her, enveloping her, then a bright flash. People were shouting and screaming, but she couldn't make out the words. And then everything went black.

• • •

Every cell in Bane's body screamed to send Orson to the Null. But Chris, not understanding, held him back. Orson lay on the floor, knocked out for the time being, and Tally was crumpled in a ball next to him. Bane broke free of Chris's hold and raced to scoop her into his arms.

Orson was coming to, and when he saw Bane, he grabbed at Chris. "Thank God you're here! I tried to stop him. He was attacking Natalia!" He touched his temple and stared at the blood. "All this time, Chris, it was him. He's the killer we've been searching for." He turned to Bane. "Don't try to deny it. You need help. We can get you someplace safe and find some way to help you. Chris? Are you listening? You must get your sister away from him." Orson lurched to his feet.

"I'm taking her somewhere where she'll be safe, Chris," Bane murmured, cradling Tally in his arms and coming to his feet. "A place where she can heal."

"You have to stop him," Orson yelled. "Chris!"

"Give me a minute, Bane," Chris said, and turned to Orson. "Tell me again what you saw and heard."

Jackie came in, took in the scene in seconds. She grabbed a throw from one of the chairs and draped it over Tally's semi-naked body.

Bane couldn't believe that Chris would trust Orson over him. He was about to slip with Tally when Jackie caught his eye. She gave her head the tiniest of shakes, then stepped away to box Orson in.

"I understand," Chris said, and Bane watched as Orson drew himself up to his full height. "You're right. For someone to commit such acts of evil, it's a cry for help. And we *will* help."

"Thank God," Orson said. "Your father would be proud, Chris. Now, Bane, hand over Natalia. I'll make sure she gets medical attention." He held out his arms, walking toward him.

"Did you really think that I would believe you over Bane?" Chris demanded, and Orson froze. "Why, Orson? Why did you do those horrible things?"

Bane could see Orson tensing to strike, and he tried to warn Chris. "What are you talking about, Chris? I could never hurt—"

"Your fucking pants are still undone!" Chris yelled. "Jesus, all those victims...women and men...and a child. And now Tally. Your own niece."

"But we're not really related, are we?" Orson spat. He stared at Jackie with hatred. "Our families should have been united with your marriage to Amy, but you had to let yourself be seduced by this cun—"

Orson flew through the air and smashed against the far wall with a crash. Bane had never seen Chris this angry before, and his power was staggering. He threw Orson to the ceiling, then brought him crashing to the floor.

"Chris," Jackie said softly.

"Look what he did to my sister," Chris seethed.

"And he'll pay for it. And for everything else." She turned to Bane. "Can you take him to the National Order? They'll be able to hold him."

"I'm not leaving Tally."

"Please. Bane? It will take you less than a minute. Don't let Chris kill him."

"Why not? He deserves death and worse."

"Exactly," Jackie said. "He deserves so much worse. But he might know things. Things that we need to hear."

Bane looked down at Tally's pale, battered face. "No," he said, juggling Tally in his arms to pull his phone from his pocket and send off a text. "They'll be here in twenty seconds," he whispered. Then, over Chris's and Jackie's protestations, he slipped away. Far away. To a secret place where no one would find them.

He ignored his phone when it rang, then chimed, and chimed again. Over and over until finally ten minutes passed into fifteen, then a half hour. He bathed Tally, cleaning her, checking that she hadn't been cut or stabbed. Bane had seen the photos of what Orson had done to the others...he didn't think Tally had been raped, but the assault would surely scar her. "But you fought back, didn't you, Tally?" he murmured, thinking of Orson's bloody temple.

He dressed her in a soft cotton T-shirt and a pair of his flannel pajama bottoms. He placed her on her side in his bed, pulled the sheets and blankets up to her shoulder, then settled next to her, holding her in the circle of his arms.

After she had healed her brother and died, only to be revived, Bane had let her go to the hospital alone. He'd failed to protect her and had nearly lost her. If he'd gone with her in the ambulance, his proximity might have given her the strength she needed to recover faster. She might not have lost her memory. Their child might still be...

It had all happened because of him.

Ultimately, he could now admit, it had been his guilt over their loss that had convinced him that she would never forgive him once she discovered the full truth. So, he had committed himself to breaking their bond. He'd removed himself from her life. Put as much distance between them as possible, as often as possible. It'd hurt like hell to leave her, but not as much as the pain of revealing that which had happened, and not mourning what they'd lost.

He wouldn't make the same mistake twice; he would give Tally all his strength to get her through this. And once she was well again, he would tell her everything. She might end up hating him, but she deserved to know the whole truth.

For the first time since being away from her, his mind felt clear. Propping up on one elbow, he examined her face. She was a mass of bruises. Her lip was split. Her cheek was cut. She didn't have black eyes yet, but she would. Gently, he probed her scalp with his fingertips and found one, then another large goose egg. She was no longer unconscious, but sleeping. She moaned when he touched the bruises on her neck, then rolled to face him, tucking herself under his chin. Bane closed his eyes, staying with her until her breathing evened.

By the time he roused himself to make coffee and light the fireplaces in his hideaway, they'd been gone six hours. His phone was dead, and he stared at the dark screen, then set it on the charger and poured himself a mug of coffee. He was taking a sip when a series of chimes went off, indicating that he had more messages than he probably wanted.

He started with the thread from Chris. They began with expletives, followed by escalating threats. Then there was a text from Jackie asking if they were okay. Finally, a group thread from both of them:

Jackie tells me to be patient. So just fucking call!

Bane looked out the window. It was dark here in the mountains, getting close to ten o'clock in this time zone. He sighed, then hit CALL on Chris's contact page. He hung up before the first ring. He set down his phone. What could he say to his friend? That he bonded with his twin sister without so much as a *Hey, is it okay if Tally and I hook up?* He ran his hand through his hair. From where he sat, he could see straight into his bedroom where Tally was still sleeping. He picked up his phone again, nearly dropping it when it rang in his hand.

Bane accepted the call, then slowly brought the phone to his ear. Back in Chicago, Chris was no doubt doing the same, waiting for the other to start. Bane cleared his throat to speak, but Chris beat him to the jump.

"Jackie says that I need to listen to you before killing you. And just so you know, I'm pissed that you put my fiancée in a position where she can't talk to me. But let's save that for later. What in the hell do you think—" Chris stopped talking, and Bane heard him muffle the phone. "Jackie says that some of this is on Tally. So, go ahead. I'm listening."

Bane took an audible breath. "First, Tally is fine. She's getting better. She's healing from tonight. And from before."

"She can heal here."

"No, she can't."

"What does that even mean?"

"Are you going to let me talk?" Bane asked, knowing he needed to make amends with his best friend, but getting annoyed just the same.

Silence answered, then the sound changed. "I put you on speaker," came Jackie's voice next, sounding pissed. "You two idiots need mediation. Now, Bane, tell Chris."

"Tell me what?"—A dull smack told Bane that Jackie had swatted Chris— "Sorry. I'm waiting."

Bane took another deep breath, then dove in, saying it all in a rush. "I love Tally. I always have. And she's in love with me. Or at least she was until she lost her memory. I should have talked to you about it. We planned on telling you after your engagement party. And then everything went ass-crazy. Tally died, Chris. She died! And then everything between us was gone. But not gone. Because I remembered. And it was killing me. And—" Bane stopped. He was so relieved to have finally told Chris, and not just because he was Tally's brother, but because he was his best friend.

"You knew, Jackie?" Chris asked.

"I guessed some of it," Jackie replied. "He's telling the truth. They were going to tell you after the party."

"That's all great, but it doesn't explain why you took my sister to God knows where."

"We need to be alone. She needs it, Chris, to heal."

"Oh shit! You two bonded, didn't you?"

Jackie gasped. "Is that even possible between a Fascina and a non-Fascina?"

Chris took them off speakerphone, and Bane knew his friend well enough to know that he was pacing.

"I need to think about this," was all that Chris said before ending the call.

Bane just stared at his phone. He set it down on the counter, then got up to check on Tally. She was snoring softly and had shifted to her back. He pulled up the eiderdown comforter, tucking it around her, then went to the other room to pour himself a stiff drink. His phone buzzed. "Chris."

"You really love her? And she loves you? I mean, I guess I don't need to ask that. But shit, Bane. You should have said something a long time ago. What did you think I would do? I'm not Torbin; you didn't need my permission. We're friends. Best friends. More. You should have talked to me."

"Yes."

"Yes?"

"To everything." They were both silent, then Bane added, "I really screwed things up."

"It's not that bad," Chris started.

"It is." Bane rubbed his temple. "When she was hurt—"

"Which time?"

Bane couldn't help himself and laughed. Chris did the same. "Thank you for that, Chris."

"No problem. Why don't you start from the beginning?"

"Elementary school?"

This time, Chris laughed first. "You've been carrying a torch for my sister that long?"

"Always."

"And Tally?"

"Not as long," Bane said. "But a long time."

"Start from when you discovered your mutual regard."

"It was by accident."

"It always is."

"We both felt this way, but never said anything to each other. And you know about the interdictions, so neither of us acted on it." It wasn't Bane's place to tell Chris about Tally's power; that was for her to reveal. So he told his friend about how they discovered that they loved one another, and how it grew, and how they bonded.

"I don't know a lot about bonding," Chris said, "but I didn't think bonding was possible for non-Fascina. Makes you wonder, doesn't it?"

"It's rare." Not an untruth, but definitely an omission. Chris was going to end up killing him, anyway, when this was all settled.

"Wow, that's useful. So, get to the part where you messed up?"

"That night, when you were hurt and Tally died, she came to in the hospital and called me Bane."

"She calls you Bane all the time."

"Not when she says she loves me, Chris. She calls me Braeden. She didn't know about your engagement. She didn't remember anything that happened between us. Not even about—"

"The bonding," Chris finished. "Shit, Bane."

"I told you it was bad. So I tried to break it...the bond. I thought—"

"Wait! What? Of all the idiotic—"

Bane had to hold the phone away from his ear.

"Okay, sorry," Chris said. "Why would you attempt something so stupid?"

"You're not going to like my answer."

"Try me."

"A lot of things went down that night. Tally was already weakened when we got to Rosegate." Bane had to word things carefully here so as not to give away Tally's secret. "We were in the alley when her house blew up. And then you were hurt. You might want to sit down for this."

"Quit stalling, Ba—Braeden."

"Just call me Bane, Chris."

"That's a relief. And I'm sitting."

"Well, that night, you died." Bane waited, but Chris was silent. "Chris?"

"I wondered about that," he finally said. "Things weren't adding up. More than just my clothes being soaked with blood. I think I saw Tally over me, but... I was over her. And then she was on the floor. What happened? How did I..."

"Come back?"

"Yeah."

"It must've been your twin-thing. And Tally does work in a hospital. She knows how to help people."

"What are you leaving out?" This time, it was Bane's turn to be silent. "Uh-huh."

"I was also being blackmailed by Janine," he admitted.

"You? How? I can't believe it. Was it because of you and Tally? Because that's not reason enough to—"

"Partly. But mainly because of Giselle."

"Ah. I see. I knew Janine had a reputation, but she really is one grand bitch, isn't she?"

"Yeah, one might say that."

"I've got your back, buddy. You've got the entire C.O.F. behind you."

"Thanks, Chris. After everything that has happened to Tally, it means a lot. It's my fault she was hurt again. I should have ridden in the ambulance with her. With our bond, she probably wouldn't have lost her memory. And she wouldn't have been so vulnerable to Orson."

"You don't get to own that, Bane. Orson drugged her."

"What?"

"That's right. He spiked her wine. The National Order was very—and I mean very—interested in where he procured the drug. They think that maybe Orson was working with one of the labs you shut down. That the group who's been taking our kind knew about Orson's...pastime. Bane, that girl who went missing, Lorna's daughter... They think he was keeping her. He owns a Chicago greystone, and the evidence there... It was... He used a dart board to find his hunting grounds. He's a sick man, Bane."

"Christ. The body at Tally's." Bane rubbed his forehead. "I should have known it was him. I should have—"

"You're starting to piss me off again, so stop. We all should have seen something. But the other stuff, yeah, you screwed up in a big way. My understanding of the bonding, especially in the beginning, is that you're weaker apart."

"I thought Tally would be better off..." He paused. He still couldn't talk about her miscarriage. Not to anyone. Not until she knew. And she had to be strong first. "I'm telling her everything when she wakes."

"Okay."

"Okay?"

"Yes. There are three people in this world that I trust completely—Tally, Jackie, and you. I know you'll give your life if it means saving hers. So yes, I'm saying 'okay'."

Bane sagged with relief.

"But Bane, Tally calls me as soon as she's strong enough. And if she wants to be at Rosegate to recover, then you will bring her home."

"Understood. And Chris?"

"Yes."

"Thank you. I love you, man."

"Love you too...Braeden."

"Fuck off, Chris," he said with a chuckle, and listened as Chris's laughter was cut off when his friend ended the call. He set his phone on the charger, leaving it on the kitchen counter. After filling two glasses with cold water, he headed back to the bedroom. He set a glass on each nightstand—one for him; one for Tally. The fire was low, so he added a few more logs. He switched off the lamp, and then climbed back into the bed and lay, staring up at the ceiling. The flickering glow of the fire sent soft shadows dancing around the room. Next to him, Tally shifted, turning and nestling against his side before settling back and breathing steadily in her sleep. He closed his eyes, and for the first time in weeks, he fell into a peaceful slumber.

Chapter Twenty-eight

Tally didn't want to get out of bed. The crisp sheets, the thick down comforter, the crackling of the burning logs, and a familiar scent that she couldn't place but that gave her comfort—all conspired to keep her from moving from her comfortable cocoon. The pillows were heavenly clouds, and she wanted to keep them forever. She would steal them and take them home with her.

Home.

This wasn't her room at Rosegate. Wherever she was, she was filled with an overwhelming sense of peace and security.

A spike of panic gripped her. Maybe she was dreaming or in a coma. Or drugged again. But then that familiar scent wormed its way past her olfactory senses, calming her. She tried to sit up and gasped at the pain. Broken ribs? How could that be? It had been weeks since the attack in the ballroom. Her ribs had been broken during CPR. Tally hadn't worried because she knew her body would heal itself in less than a day. And then it hadn't. At least not as fast as it normally did. This ache felt fresh. She focused on her surroundings.

A cut crystal glass with a bendy straw sat on the nightstand, just within her reach. She brought it to her lips and drank. Cool, clean water. It was the most delicious thing she had ever tasted.

She set the glass back down, then relaxed into the pillows, closing her eyes to think. Her ribs had nearly healed. But she hadn't been herself. She'd felt ornery all the time and had no appetite. She ran her hand down the flat of her stomach, felt it dip into the concave of her abdomen, where once she had been toned. The gesture of touching her stomach filled her with a deep sadness she didn't quite understand. One mystery at a time, she reasoned. First, she needed a bit more sleep.

• • •

Tally came awake again. Her water glass had been refilled. A posy of violets sat next to it in a little vase. Her phone was there as well. A muscular arm was draped over her, but she wasn't alarmed. Outside, it was night, and a bright fire burned in the hearth. The man sleeping so soundly next to her was Bane. No...Braeden. Tally put her head back down and tried to puzzle out why he was tucked around her, albeit on top of the blankets, and why she wanted to call him by his given name. Gingerly, she reached down and pulled up the quilt at the foot of the bed, drawing it up and over him. The movement didn't leave her gasping in pain this time. No wonder she felt safe—she was with Bane. She drifted back to sleep.

• • •

The next time she woke, the door to the room was closed, and she was alone in the bed. The water glass and violets were still there, as was her phone. The fire continued to burn in the hearth. She managed to sit up, wincing only a little. The shades were drawn, but a small sliver of daylight speared into the room. As carefully as she could, she swung her legs over the edge of the bed and discovered a pair of slippers in just her size on the rug. There was a tap on the door, and Bane stuck his head in.

"You're awake," he said, stating the obvious. He looked so nervous that Tally couldn't help but grin at him. She was immediately sorry that she did, for her face hurt something awful. Bane was at her side in a flash. "Take it slow, Tally."

"What happened to me?" Please, she couldn't have lost part of her memories a second time, could she? Panic rose inside her at the thought.

"What do you remember?"

She closed her eyes and frowned. "Playing pool. Pizza. I was mad at you." Flashes were coming back to her so fast they were making her sick. "Shareff," she said with a foul taste in her mouth. "He tried to..."

"He tried to what?" Bane demanded.

"He thinks he can blackmail me into marrying him. He suspects that I can heal people."

"What else?" Bane asked, but more patiently, as if it took great effort.

"He left. And I was tired but wanted to straighten up. Orson was there. He came in to help me. No." She covered her mouth, shaking her head as if trying to deny her memories, but it was no use. Orson. The man who had been in their lives for years, guiding them. Her uncle. "He wanted...he—"

Bane pulled her into his arms and held her close. "*Shh.* I'm sorry, Tally. I'm so sorry. You're safe now. He can't hurt you or anyone else ever again."

Every sickening detail came back to her in that moment. "Bane," she begged through a clenched jaw. "I need to get to the bathroom. Now."

He helped her to her feet, and when she was too weak to walk, scooped her into his arms and carried her. She grabbed a hand towel from the rack on the way in and retched into it. Bane set her before the toilet, lifted the lid, and she grabbed the seat and vomited. Barely anything came up, just a dribble of bright-yellow, bile-sickened water. He sat on the floor, right next to her, and held back her hair as the retching was followed by dry heaves. She cried out in pain as her ribs throbbed sharply in response to the spasms.

And when the heaves finally stopped, Bane flushed the toilet and handed her a clean towel, then went and grabbed her water. "What can I do, Tally?" he asked while she took a tiny sip.

"I need to pee," she said, embarrassed at how it made her feel to admit it. But he nodded and helped her up from the floor. He didn't leave until she could stand by herself, using the counter for support.

"Want me to stay?"

Tally shook her head. He left, closing the door behind him. With one hand, she untied her—his—pajama bottoms, then slowly lowered herself to the seat. She was afraid there would be blood in her urine from the beating she'd taken. She wiped herself, then turned to flush the toilet again, almost crying with relief that the water wasn't tinted red. Using the counter again, she hobbled to the chaise set in the corner. She managed to pull her underwear back on, noticing that they were new. Bane chose that moment to tap on the door. The pajama bottoms were in a pile around her ankles. She sighed. "Come on in."

He was carrying a stack of clean clothes. A T-shirt, loose yoga pants, bra, and underwear. "They're all new. I only slipped out for a few minutes to get them for you." She nodded, and he set them next to her. "What can I do?"

"Nothing. I need to see what he did." He frowned, but helped her to her feet, and she managed to shuffle toward the floor-to-ceiling mirror that covered one wall.

Tally didn't recognize her own face. "How is it possible to look gaunt and swollen at the same time?"

Bane didn't answer.

She lifted her chin, carefully turning her head from side to side. She was the definition of "bruised and battered." Around her throat, a necklace of contusions. She grimaced at her greasy hair and scalp and discovered two separate knots with her fingers. There were horrible black-and-blue marks on her legs, between her thighs. She lifted the hem of the T-shirt, spread her fingers over her hollowed-out abdomen, and frowned. There was a dark, angry purple-black welt where Orson's foot had connected with her stomach. Bane had looked away. She turned slightly, the dark purple welts on her side and back reminding her how Orson had kicked her.

"He put something in my wine. I couldn't fight him. Then I blacked out when he threw me against the wall." Hysterical fear clawed at her mind. "Did he rape me?" she asked, needing to know.

"No," he said, his tone absolute. "He didn't have time. And drugs or not, you gave as good as you got. I think you cracked his skull with—"

"The cue ball."

He nodded and gave her a soft smile, one filled with relief.

"I need to wash my hair...to scrub away his...I need to be clean," she finished.

He led her to the shower and supported her as she sat down on a large teak bench. He turned the nozzle away from her before turning on the water and letting it heat up. Then he handed her a bottle of her favorite shampoo. She looked up at him, knowing she looked like hell, wet and bruised and bedraggled, and did the only thing she could—she pressed the bottle back into his hands. There was a softening in his eyes, but he set himself to work, making sure her hair was wet, then lathering the ends before applying more to her scalp. He was gentle around the knots, then carefully rinsed out the suds. He repeated the steps with the conditioner. All the while, she sat there in the wet tee and underpants that he had bought for her. He draped a thick towel around her and then stepped out of the shower. His shirt was sopping wet, and Tally swallowed upon seeing the broad expanse of his back and shoulders when he stripped it off. His tattoos were strangely gone.

Across the bathroom, he pulled open a door she had just noticed, and stepped into a walk-in closet, reappearing a few seconds later in dry clothes. Then he set to work, gently buffing the water from her hair before wrapping her head in a loose turban.

"Here," he said, handing her the new clothes. "I'll be right back."

At this point, Tally didn't care if he saw her naked. She was just too tired. She somehow managed to remove the sodden shirt, knocking the towel off her head in the process, and then shrugged into the new tee. It was his and large enough to provide her with some modest cover. She didn't have the energy to pull on bra and underwear, let alone yoga pants.

Bane returned with a high-backed chair, one that looked like it had been handmade by some Scandinavian artisan.

When she shrugged helplessly at the clothes in her lap, he helped her to stand. She held onto the chair for support while Bane knelt before her as she stepped into the underpants and leggings. He was all business, she thought sadly. But then he stayed there, hand on her hip, staring through her, and she had an uncanny feeling that this had happened before. He finally roused himself to help her sit, then gently combed out her hair before taking a blow dryer to it.

She grimaced at her reflection. "I'm a black-and-blue Q-tip," she observed, then began patting down some of the frizz. She ran her fingers through her hair, splitting it into three parts to braid, but her arms were too tired, and she made a mess of things.

Bane cleared his throat.

"You think you can do better?" she asked.

"I couldn't do worse."

In the end, he did a pretty fair job of it, and Tally pulled her braid so that it draped over her shoulder. "Thank you. Again."

"You never need to thank me, Tally." He helped her up, then gave her his arm as she shuffled out of the bathroom.

"Can you take me to the window?" she asked when he started steering her back to the bed. It was slow going, but when they made it across the room, he drew back the curtains, securing them so that she could see the French doors that opened to a wide deck that appeared to float above the world. But it was the view beyond that stole her breath. "Where are we?" she asked, taking in the steep slope upon which his home was perched.

Massive pines populated the...mountain? Thousands of feet below, a crystalline lake sparkled in the sun. And snow. Pure and white and blinding.

"Finland," he admitted.

"Oh my gosh, Bane, you actually did it! You bought a fjord. Wow." He shrugged, but Tally could see that he was pleased with himself. "You said that you would do it one day," she reminisced, "and you did."

"For the record," he said, "I don't actually own a fjord, just a good chunk of real estate surrounding one."

After her parents were gone, Bane's father banished to the Null, and his mother estranged, Orson had helped them by making sure the courts left them alone. Even in their community, Child Services would never allow three unattended teens to live alone and unsupervised at Rosegate. The Corbetts were declared their legal guardians, and their inheritances put into trusts until they turned eighteen. Bane was nearly a half year older than

Chris and Tally, and when he came into his money, the Corbetts asked him what he was going to buy.

Ever serious, he answered that he was going to purchase the best education he could and invest in some real estate. Mrs. Corbett had pressed him, stating that surely he would buy something fun, and Bane, straight-faced, told them that he wanted to buy a fjord. The Corbetts assumed he meant a convertible Mustang. But later, he told Tally and Chris that he really wanted a fjord, one with a massive Viking lodge.

Tally looked up—huge, knotted timbers spanned the lofty ceiling.

She sagged a little against him, and he helped her back to bed. When she was tucked in, she patted the spot next to her and waited for him to sit. "I don't know why you brought me here." She held up her hand when he opened his mouth to speak. "I trust you, Bane. All these years, I have never known you to do anything that wasn't necessary." She watched his face closely, for he was a master at hiding his emotions. "Something is happening. It's not just that I feel better when you're around me. I feel good. Really, really good. And I can sense myself mending when you're near. You're hiding something from me, and"—ah, there it was, she thought, a flicker of guilt in his eyes—"I'm fine with that because, like I said, I trust you. But whatever it is, you are going to have to eventually tell me." She leaned back against the pillows.

He was quiet for a minute, then said, "When you're stronger."

She nodded.

"Think that you could handle some broth?"

"I'm actually hungry for once."

"Soup, then." He chuckled, then added, "Maybe some bread." He picked up her cell from the nightstand and handed it to her. "I promised Chris that you would call him."

"It's what, like two a.m. there?"

"Three," he said. "Yeah, maybe wait until after lunch."

Tally opened her phone and started reading the texts—all seventy-three of them—from Chris, wanting to know where she was, if she was alright, if she wanted him to come and get her; more of the same from Jackie, though her texts told her to trust Bane. A little odd, that. The most recent from Chris told her to call, no matter how late. She texted him instead.

> I'm safe. I'll call you at a more reasonable hour.
> Luv u, Talz.

She shut off her phone and leaned back against the pillows, closing her eyes. That's when she smelled the unmistakable aroma of freshly baked bread. A few minutes later, Bane entered the room, carrying a breakfast tray. She pushed herself up so that he could set it over her lap. The soup looked amazing.

"Chicken with rice," he said.

She took a spoonful, chewing the thin strip of chicken breast. Hints of garlic and lemon zest spiced the broth. "Delicious. Where did you get it?"

"You wound me!" He mock-gasped. "Actually, it's one of the few things I can make. That and simple yeast bread. I keep a starter in the fridge and made this dough earlier in the morning. The nearest bakery is several fjords to the south." He pulled back the napkin to reveal two thick slabs of steaming bread, buttered a piece for her, and then handed her the slice.

Tally took a bite and chewed gingerly. It was heavenly. "Next time you come over to my place for dinner and a movie, you're cooking." Then she remembered that her house was gone. "No matter," she said, more to herself than him. While she ate her soup, Bane filled her in on what he had been doing in San Francisco with the National Order.

"There's news," he started, "about Orson."

Tally set down her spoon. "The Null?"

"Not yet. Upon my recommendation, they reached out to Mayor Greene and Detective Haneluk." He pulled up a chair to the bed. "I, uh, was a suspect."

"What! I don't care what time it is. I'm calling Barney right now."

"Hold on," he said. "Barney and I talked. Tally, Orson had planted evidence to implicate me. It was pretty convincing, hearing it from Barney. Think about it, I was at the Gala with Antonia just two days before she disappeared. Barney said that it was Orson who identified her once her image was released to the task force. He could've brought me in, but he kept digging. And then, you alibied me."

"He's good at his job."

"So is Emily Sykes. She's leading the interrogation team. Apparently, Orson won't shut up about everything he's done. Still, she sensed that he was hiding something. They researched his financials—that's how they found his little hideaway house in Wicker Park. The deed was filed under Amy's name. We gave the information to Barney, and in a joint investigation, they went to the site. They found dog hair all over the place— the same as was found at a murder scene in Michigan. They found other things. Little trophies. A greenhouse with near-black roses. There were different...rooms."

Tally waited.

"He'd been keeping people in the house. One was decorated for a little girl, but had items in it for a woman. It appeared as if he'd kept a woman there for years. Her body wasn't there, but there were skeletal remains in various stages of decay spread throughout the different floors."

"That's horrible. Didn't anyone smell or notice anything? He had to have had neighbors."

"The seals he'd set were easily breached, probably started to fade once the N.O.F. stripped his powers from him."

She shuddered. "But why try to frame you?"

"I don't know. We're still working on that. Best theory is that he was part of the attempt to take over Chicago. We thought that he was working with the group responsible for the Fascina abductions. He had their serum, after all. That's what he added to your wine."

"But?"

"Remember when I told you about that night in the park, when the three men tried to take you, and then they escaped? It turns out that Orson took them and killed them. He was gleeful about it when retelling the story to Emily. But he still hasn't confessed to how he came to have the drug."

"He told me that he tortured those men, but it doesn't mean that he wasn't working with them." Tally frowned. "Bane, I'm sure he doesn't realize that I'm Fascina. He said as much that night. But my brother will eventually figure it out. I have to tell him."

"Agreed," Bane said, taking the tray from her lap. Tally snagged the last piece of bread before he set it on the table. "It's still too early there. Why don't you take a nap first?"

She snuggled in the heavenly bedding. "Can you leave the curtains open?" she asked when he started to draw them closed, and he nodded.

"I'll be in the other room if you need me." He paused before heading out. "What is it?"

"After I talk to Chris, you and I are going to do the same. I need to know why, right now at this very moment, I would rather you climbed into this bed to hold me until I fall asleep than go out of the room to do something else." There was a flicker of some emotion in his eyes. Hope, maybe? She wasn't sure.

"I'll set this in the kitchen, then come right back."

• • •

Bane placed the tray on the counter, rinsed off the dishes and loaded them into the dishwasher. He got out his phone and shot off a quick text to Chris.

> T will call in a couple of hours. She still doesn't remember anything about us. Please, let me tell her.

He set his phone on the counter, then went to be with Tally. At some point, he must've dosed off, because he woke to her calling out his name.

"Braeden," she murmured in her sleep. He put his arms around her, kissed her behind her ear, and she settled back into regular, even breathing. If the clock on the nightstand was right, nearly two hours had passed. He eased off the bed and out of the room.

There was a text from Chris saying that he wouldn't say anything about the bonding. Bane sent him a quick update that his sister was still sleeping. He surveyed the kitchen, then went to work. Tally needed to start eating again. Her body was burning through too many calories in its effort to mend itself. Chicken soup wasn't enough. He pulled out the filets from the fridge. Hers was only four or five ounces, but the protein would do her good, and he seasoned the beef with fresh garlic, salt, and pepper. He dumped mushrooms into a wire basket, then proceeded to brush the dirt from each one. They were pared and sliced in minutes and tossed into the sauté pan. The salt, pepper, and olive oil were on hand once he fired up the burner.

A few minutes later, he had a salad of mixed greens plated and an easy vinaigrette whipped up. In the next room, the sound of Tally's voice filled the quiet space. She was talking to her brother. Bane pulled the cork from a bottle of wine—a hearty Barolo—and poured a glass. He poured another, albeit smaller, serving for Tally, and then ignited his indoor grill and started the mushrooms. Running water told him that she was using the bathroom sink. Soon after, he turned at the shuffling sound of her footsteps.

"Need any help?"

She shook her head and looked to be moving a bit easier as she entered his living room to take in the opposite view. When she whistled, he smiled. His home was situated to offer spectacular views from every window, and the one she was seeing now was of the waterfall.

"I like to call it Enkelin Kyynel," he provided. "Or Angel's Tears. I won't even attempt to pronounce its real name." She leaned against the arm of the sofa to stare at him. "You're sure you don't need help?"

"I was just going to ask you the same, but it looks like you've got everything under control."

He walked over to her, carrying both a big glass of water and the small pour of wine. She lowered herself to the couch, tucking her legs under her as was her habit, and took the water. He set the wine on the end table, then pulled the coffee table closer so that she could reach it. After stoking the fire and adding more logs, he tossed the remote to her.

"There's local news—Chicago, I mean—and movies, whatever you want to watch. You could check your email."

"How do you get such good reception up here?"

"My satellite."

"Of course you have your own satellite. I guess if you have your own fjord and waterfall..."

"The waterfall isn't mine either." He laughed. "Just the view."

"Exactly how rich are you?"

"I was lucky," he said from the kitchen. "I was an early adopter in crypto." He threw the steaks on the grill and turned on the exhaust fan next to it before giving the mushrooms a toss. "How did it go with Chris?"

"I didn't tell him yet. I think I want him to watch our mom's video. Let her explain it to him first."

"Sounds like a good plan. Do you want cheese on your salad? It's baby spinach with toasted pine nuts and a light vinaigrette."

"Are you having any?"

"A little gorgonzola."

"Then I'll have a bit too."

She was watching him as he worked in the kitchen. He brought the place settings over to her, wrapped up in woven placemats, and she set the two spots. After dropping off the salad, he returned to the kitchen area where he removed the filets from the grill—hers medium-rare, and his a little bloodier. After they rested for a few minutes, he covered them with sautéed mushrooms, then set the two plates on the coffee table. "Just eat what you can. You need the iron."

He watched as she dug in. After an auspicious start, her appetite seemed to lessen.

"Like the soup, it's delicious."

"And easy. Salt and pepper. Vinegar and oil."

"And toasted pine nuts. And perfectly sliced criminis. Quit selling yourself short. I know your secret now."

He finished his dinner. She ended up eating only half of her filet, but the mushrooms and salad were gone. Bane went to clean up. He knew he was stalling, but he still hadn't figured out what he was going to say. Then his phone buzzed. It was Chris.

Keep it simple

If only it were that easy, he thought, looking over to where Tally was staring at the fire. He grabbed the bottle of wine and went to join her. She held out her glass, and this time he poured a full portion. "First and foremost," he started after he sat next to her, "is that I have to tell you that I love you." She froze mid-sip. "I always have. And never once as a sister. Then as we grew older, more. I need you to know that...that I love you...before I fill in the parts that you can't remember." He ran his hand through his hair.

"It started with a kiss. An amazing, earth-shattering, planets-colliding kiss. And then, by accident, I discovered that you're Fascina. We grew closer. You told me that you'd loved me for years but couldn't act on it because you thought you were non-Fascina, and later, because of your mom's cryptic warning." Bane knew he was rushing, but he just wanted to get to where they were now. So, he told her about how they discovered their love for one another and the incredible passion between them. Tally listened without interrupting through the entire history. "What do you remember about your mom and dad?" he finally asked.

"That they had a love like no other. They were truly connected, heart and soul. And when my dad died, my mom got sick. She tried to stay with us, but the poison was too much for her."

"It's a little more complicated than that." He took her hand. "When your father died, he took part of her with him. She died of a broken heart."

"I read somewhere once that Fascina couples can become especially connected to one another. My parents were like that—bondmates."

Bane stared at her.

"We had that?"

He nodded. "It happens when two people transcend the three levels of love. Philosi, we already had as kids. Uh, Erosa—well, let's just say, and I don't want to make you nervous, because I can completely control myself, that we had no problem with passionate love. Finally, Pragmalia, the idea that we've always loved one another—past, present, and future."

"Agapia?"

He nodded.

"So what happened when I got hurt? When I couldn't remember?"

"I tried to break the bond. It can be done with distance, but it makes one really angry."

"I see. That explains a lot. But why would you do that? If we loved each other, why try to break it?"

"So many reasons—none of which make any sense now—but mainly because I was an idiot. I was forced to work for the N.O.F. If I didn't break what we had wrought, you would've been hurt worse; you may never have healed. As for the N.O.F., it's a long story involving Janine, Giselle, and your mother. I promise to tell you everything after you've rested.

"Suffice it to say that I made mistakes. I thought I was protecting you. I ended up doing the opposite. Because of the distance I put between us, you were taking too long to heal. With the bond, when one of us is hurt, the other can help them to heal faster, just by being near them. The night of the engagement party, I should have gone with you in the ambulance. You were already so weak—I've never heard of anyone being able to bring someone back like that. And I couldn't tell Chris or Jackie. I couldn't tell them because no one but me knows that you're Fascina."

"But why didn't you just tell me? Bane, I love you. I may not remember the last few months, or this bonding, but..."

She took a breath, then yelled, "I remember that I have loved you my whole life. You're such a jerk! If you had just told me, we would've been stronger. Orson might not have tried..." She trailed off and stared at him, reading the guilt etched across his face. Her eyes softened, and she reached up to cup his cheek. "I love you, you idiot. I don't understand why you couldn't just tell me."

"Because I couldn't protect you, Tally. I couldn't protect..."

"What? What is it? I'm going crazy, Bane. Not just angry at you, but I feel like I'm missing something. Did you succeed in breaking our connection? Is that it?"

He shook his head. "You...we..." He trailed off, unable to finish, and she turned away to stare at the fire. "You gave everything you had to save Chris that night. Everything. And in the hospital...you lost..."

Slowly, her hand moved to rest on her stomach.

"Please, look at me."

There were tears in her eyes. Her face reflected the same pain he'd been feeling in his heart. "Did I know, Bane? When I saved my brother, did I know that I was pregnant? Did I knowingly put our child—"

He pulled her into his arms. "No, Tally, no. Neither of us knew. I didn't tell you because, well, with everything you had gone through, it would've been too much. And Marc...I convinced him...it didn't make it onto your chart. He didn't want you to have the added stress of people knowing we'd been together and risked having a maliker."

Bane laughed, the sound of it harsh to his ears. He couldn't help it. "No one knew you had powers. If they found out about a pregnancy... They would have put me away and made you... We didn't tell anyone."

"You saw that I wasn't getting better. I wasn't sleeping, Bane. I look like a skeleton. I couldn't eat. And something so important—" She stopped, pushing him away from her. "You had no right. All this time, I was mourning our child. Grieving, Bane. And I never even knew it!"

He started to reach for her, but she shrank away from his touch. "I need to be alone right now. Please."

She remained seated. It was up to him to vacate the room. He rose from the couch, and for the first time, saw what he'd done from her perspective.

"Was it a boy or a girl?"

"Tally..."

"A boy or a girl?" she insisted, her voice bleak.

"It was too early to tell." He stood there, rooted to the spot. "Tally, I'm sorry. I will do everything in my power to prove that you can trust me again." She didn't reply, just stared at the fire until he walked away.

"The problem isn't that I don't trust you, Bane." He stopped at the entrance to the bedroom. "It's that you didn't trust me."

"You're wrong. I trust you with my life."

"Sure," she said, almost too quiet to hear. "But you don't trust me with mine."

When she didn't say anything else, he went into the bedroom, closing the door behind him to give her the privacy and time she demanded. What he wanted to do was go back out there and hold her. And grieve with her. And help her through the loss he'd been feeling. He stripped out of his clothes, pulled on some pajama bottoms, then climbed into bed to toss and turn for the rest of the night. He couldn't even call Chris to ask his advice, since he'd left his phone on the kitchen counter.

Chapter Twenty-nine

Tally checked her phone. It was just after five in the morning. She had sat for hours staring at the fire after Bane went into the bedroom, adding a few logs when the flames had died down because all she had was a soft throw. At some point, she must've dozed off. When she woke, the hearth was burning bright and hot, and there was a down comforter draped over her.

The emotional rollercoaster of the previous night had left her more exhausted than she'd felt in her entire life. Grief over everything she and Bane had lost. Fear that they would never get back to where they'd been. Though Bane had believed that trying to break the bond was the best thing for them, he should have told her the truth. Misguided idiot. He had ended up hurting them both, more than any physical attack ever could. Then guilt washed through her—he'd been mourning their loss the entire time on his own. And in feeling guilty, she grew angry again.

Though she didn't want to, she thought about Orson. About what he'd said to her about cleaning up her disgraceful mess. If he had somehow caused... It didn't matter. Her guilt would never go away.

Up and down she went, riding the gamut of emotions. And when she'd finally cried out her tears and given in to an insane fit of laughter at her predicament, she had slumped over and succumbed to sleep. Now she wondered if she'd accomplished anything during her hours of soul searching.

What had Bane's night been like? She felt just a little petty at the thought of him tossing and turning alone. By leaving her on her own, he was trying to respect her wishes, allowing her to decide what would become of them. But as much as she loved him for it, it also pissed her off.

"So," Tally asked herself, "what do I feel? Other than anger?"

Was it hope that she and Bane could work through this, regardless of her missing memories? Relief that she could finally be herself? Had her mother been right when she'd written that Tally would *know* the right moment to reveal herself to the rest of the Fascina?

"I'm ready," she whispered to the predawn dark. And she would start with her brother. So yes, hope *and* relief.

She rose from the sofa and padded quietly to the bedroom, the down comforter wrapped around her like an overstuffed cape. Bane, asleep and facing the balcony, was tangled in a crazy mess of blankets and sheets. She eased onto the bed and snuggled up behind him, draping the comforter over them both before wrapping her arm over his waist. His breathing changed, and she counted his breaths—one…two…three. Then his fingers laced through hers. She'd made the right decision. She wasn't about to give up on him. On them. And nothing felt more right. She fell into a deep and peaceful sleep.

• • •

When she woke again, it was hours later. A heavy weight rested across her stomach—Bane's arm. She turned so that her back was to him and took his wrist, hugging it and his forearm to her chest. He stirred behind her.

"What time is it?" he asked groggily.

"Don't know. Don't care."

She felt him smile into her hair. A few minutes passed by, and she thought he had fallen back asleep. But he pressed a kiss to the back of her head.

"I didn't realize how exhausted I was," he murmured, "until you came in this morning. I mean, I knew trying to break the bond would have side effects for me, but I was so focused on you, I didn't bother to pay attention to my health."

Tally was torn. It felt so good being held in his arms, but weird. Her nerves were getting the better of her, and she tried easing away. According to him, they'd made love. Many, many times. And now, she couldn't even recall kissing him. He seemed content to hold her, but he would want more at some point.

"What's wrong?" he asked, rolling away onto his back. "You can tell me." She was about to say that she was fine, when he begged softly, "Tally, come here, please."

She turned and tucked herself against him, her head on his shoulder. He brushed her hair back from her forehead.

"We've always been able to talk," he murmured. "That didn't change when we bonded."

"I know."

"Then what's wrong?"

"I don't know how to act. You remember *things* we've done together."
She felt her face turn red, and he must have noticed, because he chuckled,
a deep rumble in his chest.

"Those *things* are impossible for me to forget," he said.

"Great for you, but I don't know what to do."

"Simple. We start over." He tilted up her chin so that she could see his
face. "There's no rush. We waited our entire lives to be together. Wooing
you again...it's a gift."

"Wooing? You are so old-fashioned."

"Courting then."

She started laughing, as he had intended, she knew. "So, what do we do?
Go on a date?"

"Yes."

"When?"

"When we get back."

"And while we're here?"

"You get to set the pace. I remember what was—is—between us, even if
you can't."

"Doesn't seem fair. I get all the firsts again. You don't." She realized at
that moment that she had made up her mind. She wanted to be with him.
The love was still there.

"Believe me, I don't mind."

"What if I want to go slow?" she asked.

"Then it'll be excruciating." She hit him on the chest, and he laughed.
"Take as much time as you need. I trust that you'll know what you want and
when you want it."

"And what if I don't know how to ask? It seems like a lot of pressure.
What if I want you to kiss me and...I'm not comfortable having to initiate
every step."

"Do you want me to kiss you, Tally?" His voice was pitched seductively
low.

A warm feeling started to zing back and forth in her chest.

He lifted her hand to his lips, then took turns kissing each fingertip.
"Because nothing would please me more than pleasing you."

She nodded and pushed up to meet him halfway, but he rose as well and
climbed out of bed. He held out his hand for her to join him. "I have almost
infinite patience, but kissing you in my bed...? Better to be over here."

He drew her against him, heat radiating from his body. She looked
everywhere but at his face, and her eyes finally settled on his clavicle. How

had she never noticed how incredibly sexy that little spot was? Or maybe she had. She could imagine herself licking and sucking him there, and her gaze flew to his, then to the bed.

"I told you it was safer over here...if we're going to take it slow."

At that very moment, Tally wasn't sure *slow* was the right pace. She could feel her pulse ratchet up another notch. Bane lifted her chin, and very gently, he brushed his lips against hers. Every nerve in her body reacted, and she groaned when he lifted away. He did it again, lingered a bit more, courted her lips to move with his. Tally pressed closer. She needed to feel the hot silk of his tongue against hers. But Bane moved back. She growled, reaching around his neck and trying to bring his mouth back down to hers.

He held her away from him, his hands firmly on her upper arms. "Wait, Tally. There's something you need to know about the bonding. And separation."

She pulled out of his grasp, turned her back on him, somewhat humiliated for being so bold.

His hands came to rest on her shoulders. "Just listen for a minute, and then I'll kiss you and not stop for a thousand years. Please."

"Fine." She plunked down on the edge of the bed.

"First, the anger you're feeling is part of what happens when people who are bondmates separate. It's like withdrawal, only filled with rage. But it's not the only side effect. There's lust, too. It's our form of the DTs. We're addicted to one another. Sex is the only fix."

She stared at him, trying to let go of that feeling that he was rejecting her.

"I thought we could go slow. But I'm not sure that I can do that," he continued, putting some distance between them. "This might scare you to hear it, but I'm barely controlling the urge to push you back on the bed and take you, hard and fast. If you press for more..."

At the thought of him keeping himself away from her, anger surged through her like a welcome heat after a freezing day. With it came a raw desire to be with him. She stalked him across the floor, advancing on him until his back was against the wall, then gave him a devastating kiss. Heat spiked in her core, then erupted when he engaged her frontal attack with equal vigor. He grabbed her hair, his gaze flicking back and forth over hers. "You're sure?"

She answered by undoing the drawstring of his pajama bottoms and shoving them down past his hips and thighs. She looked down and saw that his cock was rock hard, and she wasn't shocked or embarrassed. This was

Bane, her friend, her confidant, her lover. The man she'd loved for years. She licked her lips at the thought of him on top of her, covering her body and taking her. And when she looked at his face, she knew there would be no dialing back.

"Bed," he ordered, backing her up and toppling her onto the mattress.

Tally wanted to feel his skin against hers. She needed it like she needed air to breathe. And just like that, they were naked. "Was that me?" she gasped.

Bane nodded. "One of your many endearing talents." His lips crushed down on hers, and she tasted blood. Hers? His? It didn't matter. They only separated to draw breath. "I have to warn you...it's been a long time. I'll try to—"

"Be quiet and fuck me, Bane. We can sort out the rest later." Holy shit. Where did that come from? Her entire body was singing with her need for him. A light sheen of sweat covered them both, and they hadn't even started.

He hiked up one of her knees, opening her, and then he thrust, deep and sure and straight to her center. It was so right. So perfect. And she quickened inside. She wanted this to last but couldn't contain herself, and she arched her back, bucking her hips high.

"Slip for me, Tally," Bane whispered in her ear. "Slip, just a little."

She stared at him, seeing the pain in his eyes, pain that was present because he was holding himself back for her. She wanted nothing more than to erase that ache. So she slipped, just a bit, like he asked, and at the same time, he did the same. And oh God. It was cascading climaxes, and flowers, and chocolate, and honey, and warm baths, and steaming showers, and love. God, it was love. He was a part of her, and she was a part of him, fluid like molten silver. He came, shouting out her name, and a second later, she followed him into the chaotic firing of every synapse in her body. "Braeden!" she screamed, her cry echoing in her mind while their comingled souls pulsed.

He fell on top of her, and they rolled to their sides, still joined, even as their essences settled back. She pressed her face into his chest, listening as his lungs heaved. She hadn't been afraid. At all. It had been the most natural thing in the world. And damn, she felt *strong*. She knew there was a sloppy grin on her face, so she kept her chin tucked down. "Always like that?"

"Oh, yeah!" Bane said enthusiastically. When she peeked up at him, he wore the same ridiculously satisfied expression. They started laughing.

"I'm starving!" she finally managed. "Want me to make breakfast?"

He shook his head. "You're feeling good now, but your body is still healing. I'll cook. Bacon and eggs?"

"Toast, too?"

He nodded.

"And coffee. I miss coffee." She hadn't had a cup in days.

His grin had widened.

"What's up? Was it really that great for you?"

"No. I mean, yes. But it's something else. I'll tell you after we eat."

When he climbed out of bed, Tally nearly whistled aloud at the view he presented. He was just that hot. After he pulled on sweats and a shirt and left the room, she rolled off the mattress and went to take a shower. It was weird. She wasn't self-conscious around him in the slightest. But by the time she got into the shower, the after-sex high had begun to wear off. She washed her hair as fast as she could and then toweled off. Her energy was quickly draining as she dried her hair, and she didn't think she would have the strength to dress. Her body was still mottled with bruises, though her ribs felt much better. Tally stared at the marks on her neck, then closed her eyes to focus, willing her clothing back on. A moment later, she was dressed. Exhausted, but dressed.

She fell onto the chaise, curling up onto her side. Later, she woke to the smell of bacon and Bane carrying her back to the bed. "I'm good," she told him. "Just dozed off."

"You can eat later, Tally. You need to rest."

"I'd rather nap on the couch, if you don't mind." He pivoted out of the room, carrying her as if she weighed nothing, then gently set her on the couch. After pulling the throw over her, he went to the kitchen and came back with a plate of scrambled eggs, bacon, and toast in one hand and a mug of coffee in the other.

"Decaf," he explained. "No sense trying to fight a battle you can't win."

"Meaning...?"

"Even if you try not to, you're going to crash after eating." He pulled the coffee table closer to where she half reclined. "Be right back." He returned, setting his plate and mug on the table, and drew the overstuffed chair closer. Tally had already eaten half her eggs, and she smiled guiltily for not waiting. The food gave her a little boost, and she started asking him questions about what she had done when she'd gotten rid of their clothes. He told her about the other gifts that she had. Those that she had thus far discovered.

"And don't forget, you are a true healer...a recoder. You're gifted with sostosi." he reminded. When she looked away, he took her hand. "Tally, you are still learning. You lived most of your life with your powers suppressed. Then your mom dropped a bombshell on you just before your talents began to emerge. It must've been very difficult to handle, with no one to guide you."

"I should have known. I shouldn't have reached so far to help Chris." She resisted pulling her hand from his to rest it on her stomach. "I would go to hell and back to save my brother. To save you. But the cost..." She stared at what was left of her eggs, her appetite having disappeared.

He pushed his plate back and moved to sit next to her. "I know. But it wasn't your—our—fault. And in time, you'll see that. We both will."

She nodded. She would tell him her suspicions about Orson later.

"Hey, you wanted to know why I was grinning like a fool earlier," Bane reminded. She took one more obligatory bite of eggs. "When we made love, you called me Braeden."

"I did?"

"Yes, you did." He explained what it meant to him and that it was how he had known that there was something wrong when she woke up in the hospital.

His story had soothed her, allowing her to finish her eggs, and when he reached to take her dish, she grabbed the last piece of bacon. He took the plates to the kitchen and bent down to load the dishwasher. "So, when do you want to..." He turned to her, then stopped. "What's that look you're giving me?"

"Look?" Tally called over to him. "Oh, come on. Don't be embarrassed just because you're hot." She laughed when he scowled at her.

"I'm not hot."

"Smokin' hot."

"Tally, I'm not—"

"Licorice-whip hot."

He froze and set down the glass he was rinsing, then turned slowly to stare at her. "What did you say?"

Tally frowned. "I said, licorice-whip hot."

"I thought so." He walked back over and sat on the couch next to her. "Why would you say that?"

"I'm not sure," she started. "Maybe because of our ongoing debate. No...something else." An image formed in her mind, black and red licorice strings, braided. A test to see which was stronger. The bed in his house in Chicago. "Did we?"

Bane nodded. "You remembered something. That's huge!"

"There's only one problem."

"No problem that I can see. This is really good, Tally. It means that other memories might resurface."

"It's not that at all. It's that I can't remember if the black or red won."

"As I recall," Bane admitted, his face beaming, "you were the winner that night, not the licorice."

He leaned back, and she nestled against him. At some point, she must have dozed off, because she woke, her head on a pillow, the pillow on his lap. He was reading, and his fingers were playing with her hair. She closed her eyes, enjoying the perfection of the moment. For the first time since finding out they were bound together, an act more sacred than marriage, she sensed all the good things that came of it—the ease they felt with one another, the implicit trust, and though she didn't remember how they got there, the unshakeable love between them. A love like that of her parents.

"Yes," she whispered.

"Yes?"

"Yes," she repeated. "To everything. With you. But you'll have to tell me what I can't remember, and there are a couple of things I need to tell you. But I know that I love you, Braeden. With all my heart. So, yes."

When he didn't say anything, she rolled onto her back and looked up at him. "What are you thinking?"

"That I love you, too, Tally. And that I was such a fool for not telling you before. So much could have—"

She put her fingers to his lips to stop him. "We need to move past that. I trust you. I love you. And now I get to be wooed all over again."

He smiled, then dipped his head down to kiss her.

Chapter Thirty

She still couldn't believe that he'd actually bought a house on a fjord. Tally shook her head as she stared at the sparkling water. As distractions went, this one was stunning—the view from Bane's office rivaled the one from the bedroom. "So much for focus," she told herself as, tab by tab, she closed out the real estate websites she'd been surfing. Not a single property had sparked her interest, but virtually walking through the neighborhoods of Chicago had her craving the hustle of city life.

Chris and Jackie had made sure she knew she was welcome to move back to Rosegate. But her heart knew that the only place for her was with Bane. She hit sleep on her screen, then got up to find him.

"Caught up with your emails yet?" she asked, then plopped down on the couch next to him where he was working on his tablet.

"An impossibility," he announced, sounding quite pleased with the fact—Bane wasn't daunted by an overflowing inbox. Rather, he viewed it as a sign of ongoing success. He closed his laptop and turned to her with worry in his eyes.

Another benefit of the bonding—it kept them completely attuned to one another, so much so that it was like living with a lie detector. She wondered about her parents, wishing she could ask them how they'd handled the constant inter-awareness. It was overwhelming at times. Bane had assured her that he would always respect her privacy, and if she had something that she didn't want to share, it was as easy as not talking about it. They would figure it out along the way. Tally didn't believe it was that simple. "What's wrong?"

He gave her a lopsided smile. "I was planning on telling you later, after we ate. But I suppose now is as good a time as any." He set his laptop on the table and leaned back, drawing her next to him. "The National Order just sent the final report on Orson."

"But we already know what he's done, and how he was involved with BioGen. He's responsible for destroying my house and planting evidence there to implicate you."

"I know, but something didn't fit. I asked Emily to keep digging."

"What was bothering you?"

"Why leave evidence to implicate me, then blow it up? And why attack the other families?"

"Because he was trying to take over Chicago with the Grossomms."

Bane held her gaze.

"Oh, *he* wasn't trying. Who, then?"

"I'm not sure. Emily could find no monetary link to Orson's accounts. He seemed to have a steady income stream, one defying explanation. But I think I know how." He took her hand. "Look toward the kitchen."

She jumped up. "Is that you!"

He pulled his essence back, and she sat back down. "It's called shadowing. My father could do it. You'll eventually remember, but you once knew about it. Saved me even, when I was taken. The other night, when I left Rosegate, I went to confront my mother about Janine. She reminded me that Orson's ancestors were once in power but lost it to scandal. Your family took over the Chicago Order. It was hushed up. Very few in the community even remember it happened, but—"

"It's something your mother would know and try to use to her benefit."

"Exactly. She said the Sedges amassed their wealth illegally—Orson's great-grandfather used his ability to shadow to steal millions. That's the reason I slipped back to Rosegate that night. I suspected him of being the killer, your stalker, everything."

"You think it was for revenge? He only admitted that he was the murderer and the one who sent me the rose. Where did he get the drugs?"

"Emily thinks someone else knew about him. That they were using him. Encouraging him, even. We don't know who, but I'll find out. Tally..."

"It's time."

"You're sure?"

"Yes," she assured him. "We need to get back to Chicago. And more. I need to come out of the closet."

"There's a council meeting today," he said. "We could surprise everyone. Make an entrance...together."

"When?"

"In a couple of hours. Chris and I spoke. He's inducting the new families to the board."

Her favorite comfy sweater, one of her only garments to have survived the explosion because she'd left it at Bane's, had seen better days. Paired with her jeans, she was dressed a bit too casually for a meeting with the entire Chicago Order. Bane was similarly attired. Screw them; her outfit would have to do.

"My brother deserves the truth, and there's no time like the present. I only wish I'd told him sooner."

"I have a feeling that, deep down, he already knows. Your twin thing, remember?"

"You're probably right." She held out her hand to Bane, and he stood.

"We're going to have to deal with Janine and the N.O.F. once you reveal that you are Fascina. She'll try to tap your resources as well as mine. Keeping everything that I can do from her is a job in and of itself. And you don't remember this yet, but you told me that she knows what your mother did to you. That she somehow helped."

"We'll deal with Janine when the time comes."

Bane frowned. "I'm worried that it'll be sooner rather than later. She's sending representatives to the meeting."

"Then you'll just have to protect me, won't you?" Tally said, standing on her toes to kiss his cheek, and he grinned—they both knew that, eventually, she would be able to handle any threat on her own.

"Yes, well, I have an idea about how to do just that."

"Then no time like the present. Lay on, Macduff!" she recited.

He shot off a quick text. Then he pulled her to him and gave her a scorching kiss that left her breathless. "Hold my hand and follow me. There's one important stop we need to make first."

She took his hand. "I'll follow you anywhere, Braeden." They slipped back to Chicago, appearing of all places in Tía Ixi's living room. Her grandniece, Angela, stood next to where the formidable woman sat like a queen.

She smiled approvingly at Bane and Tally. "Let's get this over with," she stated. "You have a meeting to attend, do you not?"

"Come with me, Tally," Angela ordered, dragging her out of the room. Bane winked at her, bowed to Ixi, then slipped away. "Don't worry. He'll be right back."

• • •

Two hours later, Tally and Bane arrived at the meeting, entering together in complementary swirls of light and dark in the back of the room. Those who noticed gaped at them—the rest of the Order members were focused on the dais.

The room was in utter chaos. Shouts demanding impeachment and forced resignation were bandied back and forth. Her brother was about to lose his cool. Jackie was next to him but conferring with her family. Sides had already been drawn. Bane texted Jackie.

It's time for the truth; trust us.
Follow our lead. We'll explain everything later.

They watched as she glanced at her phone, then showed the message to Chris.

Tally squeezed Bane's hand, and they both slipped to the center of the room, a mélange of light and dark. She remained calm as people gasped at their sudden appearance. They'd just become the eye of the storm.

"See there!" someone shouted. "Another example of the improprieties being committed under your leadership." Murmurs of agreement followed.

"If a vote is made now, your family is out," Bane whispered, gauging the room. Tally turned to her brother, but not before noticing others had also suddenly arrived. They stood quietly in the back, in the shadows and observing. The National Order.

Using the same trick she had perfected over years of having people shout down her input, Tally lowered her voice and addressed her brother. The room quieted.

"What was that?" someone shouted.

"My sister has asked to speak to the Order. She is following proper protocol, unlike the rest of you." Chris nodded to her. "You have the floor."

"Thank you," she said, then turned to the assembled families. "Before I speak, can one of you please fill me in on what is going on here?"

"We are demanding that your family be removed from Chicago's leadership," Adrian Shareff boldly spoke out, a confident gleam in his eye.

"Is that all?" she asked, garnering a few supportive laughs at Adrian's expense.

"You got this?" Bane asked. When she nodded, he kissed her cheek, then stepped away to take his place next to her brother, leaving her in the center of the room, separated from everyone by the square arrangement of tables.

"You don't belong here, Natalia," Shareff complained. "You never have. It's just another way that your brother has abused his position. He surrounds himself with family, sycophants, and psychos. You cannot begin to comprehend the intricacies necessary to run an order of the size of Chicago."

"Perhaps you can enlighten me as to how else Chris has been abusing his power. Truths only, Shareff. None of your usual innuendos or gossip. We deserve specifics that back up your gross accusations."

"Specifics," he replied smoothly. "The first two just now witnessed by the entire assembly." He entered the center area of the tables, strutting like an attorney about to address a stacked-in-his-favor jury. "Do you deny that you and Bane have had carnal relations? For months?"

Carnal? Tally thought with a poorly smothered laugh. What century was he living in? Well, two could play that game. "What's wrong, Shareff? Did I wound your ego the other day when I spurned you? You propositioned me, did you not? Or did I misread your intentions as you attempted to grope me?"

His face turned dark red when a few people snickered. "I made you an honest offer, Natalia Waever, more than a Non deserves. After sterilization, you would have been well-kept. I'm sure you're easily satisfied, and I..." He stopped talking when more than a few people gasped and shook their heads in disgust at his words.

"Thank you, but no. I'll keep my reproductive rights to myself. What else have you got? Come on, Shareff, bring it on."

"You...you were all blind to Orson Sedge's activities. Your closest advisor. You allowed that repugnant man to help shape the direction of the Chicago Order."

"If memory serves," Tally reminded, "you were on the committee to help discover his identity. Did you suspect nothing?" Nods of agreement amongst the members made their way around the room. "Did any of you?"

Shareff noticed the shift and bore down on her. "It doesn't change the fact that you and Bane are fucking. A Fascina and a Non. It's disgusting. It's punishable by sterilization and worse." He raised his voice even higher. "You all saw how they arrived. Bane Caron slipped Natalia Waever into this room. He's been doing it for years. It's strictly prohibited under our laws." He grabbed Tally's arm and spun her around to face the room. "I demand a vote," he spat.

Chris started to deny the request, and Tally saw Bane lean in to whisper something in his ear. He nodded, then said, "Tally, do you deny this allegation?"

"I do not," she said, her voice clear. "But I assert that we have broken no laws." Cries of outrage sounded at her declaration.

"You whore!" Shareff screamed, swinging toward her with a raised hand.

Tally was ready and used her powers. He was stunned as the invisible force struck him, throwing him off his feet to crash land some three yards away.

"She isn't a Non," someone in the crowd shouted. "She's one of us. I'll be damned."

Shareff was on his feet, but he didn't come at her again. "That wasn't her! I don't believe it! Make her prove it!"

Tally slipped, reappearing directly behind him. "Boo!"

Shareff jumped. Many of the assembled families were shaking their heads at him. "It changes nothing. Don't forget, they allowed Orson Sedge too much access. He destroyed not only Natalia Waever's home but attacked others as well. He murdered some of our own. He even tried to blow up Rosegate. And they covered it up." He had regained some of his momentum.

"How did you know about Rosegate?" Bane asked. "The only people who knew were there that night."

"Maybe your employees aren't as loyal as you think," Shareff swore, a smug expression on his face.

There was a murmur in the crowd as Janine Almarque stepped into the ring. Whispers filled the room as those who recognized the powerful woman shared her identity.

Tally kept her eyes on Shareff as Chris welcomed Janine to Chicago. Shareff, thinking he'd been forgotten, started slinking away, but stopped when some of the Baptistes and Silvas moved to block his path. Tally waited, sensing that, like a trapped animal, he was about to flee. She imagined wrapping him tight with energy just as he slipped away.

"Very nice, Natalia," Janine praised. "Your suspension looks quite uncomfortable." She walked around Shareff. He certainly was aware that he was caught in between, for the times when his face settled back together, he looked panicked.

It was gruesome, and she grew sick that she was the cause of such agony.

"I have him," Bane said quietly, coming up next to her. Tally let go of her hold, and when Adrian settled back to himself, Bane pinned him to the spot.

"I knew the two of you would suit," Janine pronounced, as if she were responsible for it. "You should come to San Francisco with Braeden sometime. Sooner would be better." She walked over to where Shareff was struggling to break free.

"Let me loose, Bane, or I'll—" He had the wherewithal to at least stop talking when Janine began examining him like a bug under a magnifying glass. She turned her attention to those assembled in the room.

"The National Order has had this one under investigation for some time. I asked the Waevers and those present the night Tally was injured at Rosegate to keep the details of the event quiet. What many of you don't know is that Rene Grossomm and his family tried to murder Chris Waever and Jacqueline Silva in an attempt to take over the leadership of the Chicago Order. But they were not alone. In point of fact, Adrian Shareff is just as culpable, if not more."

"She's lying! I would never!"

Janine pulled out her phone, called someone, and a moment later, Emily Sykes appeared. Next to her, a cowering Rene Grossomm stared at the floor. Emily pushed him to the center of the room, and he stumbled and fell to his knees. He looked like a trapped animal, and Tally tried to find some sympathy in her heart. There was none.

"Rene," Janine called out, and he jumped. "Tell these good Chicagoans whose idea it was to usurp the rightful leader of their Order."

"It was Adrian Shareff," he croaked.

"Of course he'll say anything you want. Look at him. He's been tortured." Adrian stared out at the audience, searching for his supporters. Tally made note of those who refused to meet his eyes, lest they too be implicated.

"I set the explosives at the Fortunas home and that of Ixara Silva's, but Shareff blew up Ms. Waever's house," Rene sputtered. "He was at Rosegate the night we attacked Chris Waever and Jacqueline Silva. He left to retrieve the Corbetts, thinking he could use them as leverage. But you never returned, did you?"

"So that's how you knew about Bane and me," Tally stated. "You must have seen us in the ballroom's gallery."

"I saw you long before that. Including that little kiss you shared over a private meal during the engagement party. The two of you, slinking off together, groping like hormone-ridden teenagers. Disgusting."

"And then there was your sudden influx of money," Janine added.

"I don't know what you're talking about," he denied.

"Yes, you do. You even donated to the Lumina Foundation," Tally stated.

"Tell them where the money came from, Mr. Shareff," Janine ordered.

He clamped his mouth shut.

"It seems that Mr. Shareff has been getting paid to act as a mule," Janine provided. "He's been ferrying Fascina and non-Fascina to certain laboratories."

"It's not true!" Shareff cried.

"Yes, it is," Janine went on. "You thought we'd pin that on Orson, but he explained how you were the one who gave him the drugs he was using on his victims."

"You're going to believe a psychopath over me?"

"I've heard enough from this exhausting man," Janine stated. "Emily, take Rene back to the holding cell. Send someone to retrieve this trash as well." She turned to Chris. "I expect you to get your city back under control."

"What will happen to them?" Chris asked.

"They'll be questioned and tried. Unlike Sedge, they didn't murder anyone, so the Null is not a given. Unless we discover he had something to do with the victim found in the rubble of Natalia's home."

Shareff's eyes bulged. "That was Orson! He was trying to pin everything on Caron!" Everyone in the room fell silent. "I don't know where the body came from. I don't..." He closed his mouth, realizing that he'd admitted that he knew about Orson.

Janine *tsked*. "Most likely, we'll strip them of their powers so they can no longer make nuisances of themselves. Their accounts have already been frozen."

"June Sedge and her daughters should not be made to suffer because of Orson," Tally argued.

Janine pursed her lips, but nodded, and then turned to Chris. "The attempt on your life that night was no small feat. You are within your rights to demand the harshest of punishments. And I fully suspect he thought you to be in your home the night it exploded, Ms. Waever."

"We'll leave it to the National Order's discretion," Chris said. "But I want Bane there during the interrogation, in case they were working with others to destabilize our city."

"Of course," Janine said, standing straighter. She addressed everyone assembled. "The Waevers have had—and *always* will have—the National Order of the Fascina's support." There were many nods of agreement, but when no one moved, Janine demanded, "Why are you all still here? Go home. Think about how good you've had it under the Waever family's protection. Then come back to your next meeting with ideas on how you can help to keep Chicago independent. The Waevers can't be expected to carry the entire weight on their shoulders."

Tally had never seen the room clear out so quickly. Emily reappeared to take Shareff.

With an enigmatic smile to Tally and Bane, Janine turned to Chris. "I suspect you and your sister have some talking to do, but you should know that her heart and Braeden's are true. They are loyal to you."

"I never doubted it," Chris said. "Mom left me a letter, Talz. Seems she thought that I might start to figure things out on my own."

"Then if you knew, why didn't you say something?"

"I just found out. The lawyers dropped off a packet the day after the engagement party. But with everything that happened afterward, I forgot about it. I watched her video a few days ago. In it, Mom said you would tell me when you were ready."

"And we didn't know if Bane knew or not," Jackie added. "When Chris told me, I agreed with him that he should wait to talk to you after you returned."

Janine was eyeing them like a proud parent at a school play, except there was something a bit greedy in her expression. Tally turned to her. "Thank you for your intercession today. Will you be heading back to—"

"Well, we're not quite finished yet, are we, dear? Perhaps we could go somewhere more comfortable and talk."

"Sure," Tally said warily. "I would like to change first, so maybe in an hour?"

"Excellent," Janine stated, looking expectantly at Chris.

"We can meet at Rosegate," he suggested.

"You could stay and dine with us," Jackie offered.

• • •

After changing into something a little more formal than jeans and a sweater, Tally came out of the guest room and met Bane in his kitchen.

"Did Chris text you?" he asked, looking up as she came in.

"No, why?"

He frowned at his phone. "He said to slip back, but to the Corbett's cottage. I don't like it."

"It *is* odd. Let's get over there, then."

A moment later, they were on the cottage's porch, and before they could knock, the front door opened, and Mr. Corbett came out. He hugged her, then held out his hand to Bane.

"What's going on?" Bane asked.

"Not sure. All of the head families have been summoned to the house," Mr. Corbett said. "Chris didn't look very happy about the situation. He asked me to wait for you here and make sure to bring you in as soon as you arrived. I don't like it, Bane. These N.O.F. people are meddling in our affairs. You be careful." He turned back to Tally, smiling at her. "Your parents would be so happy to see the two of you together."

"Thank you," Tally said, as Mr. Corbett led them to the main house.

Just before they entered the dining room, he turned to her. "Remember, Natalia—you may have your mother's heart, but you are your father's daughter as well, and you have his head. Make use of it when dealing with the Almarque woman."

"Does everyone know about me?" Tally asked, as Bane put his arm around her shoulder.

"Yes, dear. But everyone *knowing* isn't the same as everyone *knowing everything*, is it?" He winked at her and then gently pushed them through the door and into the lion's den.

Chapter Thirty-one

"What's going on?" Bane asked, foregoing the niceties of greeting everyone with his usual adherence to protocol.

Janine rose to her feet, taking his measure. "There's an outstanding N.O.F. compliance issue that needs resolving, isn't there?" she asked a little too eagerly. "Despite Adrian Shareff's crimes, his accusation regarding you and Ms. Waever requires an official National Order intercession. A mere formality, you understand." She turned to Tally. "And now, Ms. Waever..."

Two men emerged from the shadows and positioned themselves on either side of Janine—as if the most powerful woman in their community even needed protection. And then Tally understood. They weren't bodyguards; they had been summoned to handle her.

Bane moved next to Tally, and she could feel the tension rolling off him. Her brother, too, came to stand by her, as the Chicago board families glanced nervously about the room.

"These two look like your supposed compliance issue is more than a formality," Chris started. "This looks like a threat. I don't care who you are, Janine, you will not hurt anyone in the Chicago Order. This is my town. My community. My family."

"That is exactly what I'm trying to ascertain," Janine asserted. "Because unless Natalia can prove that she is Fascina, family or not, she is *not* part of any community."

"You just witnessed her slip during the meeting," Chris argued. "Watched her as she contained Adrian Shareff. There's no doubt she's a strong addition to the Chicago Order."

"Yes, we shall determine how strong in due time," Janine went on calmly. "But ultimately, it matters not what you or I believe. An accusation was made during an official Order meeting. The Chicago families must have irrevocable proof."

"You know that it's nearly impossible to prove non-interference," Bane stated. "I see the game you're playing, Janine, with this reverse witch trial of yours. You will not subject Tally to your antiquated testing."

"Any one of you could have tossed her an assist," one of the bodyguards threw in, bristling when Bane took a step toward Janine. But she only arched an eyebrow at the man, and he took a step back. "Sorry, ma'am."

Tally didn't get the sense that the woman meant her any real harm. Her bodyguards, on the other hand... "Fine. What do you need me to do?"

"Tally, you don't need to prove anything," Bane insisted. When she looked at the other Chicago families, she suddenly understood Janine's wisdom—Shareff's poisoned words would always linger in their minds. Janine was scrutinizing her. She wanted something, and Tally finally understood what Mr. Corbett had meant. She had inherited Torbin Waever's gifts as well, especially his most powerful, not one that was limited to the Fascina—namely, the ability to keep a cool head. The National Order was testing her, not to prove that she was Fascina, but to determine that of which she was capable.

"I've got this," she said. "I can handle whatever they throw my way. What is it that you need me to do, grand-godmother?" she asked the older woman, reminding her of the connection she once had to Tally's mother. The bodyguard who had overstepped glared at her.

"Ms. Waever, really. Let's not make this personal."

"It already is," Tally impugned, taking a step forward. "Let's get this over with, so that I can get on with my life."

"Have some respect for your betters," the man to Janine's right snarled.

"You're a real peach, you know that?" Tally replied.

"He knows," the previously silent guard said under his breath.

"Enough," Janine interrupted. "Natalia, please come and sit with me."

"No offense, but I'll stand right where I am."

The head of the National Order sighed. "Stubborn, like your mother. I need you to let Claude escort you to another location, then once he departs, wait two minutes and slip back here on your own. No one will be able to bring you back as they'll have no idea where Claude is going to take you. Not me. Not James. No one."

"Ma'am?" the quiet bodyguard started.

"It's alright, James. Claude will be on his best behavior. Won't you, Claude?"

"Yes, ma'am." He crossed the room to Tally and held out his arm. Just as she touched it, she noticed the malicious gleam in his eye. She immediately knew why. They reappeared on a floating dock in the middle of a swamp. He got the jump on her and managed to shove her off the edge and into the murky water.

"You asshole!" she spat at him, then dragged herself back onto the dock. "What's your damage, anyway?"

"I don't like uppity little girls meddling in the affairs of adults," he sneered. "That goes for your brother and his goon as well."

He tried to immobilize her with his will, but she was ready. Shaking it off, she was about to attempt the same—no sense hiding that skill as they'd already witnessed what she'd done to Shareff. Besides, it wouldn't work on someone who could do the same. What she needed to do here was keep her cool and overpower Claude without her Fascina gifts. He couldn't report what she didn't reveal. "I've never been afraid of bullies, Claude. Do your worst."

"It would be my pleasure to put you in your place."

Then Tally realized—her greatest weapon against Claude would be her words. She would have to incite him to meet her on a physical level. She would also need a mean right hook.

"Poor widdle Claude," she taunted. "Did you miss out on a promotion to Bane?"

His eyes narrowed.

Bingo! "Get over yourself. I'm sick and tired of brutes and bullies who think they are God's gift, and when something doesn't go right for them, they blame everyone else instead of trying to improve their, ah, shortcomings." She glanced pointedly at his crotch.

He made a grab for her, but she ducked and sucker-punched him in the stomach. Claude would soon discover that she could fight as dirty as he. "Oops. Looks like you forgot that I grew up with the two biggest toughs in Chicago."

Claude was fast and, bent over, he drove forward, his shoulder slamming into her gut. She flew back several feet, thudding across the dock and earning more than a few slivers in her palms as she grabbed for the wood planking. Behind her, something large made a splash and a snap, then slithered back under the surface. No way was she going back into that water. He stalked forward again, and she kicked up her legs and regained her feet. She took up a boxer stance, held up her hand, and beckoned him forward. Cocksure, just like in the movies.

He grinned and surprised her with a left hook. She'd already ascertained that he was right-handed, and she barely managed to dodge being clocked in the jaw. His knuckles grazed her mouth, and his ring caught her lip. He recovered faster than she'd thought he would be able to after the missed connection.

"You've got some skill," she admired, landing two quick jabs to his ribs, then a hook to his eye before dancing away from him. The metallic taste of blood from her cut lip washed through her mouth, and she spat.

Claude went on the offensive again, and she let him in. When his fist came close to connecting with her ear, she decided she was tired of the game. Her jab to his throat landed with surgical precision, and he grabbed his neck, coughing and backing away. "You need a bath," she taunted, then landed a front kick to his chest. It wasn't a hard blow, but she hit him squarely in the solar plexus. His breath *whooshed* out of him, and his fingers clawed out at the air as his balance yielded to gravity, and he toppled into the swamp.

After he pulled himself back onto the dock, she gave him a moment to catch his wind. He looked up at her, then gave a curt nod. "We're done. You can go."

"I never needed your permission," she said haughtily, then returned back to the dining room at Rosegate.

Bane and Chris were shouting at Janine. It took them a moment to realize she was back. When Janine saw the condition she was in, the woman's composure looked shaken. James diffused the situation by laughing. "What does the other guy look like?" he asked, handing her a handkerchief.

"See for yourself," Tally parried when the pressure in the room dropped as Claude reappeared. His left eye was already starting to swell shut, and the angry red welt on his windpipe would eventually yield to a beautiful shade of eggplant. His breathing was still labored, and she worried that she'd done some serious damage to his chest. She was about to heal him, then checked herself. Let someone at the N.O.F. take care of him.

"Are we done?" she asked, walking from the room. "Because I need a shower."

"Not quite yet," Janine intoned. "I demand to know how you protected yourself."

"A right hook, mainly," Tally retorted, noting the approval in the eyes of the other families.

"Claude will be able to tell me everything that happened, so why stall?" Behind Janine, Claude rasped something. "Speak up!" the old woman ordered.

"She's got a mean jab and kicks like a cage fighter," he finally got out, giving Tally an appraising look.

"Unacceptable," Janine stated coldly. "Our laws state that when a non-Fascina claims to be Fascina, if said claim is challenged, they must declare their gifts."

"Why is it so important for you to know, Janine?" Tally asked. The other families were murmuring their agreement.

"Enough of this. You can answer me in private. Everyone else, leave. Now."

"I don't think so," Chris stated.

"Stay out of this, Mr. Waever. Now, Natalia, if you won't disclose your talents, then Bane will be forced to. He is in our employ, after all."

Tally smiled and snaked her arm around Bane's waist while he draped his arm over her shoulder. "My husband doesn't have to tell you anything. That's right, Janine. We got hitched."

"When did you guys do that?" Chris asked, smiling and holding out his hand to Bane.

"Right before we crashed the meeting." Bane offered.

Jackie moved in to hug Tally, but paused, crinkling her nose. "Uh...maybe after you've changed your clothes." The other board members began offering their congratulations.

Janine pursed her lips—she had lost. She regarded Tally, and then warned, her tone compulsive. "I am the Head of the National Order, and you are bound to answer to me, Natalia Waever."

"I think not," Bane interceded. "The only thing Tally is bound to is me."

Tally heard someone in the room whisper, "Cue mic drop."

"And as such," Bane continued, "you have no authority to compel either of us to talk about the other, as it could lead to potential harm against our persons. I'm sorry, Janine, but your fishing expedition is over."

"For now," she stated. She turned to the others. "I aver that Natalia Waever is a member of the Fascina Community, and as such, is beholden to our rules and strictures."

"And our protections," Chris added.

"Yes, well, thank you for your hospitality. I don't think that we will be staying for dinner, after all." Her bodyguards came to stand next to her. "Bane, we expect to see you in two weeks."

"Two weeks?" Tally asked, knowing that Bane was due back in San Francisco in three days.

"Yes, my dear grand-goddaughter. Unless you don't want time for a honeymoon. In fact, why don't you consider San Francisco as your destination?" She nodded to them all before slipping away.

Tally turned to Bane. He held out his arms, and she jumped into them. The Corbetts entered the dining room, and Tally heard the distinct popping noise of a champagne cork. After everyone toasted them, the families began to disperse.

Tally ran upstairs to her room to take a quick shower, washing away the slime from the swamp. When she returned, they all retired to the living room to sit around the blazing hearth. Bane cleared his throat. "Hey, we're, uh, sorry we beat you to the altar, so to speak."

"Tía Ixi just called us," Jackie admitted. "Sometimes it's a little scary how much she knows about the families in Chicago."

"I'm just so happy that you are finally together," Chris added. "I always knew it was meant to be, but I was worried that it wouldn't happen. These things can be fickle."

"You *knew* knew?" Tally asked, and her brother shrugged.

"It's one of a few traits that didn't get shared equally between us. You can heal, and I sometimes *know* things."

"Then let's toast to us," Jackie announced joyfully. When Tally clinked her glass against her brother's, she wasn't the only one who saw that he looked a little troubled.

"What is it, Chris?" Jackie asked.

"Nothing bad," he said. "It's only that I sense that there'll be a few rough patches ahead. But if I can predict anything, it's that we're stronger together, and we'll get through them by helping one another."

"Cheers to that, then," Tally said, lifting her glass and finishing what was left of the champagne. She and Bane rose from the loveseat. "I'll call you tomorrow, Jackie. We can talk about what you and your family need me to do for your wedding. I'm at their disposal."

"And we can also talk about the party that you and Bane will need to have to celebrate your marriage. You have to have it here—we'll take care of everything for you. Once the ballroom is restored, that is."

Chris nodded his agreement.

Bane looked at her and smiled. "It's up to you, Tally, if you want to have a party."

"I'll think about it," Tally said, "but not until after your wedding." She and Bane made their goodbyes, then slipped back to his place. He pulled her into his arms and kissed her soundly. "I love you, Natalia Waever."

"Natalia Waever-Caron," she corrected with a sloppy grin. "And I love you, too, Braeden."

Epilogue

"Let's get out of here," Bane said after the last of the wedding guests left Rosegate.

"We should say goodbye to Chris and Jackie." Bane gave her a look, and she shook her head. "They already left, didn't they?"

"Chris said goodbye and thank you, and they would call after getting settled on Île de Lune." He held out his hand, and they walked out to the driveway, where her wedding gift from Bane sat. She tossed him the keys.

The drive to his penthouse was peaceful, and Tally watched as he maneuvered her new Alfa through the city. They rode up the elevator, holding hands. For now, they'd decided to keep the penthouse and were taking their time looking for a place in San Francisco's North Beach neighborhood for when Bane had to report to the National Order. Tally hadn't told him yet, but she'd found a three-story fixer-upper on Golden Gate Avenue in the Western Addition. She rather liked the idea of finding occupants who needed a break and providing them with beautiful apartments at low monthly rates. And maybe Michelle could fly out and create a rooftop garden system for the tenants. Tally smiled. Bane would completely be on board.

Janine had accepted their proposal, and the first satellite office of the N.O.F. would be established in Chicago. There were plans to do the same in L.A., New York, D.C., and Atlanta. Bane had been working on setting up a secure network, reducing the number of days he would need to be in San Francisco. So far, Tally hadn't been tapped, but she knew the day was coming.

The elevator doors swooshed open, and she followed Bane into the foyer.

"What the hell?" Bane swore, pushing Tally behind him when they discovered James, one of Janine's bodyguards, helping himself to their best bourbon.

The man held up a finger, finished pouring, and then handed them each a glass. "I come in peace," James swore. "Let's have a seat."

"I don't think so," Bane said. "You can get the f—"

Tally took his hand to forestall his anger—James looked so weary. "We can give him five minutes, can't we?" She dragged Bane with her to the couch, and James took a chair across from them.

"Tick-tock," Bane reminded.

James took an unhurried sip of bourbon. "I have some information about Orson Sedge...information that involves both of you. I'm very sorry, Natalia, I don't know how to say this, but Orson did something to you...when you were in the hospital and—"

"I already know," she said. "So does Bane."

"I kept it out of the transcripts, and I wiped it from Orson's memory, so you needn't worry about anyone else knowing. And I truly am sorry."

"Thank you," she said, unwilling to comment further.

James nodded, then looked at Bane. "We found some disturbing evidence in the building that Orson kept. Traces of DNA. One was very fresh and very abundant."

"And..." Bane said.

"And it was a familial match to you, Bane."

"Why does the N.O.F. have my DNA?" he demanded.

"We don't. We have your father's. It seems that one of the women Orson had been keeping there is your half-sister."

"Was," Tally said, taking Bane's hand. "Her remains were found in the ruins of my house."

James shook his head. "The samples weren't a match. The body found at your house was someone else. He hasn't told us who yet. And we're not even sure he knows...he would throw darts on a map to find his victims. But the one he held captive...he knew she was related to you. It's why he took her. She wasn't random, like the others."

"Where is she? This half-sister?"

"We've no idea. But he referred to her as Missy. He claims that he didn't kill her. That he didn't have time. Janine wanted you to know." James finished his bourbon and then stood. "That day she tested you, Natalia, had it been me she sent with you, I wouldn't have attacked you. Janine can be...well...Janine. And for your part, nicely played. It's not often that she doesn't get her way. It's good for her. And I suspect, grand-godmother notwithstanding, you've earned her respect. Probably the main reason she hasn't dragged you to the N.O.F."

"Yet," Tally added.

He gave her a crooked half smile and shrugged, and there was something very familiar about the gesture. "Please pass on my congratulations to your brother and Jackie. Bane," he finished, tipping his head as he made to leave.

"Who are you?" Tally asked, taking in his dark looks and his almost avian features, features echoing those of Janine Almarque.

He shrugged and lifted an eyebrow, astonishingly like someone else Tally knew and held dear. "No one important. One more thing, Bane. I'll find the girl; I swear it."

"Why is she so important to you?" Tally asked.

"I think you've guessed that already," James said and turned to Bane. "She's my half-sister as well." Then he slipped away in a swirl of darkly colored mist.

Bane swallowed his bourbon, then swore, "My father and Janine."

The End.

ABOUT THE AUTHOR

From San Diego, where she met her Montanan husband, to San Francisco, where she married him, and then to Chicago, where her twin boys were born, the Michigander-and-wanderer-at-heart settled once and for all in Northern Virginia. There, she continues to write, work, play, and post pics of #LucyTheVizsla.

OTHER BOOKS BY NICOLE E. KELLEHER
The Heart & Hand Series:
Wild Lavender
The Queen's Dance
The Naked Moon
The Shadow Healer
Book Five Coming Soon

Visit www.nekelleher.com for more information, newsletter sign-up, and more.